Nothing Like Love

Sabrina Ramnanan

DOUBLEDAY CANADA

Doubleday Canada and colophon are registered trademarks of Random House of Canada Limited

Library and Archives Canada Cataloguing in Publication

Ramnanan, Sabrina, author
Nothing like love / Sabrina Ramnanan.

Issued in print and electronic formats.
ISBN 978-0-385-68102-5 (bound).—ISBN 978-0-385-68103-2 (epub)

I. Title.

PS8635.A4634N68 2015   C813'.6   C2014-907431-X
                                              C2014-907432-8

This book is a work of fiction. Names, characters, places and incidents are products of the author's imagination or are used fictitiously. Any resemblance to actual events or locales or persons, living or dead, is entirely coincidental.

Book design: Terri Nimmo
Cover and text images: EVA105/Shutterstock.com, De-V/Shutterstock.com
Printed and bound in the USA

Published in Canada by Doubleday Canada,
a division of Random House of Canada Limited,
a Penguin Random House company

www.randomhouse.ca

10 9 8 7 6 5 4 3 2 1

Penguin
Random House
DOUBLEDAY CANADA

Every page is for my dad,
hero,
kindred spirit,
storyteller.

IT WAS AFTER MIDNIGHT when Vimla Narine finally closed the enormous front door against the pelt of autumn rain and dragged her book bag up the splintered staircase to her rented room at the end of the corridor. She saw, in the dim lamplight, her silhouette slink hunched and weary along the paisley walls and vowed to spend tomorrow wandering the city instead of tucked away in a library cubicle, turning mouldy pages yet again. The hallway smelled of orange peels and cinnamon bark, and beneath those, the faintest hint of damp dog fur. She squinted through the haze and saw Tiberius sprawled like a black puddle in her path, and there, perched on a chair, curlers piled high on her head, Ms. Nelly, the landlady.

"A letter came for you today," Ms. Nelly said. Her blue eyes sparkled in the gloom.

Vimla stopped short; her stomach fluttered with anticipation.

"From Trinidad," Ms. Nelly said. She leaned in and whispered like she was sharing a secret. "Someone named Minty sent it." Ms. Nelly clutched the letter to her chest. "*Minty!* What a *flavourful* name!" She shuffled ahead of Vimla into her room and flopped on the bed. "Are you going to open it now?"

It had been this way since Vimla had accepted the tiny room in Ms. Nelly's two-storey home five blocks from the university. The landlady had taken one look at Vimla with her eyes full of stories and her brown skin stippled with gooseflesh and had hauled her out of the cold and into the foyer like a treasure from some faraway place. In the days that followed, Ms. Nelly made her rich lamb stews and casseroles, chocolate chip cookies and apple pies with the criss-crossed tops, in the hope that in turn Vimla would reveal how she had ended up in this city with a suitcase of ripe mangoes and a soul full of courage as her only possessions. But Vimla never spoke of her past, no matter how enticing Ms. Nelly's cooking, so that now, in their second week together, Ms. Nelly was mad with curiosity.

"In the morning," Vimla said. She extracted the letter from Ms. Nelly's quivering fingers and slid the envelope beneath her pillow. "I real tired. I get lost today, you know." She gathered up her toiletries and draped a towel over her shoulder. "I spent the morning running around the campus looking for the right lecture hall, and when I find it, the only vacant seat was quite in the front under the professor's nose." Vimla headed for the washroom. "And everybody watch me like they never see people before!" she said over her shoulder.

Ms. Nelly scurried after Vimla. "Well," she said. "You do *look* different, Vimla. Like butterscotch."

"Butterscotch?"

"Your *skin.*"

Vimla slid into the bathroom and closed the door, just missing Ms. Nelly's fingers. "Good night."

"I can't sleep until I know," Ms. Nelly said. She was pacing Vimla's room, a harried look on her ashen face, when Vimla returned wearing pajamas. "Who is Minty, and why has she sent you these?"

Vimla's gaze fell on the bed. Ms. Nelly had pried open the envelope and scattered the contents—a dozen scraps of beautiful cloth—across the patchwork quilt. She wanted to be furious with her landlady; only, she couldn't, because there was such tenderness in Minty's gesture Vimla was overcome with nostalgia instead. "No letter?" Vimla whispered. She climbed onto the bed.

Ms. Nelly strummed her fingers against her cheeks. "Nothing." Her eyes were wide, probing.

Vimla smiled. Of course. There was no need for a letter; the fabrics were Minty's message. Quickly, Vimla began to knot the pieces together, the weathered ones first, and then the new piece, a snippet of rich red silk from a wedding sari, until finally a multicoloured rope of a dozen different textures meandered across the bed.

Ms. Nelly watched, transfixed. "What does this symbolize?" she breathed. "Is this some sort of Trini-dade-ian custom?"

Vimla swept her hair to one side and divided it into three equal parts. "It's a reminder, Ms. Nelly." She held the rope of fabric against the middle part and began to weave it into her hair.

Ms. Nelly swallowed, nodded vigorously. Her curlers bobbed up and down. "A reminder to . . ." Her hand paddled the air.

"To keep going."

"Where?"

"Anywhere."

Ms. Nelly looked disappointed. "How ambiguous!" She tried again: "And do you always wear your reminders in your hair?"

Vimla slipped beneath the warm quilt and felt the trials of her day melt away. She let her eyes shut. "Turn off the lights, nuh?" she mumbled.

Ms. Nelly sighed. "Pancakes and sausages in the morning, Vimla," she said as she closed the door behind her.

Vimla rolled onto her side and her fingers grazed a strand of satin entwined in her hair. As she tumbled into sleep, her feet stirred beneath the covers and her heart quickened. Before she knew it, she was running.

The Sacrilege

Vimla Narine stole across the uneven stepping stones, the staccato ring of her silver anklets beating in time with her heart. Her mother's gold wedding earrings swung against her flushed cheeks. The sequined *phaloo* of her new sea-green sari flashed in the early-morning sunlight, undulating over her shoulder like a wavelet chasing her home. Vimla shut her eyes, sprang through the air and imagined herself soaring. She landed with grace, her silky sari pleats whispering against her calves before she took flight again. A smile lit her face and made it pretty.

Vimla followed the stepping stones through the guava and coconut trees, around the duck pens and dog kennel. She darted past the bull and cow, a stray cat swollen with young and an old rooster scratching the earth. She barely noticed her fast breath and the beads of perspiration gathering at her hairline, but she could feel the rush of adrenaline through her body, propelling her forward until she tore through the tamarind trees and the back of her home came into full view.

As Vimla drew nearer to home, she reined in her wild energy and drove it back into her soul. She willed her legs to slow their pace and filled her lungs with long deep breaths until the thudding in her ears subsided. She adjusted her sari pleats, which had shifted to the left. She tried to flatten her hair, but it leaped through her fingers and flung itself in errant waves down her back anyway. Vimla shrugged, deciding to blame her dishevelment on the heat, on the dogs, on whatever else came to mind should she be questioned. She set about the wearisome task of focusing her mind on today's responsibilities. She squared her shoulders, repeated the fourteenth times table to twenty until an almost-calm came over her, and then slowly permitted reality.

Of course she was late for the *puja*, prayer. She scolded herself for gambling with time this morning. It would be inappropriate to preface this ceremony by a quarrel with her mother. This wasn't just any puja, after all; it was an offering of thanks to the deities for helping Vimla pass her A Level exams with such success. It was important to her mother.

Vimla looked up from the swish of fabric around her toes and noticed her father, Om, reclining against a house pillar, a brass *lotah*, water vessel, in one hand. Placidness softened his round, weathered face as he stared beyond his backyard across his five acres of sugar cane.

Vimla stopped in front of him. "Pa?" She tilted her head to one side, hunting for annoyance somewhere beneath his dreaminess.

Om grunted. "Where you went? The pundit reach. Your mother looking for you." Then his frown gave way to an affectionate smile. "You looking like a fairymaid in that sari, Vims."

Vimla smiled at her father, delighted. She remembered how he had rushed to the Indian bazaar the morning her name was printed first in the *Guardian* of all the students who had passed their A Levels. "One pretty sari to match my pretty daughter with the pretty smart brain," he had said as he spread the paper open on the counter and pointed to Vimla's name. Her mother, Chandani, had said the sari was too heavy with jewels, too expensive, too grown up for a seventeen-year-old girl, and yet she swallowed her protests when Vimla draped the fabric across her body and beamed back at her.

Om shoved the lotah into Vimla's hands. "Take this. Fill it up with water from the standpipe. Pundit Anand almost finish setting up. Do fast before your mother cut your tail!"

Vimla hurried away with the lotah, grateful for a reasonable excuse for her tardiness. She was careful not to let the water slosh over the sides, more careful still to accentuate the sequined border of her sari pleats with delicate kicks as she walked toward the *bedi* assembled in the middle of the downstairs living area. Without a single spilled drop, she set the water vessel down and shone radiant in the sea-green drapes of her sari, a smile inviting compliments playing on her face.

But nobody was looking at her.

Pundit Anand, the village priest, busied himself taking inventory of the materials necessary to conduct a successful puja. Om regarded him with suspicion, searching as he always did for an oversight, while Chandani observed her husband's irreverent behaviour, her lips pulled into a straight line of petulance.

Vimla sighed quietly and moved beside her mother in front of the bedi set on the ground. The bedi was a wooden box, twenty-four inches long on each side and four inches deep. It was packed firmly with earth and cow dung and smoothed to create a flat working surface. Pundit Anand had used rice grains to decorate the top with designs and holy symbols.

Vimla watched as Pundit Anand's eyes swept approvingly over the brass *taria*, rubbed gold for the occasion. The first plate overflowed with fresh neem, tulsi and mango leaves. The second contained a myriad of fragrant articles like cloves, camphor and sandalwood incense. The third was arranged with materials Vimla thought would feel nice against the skin: a mound of soft cotton balls, an orb of red and yellow string, a dusting of vermilion powder. Fresh fruit, hibiscus, marigold and jasmine flowers filled the other trays. The fruit would be offered to the little brass *murtis*, statues of the gods, the flowers to adorn them.

Pundit Anand inhaled the burning incense deeply and pretended to close his eyes. Vimla knew he was trying to avoid meeting her father's distrustful scowl and she could see that he was peeking beneath his half-closed lids at her mother's now reverent expression with an opportunist's beam. It was common knowledge in the district that Vimla's success would bring greater academic opportunities, and that unlike many of her peers, she had the potential to truly excel. But according to Pundit Anand, if Vimla was to be successful, she needed her planets completely realigned, all the holy deities appeased and all the evil spirits dispelled from her home. He had warned Om and Chandani that such services did not come cheap these days. Vimla saw Pundit Anand's mouth turn up in a half-smile and then vanish.

She rolled her brown eyes. She would succeed in life because she was bright, not because she offered a jasmine flower at the feet of Saraswati Devi. In the nights leading up to the exams, when Vimla had studied by the light of an oil lamp, she hadn't had time to pray. There had been too many formulas to memorize, too many practice compositions to write, to dither in front of the altar with expansive supplications. She had read until her eyes burned and then read some more, until there wasn't anything that could surprise her on the exams.

Pundit Anand gestured for the Narines to sit before the bedi. He fixed his lips into a puckered O and summoned the holiest *aum* he had in his belly. It vibrated through his body and out the tunnel of his lips. His eyes twinkled at the effect, and the half-smile appeared again, barely peeking out from beneath his silvery-grey moustache. Then Pundit Anand fell into a jumble of Sanskrit mantras that had travelled a treacherous journey over time and dark waters in fragments from India to Trinidad.

Vimla wondered vaguely if broken prayers worked.

While her parents and Pundit Anand prayed, Vimla fidgeted with the sequin border at the hem of her sari, turning it inside out and flipping it back over again. She twisted the sequins on their gold thread until they became loose. She trailed her finger along the hem softly, thinking how much the sequins looked like green fish scales. When she grew tired of this, Vimla plucked a jasmine blossom idly from the brass plate of flowers and threaded it into her dark wavy hair, wishing she had a mirror to glimpse her reflection in.

Vimla heard a chuckle beneath the drone of chanting beside her. She dropped her hands into her lap and looked up to find Krishna Govind, Pundit Anand Govind's son, padding across the concrete on bare feet toward the bedi. He had entered through the iron gates, left open by her father, and removed his slippers so as not to disturb the puja. Krishna was dressed in a simple white cotton *kurtha* pajama, a shirt that fell to his knees, and a pair of matching, loose-fitting pants. Tucked beneath his arm was a bundle of wood, five inches long and wrapped in yellow cloth. He set this bundle and his slippers down and then seated himself across the bedi from Vimla on a piece of white fabric spread earlier for him by Chandani.

Vimla glanced at her parents, then at Pundit Anand, but they were still chanting mantras with their eyes closed and their palms pressed together. She shrugged at Krishna, slipped another jasmine blossom into her hair and smiled.

Krishna shook his head, smiling back at her as he loosened the knot that held the wood together. He began to place the pieces of wood in the family's *havana kunda*, a metal container used for fire rituals. While he worked, his gaze travelled the embroidery and sequins that roved the curves of Vimla's body. He lingered longer on the soft sliver of flesh Vimla's sari blouse exposed at her midriff as she reached to slide a third jasmine flower into her hair. And when she looked at him with her cocoa eyes, fringed with thick dark lashes and full of mischief, Krishna blew her a kiss across the bedi.

Pundit Anand, Chandani and Om bowed their heads in unison then, opened their eyes and placed the wilted petals between their sweaty palms at the feet of a brass deity sitting on the bedi. Vimla snatched the jasmines hurriedly out of her hair and did the same, her face burning as Pundit Anand shot her a sidelong glance.

Pundit Anand took a deep breath and launched into a fresh string of mantras, rocking back and forth as the prayers tumbled out. He swept his hand over the havana kunda, nodding to Krishna to set the wood inside ablaze. Then he gestured for Om and Chandani to drop melted ghee, clarified butter like molten gold, from a spoon into the flames as he called upon the deities one by one to accept the offerings made to them in the fire.

Vimla and Krishna watched each other through the dancing flames and the black, choking smoke uncurling into the space between them; they exchanged brazen smiles under the noses of their parents and over the heads of the miniature brass gods on the bedi.

Thinking back on this day much later, Vimla would understand: this was the pivotal moment in her and Krishna's relationship. The moment when the gods witnessed their audacious sacrilege. The moment it was decided a torrent of misfortune would rain down upon the pair.

And while the destiny of their children was being transformed, Pundit Anand Govind and the Narines chanted 108 names of a god who was no longer listening.

Chance Market

C hance Market was already vibrating with activity at 5 a.m. Vimla zigzagged through the rows of stalls in search of a vacant space to sell her father's long beans.

"Here, Pa!" She waved her arms at Om.

Gloria Ramnath, dressed in a new pink dress, bumped Vimla with her wide hips. "Eh, gyul, move from here. I selling my eddoes at this stall." She heaved a heavy bag of eddoes off the floor and plopped it onto the stand. "Go and find a next place to play."

Vimla stared at Gloria. She wore ten rings on her fat fingers and three chains like gold ropes around her bull-like neck. Her earlobes were stretched by the weight of gaudy earrings that dangled to her shoulders, and on her toes—Vimla flinched at the sight of hair on them—Gloria wore silver rings fashioned like coiling snakes. Her son was a jeweller in Port of Spain, and everyone knew it.

"Auntie Glory, this is my father's stall." Vimla pointed to the scale she'd placed on the splintering wooden stand to secure the spot for Om.

"Where is Fatty-Om? I ain't see him anywhere, and nobody can miss Fatty-Om when he walk into a place." Gloria chuckled and her gold-draped bosom danced up and down. She untied her bag of eddoes and pushed it on its side with a *thump*, rolling the brown hairy vegetables out onto the stand with her pudgy fingers.

Vimla stepped back and assessed Gloria's bulk, lingering on the hanging flesh at her forearms and the triple layer of fat at her chin. She screwed her face up at the woman. "That's *Mr.* Om Narine, to you." Vimla nodded to her father, whom she could see out of the corner of her eye making his way up the middle aisle. "And he's right there . . . Auntie *Boobooloops,*" she muttered.

Gloria dropped an eddoe and placed her meaty hands on her wide waist, bending forward so that Vimla saw the endless line of her cleavage. "Boobooloops!"

Om arrived and wedged himself between the stalls. He dropped an armful of bags on the stand around his scale. "Morning, Glory."

Gloria glared at Om. "Your daughter just called me 'Boobooloops.'" She pointed a finger at Vimla.

Om stared at Gloria for a moment and then looked to Vimla for an explanation.

"Pa, she called you 'Fatty-Om'!" Vimla folded her arms.

Om chortled. "That's my name, Vims. Everybody does call me 'Fatty-Om.'" He massaged his gut and hula-hooped his waist.

Gloria gloated. Vimla's face darkened. "Well, I don't think *she* should call you that, Pa. Look at she! She have no neck! And besides, she try and t'ief this stall from me." Vimla narrowed her gaze at Gloria.

Gloria turned to the neighbouring merchant, who was eavesdropping as he prepackaged his hot peppers: two shrivelled peppers and three ripe peppers per bag. "Eh, Bulldog! You hearing this?" Gloria demanded.

Bulldog shrugged. "Glory, you t'ief the stand from the girl."

Another woman behind Vimla spoke up. "You slam down your bag of eddoes on she table like if you own Chance Market when you know Fatty-Om was coming."

Gloria puffed herself up even bigger. "Child, you hear that? That auntie call your father 'Fatty-Om,' too." A smirk settled on her thin lips.

Vimla scowled. "That auntie only have one chin!"

Some people chuckled, but an older granny stood slowly from her perch and pointed a shaky finger at Vimla. "Mind your elders." Her voice crackled when she spoke and the words came out slow. "Why you come here? You should be home learning to cook *paratha roti* for your husband."

"I ain't married."

Granny smiled, showing the dark gaps of missing teeth. "Because you can't cook paratha roti."

Onlookers laughed again as they arranged their produce on their stalls. Om sighed. "Vimla, tell Auntie Glory you sorry and let we find a next stall fast before this place full up." He glanced around the giant tent for a spot.

Vimla's mouth fell open. "Pa! This is our stall, and she—"

Om gathered up his bags of long beans and headed for the

last vacant stand he could see, leaving Vimla and Gloria glowering at each other. Vimla lifted the produce scale into her arms.

"Take the damn stall, you fat water buffalo."

By six o'clock, the tent was overflowing with vendors and shoppers. Om and Vimla had set up their stall in the far right corner close to the exit. The flap of the tent was peeled back, allowing warm yellow sunshine to pour onto Om's long beans.

"Golden bodi! Get your golden bodi!" he hollered, as people ambled by with baskets slung on their arms.

When she wasn't stuffing bags with long beans or making change for customers, Vimla scanned the bustling tent for Minty. She searched for a milky, moon-shaped face in a sea of tanned farmer families, or a black glossy ponytail of unusually needle-straight hair. Vimla peered around elbows and over shoulders from where she sat, peeked in between chatting friends and around obstructing heads.

Om tapped Vimla on the shoulder. "Go buy some garlic and some 7 Pot Pepper." Vimla sprang to her feet as Om deposited a few crumpled bills into her open palm. "*Hot* pepper, Vimi." He gazed across the tent, assessing the various pepper vendors. "Don't go by she." He pointed to a woman in polka dots. "She does sell sick, squingy-looking pepper. Don't go by he." He pointed to a man with a zigzag part in his hair. "He does t'ief peppers from Chaguanas Market and sell them here. Don't go by Bulldog neither."

"Okay, Pa." Vimla squeezed her way past Om.

"Vimla!" he called after her. She turned back. "7 Pot Pepper. *Hot* pepper."

Vimla rolled her eyes and sidestepped a cluster of shoppers. She weaved leisurely through the rows of fresh produce, past piles of shiny eggplant, green figs, yellow plantain and halved pumpkins with gold-orange flesh. The smell of ripe papaya, watermelon and sweet juicy Julie mangoes wafted through the air, tantalizing buzzing flies. Vimla swatted at one fly as it zipped past her and landed on the top of a tangelo pyramid. The tangelo vendor waved the fly away and it took off again, making circles in the air and then alighting on the bumpy skin of a green karela.

The tent was bursting with market prattle. Everywhere people haggled, gossiped and hollered to their neighbours at a distance.

"Eh, man, give me a good price for this coconut, nuh?"

It was Rajesh Gopalsingh, Minty's father. Vimla drew nearer.

"That is the coconut price!" The bald coconut merchant gestured to his cardboard sign, shrugging, as if the price was etched in stone.

Rajesh sucked his teeth. "Come, nuh, man. This is robbery."

The merchant shook his head, which shone with perspiration.

"This coconut have gold inside?" Rajesh held the young coconut to his ear and shook it so the water sloshed around inside. He turned it over in his hands, pretending to examine its shape, knocked it randomly with his giant knuckles, rubbed it with his callused fingertips. "Genie? You there?"

The merchant grabbed a bag from behind his stall. "Man, just take the damn coconut. I losing all my hair listening to your shit-talk." He mopped his head with a handkerchief.

Rajesh beamed at the merchant and bought four green

coconuts. The merchant showed his teeth in what was meant to be a smile, stuffed the bills in an old cookie tin and slid it behind his stand with his foot.

Vimla followed Rajesh down the aisle. He cleared a path through the throng with his broad chest and broader status in the district. He nodded to important men and stopped to greet elders on his way to his wife's alterations stand. Vimla darted past him and flung her arms around Minty, who sat on a chair with a book in her lap.

"Vimi!" Minty said.

Sangita, Minty's mother, eyed the pair warily.

"Hi, Auntie Sangita." Vimla brushed Minty's mother with a careless kiss on the cheek and squished herself next to Minty on the chair. "You studying for your A Levels in the market?"

Minty gave Vimla a sheepish look. "Yeah," she said, closing her book.

"Vimla Narine, don't try and put style on we. You must be study whole day and night to pass all your exams so." Sangita was measuring a piece of orange cloth. "The A Levels no joke." She draped the tape measure around her neck and ripped the cloth in a perfect line down the middle.

Vimla shrugged. "Not really. I didn't study plenty."

Sangita fixed Vimla with a stern gaze. "Vimla, I find you getting real fresh these days."

Sangita drew near the girls, giving Vimla an appraising once-over. "Come, Vimla." She put the pieces of cloth down and reached for Vimla's wavy ponytail. "You must oil your hair and plait it to keep it neat." She began weaving a braid into Vimla's thick unruly mane.

Vimla made to rise from the chair, but she was tugged backward by Sangita, who insisted on braiding her hair to the very ends.

"Look at Minty's hair. Look how tidy and shiny she hair is!"

Vimla glanced sideways at her friend. Minty's hair was straight and fine, unlike Vimla's wavy, coarser tresses. It felt unfair to compare the two. "She hair different from my own." Vimla craned her neck over Sangita's stall to see the sari blouses she was stitching. "I like that blue one, Auntie. Who is that for?"

Sangita pursed her full, sensual lips. "Vimla, you too fast!"

Minty lowered her eyes, but Vimla grinned, unfazed. "Definitely not for Gloria-Booblooloops. She boobies too big for that blouse!"

Rajesh, who was counting the money Sangita had received, glanced up and grunted. "That is true."

Sangita pursed her lips tighter, snatching the bills from Rajesh's massive hands and handing some to Minty before stuffing the rest into her blouse. "You does encourage such nonsense, Rajesh."

He grunted again and nodded over Sangita's shoulder. "Look, Pudding selling crab." He pointed to the entrance of the open tent, through which he could see his cousin with his crabs at the side of the road. "I gone." Rajesh sauntered off.

"Minty, take this and go and buy a pound of currants and some paw-paw."

Vimla hooked her arm in Minty's and began tugging her in the direction of a papaya stand. "I go show she where it is!" Vimla said. She didn't turn to see, but Vimla knew Sangita was frowning after her.

Minty allowed herself to be dragged away. "Vimla! You brave to talk to Mammy so."

"Your mammy would call it 'boldface.'"

The girls giggled as they manoeuvred around knots of hagglers and gossiping vendors. After they had purchased garlic, pepper, currants and papaya for their parents, Minty and Vimla joined Rajesh and Uncle Pudding.

"Get your fresh crab!" Pudding cried. "Everybody eating fresh crab tonight except you!"

Vimla and Minty peered into Uncle Pudding's crab crate. The crabs scuttled over one another, snapping their claws and grasping at anything within reach. They snatched at legs, climbing and toppling over their neighbours in pursuit of freedom. Some landed on their backs, flailing hairy legs in the air; others landed on their bellies, only to try to escape again. But always the crabs fell back to the place they began, until Uncle Pudding yanked them out and flung them on his stall to be cleaned.

Minty placed a hand over her nose to block out the fishy smell as Uncle Pudding scraped the hair off a crab's legs with meticulous strokes of his knife. "You see this crab, Minty? When I done scrape out the hair"—he flipped the crab over and pointed at the crab's underbelly—"I go clean out the guts, and this crab go be ready to sell."

Minty's fair face paled further.

Uncle Pudding's knife grazed over the crab's legs swiftly as he spoke. "You ever see a crab man clean a crab like your Uncle Pudding, Minty?"

Minty shook her head.

"You want to try and chop it up?"

A man in a dirty vest and yellow shorts weaved up the walk. "Pudding, give me two crab for free, nuh?" He braced on the board that Pudding was cleaning his crab on and slapped Rajesh hard on the back. "Raj, when last I see you, boy?"

Rajesh remained rooted in his spot despite the slap. "Puncheon, how you could be drunk at six thirty in the morning?"

Puncheon laughed and draped an arm around Rajesh's shoulders, exposing a sweaty armpit. "Who drunk? Me?" He sucked his teeth.

Vimla and Minty inched back. They made their way out of the tent and began to browse the stalls that lined the side of the road. Slippers, cast-iron pots, rolling pins and pot spoons lay in the sun on wooden stalls or on newspaper on the ground. Men and women sat beside their goods, fanning themselves in their best market wear and calling out to shoppers who swarmed the side of the road like bees.

Across the road, Vimla spotted a doubles stand. She watched hungrily as a woman heaped a spoonful of curried chickpeas and a dash of pepper sauce in between two pieces of flattened, fried dough and wrapped the sandwich in wax paper for a waiting customer. Her hand flew to Minty's arm. "Is him!"

Minty squinted against the sun. "Him who?" There were dozens of people milling about the place.

"*Krishna*. Pundit Anand Govind's son. He buying a doubles. Look." Vimla glanced both ways and darted across the busy street, with Minty running after her. They positioned themselves behind a pair of men shucking corn.

Krishna, five foot ten, beamed down at the doubles lady. "Thank you, Auntie," he said, handing her some money. His deep brown eyes crinkled at the sides when he smiled.

The doubles lady batted her sparse eyelashes at him. "That's all right, son. Tell me, your father find a girl for you to marry yet?"

Krishna leaned forward some. "You available?"

The doubles lady giggled and waved her hand at him. "I too old for you, dahling," she cooed.

He took a step backward, his hand flying to his heart. "Well, if I can't have you, I go take two more of your doubles then." He fished into his trouser pocket and pulled out some more bills. "Not too spicy this time."

Delighted, the doubles lady whipped up two more packages, oozing with chickpeas. Krishna thanked her, turned on his heel and headed straight toward Vimla and Minty.

"Pretty gyul." Krishna handed Vimla a package and winked. He turned to Minty. "How you going, Mints?"

The girls stared back at him, doubles in hand, speechless. He laughed. "What happened? I have *channa* on my face?" Krishna wiped his large hand over his smile, brushing the invisible chickpeas away.

"Sita-Ram," Minty said.

"How you so formal today, Mints? Like you and me is strangers now?" Krishna made to pinch her arm playfully but then remembered where he was and shoved his hand in his pocket instead.

Minty shrugged. Then: "How you know we was here? And how come you buy this for *we*?" When she took a big bite of her treat, sauce drizzled over the side of her hand and down her wrist. "Mmm . . . thank you," she said through a spicy mouthful.

"I been watching Vimla for the past hour," Krishna said to Minty, nodding at Vimla with a roguish smile. "When she finally notice me, she was giving me a hungry look, so I decide to buy my girl a snack—and one for she co-conspirator, too," he added. "How I could let two sweet girls starve?"

Minty looked away, embarrassed, but Vimla stared up at Krishna as if he were the only other person in Chance market. Krishna took a step closer to her, so close the faint hairs on his arm grazed her skin. She inhaled the soapy scent of him, trying to extract it from the market smells and hold it in her lungs for as long as possible. Krishna inched nearer still and lowered his voice. "I left something for you with the fig man. Tell him I send you and then get back in the tent—Sangita looking for allyuh." He gazed over her head while he talked, scanning the road and the produce tent across the street.

She could feel her heart pounding. If she shuffled just a step forward, she would brush against his muscular arm. The thought caused her cheeks to burn all over again. As Minty devoured her doubles and hummed the latest film song, Vimla started to ask Krishna what he'd left for her with the fig man. But Krishna had already turned away, whistling as if the conversation had never occurred.

Jammette

Sangita Gopalsingh paced back and forth before the wrought-iron gates of her home, her white nightie swishing in the late-evening breeze. The moon looked like a fat dull thumbprint in the sky, smudged between heavy clouds on either side. She thought of the god that had pressed the moon into the sky that way, trapping it, allowing it to languish in the moving and swelling clouds.

Sangita clasped her hands around the bars of one of the gates and peered into the shadows, hoping to catch a glimpse of Dr. Mohan riding his bicycle home after a late day. She wanted him to ring his bell and wave at her. She wanted him to see her in her transparent nightie and make an inappropriate comment about how spicy she looked. She hoped Dr. Mohan would bicycle by when her hair was still wet from her bath; he'd liked the damp black waves snaking down her back and coiling at her waist the last time. Sangita traced a slender finger over her hairline, down the side of her smooth face and hovered over her full mouth, the way Dr. Mohan had once done with his lips. A frisson of longing shot through her body. She rested her head against the gate and sighed into the night.

Flambeaux bounded from a pile of bricks stacked against the fence that divided the Gopalsinghs' property from their neighbour Faizal Mohammed's, and landed in a silent crouch just inches from the frilly hem of Sangita's nightgown. She caught the movement out of the corner of her eye and watched as Flambeaux uncurled his spine one vertebra at a time, until he was sitting tall on his haunches, his two front paws placed lightly on the ground.

"Shoo!" Sangita waved her hands at the cat.

Flambeaux gave the three sleeping mutts sprawled across the floor a cursory glance and then fixed Sangita with his glowing hazel eyes, sweeping his bushy orange tail back and forth across the concrete like a coconut broom.

Sangita frowned. "Don't watch me so, Flambeaux. I does get lonely." She floated to the flour sack that was Rajesh's hammock and collapsed onto it, careful not to upset the cup of Ovaltine she'd placed on the ground earlier, now cold and unappetizing.

Flambeaux narrowed his gaze.

"Humph! You no better. You does have this Mrs. Cat and that Mrs. Cat coming to my house to make kittens with you. My house look like a cat motel, Flambeaux."

Flambeaux yawned and squinted.

Sangita was just about to pull herself out of the hammock and make her way to her bedroom, where Rajesh was fast asleep, when she heard a rustle in the darkness. Flambeaux started, flicked his gaze from Sangita to somewhere beyond the gates. He took one tentative step forward, keeping low to the ground like a prowling tiger.

Sangita shook her head. "Don't go and scrap with a next cat, Flambeaux. Keep your tail home." But as Sangita picked up her small oil lamp and made for the stairs, she heard it: the distinctive sound of a girlish giggle muffled by . . . a hand? A kiss? She pivoted on her heel and flew back to the gates like a frantic ghost moving through the night. Who was there? Was it Dr. Mohan with Shantie Ramdeen? She held the lamp high, flooding the dark road and the bushes beyond in pale yellow light. Flambeaux took off in a flash; he squeezed his sleek body through the bars of the gates and disappeared in the direction from which the sound had come.

Sangita gasped when her eyes fell on the pair. They were darting toward the ravine, hand in hand, trying to escape the lamplight. They hovered low, covering their faces, but Sangita had got a good look and there was no mistaking who she'd seen. When finally their silhouettes—so close, they were almost one—disappeared into a forest of leafy mangrove trees, Sangita felt the injustice of her dull marriage rise and gorge itself on the last of her common sense.

"Jammette!" she shrieked. "Jaaaammmeeettteee!"

The sound of Sangita's sharp insults roused the dogs from their slumber. They sat up, startled, and began to bark wildly, gnashing their teeth at the darkness and joining in a harmony of fearsome growls and distressed barks. They pawed at the gates to be let out, paced back and forth at the prospect of tackling an intruder. They made such a commotion that somewhere down the road a neighbour yelled, "Allyuh shut your dogs up, nuh? A man trying to catch some blasted sleep here!" Other neighbours began lighting lamps and peering out of their homes. "Sangita! Allyuh all right?" Faizal Mohammed hollered from next door. Sangita saw him push an empty Coca-Cola crate up against the window and perch on top to get a better look at the fuss below. She tried to hush the panicked dogs and hurry back to bed before Rajesh awoke, but he met her on the steps, shirtless, cutlass in hand.

"What happened?" He pushed past her; the dogs barked at his heels.

Sangita whisked her heavy hair out of her face and plaited it skilfully. She didn't hesitate: "I see Vimla Narine go in the ravine." She crossed her arms over her heaving bosom, hoping Rajesh wouldn't notice her bare body trembling beneath the nightgown.

"Vimla? What she gone there for at this hour?"

"Rajesh, I look like a seer woman to you?" Sangita shoved the lamp at her husband and steered him toward his bike, which was leaning against a concrete post. "I ain't know why she run away, but I know I see she and I know who I see she with."

Rajesh stopped wheeling his bike toward the gates and held the lamp up so that the glow of light fell directly on Sangita's face. "What you mean? Who she with?"

Sangita fixed her husband with a grave stare. "Krishna," she said, "the pundit's son!"

"Krishna?" Confusion tugged at Rajesh's square face. "The two of them alone?"

Sangita nodded, a terse incline of her chin. She bit down on the tip of her tongue, waiting for her husband to process the severity of the situation. The seconds dragged on. Sangita tasted coppery blood in her mouth.

"Shits, man!" Rajesh fitted the sharp cutlass into the elastic waist of his shorts so that it jutted out the bottom. Then he climbed on his bicycle and shifted the flat blade onto his thigh before pushing off the ground with his left foot. "Open the gates, Sangita, I going to fetch them."

When her husband had pedalled away, Sangita wrung the end of her braid in her hands and shuffled up the stairs to change into something more appropriate, grateful Vimla's scandal had eclipsed her own unsavoury intentions. She mounted the steps and peeked into Minty's room, where she found her daughter sitting upright in bed. Sangita moved closer, suddenly wanting to touch the youthful skin on Minty's face, to climb into bed with her and be a good respectable mother; the sort of mother who soothes her child from the din of angry dogs, not the sort who steals from her husband's bed in search of passion.

Minty sat with her knees pulled up to her chest and Sangita could see she was shaking. "The dogs frighten you, *beti*?" She moved to the bed, stroked a tendril of damp hair from her daughter's forehead. As Minty flinched, a cloud scudded past the moon, allowing a few beams of light to slice through the window and cut across her face. Reproach sparkled in her eyes.

"Who you call a 'jammette,' Mammy?" Minty asked.

Sangita pressed her full lips together in a firm line. She didn't like her daughter using such crude language and she told her as much.

Minty sprang from bed and dashed barefoot to the window. In the distance torchlights blazed bright against an inky sky and five figures trudged from the underbrush by the ravine.

Sangita looked over her daughter's shoulder. She recognized Rajesh's stocky build, Om Narine's protruding gut, Faizal Mohammed's long-legged gait and the stooped shoulders of a disgraced young man—Krishna. The fifth figure was slighter than the rest. She walked at Om's side, hugging herself as she went, a crumpled curtain of black wayward hair hiding her down-turned face.

Minty wheeled on her mother, eyes flashing. "Mammy, look how you get Vimla in trouble!"

Sangita faced her daughter. "Minty, Vimla is seventeen years old! What business she have rollicking with the pundit's son in the bush? She is a loose little jammette!"

Minty's expression was stony. "As much business as *you* had *rollicking* with Dr. Mohan. And Faizal Mohammed. And—"

Sangita cuffed Minty across her mouth before the rest of her paramours tumbled out into the night.

Faizal Mohammed's Barrel Bath

Monday August 5, 1974

....

CHANCE, TRINIDAD

Faizal Mohammed swung his long legs to the floor and extended his arms in a luxurious diagonal stretch. "Praise Allah!" He leaped to his feet and peered out the window onto Kiskadee Trace. A mangy stray dog blotched with black patches trotted up the deserted road through the early-morning gloom, raising dust in his wake. He stopped abruptly in front of Faizal's home and squatted in the dirt to nip at a family of fleas on his underbelly before carrying on. Faizal surveyed the road again, narrowing his eyes and straining at the shadows, peering into the front yards and windows of every home he could see from his bedroom. There was no movement, not even the kiskadees had stirred awake yet. He nodded with approval and set off to make ready for his morning prayers.

After zipping into his second room, Faizal crouched before the large wire cage he'd built with his own hands. "Allahu Akbar," he purred, lifting the white sheet that covered the cage and bringing his face close.

Sam, Faizal's blue-and-gold parrot, squinted back at him and then bobbed up and down on his perch. "Allahu Akbar. Allahu Akbar."

Faizal beamed as he unlocked the cage door and allowed Sam to step onto his extended index finger. He bounded down the stairs and set Sam on the floor then rounded the corner to his bathroom. The room, separate from the house, was a chamber of three walls constructed from large sheets of silver galvanized steel. The open side faced the back of Faizal's home, allowing two feet of space between the house and one wall for him to slip in and out of. The structure had no roof so that rainwater could fill his oversized rain barrel. A frangipani tree arched over the bathroom, creating a spectacular leafy awning with fragrant white blossoms.

This morning, the barrel in Faizal's bathroom was half filled with rainwater. He fished a soggy leaf and a sopped flower out of the water with his long fingers and tossed both over his shoulder, just missing Sam. Faizal felt a sharp pinch at his ankle and apologized profusely to his parrot, who squawked in return. Then, with magnificent agility, Faizal gripped the sides of the barrel and hoisted himself up so that his tucked knees hovered just above the barrel's mouth. "Praise Allah," he said, and plunged into the rainwater. Sam stomped about in the water that cascaded over the edge to puddles on the cracked concrete ground, spreading his wings wide and chuckling in the back of his throat.

Inside Faizal's rain barrel was a crescent moon bench fastened to the sides with brass hinges. Constructed with his own hands, this movable bench allowed Faizal to sit or bob around freely, depending on his mood. This morning Faizal pulled the bench down and sat quietly on its edge as the chilly water seeped over his shoulders to his chin.

He wondered, not for the first time, what his neighbours would think if they knew he bathed in his rain barrel instead of using the standpipe like everyone else. The secret sent thrilling zings through his wiry body; he loved to know what others didn't. And Faizal's rain-barrel baths were a particularly safe secret, as he was the only Muslim in the district, the only one who rose before the cock's first crow, before the sun peeked over the horizon, to wash, and to praise Allah.

Faizal reached for his bar of blue soap in a dish cut from a scrap of galvanize screwed to the outside of his barrel. As he lathered his arms, he thought of last night's curious melodrama with Krishna Govind and Vimla Narine. How fortunate to live nestled between the Narine and Gopalsingh residences, to be called upon at the climax of the crisis to search for the runaway lovers! "A pundit's son and a village prize pupil—what a delicious disgrace, Sam!" Faizal hauled one leg out of the water and balanced his heel on the rim of the barrel so he could soap between his toes. "And I was *there*, Sam. I see everything." He switched legs. "You know, is a damn shame a nice girl like Vimla go and shit up she reputation over a jackass like Krishna Govind." Faizal rubbed the soap into his armpit hair until blue lather oozed through his fingers and dribbled down the side of his body. "I mean, I ain't know he too good, but I hear he does knock about all over Chance instead of studying he scriptures like a pundit's son should. But if you ask me, half the damn Hindus in this place is a bunch of crooks!" He swished back and forth in the water, watching blue and silver bubbles spread over the surface. "Except Sangita Gopalsingh."

"Praise Allah! Praise Allah!" Sam puffed his blue-and-gold body up. "Praise Allah!"

Faizal glanced at his parrot over the side of the barrel and then up at the sky through the canopy of frangipani branches. The ashy grey heavens had turned a faint mauve. "Mangoes!" he exclaimed. His hands flew to his dry hair. After filling his small chest with air, Faizal pinched his nose and plunged into the barrel, soaking Sam. He stayed submerged for thirty seconds, drowning out Sam's frenzied shrieks, and then burst into the balmy morning air with another splash. Sam scurried away, flapping his drenched wings and screeching.

Once Faizal had dried himself and smoothed coconut oil into his puffy hair, he slipped into a fresh white kurtha pajama, grabbed one of seven prayer mats around his tiny house and darted to his garden. "Come, Sam!" he called over his shoulder.

"Shut up! Shut up! Shut up!" Sam hollered back as he scurried after Faizal into the back garden.

Faizal unrolled his prayer mat in the savannah grass between two young hibiscus trees, their peach and white blossoms still beaded with morning dew. He pressed the curling edges of the mat tenderly down. It was green, covered in specks of gold. For a split second he admired the thread work, and remembered the soft hands that had embroidered it.

Sam scurried onto the prayer mat with the blue-green feathers on his head raised in angry spikes. When Faizal stooped to stroke his ruffled plumage, Sam tipped his head back and nipped Faizal's finger hard with his black beak. Shrugging, Faizal turned to Mecca, opened his hands before him like a book and sped through his prayers. This morning Sam refused to join in, but as Faizal lowered his forehead to the mat reverently, Sam mirrored him. Then the bird strutted off, muttering.

When Faizal Mohammed rose from his last prostration and opened his eyes, he found himself staring into a luscious bosom the colour of rich caramel.

"Good morning, Faizal. I hope I ain't interrupt your prayers."

"Sangita." Faizal got to his feet, gathered his prayer mat off the ground and rolled it up. Just behind Sangita, ribbons of coral were stretching across the sky and a dazzling amber sun was casting its first rays onto Chance's silver roofs. Faizal allowed himself a smile; she had timed her arrival carefully. He noticed a notebook tucked beneath her arm, and a piece of red thread clinging to a shapely hip. "Working early, I see." He gestured to the kitchen, which backed onto his garden. "Come. Let we have some coffee."

Sangita glanced at the thin gold watch on her wrist and then over the fence at her house. She bit her lip and blinked her black slanted eyes at Faizal, letting her gaze trail quite obviously over his lean body. "A quick coffee while we discuss. Half a cup." Her pink lips turned up at the corners. "Just a sip." She sashayed past him to the kitchen. Her cream skirt swished at her calves.

Faizal put a pot of water on the stove and set two blue enamel cups on the small counter, watching out of the corner of his eye as Sangita crossed and uncrossed her legs. He cleared his throat and she looked up at him.

"Faizal," she began, flipping open her notebook. She retrieved the pencil from her hair, letting it tumble like soft silk down her back. Faizal swallowed. "Did the money for the burgundy-and-red prayer mats come in as yet?"

He poured the steamy coffee into the cups and brought them to the table, accidentally brushing Sangita's ankle with his toe. "Sorry—and no, because I ain't take them to my store as yet. The mats are scheduled to be picked up today. I go have your payment for the embroidery by tonight."

Sangita scribbled this information into her notebook as if Faizal hadn't told her this a week ago.

"Your designs was real nice, Sangita. They getting popular. Everybody who sees one of my mats with your needlework does put in an order."

Sangita puckered her lips and blew the steam from her coffee before taking a sip. Faizal noticed the top two buttons of her cream-and-powder-blue blouse were still undone. His eyes lingered there until she placed her cup down and shut her notebook abruptly, snapping his attention back to her exquisite face. A sheen of perspiration glowed on her skin and the hairs around her high cheekbones curled in the warm kitchen. Faizal sat back in his chair and waited.

"Faiz-al"—she sang his name—"tell me what happened last night."

He knew she hadn't really come about the prayer mats. "Last night?" He feigned confusion.

Sangita swatted his hairy arm with her soft fingertips. "Faizal Mohammed, don't play stupid!"

He moved to throw open the tiny windows, distracting himself from the burn of her touch on his skin. Taking a deep breath as a rush of dewy airy blew into the kitchen, he said, "Didn't Mr. Rajesh Gopalsingh share all the details with his pretty wife last night?"

Sangita arched an eyebrow at him.

Faizal knew he was being petty, but he couldn't help it. She had been teasing him for years. They had been teasing each other for years.

"I was sleeping when he come home." She lowered her gaze and Faizal knew she was lying.

"Hmm. Well, maybe later, nuh?" He pretended to be interested in two birds flitting after each other in a tree outside the window. "When I get back from the shop tonight, I go tell you."

She stared at him. "I can't come back here *tonight!*"

Faizal pushed his chair back. "Come to the shop."

"In Port of Spain? *How?*" She rose, too, but still she had to look up to meet his eyes. "Just tell me if you see them kiss. What were Krishna and Vimla *doing* by the ravine?" She gathered her heavy hair on top of her head and slid the pencil from the table back in its place.

Faizal grabbed Sangita's narrow waist and pulled her close while she fiddled with her hair. She gasped, letting her hands fall to his chest but never pushing. "Faizal—"

"I found them like this." He lowered his face close to hers, deliberately, until he could feel her warm breath. She parted her lips and leaned into him as he drew her nearer, until their mouths were only half an inch apart. Then he released her, suddenly, and stepped away. "Just like that. That is what I see."

Pink crept into Sangita's cheeks. She puffed at a tendril of hair that had fallen free of her careless upsweep and took a step back from Faizal. After buttoning her blouse hurriedly, Sangita snatched her notebook off the table and brushed past him. "You can leave the money with my husband when you get it," she called over her shoulder. Faizal knew her words were meant to sting, but the breathlessness in her voice pleased him. He smiled after her, watching as she weaved through his frangipani trees with their great white-and-yellow blossoms and slipped, soundless, into her own yard.

The Rude Awakening

Monday August 5, 1974

. . . .

CHANCE, TRINIDAD

Vimla opened her eyes and rolled onto her side. She listened to the kiskadee morning call and watched the flutters of black and yellow in the guava and tamarind trees at her bedroom window. They trilled and rustled in the treetops, cocking their heads at impossible angles and announcing their presence to the world: *kis-kis-kiskadee!*

Vimla blinked at the blue sky from her bed until slowly a feeling of foreboding stirred awake and spread thick and oily over her heart. Memories of last night burst in her mind in dreadful detail. She covered her face with her hands and curled into a tight ball as the image of her father hovering over her and Krishna with a torchlight held high flashed through her mind. Vimla groaned from her soul. He had looked so injured.

She reached under the pillow beside her and retrieved the conch shell Krishna had left for her in the market on Saturday.

It was the length of her hand, a glossy shell of peach and ivory swirls. She ran her fingers over the ridges and sharp points and inside the shell where it was as smooth and cool as marble. She held it to her ear the way Krishna had shown her and heard the ocean rise up and crash against an invisible shore. Vimla had seen conches a hundred times before—during prayers pundits blew into the shells like trumpets—but she hadn't known that the sound of the ocean lived inside them, too.

"What you hear?" Krishna had asked when he'd given it to her.

"Water. Energy. Something powerful," Vimla said. She put the shell to his ear. "What you hear?"

"The ocean. Freedom. *You.*"

Vimla still wasn't sure what Krishna had meant by that, but it made her feel special and cherish the conch that much more. She took it away from her ear and tucked it back under the pillow.

"Wake she up, Om! Wake she up so I can kill she!"

Startled, Vimla scrambled to her window and peered behind the house, where Chandani was untying the goats from their stall. The kids bleated and pranced about the moody ram goat and he lowered his head and butted one away.

Om took the ropes from his wife's hands and led the goats toward the field to graze. "Vimla!" he bellowed as he walked away. "Get up so your mother can kill you!"

Vimla leaned against the wall and closed her eyes. How many Saturdays had she pretended to go to Port of Spain for exam preparation classes, only to steal away with Krishna when she arrived? How many times had she and Krishna hidden in her father's sugar cane to exchange a quick word, a nervous kiss? Vimla groaned. She had become careless in the past few weeks under Krishna's self-assured care, taking bigger risks, meeting him at ungodly hours closer and closer to home. She let the back of her head rap against the wall as she sank to the floor. What would she do now?

The stairs creaked and Vimla froze. She heard footsteps draw nearer then stop outside her bedroom door. She held her breath as the door was thrown open with a crash. Chandani stood four foot ten and frightening in the doorway. Her eyes, red and puffy—presumably from a night of crying—bulged from her small face in fury now. She breathed in through her nose and out heavily through her mouth. Gripping the sides of the door frame with her tiny hands, Chandani leaned forward and peered down at Vimla cowering on the floor. "What the ass is wrong with you?"

Vimla's heart struck irregularly against her chest. "Ma—"

"You want to get married?" Chandani shot across the room and stood over her daughter. "Hmm? That is what you want? Well, why you didn't tell me that, Vimla? I go find somebody for you to marry!"

Vimla stared up at her mother, wide eyed. "I done pick Krishna, Ma."

Chandani gasped and swiped at Vimla, who threw herself across the floor to avoid the blow. "Pick? Pick!" Chandani looked mortified. "You feel Krishna is a sweet sapodilla you could just *pick* from a tree?"

Vimla winced. As bright as she was, she often expressed her thoughts unfiltered. This was one of those times Vimla wished she'd kept her opinions private. "Ma. I sorry."

Chandani sat on Vimla's bed. "You sorry, Vimla? Tell me what you sorry for."

Vimla swallowed. This was a trap. There was no way to win an argument with her mother, and in truth, she wasn't sure what she was sorry for yet. So Vimla waited for her mother to continue, which inevitably she did.

"No more walking about for you, you hear? Concentrate on university applications. Unless it have Krishna and tra-la-la-ing with man in the bush on your syllabus, you better not study that again!"

Vimla's mouth dropped open.

Chandani made for the door. "And while you waiting to hear back from schools, you go cook and clean and wash, mind the goats and the cow and the bull and the fowl." She counted these tasks off on her childlike fingers. "In the meantime, Vimla, I go work hard, too. I go search high and low, upside down, round and round, to find a boy as dotish as you for you to marry." She brushed her hands against each other. "I done talk," she said, and walked away.

Vimla followed her out of the room. "What about Krishna? To marry."

Chandani halted mid-step and her back went rigid. Vimla began to edge away even before her mother spun around and pounced at her like a vicious cat. "Krishna? Vimla Narine, what the ass make you think Krishna go marry you now?"

"He love me."

Chandani flinched. "It ain't have nothing like love here!" She gestured to the sunlit hallway. Vimla wasn't sure if her mother meant this house or Trinidad, but she didn't dare ask. "Your reputation ruined, girl. The Govind family ain't go want Krishna to marry you now."

Vimla stared, dumbstruck, at her mother, who sucked her teeth, stomped into her bedroom and slammed the door.

A Pundit's Plea

A nand sat on the *mandir* floor by the concrete lattice window with his legs folded beneath him. A diamond patchwork of sunlight and shadow fell across his back and sagging shoulders; a mellow breeze drifted through the open spaces, ruffling the fine silver hairs on the back of his neck.

Anand hadn't worn his elaborate priestly attire this morning. Instead he had dressed in grey slacks and a simple cotton kurtha, with the sleeves rolled up to his elbows. He'd tucked his *mala*, a string of 108 prayer beads, inside his collar and kept his gaze fixed on the ground as he'd hurried up the main road, slipped through the mandir's back door and sat. Now that the doors were locked and he was alone, Anand could have this conversation aloud.

He turned his bloodshot gaze to Mother Lakshmi, goddess of health, wealth and prosperity. "Karma?" His sleepless night hung in pouches under his eyes. His lids drooped with the weight of them.

The marble goddess, swathed in fuchsia, pink and gold, sat in her expansive lotus throne with her right palm turned toward Anand, proffering blessings. Sunlight dazzled off the gems sewn into her silk sari, lending her marble expression a celestial glow. She smiled at him the way she always had, but for Anand something had changed.

He took a deep breath before he continued. The place smelled of yesterday's prayers: sandalwood and smoke, cotton wicks burning in pools of rich yellow ghee. "I dedicate my life to your service and this is my reward?" He leaned forward and squinted at the murti as if to make sure she was listening. "This mandir is my second home. I does come here and clean your altar and chant your mantras. I does come here and per-form pujas with such devotion. How many *diyas*, clay pots, you think I light at your feet?" He frowned as if he were remem-bering. "Plenty—and that ain't counting my past lives!" He stared directly into Mother Lakshmi's marble eyes, daring her to disagree. "And see how lovely you look in that pink sari! Who does adorn you in such nice-nice clothes?" He arched a silver dishevelled eyebrow at Mother Lakshmi. "Is me self who does do it. Me self!"

Anand sat blinking at the murti for some time. Silence loomed like a concrete wall between them. He sighed, letting the exhale whistle between puckered lips, and then, grumbling, unfolded his legs and hauled himself to his feet. When he took a deliberate step forward, a prickly sensation surged through his toes and shot across his sole. Anand swallowed a curse and shifted his weight into the other foot. He glowered at Mother

Lakshmi as blood rushed back into his smarting toes. Was She toying with him? He was in no mood.

Anand marched to the altar and poured ghee from a jar into a freshly washed diya. Between thumb and forefinger, he twirled a cotton ball into a wick and drowned it in the clarified butter. When he set the wick ablaze with a match, the orange flame flickered in the small diya, elongating as it stretched toward heaven and then settling into a plump, upside-down teardrop. Anand gestured to the diya and then looked into Mother Lakshmi's eyes. "You see? A next one. You paying attention?"

He stooped and gathered a handful of flowers in his left hand from a taria he had filled from the small garden behind the mandir. "What you think people saying about me, Ma?" He placed a burgundy dahlia at her feet. "Them probably wondering how a devout pundit like me could raise a son to do such *nastiness*." He hissed this last word as he tucked a delicate jasmine into the fold of a sari pleat. "I feel so shame." He shook his head. "Shame, shame, shame. How Krishna could disgrace me so?" He threaded a few daisies into her gold crown with a practised hand. "How I could show my face to the people when my son do what he do with *she*?" He groaned as he slid an orange immortelle blossom between the marble fingers of Mother Lakshmi's raised hand. Then he stopped and cocked his head thoughtfully. "How *you* could allow this to happen to me?"

When the goddess was decorated with fresh flowers, Anand plucked three incense sticks out of their box and held them into the diya's flame. As they caught fire, he waved the flame out with his other hand so that the orange glow dissolved into ribbons of fragrant grey smoke. He inhaled deeply and then deposited the incense sticks in their brass holder at Mother Lakshmi's feet to purify the air around her. He opened his arms, palms facing upward. "So what can I do? My reputation as a pundit, as a leading man in this district, is in jeopardy. My earnings is in jeopardy." He pressed his right hand to his chest as if to soothe a sudden spasm of pain there. "And Krishna and this girl, they responsible. Tell me what to do."

Anand sat by the window again, folded his legs beneath him, interlaced his fingers in his lap and waited for an answer. He closed his eyes to meditate, but instead he drifted in and out of a restless sleep, waking sporadically to find his chin resting on his chest or his head lolling to one side. In those cruel intervals of wakefulness, Anand thought of the promise he had made to his own father: that he would be known as a well-respected, much-sought-after pundit and honour the Govind legacy born from six generations of learned Hindu priests. That memory was always followed by Krishna's handsome face, sunny with the carelessness of youth. Anand rubbed the throbbing at his temples. Krishna was failing him, and by extension, he, Pundit Anand Govind, was failing.

Anand gave up trying to sit and meditate. As he lay back in the dappled sunlight beneath the lattice window, his mala fell across his throat like a noose and pinned itself beneath his left shoulder. He raised his head, slipped the mala off and began moving his fingers deftly over the rough beads, his gaze trained on the ceiling. But the prayers wouldn't come. They got lost, or discouraged somewhere between his soul and his mouth, so he fiddled with his prayer beads thinking of things other than God.

Anand didn't fret about his mortality the way most other men his age in the district did. He had always led a virtuous life, beginning and ending his day with prayers and facilitating pujas for other people in between. He saw himself as a holy middleman, a liaison to the Lord, and naturally received a bountiful cut of the common man's blessings. His body, a vessel for his pure soul, was equally immaculate. Never had a drop of alcohol or morsel of meat touched his tongue. He was devoted to his wife, Maya; he had passed everything he knew of Hinduism on to Krishna. He had done good karma in the physical world, and when *Bhagwan*, God, decided to take him, he was ready. That's how he had thought of death. Up until last night.

Anand had even been willing to leave the matter of Krishna's marriage to Maya should he pass before that time came. He never doubted there would be an abundance of eligible young ladies from good Hindu families, eager to marry his son; never imagined that Krishna would do anything to befoul the Govinds' good name. But Anand had been wrong. Now there was no room for complacency in his life. He could not afford to slip quietly into his golden years. He had to ensure Krishna married well and that his family's good name was restored. Hadn't this been his life purpose?

"Hello?"

Anand heard a rap at the door. He stiffened.

"Baba? You there? Is me, Gloria. I come to do my morning prayers!"

Anand lay still and continued to stare at the ceiling. It was black with smoke and the old fan was coated with a film so thick he could mark his initials in it. And he should. That fan was as much his as this temple was. He was Pundit Anand Govind of Chance, after all. He chewed his lip. Had he asked Krishna to wipe down that smutty fan? He couldn't remember now.

Gloria jiggled the door handle. She rapped on the door again. "Well, this is real strange." Her voice glided in through the window. "Since when the pundit does lock up the mandir in the morning?" The door rattled in its frame and Anand grimaced; she was throwing her weight against the old wood.

"Ba-baaaa!" Gloria sang as she walked around the side of the building.

Anand held his breath. He wished she would go away and leave him to his thoughts. He would never hear Bhagwan's answer with all the racket Gloria was making.

Suddenly the pool of sunlight in which Anand was lying was eclipsed by a long shadow. "Baba?" Anand shut his eyes. Gloria was kneeling on the ground, peering through the diamond latticework at Anand's prostrate body.

Anand knew he should sit up and greet her, but for the first time in his life he did not feel like fulfilling his duty as village pundit. He couldn't when his own life wanted mending, when he was in as much need of Bhagwan's grace and guidance as Gloria or anyone else in Chance. Anand remained still.

"Oh gosh!" Gloria shrieked. "Pundit Anand sleeping in the mandir." Gloria fitted her mouth into a diamond cut in the concrete wall. "Ba-ba! Ba-baaaa! Wake up!"

Anand began singing Bhagwan's praises in his head to distract himself from breathing.

"Baba? Pundit Anand?" Her voice grew small. "Oh shames! This pundit gone and dead in the mandir!" She clicked her tongue against the roof of her mouth. "All that sexy-news about Vimla and Krishna must be kill the man."

Anand felt sunlight flood over his skin again as Gloria flew from the window in search of an ear to tell the tragedy. He opened one eye and then the other and then filled his hungry lungs with air. Anand thought about running after Gloria to explain that he had only been meditating, but he couldn't bring himself to do it. It was cruel, he knew, to let people think he was dead, but fate had been cruel to him, too, and this morning Anand's heart was tired and cold.

He sat up and slipped his mala back over his head. He had to leave the mandir. It wouldn't be long before the closest neighbours were swarming the place in search of him. "Gloria Ramnath already hear about Krishna and Vimla," he muttered, rubbing his hand over his face and tousled hair. "Ma"—he turned to Mother Lakshmi, his voice strained— "what answer you have for me? How to fix this?"

Mother Lakshmi stared vacantly back at him, but the orange immortelle balancing between her fingers tumbled to the floor.

A ghost of a smile played at the corners of Anand's lips. He nodded. "So Vimla must fall, too." Anand smoothed his kurtha and blinked his tired eyes at the altar. He nodded. "Of course, of course, Ma. Is only fair. Is only just. And I know the right person to help me—Headmaster Roop G. Kapil." He clapped his hands and bowed hurriedly. "Sita-Ram. We go talk later!"

Anand stalked past the altar and swung his arms with purpose. In the *whoosh* of his movements the diya sputtered and died.

The Immoral

Monday August 5, 1974

....

CHANCE, TRINIDAD

"We didn't raise you so, Krishna." Maya sniffled into a paisley handkerchief. "With no morals. Without a ounce of shame." She shut her eyes and shuddered as if his very presence on the veranda repulsed her. And yet he couldn't leave her alone. She needed someone to absorb the grief spilling out of her, and his father—Krishna dropped his head in his hands—hadn't the patience for Maya's laments this morning. He'd left early in a temper of his own, muttering about Krishna's ingratitude and boldfaced stupidity as he'd slammed the gates shut behind him. And so Krishna sat in quiet shame and watched the pink paisleys on Maya's handkerchief turn deep rose with tears.

Maya looked off into the distance. "What you see in that girl? What she have so special to make you throw away everything me and your father work to give you?"

Krishna thought back to the first time he'd seen Vimla. It had been at the Gopalsinghs' annual Ramayana and Vimla had sat among the dozens of guests under a yawning white tent listening—or pretending to listen—to his father's *katha* on Shri Ram's fourteen-year exile from his beloved city. He noticed that while the other devotees watched Pundit Anand's face animate with devotion as he told this ancient story, Vimla's eyes remained downcast as if she were watching something fascinating on her lap. And when the devotees joined in song with his father, Vimla's sweet lips mouthed the wrong words without the slightest inclination of shame. Krishna spent the course of the night observing her peculiar behaviour, and admiring, much to his surprise, the way the careless waves of Vimla's hair danced around her face in the humid night. It was only later, when the Ramayana was finished, and rice and karhi and spicy curries were being spooned onto sohari leaves for dinner, did Krishna walk casually by Vimla and discover that she had nestled a miniature periodic table into her sari pleats and that all night long she had been committing the elements to memory and, quite cleverly, reciting them aloud.

"Krypton," Krishna murmured, handing her a bag of warm *prasad*.

Vimla glanced up at him. A conspiratorial smile bloomed on her face. "Kr 36," she replied without hesitation. Her fingers brushed his as she accepted the prasad and in that touch sprang the unforgettable pulse of her liveliness.

Krishna looked up at his mother's drawn face. He couldn't tell her this now. No explanation, no apology, could undo the fact that he'd covertly pursued a romance and blackened the Govind name.

"Maaa-yaaaa! Oh gosh, Maya!"

Krishna sat up straight. "What the——?"

"Maya Govind! I sorry, gyul. I so sorry!"

Krishna and Maya leaped to their feet and peered over the veranda. There was Gloria Ramnath lumbering toward them, wheezing audibly and waving her arms in the air.

Maya flapped her handkerchief at Gloria from above. "Shh! What you carrying on so for, Glory?" She nudged Krishna toward the stairs. "Go and open the gates for that silly woman before she wake up the neighbours."

When Krishna let her in, Gloria threw herself against his chest so that he stumbled backward. "This go fall on your head, son!" she wailed. "But I know you is not to blame. Is that hot-mouth Vimla who cause all of we grief."

Maya's hand flew to her mouth; she was appalled. Gloria was a sopping mess. Her dress was plastered to her body with sweat, tears streamed down her cheeks and snot pooled in the hollow above her upper lip. "Gloria." Maya stuffed her damp handkerchief into Gloria's hand. "Hush your mouth, nuh, gyul!" Maya's eyes, red from crying, flashed angrily. "You must not have any shame yourself, coming to my house at this ungodly hour to meddle in we business!"

Even now, Krishna thought, Maya was determined to salvage her status in the district. She would not allow the likes of Gloria Ramnath to trumpet her downfall in a show of put-on grief.

Gloria gasped like she'd been slapped and peeled herself off Krishna's chest. "Pundit Anand Govind collapse in the mandir," she sobbed. Gloria brushed the soup of bodily fluid from her face with a pudgy, ringed hand and stared back at them like a child, chastised and heartbroken. For a moment Maya and Krishna stood dumbfounded.

"He look dead. I think he gone and dead," Gloria said. And then she burst into fresh tears.

Krishna's heart was in his throat. It beat so intensely his whole body seemed to judder, or maybe that was the car flying down Kiskadee Trace, endlessly uneven and pockmarked. Gloria blubbered on about her morning puja, how she had discovered Pundit Anand sprawled pitifully across the mandir floor; her son in Port of Spain, although a jeweller, could revive Pundit Anand if only he lived in Chance. Maya listened to all this with the fingertips of one hand pressed firmly into her lips and the other hand gripping the door handle until her fist turned white.

The district went by in a whir of houses painted in pinks, yellows and blues. Brushwood and flowers stirred sleepily in the mid-morning breeze. Cows and goats grazed their way through fields, lifting their heads just briefly as the car rattled by. Laundry snapped on makeshift clotheslines. Palm fronds splayed like fingers against the sky and filtered the blazing sun. Krishna flew past Vimla's house and the cane field that was their meeting place, past Minty's house—Minty, their faithful lookout until the very end—and over the bridge that once sheltered all three from an afternoon of rain. The mandir stood in the distance. Krishna recalled watching Vimla walk through the door at her mother's side Sunday after Sunday on the pretense of devotion. These memories, once full of perilous joy, now choked him with guilt. He couldn't help but think every meeting, every small betrayal, had led him closer to this fatal moment.

"Krishna!"

Krishna glanced sideways at his mother, who leaned on the dashboard, squinting against the sun's glare.

"Slow the car down before you kill your father!" she exclaimed.

Krishna was about to ask her if she was crazy, when he made out Anand standing in the middle of the road, looking as menacing as ever. Krishna hit the brakes and the car swerved before screeching to a halt. The smell of burned rubber floated on the sultry air.

Pundit Anand marched around the car and slammed his fist on the roof. "Who tell you to drive my car?" he asked.

"I thought you dead in the mandir," Krishna answered, and he knew how ludicrous he sounded. He was aware of Gloria Ramnath slouching against the back seat and trying, unsuccessfully, to appear inconspicuous.

"You can't kill me so easy," Pundit Anand said. "No matter how hard you try."

Krishna's shaking hands fell away from the steering wheel and into his lap. "I wasn't trying to kill you."

"True?" Pundit Anand arched a dishevelled, grey eyebrow. "You could have fooled me. You nearly ain't stop the car." He opened the door. "Get out."

"Come, Anand, let we go home," Maya coaxed. She glanced in the back seat at Gloria, who was observing the intimate family moment with unabashed interest.

"Not yet. I have business to discuss with Headmaster Roop G. Kapil," Anand said. He rubbed his palms together then clasped them behind his back.

Krishna caught the spiteful shadow that crossed his father's face and now he found his guilt forgotten. "What? What business you have with Headmaster Roop G. Kapil?" Although he suspected what mischief his father was up to and worried that Vimla would suffer for it.

Pundit Anand scowled at his son. "Krishna, you didn't hear me tell you to get out the car?" A vein throbbed in his neck.

Krishna abided, his gaze as cold as Anand's.

Anand slid into the driver's seat, cranked the ignition and looked over his shoulder. "Good morning, Gloria." His moustache lifted and revealed his most virtuous smile.

Gloria sat forward. "Baba, I was so frightened when I see you lie down in the mandir so."

Anand nodded. "I was in a deep meditation, Glory. Did you call for me?"

"I did, Baba!" Gloria said. She gripped Maya's headrest to pull herself closer. "And when you ain't answer, I thought Bhagwan take you for Heself."

"Not yet." Anand turned in his seat to face Gloria. "It is my *dharma*, my duty, to serve in this world until at least eighty. Chance needs me—good-good people like you need me. Ain't?"

Gloria's nods were so vigorous she crushed her chins against her neck and made still more folds. "You know, Baba, you is the best pundit in Chance and in the whole world. I know I could always count on you." She wiped the perspiration beading at her hairline with the back of a hand and continued. "Some people say you too greedy for a pundit."

Pundit Anand frowned and his moustache drooped to his stubbled chin.

"And some people say you does be sending money to

Venezuela steady, like you mix up in some kind of drug activities."

Maya groaned audibly in the front seat.

"But I never believe that kind of gossip, Baba. You is my pundit. You are God's gift!"

Pundit Anand cleared his throat and paused, and Krishna knew it took all his resolve not to ask the names of the gossipers. "Thank you," Anand finally said. "I go drop you home now, Gloria. And tomorrow morning first thing, I go do your puja. I wouldn't forget." His smile was tight, but Gloria didn't seem to notice.

She beamed at Pundit Anand. "Yes, Baba. Thank you so much, Baba."

Anand glanced up at his son through the window. "And you—find yourself home."

Krishna wanted to protest, but Maya's eyes pleaded against it. And then there was Anand, who, despite his malice, looked so desperate and haggard hunched behind the steering wheel Krishna couldn't bring himself to disobey him yet again. He turned on his heel and headed for home, realizing it did not matter what he did now: someone he loved would be hurt. As he strode past Vimla's house with his head down, Krishna murmured an apology for the part he'd played in her undoing and for the part his father would play to ensure her defeat. The wind carried his words into the treetops, leaving Krishna feeling more helpless than ever. With every step closer to home, Krishna knew that however torn, however heartbroken he felt, for Vimla it would be much, much worse.

Headmaster Roop G. Kapil

Monday August 5, 1974

....

CHANCE, TRINIDAD

Vimla and Chandani arrived at Saraswati Hindu School at 8:30 a.m. They immediately spotted Headmaster Roop G. Kapil sitting under a tamarind tree, a notebook lying in his lap and a pen poised over the open page. He wore a crisp, pale-blue shirt, unbuttoned at the collar, and a pair of brown trousers, rolled up to the ankles to avoid the dust. Hooked and swaying from a lower branch was the headmaster's brown blazer, and in the blazer breast pocket a pale-blue handkerchief to match his shirt. He read his notes aloud, crossing lines out and scribbling additions into the margins. Every time he modified his work, he went back to the beginning and started anew.

Chandani smoothed her hands over her hair and touched

the thick knot at her nape as she neared the headmaster. "What he jacket doing swinging in the tree like a howler monkey?" she mumbled.

Vimla didn't answer. Her mouth was dry. Her palms were damp. She knew in her heart what Headmaster Roop G. Kapil had called her here to say and all she wanted was to go back home and crawl into her lumpy bed.

"Good morning, Headmaster," Chandani said as they approached the tamarind tree. Vimla watched Chandani, in her peach dress, smile sweetly at the headmaster as though there was great peace in her soul.

Headmaster jumped and his notebook toppled into the grass at his feet. "Sita-Ram and good morning." He busied himself with tucking his pen behind his ear, unfolding his pant cuffs and unhooking his blazer from the nearby branch. "I suppose is eight thirty already," he said, slipping the blazer on. He whipped his notebook off the ground, dusted it off and adjusted his handkerchief so that it peeked out a little higher from his breast pocket. "Come, come"—he gestured to the pair—"let we chat in my office."

Headmaster Roop G. Kapil kept his eyes fixed forward and walked the twenty feet to the school doors in silence. Vimla watched his thin brown face out of the corner of her eye, noticing how he tensed and relaxed his angular jaw as he went. A nervous tic? She couldn't be sure. She had only ever seen Headmaster composed and confident. As he drew near to the door, his greying hair, feathery as a child's, fluttered in the breeze and fell over the left lens of his gold-rimmed glasses. He stole a glance at Chandani behind the veil of his hair before brushing it away.

Headmaster Roop G. Kapil unlocked the school doors and led them down a long corridor. Vimla knew the way well. She had sat in each of the seven classrooms along that hallway throughout her primary school days, written the solutions to math problems on every blackboard in the school. The classroom doors had been left open so that sunshine streamed in through the windows and spilled into the hallway, lighting the route to the headmaster's office. As she trailed behind her mother, Vimla inhaled the smell of chalk dust and felt a sudden longing to slip into an empty classroom and sit at one of the long wooden desks made for three.

They arrived at the end of the corridor, where Headmaster Roop G. Kapil's name was etched on a nameplate beside the door. He jiggled a key in the lock and pushed the heavy door open. "Please sit," he said, as he made his way around the oversized desk.

The thick oppressive heat pushed Vimla into a chair. She looked around while the headmaster retrieved his pen from behind his ear and flipped through his notebook. The bookshelf, mounted high on the green wall behind the desk, sagged with dozens of texts arranged in alphabetical order. The spines had faded under the unrelenting sun pouring in through the lattice windows, rendering them worn and weathered. A silver fan stood next to the headmaster's chair. Unlike the books, it appeared new and shiny, and Vimla wished he would turn it on. She could feel pinpricks of sweat at the back of her neck and the clamminess in her hands seemed to spread across her entire body. In those excruciating moments while she waited for the headmaster to speak, Vimla felt like she was wilting in her chair. She watched his face, leaning forward every time he silently mouthed something or opened and closed his lips. It was if he were rehearsing his dismissal speech right in front of her. Vimla wanted to grab his shirt collar and shake the terrible news out of him. At least then she could put the agony of waiting behind her and deal solely with the embarrassment of her many losses since Krishna.

Headmaster Roop G. Kapil cleared his throat and began in the loud voice he used to address school assemblies on the front lawn. "As you know, Saraswati Hindu School holds a high standard of education for the children in this district." He folded his hands over his notebook, looped his thumbs clockwise and then counterclockwise.

Vimla jiggled her knees until Chandani's firm hand stilled them. Chandani sat on the edge of her seat, her feet flat on the ground, her back erect, her chin raised. "I agree," she said. "That is why I send Vimla here." A syrupy smile coated the lie; they all knew the next closest Hindu school was in a different district.

Headmaster wet his lips, tensed his jaw and relaxed it again. "I called you both here to discuss the teaching offer I made Vimla after she passed she A Levels—"

"Is a real honour, Headmaster," Chandani said.

Vimla stole a curious glance at her mother. This wasn't the same woman who had railed through the night over Vimla's carelessness. There was something different. It was in the tilt of her head as the headmaster spoke and the curve at the corners of her lips. It was in the unfamiliar tone of her voice, neither impatient nor self-righteous. It was in the way she leaned forward, a subtle hinge of the hips, as if she were hanging on his every word. Vimla wondered what trick Chandani was playing on Headmaster Roop G. Kapil.

A weak smile wavered on the headmaster's lips. He shifted in his chair and sighed. "Mrs. Narine, at the time of the offer—"

Chandani clapped her hands to her chest and gasped as though she'd just remembered something. "Headmaster, you see Vimla name in the paper?" She beamed across the desk at him, her eyes twinkling. "I sorry I forget to bring it for you."

Headmaster Roop G. Kapil removed his glasses and massaged the bridge of his nose with his thumb and forefinger.

Chandani stroked Vimla's hair and her fingers snagged in a tangle of curls. "We so proud of she. So, so proud."

Vimla clasped and unclasped her damp hands, wondering if there was a shred of truth to anything her mother said. Tentative seeds of hope stirred in her belly. She wrapped her arms around them to keep them safe.

Headmaster Roop G. Kapil swallowed and tugged at his collar with a ringed finger. Sweat beaded at his sideburns. He was melting in his blazer.

"And you know, Headmaster," Chandani began again, widening her smile.

Headmaster Roop G. Kapil held his hand up and dropped his gaze to his notebook. "Mrs. Narine . . ." Resolve and weariness tightened his voice. "After some deliberation, we have decided to withdraw our offer for the teaching vacancy in September due to Vimla's recent indiscretions."

Vimla watched the headmaster exhale slowly, forgetting to breathe herself. For a moment, no one spoke. Vimla saw Chandani's eyes narrow, her face darken, and she knew that all her mother's false sweetness had fallen away.

"Roopy, who is *we*?" Chandani's voice was clipped.

Vimla's stomach lurched. Had her mother just addressed Headmaster Roop G. Kapil as *Roopy*? She looked at the man whose very presence frightened the school children into obedience. As his face turned red, a droplet of sweat trickled the length of his sideburn and down his chin. "When I said 'we,' I meant the school." He removed his blue handkerchief and mopped his face.

Chandani sprang to her feet. "Who is 'the school,' Roopy? Cut the bullshit, nuh, man!" She leaned over the desk so that her face was inches from the headmaster's. "Ain't you mean Pundit Anand decide to withdraw the offer?"

Headmaster pushed his gold-rimmed glasses up on his nose and looked away. "Chand," he said, rolling his chair back a few inches.

Vimla's eyes grew wide. *Chand?*

"People talking about Vimla all over the district. How can we—the school—let she teach here? The parents go get vexed. Think of Saraswati Hindu School's reputation."

Vimla was startled by the imploring quake in Headmaster Roop G. Kapil's voice. Chandani pointed a finger at Vimla. "Is people talking about she alone?"

Headmaster lowered his eyes and fiddled with the pen lying across his notebook.

"Ain't people saying that Vimla get catch with Krishna, Pundit Anand Govind's son? And Pundit Anand Govind have plenty influence at Saraswati Hindu School, ain't so?"

Headmaster started to stammer a response, but Chandani wouldn't hear it. "How a man like you become a headmaster?" she demanded.

Vimla gasped. "Ma!" She grabbed her mother's reedy arm.

Chandani shook Vimla's grasp off. "You could never make up your own mind, Roopy," she said. The veins in her neck throbbed. "You did always rely on the opinions in books, the advice of other people and that damn, stupid notebook of yours for everything." She picked up the notebook and hurled it at the lattice windows.

Vimla covered her mouth, horrified. She felt faint in the suffocating office.

Headmaster whisked his notebook off the floor and buttoned his blazer over the perspiration seeping through his shirt in patches. "Mrs. Narine, I am sorry you are upset. Perhaps Vimla could find a next opportunity elsewhere. Plenty universities go want she. Perhaps something abroad? Canada? England? We wish you luck, Vimla." He looked directly into her eyes for the first time and she saw sadness not unlike her own flicker behind his gold-rimmed glasses.

Rum Shop Blues

Om trundled up the side of the road with his head lowered and his fleshy arms swinging through the humidity. He puffed as he went, mopping the perspiration from his sideburns with his hands. He had been walking only a few minutes and already the off-white T-shirt he wore was damp and turning ochre under his armpits. Om could see, out of the corners of his eyes, people watching him as he went. He pretended he didn't notice his neighbours, resisted the natural urge to raise his hand and call out to them. Instead he thought of Chandani sprawled in resolute defeat across their bed, and Vimla attending to her numerous chores with forlorn eyes. He couldn't take it anymore; he'd had to leave. They had driven him away with their misery and their scandal, and it was their fault he was here. Om turned off the road and lumbered into Lal's Rum Shop.

It was a small bar, with seating for no more than twelve men at a time. Plastered against the Caribbean-blue walls were Carib and Stag Lager posters, and just behind the bar Lal had tacked dozens of bikini-clad beauties and a miniature photo of Lord Shiva offering blessings to Lal's drinkers. A silver radio—Lal's most prized possession—played the latest chutney song and drowned out the incessant drone of circling flies.

"Om!" Puncheon slid off his rickety brown stool and wobbled to his friend. "*Hari Om!* Fatty-Om!" he sang. His shirt was crumpled and buttoned askew, the front tucked neatly in his pants and the back hanging, pathetic pink coattails, over his rear.

Om offered Puncheon a weak smile and heaved himself onto a stool. "A bottle of Old Oak and two glasses, Lal."

Lal nodded, wiping his hands on a dishtowel. He plucked a bottle of rum off a shelf and slid it across the bar toward Om. "Enjoy, Boss," he said.

"Eh, Om, that extra glass for me, boy?" Puncheon slapped his hand on Om's back, climbing up next to him. He reeked of a lifetime of drink.

Om poured a shot and a half of rum into each glass and handed one to Puncheon, who grasped it, red faced. He downed his drink in a single gulp and held out the glass for a refill. "You is a good friend, Hari-Om-Fatty-Om. So what happened to you, boy? Why you ain't picking ochroe today?"

Om snorted, his shoulders slumped. "You mean, you ain't hear?"

Puncheon twirled his coaster and it spun off the bar onto the floor. "Hear what? About Vims and Krish? Yeah, man! Of course I hear. But what that have to do with picking ochroe?"

Om finished off his drink. "Who you hear from, Punch? Is only eleven o'clock in the morning."

"Lal tell me."

Om glanced at Lal, who had the courtesy to look shame-faced. "Where you hear, Lal?"

Lal began wiping down his bar. "I hear from Bulldog, who hear from Kapil, who hear from Dr. Mohan, who hear from Sangita Gopalsingh."

Om nodded. "Sangita Gopalsingh," he muttered.

"Eh, man, that woman real beautiful, ain't?" Puncheon grinned. "Every time I see she, I does want to hug she up and kiss she up and rub she up and love she up. But she always looking so sour-sour like she suck a pound of lime. She need some good Puncheon in she life. That is what she need."

Lal shook his head. "One of these days, Punch, Rajesh go carve you up with he cutlass and scatter you across Trinidad."

Puncheon shrugged. "One of these days, I go get sober. One of these days, Om go get thin."

Om and Lal laughed.

"So what you going to do, Boss?" Lal leaned on the counter, his eyes sincere. "Talk to the Govinds? Ask them for Krishna to marry Vimla?"

Om shrugged his heavy shoulders. "Chandani don't think they go take Vimla."

Lal poured Puncheon and Om another drink and added a splash of Coke this time. "How you mean? Vimla real smart, I hear. She real pretty, too. You and Chand is good people. Why the Govinds wouldn't consider a match?"

Puncheon jumped to his feet and threw his hands in the air. "Hold up! Hold up! You say Vimla smart, Lal?"

"You ain't see the paper?" Lal had saved himself a copy. He slid it across the bar to Puncheon.

"If Vimla so smart, why she sneak right in front she mother house to meet she boyfriend? She sound like a real stupidee to me."

Om shot Puncheon a warning look and Puncheon climbed back onto his stool.

Om decided to change the subject. "Boy, Chandani ain't cooking."

Puncheon gasped. "What happened to Chand—she two hand break?" He glanced upward. "Lawd, Father!" Then he tapped his empty glass on the bar. "Pour me a next drink, Lal. This is real tragic news I hearing!"

"No, Puncheon, she hand ain't break."

"Then how come she ain't in the kitchen? She two foot break?"

"No, she gone on strike, you jackass!"

"On strike?" Puncheon dropped his head into his hands. "Man, what I hearing? You let your wife go on strike? What the ass kind of thing is that?" He whacked the bar with his hand. "I getting stressed out, man. You driving me to drink."

Lal laughed at Puncheon's theatrics. "You full of shit, Punch."

"But really," Puncheon continued, turning to Om, "you need to go home and beat some sense into Chandani, and when you done that, beat some shame into Vimla, and when you done that, come back here and buy a next bottle of rum for we to celebrate with."

Om gulped his drink. His limbs felt loose and light now, and suddenly the chaos unravelling in his life seemed less important. He looked at Puncheon, who was dancing in his chair to a song on the radio, arms in the air, eyes closed. It was in moments like these that Om understood why Puncheon went through life intoxicated. He thought fleetingly about his ochroe drying in the sun; he thought about his daughter, who had betrayed his trust; he thought about his wife, who had abandoned him for her grief. "Bullshit," he slurred.

Puncheon opened his eyes. "Yes, man, real bullshit. Fatty-Om, you want me to go and beat Chandani for you?" He slipped off his stool and staggered to the door. "But allyuh don't wait for me." He looked over his shoulder with a wicked grin. "Because when I done deal with Chandani, I going to visit my sweet little Julie mango, Sangita." Puncheon laced his fingers behind his head and thrust his pelvis back and forth.

He made it to the main road before he collapsed in the heat and had to be carried back into the shop.

Chandani's Strike

C handani's strike stretched on for days. She stopped greeting the sun in the mornings; she no longer offered flowers to her little brass murtis. She refused to wash the wares or tend to her fowl, neglected the laundry and her coconut broom. She spoke to no one except herself, and even then her words were mumbled and indecipherable to Om, who eavesdropped from the other side of the bedroom door.

Om coped with Chandani's neglect the only way he knew how: he delegated her tasks to Vimla. But on the third evening Chandani shut herself up in their bedroom, Om roused her gently from beneath the coverlet. "Chand, I working real hard all day, and three days I come home to Vimla's burn-up roti. Get up, nuh, Chand, and cook something nice for me." He rubbed his massive belly with a callused hand.

Chandani had drawn the curtains, but the relentless tropical sun shone through in faint beams of watercolour yellow, a spotlight for dancing dust particles and buzzing flies. She lay in bed, staring at the ceiling, her hands folded neatly over her stomach. Her long hair, usually oiled and shining, spread across Om's pillow in dry, lifeless tangles. She looked like she was waiting to be lowered into the earth and this worried Om. He hovered over her, waiting for a response, pressing the weight of his belly into her small frame. Her gaze remained fixed on the ceiling beams until Om retreated down the stairs, miserably massaging his rumbling belly.

The following day Om found Chandani sitting on the only chair in their bedroom, staring out the window onto their acres of cane. He moved beside her and laid his large hand on a sagging shoulder. "Chand, you cooking today? I tired eating doubles. I wasting away here."

Chandani eyed Om's gut and then turned away again. He stood there for a while, waiting for her to say something, to move more than an inch this way or that, to scowl, even to sigh. She did nothing. This was not the woman he had married.

The next day Om lumbered up the stairs and found Chandani standing in the middle of the room, studying a photograph on the wall: Vimla as a baby. Chandani was dressed in black and this time her hair was knotted into a severe bun at her nape. Today she looked like she was attending someone else's funeral. Om groaned loudly to announce his presence and then flopped onto the bed. It creaked under his weight, and continued to whimper as he sprawled his giant limbs into a starfish position across it.

Chandani studied Vimla's laughing eyes in the picture.

"Chand, I wouldn't ask you to cook anything today." He rubbed his stomach luxuriously. "My belly full."

Chandani traced Vimla's lopsided smile with a finger.

"In fact," he went on, "you don't have to cook for me ever again. You could just sit up here and rest forever."

Chandani didn't move, but Om knew she was listening now.

"I went over to Sangita and Rajesh Gopalsinghs' house for lunch and dinner. Sangita invite me when she see me buying doubles at the doubles stand today. It was a good thing—"

Chandani whirled on him then, her eyes ablaze.

Relief zipped through Om, but he wanted more. "A real good thing she see me buying street food and invite me over. I was getting tired of eating oily doubles every day." He paused for a moment, just before the climax. "She send some food for you, too. She know you ain't cooking much these days."

Om noted the rise and fall of Chandani's small chest with glee. She was breathing heavily now.

"You should ask Sangita how she does make she coconut chutney, Chand. It have a different kind of zing than yours," he mused.

Chandani moved then, swiftly down the stairs and into the kitchen. She made a racket with her pots and spoons and all her stomping about. Om chuckled; the bed squeaked. The kitchen din went on for some time and Om wondered if Chandani was whipping up another dinner for him, something to top Sangita's, he hoped. He licked his lips in anticipation.

Chandani returned minutes later with her dutiful *belna* in hand and a deep scowl on her lips. Om smiled. How beautiful she was. But when she charged toward him with the rolling pin raised high above her head, his smile faltered. He received a solid blow to his belly before he managed to haul himself off the bed. When she raised the rolling pin to strike again, he caught it in his giant hand and the sharp sting of the slap quivered through his fingers. Om wrenched the belna from her grasp and stuck it gruffly in his back pocket and then hoisted Chandani over his shoulder, kicking and quarreling. Down the stairs they went, straight into the kitchen. Om set his wife down in front of the stove. He retrieved her belna from his back pocket and handed it to her, which she accepted.

Chandani began to make dough, mixing water into a small basin of flour as she raged on. How could Om have added to her humiliation? First Vimla was discovered gallivanting in Chance's bush with Krishna Govind, then Vimla lost her teaching job at Saraswati Hindu School and now Om was taking meals cooked by the neighbours! She would die with the legacy of an unfit mother and wife, she declared, kneading and punching the dough.

Om looked on from the kitchen table, satisfied. He strummed his fat fingers on the red-and-white plastic tablecloth to the tune of his wife's rage.

"You *coonoomoonoo!* It was Sangita who see Vimla that night!" Chandani said, stabbing the air with her belna as she cut Om down with her razor stare. When Om looked back at her blankly, Chandani attacked the dough with aggressive sweeps of the rolling pin. "Sangita go spread the news for all of Chance to hear: Chandani Narine have a jammette for a daughter and a greedy jackass for a husband." She peeled the dough off its smooth surface, sprinkled some flour onto the counter and dropped the dough back with a slap. When it was made smooth and flat under her abuse,

Chandani expertly transferred it to the flat, cast-iron pan, a *tawa*, to cook.

Om was not bothered by the insults. In fact, he found himself aroused by the pairing of belligerence and culinary skills. When Chandani tilted the tawa at an angle off the stove burner so that the dough swelled into a delicious balloon, Om felt a similar hot rising and swelling in his body. Chandani quickly flipped the inflated roti over on the tawa and grimaced at him. Om smiled back at her adoringly. He had missed her.

That evening Om and Chandani ate and cussed, respectively, well into the night. A stranger might have found their relationship dysfunctional, even borderline abusive, but to Vimla, who lay listening in the hammock just outside the kitchen, they were a perfect picture of love. She pulled the sides of the flour bag hammock up around her body, the rough textile scratching against her exposed arms. But the makeshift cocoon didn't ward off her loneliness; in fact, it only made her isolation more pronounced.

That evening the sun dissolved so quickly into the cobalt sky Vimla felt cheated. Now the only light escaped from the kitchen and cast itself in a scalene triangle on the dark concrete beneath the hammock, pointing accusingly at her. Everywhere else there was blackness. Amid the nighttime noises she heard the swish of the island breeze stirring some leaves awake, and from every direction the ceaseless cry of the cicada, competing unsuccessfully with Chandani's tirade. Vimla let go the ends of the hammock. She dropped a long leg over the side and pushed off on the concrete with a bare toe.

She swung like that in the darkness for a while, surrounded by bush, suspended in thought until the last triangle of light vanished from the floor and Om and Chandani marched up the stairs to bed.

The News

Vimla led her father's cow and bull into the field by two fraying ropes. This was the best part of Vimla's day. It didn't matter that the sun beat down mercilessly on her, or that her only company was two sad-eyed animals that grew increasingly moody in her presence. Vimla could escape her mother's reproving looks in the field and that was all that mattered.

Of course, that didn't mean she was happy. She had lost her chance at happiness the moment she lost touch with Krishna. After that, life had become unbearable. Vimla knew she had disgraced her parents; that her name was on every gossip's tongue in the village; that she would never teach at Saraswati Hindu School. But it was the absence of Krishna Govind from her world that shook her to the very core.

She sighed, absent-mindedly shooing a fly from the cow's

ear. The cow moaned deep in her chest as if to say she, too, was above the company of Vimla Narine.

"Vimi!"

Vimla heard Minty's voice before she saw her hiding at the edge of the sugar cane.

"Minty, what you doing here?" Vimla dropped the animals' ropes and leaped through the savannah grass toward her friend, flinging her arms around Minty's clammy neck.

Minty hugged Vimla quickly then pulled her to the ground.

"I sorry." Minty rocked back and forth on her haunches, her meaty elbows resting on her knees. Her smooth, milky skin was pinched by adult-worry, and there were faint shadows beneath her black, almond-shaped eyes. She usually kept her sleek hair in a neat plait that wound down her back, but today her mane spread across her back like a veil.

"What you sorry for, Mints?"

The dimple in Minty's chin quivered. "It was my mother who tell everybody about you and Krishna." She wrung the hem of her dress.

Vimla sucked her teeth. "Gyul, I done find that out already. I can't keep a secret from Trinidad, and Trinidad can't keep a secret from me." She smiled at Minty to show there were no hard feelings.

Minty's shoulders sagged in relief, as if she'd been balancing the guilt across them for days, and her pinched expression slackened just enough to show the rosy glow of a young teen-aged girl. Suddenly her eyes lit up. "So, how was it?"

Vimla brushed the back of her hand across her perspiring forehead. "How was what?"

"How was Mr. Pundit . . . in the bush?" Her lips twitched with mischief.

Vimla giggled. "You so fast, Minty." She looked away. "We ain't do nothing except talk."

"Talk? What allyuh talk about?"

Vimla shrugged. How could she tell Minty that she and Krishna had spent hours planning their lives together? She shivered despite the heat; their plans hadn't even made it through the night.

"Minty, suppose your mother catch you here? She go cut-cut your tail if she know you talking to me."

Minty stared at Vimla, her mouth drooping at the corners. "I come to tell you something."

Vimla caught the pity in her friend's eyes. She swallowed hard. "So, he getting married."

Minty nodded. "Soon."

"To who?"

"A girl called Chalisa Shankar from St. Joseph."

Vimla's stomach lurched. She had known this would happen, but she hadn't expected it so soon. She'd lain awake night after night wondering if Krishna would be picky about his bride, if he'd try resisting the marriage altogether, if he'd suddenly miss her and come for her in the night. But the fact that Krishna hadn't put up a fight, had resigned himself to a loveless marriage, hurt Vimla so much she thought her heart would stop beating right there in the field.

"Are you sure? How you know?"

"Auntie Maya tell my mother so." Minty lowered her gaze. "She rather Mammy be she friend than she enemy—Mammy know too much about you and Krishna, you see."

Vimla understood. She could still hear Sangita Gopalsingh's shrill voice in the dead of the night calling her a jammette for all the neighbours to hear. Vimla shuddered.

"But so fast, Minty?"

Chalisa nodded. "Chalisa's parents dead in a car crash two years ago. They tumble off a cliff and the car burst into flames."

Vimla's eyes widened.

"She old nanny does mind she now and want a marriage fix for Chalisa before she and all dead. They was looking for a good Hindu boy from a good Hindu family. When they meet Krishna, they arrange everything one-time."

Vimla scowled. She picked idly at the grass. "What else?"

"Chalisa and she small brother have plenty money. They inherit big-big orange estates after they parents dead. Mammy say they more rich than Nanny self!"

"Oh." Vimla brushed her mop of unruly hair over her shoulder. "Chalisa Shankar. She pretty?"

Minty looked her square in the face. "She like a old crapaud."

Vimla burst into tears. Krishna was too vain to marry someone who looked like a frog; Minty was the worst liar she knew.

Chandani looked like she'd been chewing a sour green mango when Vimla returned thirty minutes later. She rounded on Vimla the moment her slippers slapped against the concrete of the house. "People is laughing at we!" Her spittle rained down like missiles.

Vimla stared back at her dumbly. She was still digesting the news of Krishna's marriage.

"That pork-*chamar* Pundit Anand is marrying he duncy-head son to a next little jammette from St. Joseph!"

Vimla should have been appalled by her mother's foul ejaculations, but by now they were as commonplace as the kiskadees' evening song. She wasn't surprised Pundit Anand had been reduced to a blasphemous pork-eating fiend, that Krishna's future wife had acquired the same slack status as herself; her mother saw good in no one these days. Vimla manoeuvred around Chandani to the standpipe for a cup of water, but Chandani trailed behind her, the veins in her wild-turkey neck throbbing with every livid heartbeat.

"Those kiss-me-ass people invite the whole island to the wedding—*except we!*" Chandani stomped her skinny foot, scattering a knot of pecking hens that had wandered boldly into the house.

Vimla, hot and pitifully heartbroken, downed the cool water in her peeling enamel cup and dropped it with a clatter to the floor. "I go stop that wedding, Ma!"

Chandani recoiled as if she'd been cuffed. Then she removed her slipper and lunged madly at her daughter. "Blasted—ungrateful—little—wretch!"

Vimla took off around the house, sweating and crying. She had never seen her mother move so quickly in all her life, never seen her so determined to injure. She considered sprinting into the street in the hope a neighbour would come to her aid, but the truth was, Chandani's invective would faster draw cheers and applause than sympathy from the district. She circled the house another time, hoping to tire her mother out instead.

"You ain't embarrass me and your father enough? Keep

your ass home, you hear me?" Chandani launched her old slipper into the air like a discus and hit Vimla square in the backside.

It was two days and two nights before the entire district caught word that Krishna Govind was going to marry a pretty girl named Chalisa Shankar from St. Joseph. Chance began to vibrate with a special kind of energy; people anticipated this wedding like no other. Many thought this would be the biggest wedding the district had ever seen, since pundits tended to marry their children with even greater ceremony than the average Hindu family. Others felt honoured that Chance was hosting the likes of Chalisa Shankar. But most people were excited because they knew the sensational scandal that was the catalyst for this hasty wedding.

All of this was according to Minty, who quickly became Vimla's eyes and ears outside the Narine residence. Minty accompanied her mother everywhere, gathering gossip from the parlour and the market and committing it to memory. At home she became an inconspicuous fixture in the kitchen, peeling potatoes or chopping onions while her father disclosed what he'd heard in the rum shop that evening. Minty learned to listen to outlandish speculation about the Govind, Narine and Shankar families with a veil of aloof blankness shrouding her unease. She was the perfect spy and she delivered all the news to Vimla in the cane fields with generous pieces of sugar cake to sweeten the shock.

Dr. Mohan wondering if Chalisa Shankar know about you, Vims.

Faizal Mohammed think you pregnant.

Puncheon say Pundit Anand hire he brother to paint they house pink for the wedding.

Patsy say Pundit Anand send Krishna away from Chance to save he from the "little obeah witch, Vimla."

Gloria say the Shankars have five orange estates in St. Joseph and that they does wipe they backside with all the extra money they have.

My mother say your mother gone mad and slap up Headmaster Roop G. Kapil.

Vimla barely reacted to the gossip until the day Minty told her that Chalisa Shankar wanted to meet her. Vimla scowled and sucked her teeth at this. "Why I should meet she?" But the truth was, Vimla was just as fascinated by Chalisa Shankar as the rest of Chance. She wanted to see if Chalisa was really as clever as everyone claimed, if her hair really did fall in perfect inky helices down her back. She wanted to hear Chalisa speak, witness her breathe, touch her. She had to be certain that Chalisa was real, this woman who had snatched Krishna away. And of course, Vimla was pleased, too. It was a victory—however small—that Chalisa had learned who *she* was, that Chalisa had an interest in knowing *her.*

Vimla licked the sugar from her fingers. "Tell she I busy."

"Busy!" Minty's eyes bulged. "I can't tell she that."

Vimla narrowed her gaze at her friend, who blushed and stuffed her mouth with the last of her sugar cake so she wouldn't have to explain herself.

"So you fall in love with she, too!" Vimla tossed her wild tresses over her shoulder. "Tell your friend Chalisa I busy, and that's that!" She dusted her dress off and stalked like a wild animal toward home, leaving Minty crouching, bewildered, amid the tall cane stalks.

That night, when the cicadas were screaming Trinidad to sleep, Vimla lay awake thinking about Chalisa Shankar. She wondered if Krishna was thinking of her, too, and the thought sent a firecracker of pain through her chest. She tossed on her squeaky mattress, flinging her arms and legs out like a woman crucified, the conch jabbing her ribs. Perspiration trickled between her breasts and collected in her navel as she watched a lizard scurry across the ceiling into a pool of white moonlight. The island breeze lifted Vimla's curtains and whispered something ominous into the room before it disappeared again. Her feistiness had melted away with the day's sun, and now she lay whimpering so piteously even the lizard stopped and took notice.

Krishna and Chalisa's wedding was like an oncoming hurricane and the eye of the storm was watching Vimla. She would go to the wedding—she knew that much; Vimla had to see the marriage for herself before she could move on with her life. But what did moving on with her life mean? What would she do when the last sad wedding song was sung and the last drunken reveller staggered home to sleep? She wondered if Chance—Trinidad—was big enough for her and Chalisa.

Vimla rolled out of bed and crept into the hallway. She glanced at her parents' closed bedroom door. Om's booming snores were all but rattling the door frame, but she was certain her mother's wiry body was stretched stiff across the mattress, her gaze fixed on the ceiling beams.

Vimla stepped out onto the veranda and leaned against the iron railing. Dark palm trees danced eerily in the midnight breeze, like they were conjuring spirits, or spirits themselves. A raindrop landed on her cheek, and the wind grew bolder in the black-green foliage about the house. Another drop, fatter this time, fell on Vimla's shoulder and dribbled down the length of her arm. She inhaled the familiar smell deeply. Suddenly the sky over Trinidad opened up and a downpour of rain spilled onto the island. Vimla tilted her head back and glared at the sky as a gust of wind whipped at her hair. She gripped the railing, filled her lungs with air and wailed, "Krrriiisshnaaaa—and—Chaaaliiisaaaa—I—haaate—youuu!"

Then she slipped back inside and decided that she would meet the young woman she hated after all.

The Orange Orchard

Chalisa stood frozen under an orange tree like a dancing figurine whose music had stopped. Her back was turned to him, the fingertips of her right hand touching the side of her averted cheek, the palm of her left hand resting against the uneven bark of the tree. Her spine was straight, her slender shoulders squared against the world, one ear tilted in the direction of his footsteps.

They were in one of the Shankars' orchards, fifteen acres of lush treetops heavily studded with swelling oranges and delicate white blossoms. In between the rows of trees, stippled sunlight fell across the ground like a carpet of stars. A butterfly sailed through the hazy air, rich with the scent of earth and sweet citrus. Krishna followed the malachite's flight, noting the striking green and brown markings on its diaphanous wings. When it disappeared in the thick of trees, he returned his attention to Chalisa and found her in the same pose, listening, quite obviously, to the sound of his tentative footfalls.

Krishna stopped and looked over his shoulder. He could just make out the blue-and-white house Chalisa's Nanny lived in, tucked behind a knot of old orange trees; just hear her scratchy sandpaper chuckle at some joke his father had told. They were sipping tea, Nanny and his parents, knitting his life to Chalisa's with grand wedding plans while he came upon her in an orange orchard like a vagabond looking for some stranger to pin his affections on. Krishna laughed, despite himself, shaking his head at the absurdity of this moment. He knew nothing of Chalisa Shankar other than she was rumoured to be beautiful, her parents had died in a car crash and she came from money. He rubbed his freshly shaven chin with the palm of his hand. The rumours were of no consequence to him; he had plans to marry Vimla.

Krishna thought of her now. Vimla's big doe eyes, Vimla's impish smile, Vimla's pluck. Guilt knocked at his conscience. The magnitude of this moment suddenly struck him. While he trod through this lovely orchard toward his betrothed, Vimla was held captive in her own home. He wondered what she would think of him if she could see him now. He swallowed and looked around the quiet orchard. The trees seemed taller, denser, than before; they seemed to rise up and gather about him like an army.

Just then there was a rustling in the leaves overhead. As Krishna glanced up, a young boy bounded from a thick branch and landed at his feet. The boy straightened himself, adjusted his glasses on his hooked nose and folded his arms over his little chest. "Avinash Shankar," he said, blowing a tuft of hair from his eyes. "Chalisa's brother. Six years and three-quarters. Your chaperone." His eyes were round and luminous behind his glasses. He was small for his age and the soft, feathery hair on his head just barely measured up to Krishna's belt buckle.

"Is nice to meet you, Avinash Shankar."

Avinash took a step back and let his eyes travel from Krishna's wavy hair to his brown shoes. He tried to whistle, but he blew too hard and spittle sprinkled on his shirt. "You real tall," he said solemnly.

Krishna knelt in the dirt so that he was eye level to Avinash. "What about now?"

"Better." Avinash wiggled his hook nose. "You could see over the trees?"

Krishna pretended to consider. "Almost."

Avinash's face brightened with an idea. "I could sit on your shoulders and see for myself."

Krishna crouched lower to the ground and allowed Avinash to clamber up his back and sit on his shoulders. Krishna rose slowly as Avinash squealed with delight and hooked his legs beneath Krishna's armpits. "I could see plenty more orange from up here. Oh! Look, a parrot!" The bird took flight in a whir of green and yellow. "I could see Gavin, too. Hi, Gavin! I could see you picking oranges, Gavin!" Avinash cried, waving his arms in the air, rocking back and forth on Krishna's shoulders.

Krishna took a few more steps with the boy on his shoulders and then lowered him to the ground again. Avinash grinned up at him. "I almost touch the sky up there! And I see my partner, Gavin. He does help Nanny pick the oranges in orange season."

Krishna smiled at the boy. "And what you does do in orange season?"

"Watch Gavin and his friends see about Nanny's oranges—watch Chalisa sing and dance—play marbles and jacks—teach my dog tricks," he said, counting on his little fingers as he walked toward his sister's turned back.

"Does your sister sing and dance?" Krishna asked.

Avinash nodded eagerly up at his new friend. "Yes! All the time." He doubled his efforts to keep pace with Krishna's long strides. The plumes on his head wafted in the wind. "You go like she. Plenty boys does like she because she pretty. Kevin, Anil, Benjamin, Gavin . . ."

Krishna hid a smile. This was a boy who couldn't be trusted with secrets. "Even Gavin?"

Avinash leaped in the air. "Especially Gavin! He does call she 'Dream Girl.'"

Krishna raised his eyebrows in surprise. "'Dream Girl'? After Hema Malini?" He thought of the famous Indian film star and wondered just how attractive this Chalisa Shankar was.

"Yep." Avinash began to trot backward in the grass, looking up into Krishna's face. "Your skin does ever turn blue? You remember to bring your flute?"

For a moment Krishna was confused, and then he realized Avinash was comparing him to the Hindu deity Shri Krishna. "No, I doesn't turn blue and I can't play the flute."

Avinash looked disappointed. "Oh. Nanny say so."

Krishna raised his eyebrows. "She did?"

"Yeah. Nanny tell we that you was playing your flute under the moon one night for some girl named Vimla."

Krishna stopped in his tracks and looked down at the boy.

He felt his pulse quicken. "You sure Nanny say that?" But he didn't have to ask; Krishna knew it was true. Avinash had said Vimla's name. This was a story he had been told. What Krishna didn't know was why Nanny would be willing to wed her granddaughter to him if she knew about Vimla.

"Yes. She say that. That is why I thought you would bring a flute today, to play for Chalisa."

"Maybe she go like me even without the flute," Krishna said, although he didn't care either way.

Avinash's eyes grew round again. He pursed his small mouth and shook his head. "Chalisa say she ain't want to marry no pundit. Next time bring your flute." He scampered ahead, calling out to his sister.

She whirled on him. "Avinash! What you doing here?"

Avinash threw Krishna a sheepish look. "Nanny send me to chaperone."

Chalisa laughed, but it sounded lonely and hollow in the open orchard. "A chaperone?" And then a flicker of suspicion crossed her face. "Avinash, what you tell Krishna?"

The boy lowered his eyes and inched away. "Nothing."

Krishna stepped forward. He flashed his most charming smile at Chalisa and placed a reassuring hand on Avinash's small shoulder. "Your brother was telling me all about his dog." He hoped she wouldn't ask him the dog's name. "And Avinash challenged me to a game of jacks later." He extended his hand to Chalisa. "Krishna," he said, turning his full focus to her.

Avinash darted behind a tree.

Chalisa's golden-brown eyes were traced with black kajal and they glowed at him with alarming intensity. Her high cheekbones and peaked bow lips had been brushed with a soft peach colour that almost looked natural against her fair, creamy skin. Her hair was parted down the middle and hung in heavy spirals over one shoulder. She was dressed in a white-and-brown paisley blouse tucked snugly into a pair of high-waisted bell-bottoms. On her feet were the tallest white platform shoes Krishna had ever seen and she balanced easily in them, as if they had been crafted for her feet alone. She placed a hand on her hip and tilted her head to look into his face, something akin to scorn swimming in her eyes.

Krishna ran his hand through his wavy hair and forced a smile. She was absolutely stunning, but there was a haughtiness about her that unnerved him. That and he didn't appreciate her indifference to his presence in the orchard. Already he resented her for playing a part in entrapping him in this marriage—however innocent—and now she had pricked his pride.

"Is nice to finally meet you." The corners of Chalisa's mouth turned up in a half-smile; the flecks of gold in her eyes glittered.

Krishna ignored the lie and fell into step beside her.

The pair exchanged pleasantries as if this moment were not the beginning of their lives together. Now and again Avinash marched between them, until his attention was taken away by an interesting bird or bug or butterfly. Chalisa grazed the leaves above her head with her fingertips as she walked, her pretty face entranced by her thoughts. "Nanny says you are a pundit. Is true?" she asked, tiptoeing to press her nose against a cluster of ripe oranges.

"Almost. I have a year or two again to study before I could start doing pujas on my own."

She plucked one of the oranges and twirled it in her hands.

"Oh. Should I call you 'Pundit Krishna,' then? Or 'Baba'?" She made a face. "It make you sound old."

"Call me 'Krishna.'"

Chalisa shrugged as if she had no real intention of calling him anything at all. She flipped the orange from one hand to the other. "Tell me if I wrong—didn't Shri Krishna have many lovers?" Chalisa tilted her head to the side and pretended to think. "I believe he did. He liked to seduce the cowherds with his flute-playing. They would meet in the woods under the moon and dance and sing and make passionate love." She tossed the orange to him and arched an eyebrow. "Ain't that is right?"

Krishna would have agreed if not for the reproving under-current of her words. Instead he said, "In the Bhagavad Gita, Shri Krishna teaches us about our life purpose and *duty* in this world." He emphasized the word to remind Chalisa his union to her was a burden set on his shoulders by his parents.

Chalisa ignored Krishna's slight and continued with her train of thought. "You have many lovers, ain't?" She started to walk again, but her eyes never left his face.

He regarded her warily. "No."

Chalisa's laugh rang like a distant bell in the sprawling orchard. "Then you must have one special lover. Shri Krishna had the beautiful Radha, and you have . . .?"

"Just you." He said it to irritate her and he was successful. As she eyed him with disdain, he knew she longed to berate him for his relationship with Vimla and yet she couldn't. To mention Vimla's name would be to admit that she herself had not been his first choice, and from what Avinash had told him, Chalisa was the first choice of many admirers.

Avinash pushed his glasses up on his nose and wedged his way in between the pair. "Chalisa, why you don't sing for Krishna."

"Avi, go on and see if lunch ready." Chalisa shooed her brother away with her hand.

"That is a good idea, Avinash. I would like to hear Chalisa sing," Krishna said.

Avinash hopped up and down. "Sing one of Dream Girl's songs, Chalisa." He threw his arms around his sister's narrow hips. "Chalisa go be a famous Indian film star one day!" he exclaimed.

Chalisa tapped Avinash on the head. "Shh!"

Krishna raised his eyebrows at her. "A film star?"

Chalisa flicked the hair off her shoulder so that it cascaded down her back. "Yes. I can sing and dance as good as any Indian film star—Hema Malini, Helen, Zeenat Aman . . ."

She sounded like Avinash naming off her suitors. "Them actresses does lip-synch. You know that?"

Chalisa sniffed. "Then I is even *better* than them."

"Is that why we meeting in this orchard?" Krishna laughed. "To sing a duet? To play hide-and-seek behind the trees?" He lunged behind the orange tree to his right and peeked out the other side at her, laughing.

Chalisa fixed Krishna with a penetrating gaze that tore right into his soul. "I wouldn't waste my talents on you," she snapped.

Avinash looked up at them, his small face crumpled in worry.

"But you plan to marry me?" Krishna asked, and now he was serious. "Why Nanny want we together? We is two strangers. A pundit and a film star . . ." He looked mystified. "That ain't really match."

For a second Chalisa seemed about to answer, and then she changed her mind. She stood in her white platform shoes with her Cupid's-bow lips pressed together and her tawny eyes shielded by a fringe of black lashes, like a doll.

Krishna shrugged, shoved his hands in his pockets and walked back to the house. He had no intention of marrying her, anyway.

The Reverie

Krishna turned his back on the retreating shore as *The Reverie* glided out to sea. He wasn't interested in waving goodbye to his father, whose sour expression had turned triumphant when they'd reached the port, or to his mother, whose left hand was permanently pressed to her lips, damming her objections to sending him to Tobago. He didn't want to see Trinidad fade away in the distance, didn't want to be reminded that he was putting thirty-six kilometres of sea between himself and Vimla. Krishna wouldn't let resentment or heartache spoil this voyage. How could he when the day was so beautiful?

He reclined against the railing at the boat's stern, hands in his pockets, and watched the early-day's sun glitter off the expanding Caribbean-blue water. The sun warmed his body like a lingering embrace. A sprightly breeze played in his hair and billowed his shirt front. He became aware of how much the steady lapping of waves against the sides of the small vessel was like his own pulse. A smile spread across Krishna's face, slow and deliberate, like *The Reverie*'s voyage.

"Welcome aboard!" a voice called.

Krishna dragged his gaze from the ribbon of cerulean blue where the sky met the sea and scanned the boat for a face that fitted that rich, throaty voice. The tourists turned their pink faces to the bow, so that all he saw was the backs of wide-brimmed sun hats and a rainbow of foreign, blond, brown and rust hair. Abandoning his bags at the stern's railing, he slipped in beside a slender woman with freckles on her arms. She turned to him, inclining her head in the captain's direction. "How long does it take to grow dreadlocks like that?" she whispered in an unfamiliar accent.

Krishna shrugged and inched closer.

"My name is Captain Dutchie and this," the captain said, letting go of the steering wheel and spreading his arms wide, "is *The Reverie*." He flashed the carefree smile of a man who knew how to live. "We are heading to Tobago. If you are on the wrong boat, jump now."

A ripple of mirth sounded over the waves. Krishna manoeuvred around a couple holding hands and made his way to the front of the group. Captain Dutchie's dreadlocks, he noticed, were reddish brown from the sun and cascaded down his back like thick marine ropes. The strong notches on his dark arms glistened with the sheen of cocoa butter, and he smelled distinctively like the sea. Not a sharp fishy smell, but a fresh fusion of sea air and freedom.

"We will be stopping at Buccoo Reef to see the Coral Gardens, at which time I will ask you to have a seat around the glass bottom of the boat," Dutchie said, his eyes glistening like black onyx.

All heads swivelled to the deck's centre, where the bottom of the boat had been fitted with an eight-by-ten-foot glass floor. Wooden benches were secured to the deck around the perimeter of the glass, allowing the tourists an opportunity to observe the tropical marine life beneath them.

"We will be stopping for an hour of snorkelling and then drop anchor at Store Bay in Crown Point, Tobago, for the afternoon. Anybody have questions?"

A man with red, peeling shoulders raised his hand. "George Moncton," he said by way of introduction. "Is this thing safe?" He glanced at the dozens of fluorescent life jackets slung up in a net overhead.

Dutchie laughed. He steadied the wheel with his hip and gathered up a fistful of dreadlocks. "Is a little late to be asking that question, George," he said, winding the locks around the rest of his hair to create a fat ponytail.

George smiled a strained and worried smile.

Dutchie took the wheel again. "*The Reverie* is a small tour boat, but she's sturdy and reliable. I never had to use the life jackets in an emergency—those are for beginner snorkellers," he said, nodding with his chin to the jackets.

George's shoulders relaxed.

"Captain Dutchie!" A young woman behind George waved her hand in the air. "What's in the cooler?" She squeezed her way to the front, giving the small group a good look at her bikini-clad body. Krishna wondered what purpose the sheer yellow sarong wrapped around her slender waist served.

Dutchie raised the cooler's lid with his big toe, giving a

glimpse of a bottle and plastic cups wedged in a bed of ice. "Rum punch, my darling," he said, winking. "For after the snorkelling."

The young woman hopped with delight, showing off the buoyancy of her breasts. Krishna snickered to himself, thinking: in the case of an emergency, she probably wouldn't need a life jacket.

"Can we go upstairs?" a child asked from beneath his oversized sun hat. He fidgeted with the plastic orange binoculars around his neck. His mother, a woman with deep-set green eyes and flowing auburn hair, placed a hand on his shoulder, ogling Dutchie like she was devouring him in her mind.

"Yes, of course. Please." Dutchie gestured to the ladders on either side of the bow. He nodded to the mother as she sashayed past him. "There are sun chairs up top. Make yourselves comfortable. The view is pretty from there." He flashed a sparkling smile. "I'll check back in with you soon."

The tourists were dismissed and moved cautiously over the swaying deck. Krishna watched them don sunglasses and apply suntan lotion. A group climbed to the upper level, while others found a spot at the wraparound railing and looked out at the sparkling sea. It felt strange discovering a part of his country for the first time with these foreigners and he wondered how many hundreds of overseas visitors had seen Tobago before him.

"Eh, what's your name, Boss?" Dutchie held his hand out to Krishna, interrupting his thoughts.

"Krishna." Dutchie's grip closed around his, firm but friendly.

"But what you doing on my tour boat, Krishna?" Dutchie glanced at Krishna's khakis and crisp, white button-up shirt.

His lips twitched, but there was nothing cruel in his amusement.

Krishna glanced down at himself, too. He grinned. "Going Tobago."

Dutchie raised an eyebrow. "You look like you going to church, man." He laughed. "When I tell the passengers to jump if they on the wrong boat, I was talking to you."

Krishna noticed Dutchie had fallen into his colloquial tongue and it pleased him somehow, like a quiet understanding had passed between them.

The captain guided the steering wheel with an extended finger. "Don't think I ain't see them big bags you tote on my boat. I know them ain't have no snorkelling gear, Boss."

A sheepish expression crossed Krishna's face. He ran his hands through his wavy hair, unsure how to explain that his father had been too cheap to buy a plane ticket, or to pay for passage on the real ferry. How could he tell Dutchie without offending him, or embarrassing himself, that this four-hour journey on *The Reverie* was part of Krishna's punishment for shaming his father?

Dutchie gazed past Krishna. "Boss, take the wheel. It look like George sick." He slapped Krishna on the back and walked away. Over his shoulder he said, "Don't shit up your khakis, nuh, man. I ain't care what you have in them bags as long as I ain't going to jail for it. From the time I see you with that white-white shirt and luggage, I done know you was t'iefing passage to Tobago on my boat." He chuckled, shaking his head of dreadlocks as he walked away.

Krisha took the wheel in his hands, surprised at how natural it felt. He enjoyed the rock of the vessel beneath him, the sporadic spray of the sea on his face, the fluidity of his whereabouts in the world. But a whisper of guilt nagged at his conscience, and the more he ignored it, the more insistent it became.

Vimla.

The waves lapped to the rhythm of her name.

Vimla.

The wind carried her name to his ears.

Vimla.

The last time he had seen her, they had lain on their bellies in the dark and dared to unfold the future blueprints of their lives. Vimla would teach at Saraswati Hindu School and perhaps attend a university in the city the following year. Krishna would continue his pundit work under his father's tutelage and carry on the family legacy. In a year, when they were more established, they would marry and start a family. Vimla wanted a boy. Krishna wanted a girl. Vimla wanted a house on a hill. Krishna wanted a house by the water. He smiled now, remembering the heat of her elbow next to his, the brush of her hair on his cheek, the undercurrent of excitement in her quiet murmurs, the sweet sound of her muffled giggles. Krishna leaned his weight against the steering wheel and stared, unseeing, at the endless blue. They would have made it happen, he told himself, had Sangita Gopalsingh not played the hand of fate.

Bitterness boiled hot inside him and suddenly he was standing in his bedroom with his father again. "You mad if you think I marrying Chalisa Shankar!" he had exclaimed earlier that morning.

"Hush your mouth, you hear?" Anand rounded on him. "You go marry she. And while I fix up the wedding, I sending you to study in Tobago!" The veins beneath Anand's eyes throbbed as he shoved a few articles of clothing into a bag.

"Straight to your Auntie Kay's house. Away from *she*, away from Chance!"

"For how long?"

Anand zipped the bag roughly. "Until this scandal die down. Until I organize the wedding and thing with Nanny." He eyed his son, scowling. "You behave like a real scamp, boy."

Krishna folded his arms over his chest. "And what make you think Auntie Kay go want me to stay with she?" he asked.

Anand froze. "Eh!" he said, eye twitching. "It ain't matter if she want you or she ain't want you—she getting you."

"Why?"

"Because she costing me a damn fortune, that's why." He sucked his teeth, stroked his moustache. "And stop asking me so many questions!"

Maya, Krishna's mother, stood in the doorway covering her mouth with her hand, her round eyes brimming with tears.

Krishna sighed. "Pa, is not really a scandal if you marry we." He leaned against the windowpane and shrugged. "We was going to marry next year anyway."

Anand stared at Krishna, aghast. He dropped the bag of clothes to the floor and pointed a trembling finger at Krishna. "Listen good: you and Vimla Narine ain't marrying. No sneaky girl like she go ever take the Govind name."

Krishna stood up straight. He looked to his mother for help, but she averted her eyes. "She is a good girl, Pa. A smart girl, too," he said, turning back to Anand.

"Too smart for she own good, creeping away in the night and fooling she parents." Anand left the room and returned with the Ramayana in his arms. He set the holy epic on Krishna's desk. "Too smart ain't good, Krishna." He slipped out of the room again and reappeared with the Puranas. "Medium is all right," he said, placing this text on top of the Ramayana.

"So you want me to leave she?" Krishna sighed. "Pa, why you bringing those books here?" He followed Anand to the door, throwing Maya an exasperated look.

Anand re-entered the room, holding the Bhagavad Gita to his heart and nearly colliding with Krishna. He added the book to the growing pile of texts. "You ain't leaving she, Son. I sending you away from she." Anand smoothed a hand over the Bhagavad Gita's cover. "And these books are for you to study while you in Tobago."

Krishna shook his head. "Impossible."

Anand paused mid-step on his way out the door again. He turned on his heel and arched a bushy eyebrow at Krishna. "Impossible?" He wagged his finger at his son, a sardonic smile playing on his lips. "You and Vimla marrying is impossible. Studying these scriptures?" He smiled. "Possible." And then he was gone again.

Krishna sat on the edge of the bed and raked his hands through his hair. He waited for Anand to reappear, an objection burning on his tongue.

"Because when you go to Tobago," Anand continued, one Vedic text tucked beneath each arm, "is only studying for you." He added the Vedic texts to the others. "No beach, no liming with friends, no nothing except"—he gestured to the pile he'd made on Krishna's desk—"studying. Oh—" Anand hurried out again before Krishna could open his mouth. "I forgot the Mahabarata!" he called from across the hall. "The Mahabarata is about virtue and following one's path of duty." He shuffled through the doorway and pushed the book into his son's arms.

"As you know, the Bhagavad Gita is part of the Mahabarata, so you can read that text twice. A bonus!" Anand's eyes were wild. "And guess who stars in these scriptures? Hmm?"

"Shri Krishna," Krishna mumbled, offloading the text onto the others.

Anand placed a palm on his son's cheek. "And what is your name?"

Krishna sighed and looked imploringly at his mother again.

Maya shook her bedraggled mane of grey fly-aways. "You drive your father mad," she sobbed. Then she pressed her fingers against her lips anew.

Dutchie reappeared at Krishna's shoulder. "Boss," he said, "you lost?"

Startled, Krishna dropped his hands from the wheel. "What?" He gazed at the sea, but it was useless pretending to differentiate this stretch of blue from the one *The Reverie* had bobbled over a minute ago. Krishna shrugged. "I going the same direction you was," he said.

Dutchie gave Krishna a knowing smile. "Relax! Tobago over there." He pointed straight ahead, but all Krishna saw was the sky balancing on the sea. "I mean you lost up here." Dutchie tapped the side of his head. He whipped a few loose locks over his shoulder. "She must be pretty. What she name?"

"What?" Krishna blushed, feeling foolish.

Dutchie furrowed his brow at Krishna. "What happened to you, Boss? You going deaf?" He lowered his face three inches and bore his black onyx eyes into Krishna's. "WHAT IS THE GYUL'S NAME?"

Krishna shoved his hands in his pocket and appeared oblivious. "Whose name?"

"Don't play the ass," Dutchie said. "Tell me the girl that have you looking so lost, or I go make you sit with George and pat he peel up back all the way to Tobago."

Krishna shook his head, laughing. "All right!" He squinted against the sun. "She name Vimla."

Mischief twinkled in Dutchie's black eyes. "What? I can't hear you over the engine noise, you squeaking like a little mouse!"

Krishna stared at Dutchie, incredulous. "It seem like *you* going deaf!" He filled his lungs and yelled. "The girl's name is VIMLA NARINE!"

Stillness fell over the boat. Krishna looked at Dutchie. Dutchie looked back at Krishna, grinning. He had killed the engine just as Krishna yelled Vimla's name. The other passengers on the lower level of the boat turned to stare. Krishna blushed again, deeper this time.

Dutchie clapped his hands. "Thank you for your attention," he said, turning his back on Krishna and taking three strides to the glass bottom of the boat. "We have arrived at the Coral Gardens. Have a seat."

A froth of bubbles gathered in the corners of the glass as *The Reverie* drifted quietly over the waves. Through the blue-green water a sprawl of colourful coral came into view. Dutchie peered over the heads of his passengers, one foot on the bench, and named the plant life oscillating in the deep.

Krishna admired the rambling orange elkhorn coral and the intricate yellow network of brain coral. A parrot fish glided by in a whir of colours, a school of bright-blue chromis flitted like a single entity through a forest of antler-like staghorn coral. George cried, "An angelfish!" And everyone leaned to the left to watch a hungry angelfish feeding off the algae stuck to the bottom of the boat.

Krishna could not hide his enthusiasm. Soon he began to point marine life out to Dutchie. "Is that star coral? Look, a grouper. That fish hideous, boy! And watch over there—is a manta ray! Watch how he flying under the water." And to Dutchie's delight, Krishna was right each time.

When Dutchie announced that they were in a good spot for snorkelling, the eager passengers abandoned the benches and pulled on their snorkelling gear and life jackets. The mother of the young boy asked Dutchie to help her adjust the straps on her life jacket. Dutchie tugged at the straps around the front, jostling the woman's large breasts and trying to hide his pleasure behind a curtain of dreadlocks.

"Mommy, you need a bigger life jacket," her son said, peering through his binoculars at Dutchie and his mother.

The woman reached out and hushed her son with a hand to his shoulder again. "This one's fine—right, Captain?" She gazed into Dutchie's face, her lips curved in a salacious smile. "I just need to shimmy a bit." And shimmy she did.

Krishna chuckled as Dutchie's expression dissolved into flagrant desire. The woman helped her son down the ladder into the water, and she slipped in after him, as lithe as a mermaid. Dutchie motioned to Krishna to join him at the bow. "You vexed, Boss?"

Krishna shrugged. "What I go vex for?"

Dutchie nodded. "Good. So tell me"—he wiped the beads of perspiration from his hairline—"why you really going Tobago?"

Krishna shrugged, staring after the snorkellers. "My father sending me Tobago to study."

Dutchie's eyes bulged. "To study!" And then they crinkled at the corners as he laughed, one hand on his chest. "Is only one thing you studying while you in Tobago and that's Vimla. Let me guess." He leaned his forearms on the railing. "You left she back in Trinidad."

Krishna rubbed the stubble at his chin. "Yeah." It was hard to hear someone else say it: he had abandoned her.

Dutchie cupped his hands around his mouth. "George, don't swim too far out. I don't feel like playing hero today!" He turned back to Krishna. "That man need a wife." When Krishna gave him a half-hearted smile, Dutchie retrieved the bottle of rum punch from his cooler. He scooped ice into a cup and filled it to the brim with the pink drink. "Here." He passed the drink to Krishna.

Krishna waved the cup away. "No, thanks. I don't drink, man."

Dutchie shrugged, taking a swig of the drink himself. "You could swim at least?"

Krishna smiled. "Like a barracuda."

Dutchie stepped back and made a sweeping gesture toward the water. "Well, let we see, Mr. Barracuda."

Krishna looked down at his starched shirt and hesitated.

Dutchie sucked his teeth. "Listen, right now, you ain't in Trinidad and you ain't in Tobago. You floating somewhere in the middle." He downed his drink and tossed the cup back into the cooler then let the lid fall closed with a bang. "While you in limbo, enjoy yourself, Boss. This moment wouldn't come again and it wouldn't last forever."

Krishna thought of his father's oppressive demands, of the smirk that peeked from beneath his silver moustache when he'd handed Krishna his ticket for *The Reverie* Tobago Tour. Krishna thought of what waited for him in Tobago: an unfamiliar aunt's dwelling and long, lonely days of studying in a place without friends, without Vimla. Suddenly he didn't want to be in either place. Suddenly the tiny belt of sea between the islands felt like home.

Abandoning his inhibitions, Krishna stripped off his shirt, rolled his pant legs above his knees and sprang off the edge of *The Reverie*. He whooped as he soared through the air, flailing like a fledgling, his face turned to the sun. He dropped into the sea in a chaos of sprays and limbs and then gathered grace and glided deeper. A school of creole wrasse zipped by him, their violet bodies grazing his fingertips as he reached and propelled himself forward. He felt weightless. The sea gurgled in his ears. As he took in the jewel-toned fish and assortment of peculiar-shaped coral, he had the odd sensation of discovering another world. In the dizzying moments just before his last breath ran out, Krishna understood that the sea would become a part of his life. He pushed down in the water and rose toward the sunlight, bursting through the surface with a splash.

"Yes, Mr. Barracuda!" Dutchie cheered from the boat.

Krishna flipped on his back, cradled by the sea, and smiled at the cloudless sky.

Maracas Bay

Saturday August 17, 1974

....

MARACAS, TRINIDAD

T he sun was just setting when they arrived at Maracas Bay, a swirl of cherry and pineapple Solo drifting lazily on the horizon, tinting the water pink and gold. Hilly mountains, draped in tangled foliage, rose up around the deep inlet, nestling kilometres of sandy shore between them. A pair of birds glided like black shadows across the glittering water, landing in a snarl of leafy mangrove trees that lined the mountain's edge and hunched with age toward the rising surf. And everywhere, tall palms stretched to the heavens, vacillating in the salty breeze.

Vimla stood at the shore, mesmerized by the dark-green surf as it crept toward her toes and ebbed in frothy white foam. She hiked the bottom of her floral print dress up and tied it in a knot at her knees then slipped free of her sandals and marched to the water's edge. Small rolling waves surged over her feet, loosening the sand beneath them, so that when the water retreated again, she nearly lost her footing. Vimla giggled quietly to herself, and then, realizing there was no one she needed to be quiet for, hooted wildly at the dying day. The sea roared back and sprayed her from the waist down.

Minty slapped across the shore behind Vimla as she withdrew the silver pins that held her hair in a bun at her nape. She pressed the pins between her lips and twisted her silky tresses into an even tighter coil than before. "Look at Faizal," she mumbled.

Vimla snatched the pins from Minty's mouth and flung them into the water.

"Vimi!"

Vimla pulled Minty's hands away from her hair. "Shake your head. Stop wiggling. Just do it!"

Minty tossed her head and let her hair spill down her back like a waterfall. "You did that just like your mother. Pretty."

Minty turned away quickly to hide the glow on her hot cheeks. "Look at—"

"I see him. That is one vexed little matchstick of a man." Vimla giggled.

Faizal Mohammed sat darkly on his prayer rug in the sand with his lanky arms wrapped around the knobs of his knees.

"How you get him to bring we here—and keep he big mouth shut about it? You promised to tell me when we reach the beach."

Minty paused; a shadow crossed her face and faded away. She dipped into her pocket and retrieved a thick gold chain. It dangled from her index finger and Vimla steadied the twirling initials with her pinky. *F.M.* She shook her head. "Where you find Faizal's chain, Minty?"

Minty slipped the chain over her head and began to tread through the water again. "In Mammy's bedside table."

Vimla gasped and then wished she hadn't. Poor Minty.

"Faizal waved he Qur'an in my face and said Allah did not condone adultery," Minty called over her shoulder, "but I show him he chain, and remind him that my father is not a forgiving man. I never see Faizal shut up so fast."

Vimla laughed, catching up to her friend, then sobered quickly. "Minty . . ." She was watching the oncoming waves as they rose restlessly before crashing into her bare shins. "If they get home before we do . . ."

Minty threaded her arm through Vimla's. "Our parents? Then we might as well drown each other in Maracas Bay."

Vimla squeezed her eyes and shook her head. "But they wouldn't. Is Krishna Janamashtami. They go stay in the temple till at least midnight. They do it every year, right?" Vimla shrugged, her smile sheepish. "They praying for me. They go stay until Pundit Anand ready to lock up the mandir and go home."

The girls fell silent for a moment, and then: "Suppose Chalisa ain't come?" Vimla kicked at the water. "You feel she fooling we?" Her eyes travelled the horseshoe shoreline. Except for Faizal Mohammed, who was lying on his belly, reading his worn Qur'an now, the beach was deserted. Fear set panic ablaze inside Vilma.

Minty's lips turned down at the corners. "Don't frighten, Vimi, Chalisa go come before it get dark." She glanced worriedly at the deepening sky and the sun that was melting into a yellow pool in the sea.

Vimla waved her hand with impatience. "I look frighten to you?" She clenched her jaw and dug her feet firmly into the sand, toes burrowed deep in to ground her.

As Minty wandered farther up the beach, she discovered a grotesque chunk of driftwood washed up on the shore. It was a labyrinth of thick, unyielding gnarls, sprawling across the beach and twisting heavenward. Weather-worn brown and grey with age, it was uneven and craggy to the touch. Minty walked around the intricate arrangement of contorted knots, ducking beneath arches and sinking her feet into the patches of cool sand shaded from the sun. She placed one foot on the base of the driftwood anchored deep into the earth, grasped a limb overhead and swung herself up. "Vimi!" She waved her arms wildly.

Vimla tore her gaze from the sea and spotted Minty perched high on the mammoth driftwood. She trudged along the beach, ignoring Faizal Mohammed's wary stares, until she arrived at the base of the structure. Clasping Minty's outstretched hand, Vimla pulled herself up onto a particularly thick snarl. The girls sat in silence for an hour as the sun switched shifts with the moon and the sea rolled and tumbled to the shore with increasing liveliness.

"What o'clock it is? Chalisa supposed to reach here half six."

Faizal reclined on his prayer mat and crossed his arms over his narrow chest. "I's not your timekeeper. I agree to bring you to Maracas Bay and take you back home to Chance. That is all. Don't mix me up in this stupidness."

Vimla sucked her teeth haughtily and plunked into the sand beside Faizal. "You love to mind people's business, Faizal Mohammed. You is the biggest maco in Chance. In fact, you—"

Faizal pulled the edge of his prayer rug out from under Vimla's foot.

"Vimi." Minty's hot hand closed around Vimla's arm. She was gazing at headlights in the distance; they flickered as the car jounced across the last stretch of Trinidad's North Coast and began its descent to the bay. "She reach."

Vimla's heart knocked violently in her chest. She suddenly became conscious of her wind-whipped hair, and the gritty wet sand wedged between her toes. She looked down at her clothes; she had on her best: a floral salmon-coloured cotton dress with sleeves to the elbows and a hemline that fell below her knees. She had pressed the dress carefully the night before, but now it was wrinkly from the long, bumpy ride up the mountain in Faizal Mohammed's car. She tried to smooth it, but defiant creases resembling her mother's angry scowl remained fixed in the fabric. Vimla closed her eyes and did something altogether astonishing: she began to pray.

The black sky had swallowed up the last rays of the sun now and a pearly crescent moon hung among a shimmer of faint stars that winked at the odd trio on the beach. The changing winds wrestled cruelly with Vimla's hair, leaving knots where there should be waves and sending wild shivers through her body. She squeezed her eyes tighter and began to rock back and forth for warmth. She heard the robust hum of the car engine as it drew closer and saw brilliant crimson behind her eyelids as the headlights cast two pools of dazzling light onto the sand where she sat. Vimla straightened her back and raised her chin in the spotlight, waiting for the other player to take her place.

Faizal reached around Vimla's back with his long, gangly arm and poked the bottom of Minty's foot. "Wake she up," he hissed loudly.

Chalisa Shankar stepped from her driver's car then. The car's yellow high beams played off her black hair, giving her an otherworldly glow. "No, don't wake she." She studied Vimla's defiant face with interest. "She look like a meditating goddess." Chalisa met Faizal's and Minty's gazes one at a time, nodding almost imperceptibly. "Good night."

Faizal whistled under his breath. "I find she looking like a witch. Be careful she ain't cast a spell on you!" He adjusted himself more comfortably on his prayer mat and gave Chalisa a charming smile.

Vimla's eyes flew open and her terrifying glare speared Faizal to his mat. "Shut up or I go feather your parrot and stew his ass up real nice when we get home."

Faizal recoiled. "You see?"

Chalisa's Cupid's-bow lips curved into an amused smile. "Vimla"—she floated forward on slender legs and curtsied into a sitting position in the sand—"so you does eat meat." She reached for Minty's hand and squeezed it.

Minty beamed; Vimla growled softly in the back of her throat like an agitated old dog.

"That is surprising for somebody who want to marry a pundit. Not so?" Chalisa said.

Vimla loathed the teasing in her voice. "You late." She raked her gaze brazenly over Chalisa from head to toe in search of a flaw, but Chalisa's inky hair really was a mass of enchanting unspoiled spirals; she was tall and graceful; her voice was sweet, her smile brilliant, however insincere. Vimla leaned forward so that her bottom lifted just slightly off the sand, and searched Chalisa's face for a mole, a blemish, a faint moustache. Any defect to make Vimla feel whole. She plopped down again with a huff, and flicked her gaze like an angry cat from Chalisa to Minty and then back again. "So what allyuh want from me?" She sat up tall and folded her arms tightly across her chest.

Chalisa set about fixing her gleaming white skirt just so on the sand. "What *you* want from *me*?"

Vimla's eyebrows arched like birds' wings in flight, and then swooped low and gathered in a peak at the centre so that darkness fell over her chocolate eyes. Angry accusations ricocheted wildly against each other in her mind, but before she could snatch the right one to hurl in Chalisa's face, Chalisa was laughing at her, showing off the sickle-shaped dimples in her cheeks and her even white smile.

"Is seven o'clock, Vimla. You travelled from quite Chance halfway across Trinidad, up a mountain road to a deserted bay on Krishna Janamashtami"—she looked sideways at Faizal Mohammed, who was lying on his belly on his prayer mat with his chin cupped in his hand, studying Chalisa—"with a very peculiar driver. You want something from me as much as I want something from you." Chalisa lifted and dropped her right shoulder in a delicate shrug.

Vimla's ears grew hot. She was conscious of Minty shifting uncomfortably on the sand and Faizal Mohammed swinging his legs in happy circles behind him. She imagined shoving a fistful of sand in Chalisa's beautiful mouth and stalking away. Would Minty and Faizal Mohammed follow? Vimla had her doubts and she couldn't risk looking more foolish than she already did. Instead she spread her hands, palms facing up, and said, "You right—"

Minty exhaled the breath she was holding.

"I want *you* to haul your scrawny backside back to St. Joseph and stop prancing about Chance like some hoity-toity town girl come to marry Krishna, when we all know"—Vimla gestured to Minty, Faizal Mohammed, and Chalisa's driver, who was lounging against the car—"that he mother and father forcing him to marry you because he can't marry me. *That* is what *I* want from *you*."

Chalisa's smirk morphed into a straight line. The light in her eyes went out. Still, Vimla wasn't satisfied.

Chalisa folded her smooth hands in her lap. "Mm-hmm. I hear about this temper of yours."

Vimla glowered. Who had been discussing her temper with Chalisa? Minty? Krishna? She felt betrayed either way.

"Vimla, let we be friends, nuh?" A ringlet, lying loosely against the coffee cream of Chalisa's neck, stirred in the wind and uncoiled itself in the air. She snatched the loose strand back from the night and tucked it adroitly behind her ear before continuing. "That is why I come here."

Faizal scoffed. "You come all the way to Maracas Bay to make friends with *she*?" He pointed a thumb at Vimla. "This girl mad in she head." Then he pointed at Minty. "That one, too. The two of them kidnap me and t'ief my car."

Chalisa ignored Faizal Mohammed as though he were beneath her. "Come," she said to Minty and Vimla. She stood up so smoothly it looked as if the wind had raised her up and lowered her back down on her feet. "Is a matter of setting our lives straight." She extended a hand to Vimla, who stared up at her, bewildered.

Vimla grasped Chalisa's hand, despite herself, and before she knew it, she and Minty were being led down the dark deserted beach toward the raucous waves. Chalisa's hand felt like silk against hers; it made Vimla's heart ache to think that Krishna had held both their hands, knew whose was softer, more delicate, and had decided whose hand was more worthy of holding. She felt frumpy in her crumpled salmon-coloured dress and foolish for thinking she was any match for Chalisa Shankar. She gulped deep breaths of the wind in an effort not to collapse on the beach and bawl into the sand.

When they reached the shoreline, Chalisa drew Minty and Vimla into the water, knee-deep. "You does swim?" She teetered and caught her balance again, extending her long slender arms out to the side.

Vimla looked narrowly at Chalisa. "We ain't have time to swim."

Chalisa lifted her skirt to her thighs and slid deeper into the chilly water. Her white blouse and skirt glowed against the darkening sky and the end of a long ringlet trailed behind her in the black water like a brush in paint. She waded through the restless waves with remarkable poise and purpose as if she were an extension of the sea.

Minty gazed, awestruck, after her.

Chalisa glanced back at the girls, who stood huddled, waves crashing at their knees and drenching the hems of their skirts. "You have time now." She sank so that the sea kissed the lobes of her ears and she was no more than a striking face floating on the water.

Goosebumps upon goosebumps spread up and down Vimla's arms and legs, but inside she burned so hot she thought she might explode.

What if she strode through the water and forced Chalisa's smiling face under the waves? What then? What if she followed Chalisa and learned to glide like an ethereal fairy-maid, too? She loathed and admired Chalisa. It made her stomach roil.

"Hey!" The girls turned around slowly, steadying themselves against the wicked undertow. "Heeeyyy!" Faizal was sprinting on spindly legs across the beach toward them. "Allyuh mad or what? Get out of that blasted cold water!" He lifted his bony knees high and flapped his skinny arms as he ran. Chalisa's driver, still leaning on the car, gazed at Chalisa as if she were the very moon.

Chalisa floated closer to the girls, but she looked directly at Vimla. "Is no sense vexing with me. We need to help each other."

Vimla stiffened as a gust of wind tried to push her down. "What you could really help me with?"

Chalisa smiled at Vimla, weaving her arms back and forth in the water, making wavelets within waves. She ignored the exasperation that crossed Vimla's face. "Vimla, come into the water."

"Why?"

"Because then there will be nothing between us. There will be no Krishna, no wedding—"

Vimla bit her lip hard.

"No rumours, no gossip. Just us. Just three young women negotiating the same tide." Chalisa stood up, dripping in the cool night breeze. Her white blouse clung to her slender body and her mass of black hair lay heavy on one shoulder. She took hold of Minty's elbow and gently guided her deeper into the water.

Minty squealed as she submerged herself in the sea. "Come on, Vims, before is time to go."

Vimla stood alone, watching her best friend wade away with Chalisa Shankar. She glanced over her shoulder; Faizal was drawing nearer. He marched with resolve, sharp angles poking the night. The sprinkling of faint stars played peeka-boo from behind the swirling clouds. Vimla felt the push and pull of the tide at her feet, coaxing her one way and then the next.

Chalisa ignored Faizal's shout, pushing off the sandy floor with her toes into a back float and surrendering her body to the rock of the sea. "I ain't love him, Vimla," she said to the sky. "I ain't even like him self."

Vimla stared at Chalisa's drifting body, aghast. "But allyuh marrieding!"

"Who tell you that?"

Vimla and Minty exchanged glances. "Everybody say so."

"Everybody wrong."

Vimla shivered. She didn't know if she could trust Chalisa Shankar, let alone befriend her. In the end it was Minty who persuaded her to let go of her reservations, if only in that moment. "Come on, Vimi," she pleaded. "We done come so far."

And she was right. They were a far, far way from home, and that's when Vimla knew that she would go yet farther before this journey was through.

She trod gingerly into the bitter cold water toward Minty's outstretched arms, and allowing herself a tentative smile, Vimla ducked below the surface of the black water just as Faizal arrived, cursing and flailing at the shore's edge.

Bhang!

Puncheon sauntered to the rusty gate hanging unhinged and lifted it away to allow his visitors through. *"Jai* Shri Krishna!" Glory to Lord Krishna.

Om and Rajesh stepped through the gates and looked around the cluttered courtyard with curiosity. A single light bulb dangled from a house beam, attracting moths. They circled the glow, flinging their papery bodies against the hot bulb, creating soft clinking noises until they tumbled to their deaths. Three old chairs were set around the circumference of light cast by the bulb, and in the middle of the circle was a mysterious circular object covered with a cloth. In the shadows lay haphazard piles of wood and scraps of galvanized steel, a bike with one wheel, two old tires and a three-storey pyramid of rum bottles with the labels peeled off.

"Punch, you make it to the mandir yet?" Rajesh lowered

himself into one of the creaky chairs and stretched his slippered feet into the circle.

Puncheon was wearing his finest kurtha this evening, the one with the three faux diamond buttons at the collar and gold embroidery at the cuffs. He smoothed the white cotton shirt, yanked up his loose pink Hawaiian shorts and stood up straighter. "How you mean? I went to the temple yesterday."

"Yesterday? Krishna Janamashtami is tonight, Puncheon. We taking you to the mandir. Put on a pants and let we go."

Puncheon stroked his chin the way he did when he had an important point to make. "The calendar is a complex thing, Om. Today is yesterday in India, ain't so? I already gone to the mandir yesterday. I fast and everything."

Om brushed a hand through his thinning hair. "Puncheon, I going to lie down in this hammock while you get ready. Do fast. Chandani and Sangita waiting for we and Chandani think is bad manners to show up in the mandir late." He hefted his leg over the holey hammock that hung from the ceiling beams and made to sink in.

"Nooooooo!" Puncheon caught Om's leg and swung it with surprising strength away from the hammock so that Om twirled and landed, stooped over, with a *thud* on the ground.

"Puncheon! What the ass wrong with you?" Om righted himself with a scowl.

"Sshhh!" Puncheon pressed a finger to his lips.

Om opened the ends of the hammock and peered inside. "What a big man like you doing with a litter of kittens in he hammock?"

Puncheon folded his arms over his chest, his bottom lip jutting out. "I find them."

"Where?"

"In the bush behind my house."

"Don't you think the mother looking for she young?"

"Not really."

"What you mean, 'not really'?"

"I kill the mother."

"You what?"

"I run she over with the tractor by accident one night."

"But you ain't have a tractor, Puncheon."

"I was driving somebody else tractor."

"Whose?"

"I can't tell you because I t'ief it."

"It only have three people with tractors in the district, Punch. We go find out eventually."

"Not really."

"What you mean, 'not really'?"

"Allyuh wouldn't find out unless I tell allyuh whose tractor I t'ief because it happened last week and nobody come looking for me yet."

"Whose was it, then?"

"It was yours, Raj."

Rajesh turned red. "Puncheon, how many times I tell you don't sneak on my property when you charged up? Last time you tie up Om's goats in my kitchen and Sangita get real vexed!"

Puncheon looked down at his cracked, bare feet.

"And how come my dogs didn't run you?"

Puncheon smiled. "I does visit so often them dogs grow to love me, Raj. I even let the wild black one ride in the tractor with me and drink my rum."

Raj swiped at Puncheon, who scampered away holding his shorts up.

Om nodded to the covered object on the ground. "What you have in there? More kittens?"

Puncheon hovered over the object protectively. He lowered his voice and looked around. "Where Sangita, Rajesh?"

"In the mandir."

Puncheon turned to Om. "And where is your striking wife?"

"Chandani is in the mandir, too, *waiting for we!* Now do fast! Let we go!"

"You sure they ain't going to show up here looking for allyuh?" Puncheon's red eyes shifted from Om to Rajesh.

"No!"

Puncheon nodded and whipped the cloth away to reveal a clay mortar balancing on two old bricks. He lifted his long kurtha out of the way and withdrew the pestle from the back pocket of his Hawaiian shorts. "I work hard all day." He stirred the air with his pestle and screwed his features up in exaggerated exertion.

Rajesh and Om leaned forward and saw that the mortar was filled with murky green slime.

"Cow shit, Punch?"

"It's bhang!" Puncheon jumped in the air and whooped. "Bhang! Bhang!"

Om rubbed his head and for an explanation looked at Rajesh, who shrugged his expansive oxen shoulders in response.

"On Maha Shivaratri, people does drink bhang. It's Lord Shiva's favourite beverage. Mine, too." Puncheon sat back on his haunches and stared, starry eyed, into the gooey liquid the way a girl might stare at her reflection in a pool of clear water.

"I thought yours was rum."

Puncheon smiled faintly. "That, too." Suddenly he sprang to his feet and sped to the kitchen. He returned with three mugs. "This better. Bhang make with grind-up cannabis buds and spices and milk and some other things. They say Lord Shiva does drink this to meditate. Is what he does use to transcend space and time and the cycles of creation and destruction."

Rajesh raised his eyebrows. "Who tell you that, Punch?"

"A friend. He give me the recipe and teach me all about it." Puncheon lifted the heavy mortar with steady hands and tipped it over each mug until every last drop of the elixir had dribbled out.

"Puncheon, is not Maha Shivaratri—is Krishna Janamashtami! You mix up your dates, boy."

Puncheon paused, a mug in his head. He shrugged. "That ain't matter. God is God is God!"

Om took his mug from Puncheon. "One drink and then we leaving." He glugged deeply, resting his palm on his gut and slouching into the wobbly chair.

Puncheon clinked mugs with Rajesh, who grunted a thank-you, and guzzled his own drink like a thirsty animal.

"This thing taste like drain water, Puncheon."

"Shut your ass—when last you drink drain water, Om?"

Rajesh closed his eyes. "I think I remember hearing my father talk about this bhang. Is a common thing to drink in India."

Puncheon nodded. "It is a *sacred* thing. Ask Pundit Anand." He wiped his mouth with the back of his hand and set his mug on the ground.

"You could ask him when you see him tonight. Now, go and change out of those blasted pink shorts and let we go."

"Punch, ain't this drink supposed to make you feel high? I ain't feel a damn thing."

Puncheon moved his chair away and sprawled on his back across the concrete. "Wait, nuh, man. Five minutes."

Rajesh and Om settled deeper into their chairs, stared blankly across the dim courtyard and waited.

Krishna Janamashtami

Sangita sashayed into the small village mandir, the soft pleats of her peacock-blue sari sweeping the floor at her feet. She lowered her gaze like a demure Indian bride as she walked down the aisle, peeking from below the thick fray of her lashes at the men and women who ogled her in a mixture of lust and envy. She wished Faizal were there; he would appreciate the design of her close-fitting sari blouse with the hand-sewn pearls, and her opulent sari phaloo twinkling in the diya light. He would like the way she let it cascade over her arm like an Indian film star instead of draping it over her shoulder or, worse, her hair. But more important, he would see how delicious she looked and be sorry for embarrassing her the other morning. Sangita sighed quietly; she wondered what—or who—Faizal was busying himself with on this auspicious night. The thought troubled her, but as she glanced at the altar, she reminded herself that it was Krishna Janamashtami, Lord Krishna's birthday, and she had come here to pray. She shook her seedy thoughts away, sending the bejewelled gold earrings at her lobes springing against her cheeks, and forced piety into her lonely heart.

The life-sized marble Shri Krishna and Radha murtis stood with their arms entwined in an embrace. Radha gazed up at her lover, lost in his beauty; Shri Krishna stared back at Sangita, one foot crossed in front of the other with a golden flute at his flaking pink lips. A magnificent peacock feather extended from his black curls, and ropes of pearls hung around his neck. His eyes were frozen with mischief and laughter, as if everything that passed before his gaze was beloved to him.

Sangita pressed her palms together at her heart centre, bowed before the murtis and seated herself against the back wall of the temple. Perhaps if she prayed hard enough, she would find more love in her life.

The modest temple overflowed with Hindus from the district. They squeezed themselves into various seated positions across every square inch of the carpeted floor, crushing their finest dresses and kurtha pajamas beneath them. The *kirtan*, music group, at the front of the temple, led the congregation in a string of chants and *bhajans* glorifying Lord Krishna as they pumped the bellows of their shiny harmoniums and drummed lively rhythms on the taut skins of their *dholaks*. People clapped and swayed, fanned themselves against the heat and swatted at fat, guzzling mosquitoes with surprising patience as they waited to celebrate the birth of Bhagwan Shri Krishna.

Sangita shifted uncomfortably on her bottom, and let her gaze meander around the temple. The altar shone with dozens of blazing diyas. They flickered in the *whoosh* of comings and goings as people offered jasmines to, and prostrated before the feet of, Shri Krishna at random. Older women fussed over the diyas, drizzling melted ghee around the cotton ball wicks to keep each flame ablaze. Burning sandalwood incense uncurled into the air, blackening the newly whitewashed walls and peeling plaster on the ceilings. A tired fan swivelling over-head pushed the hazy air around the room, sending the pink and white crepe paper decorations on the ceiling a-flutter.

Sangita yawned.

Pundit Anand Govind appeared at the altar, draped in a brilliant saffron cotton shawl dotted with red aums. He smiled at the congregation, his little eyes dissolving into a hundred crinkles. Everyone stopped singing and the harmo-nium and dholak players shifted the microphones away from their instruments so that the music grew soft and distant, as if drifting in through the open windows from a far-off place. Pundit Anand folded his hands and bowed to the villagers.

"Devotees, it is midnight, the hour of Bhagwan Shri Krishna's incarnation. I invite you to come to the altar to rock the *palana* and offer flowers and incense to our Lord in his infancy." Pundit Anand gestured to the red cradle, in which a miniature painting of the baby Bhagwan Shri Krishna was nestled, his hands in a pot of butter.

Pundit Anand lifted his voice and made grand gestures of importance as he spoke. "Our scriptures tell us that on this night"—he punctured the air with his pointer finger—"on this holy night, our Bhagwan Shri Krishna was incarnated to dispel the earth's evils and teach us the path of righteousness. Let we rejoice in his coming!"

Pundit Anand smiled warmly. "You are all blessed for fasting today. Many of you have eaten only fruits and milk, some of you nothing at all. But the real fasting begins in the mind!" He tapped his finger against his greying temple; his moustache twitched. "Those of you who remain pure of heart and abstain from negative, unsavoury thoughts will receive Bhagwan Shri Krishna's choicest blessings." He paused, gazing across the sea of villagers, lingering longer on those with the deepest pockets. "You are invited now to form a line up the aisle and make your offering to Bhagwan Shri Krishna." He smiled, adjusting his saffron shawl, and took up his position next to the palana.

At once the kirtan group resumed their music making, and the entire temple vibrated with a new, more vigorous, energy. One by one, people rose to their feet and then picked gingerly through the crowd to join the line, until devotees dressed in kaleidoscopic colour snaked from the altar to the back of the mandir like a rainbow's arc.

Sangita fell into line behind Chandani. Her neighbour wore a stiff lilac skirt and blouse, stitched from a sari. The skirt draped like cardboard from her hips to her ankles. A plain white *dupatha* was pulled onto her head, just hiding the knot of stark black hair at the nape of her cane-stalk neck. She shuffled forward on wooden legs, her eyes fastened on the slobbering baby slung over the shoulder of the woman in front of her.

Sangita touched Chandani's elbow softly. "Sita-Ram, Chand."

Chandani turned and her piggy eyes squinted so small it was as if she were trying to squeeze the image of Sangita out of her sight. "Sita-Ram." She cleared her throat. "And thanks for sending the food last week." But her gratitude sounded like an accusation. She strained the muscles in her face to produce a smile; the result was an unfortunate grimace.

Sangita swept Chandani's thanks away with a flick of her wrist, sending a dozen gold and peacock-blue bangles tinkling. "I was happy to do it, Chand. So tell me, how is Vimla?"

The woman with the baby moved away then and Chandani arrived at the front of the line. She turned her tense back on Sangita as if she hadn't heard the question, and found herself staring into the crinkly face of Pundit Anand Govind. Something akin to dread flashed through the old priest's watery eyes as Chandani climbed the altar steps and stood opposite him on the other side of the palana. Sangita noticed the tremor of blue-green veins peeking from the white wisps of hair at Pundit Anand Govind's temple, and the left side of his moustache droop in a faint, almost imperceptible frown. His gaze shifted to the congregation then back to Chandani, and in that millisecond respite, he recovered his pious smile. He handed Chandani a handful of flower petals to place in the cradle; as if his son hadn't been caught with her daughter by the ravine; as if he weren't marrying his son to another girl and abandoning her daughter's reputation to the village gossips.

Chandani sprinkled the flowers over the picture of baby Krishna and, without instruction, took the brightly blazing diya from Pundit Anand's open palm and waved the fire in three circles in front of the picture before setting it down again. She rocked the palana gently, lingering for a moment as if a live child were gurgling within. A wistful look crossed her face. When she was finished, Chandani clasped her small hands and bowed at the waist in front of the palana.

Sangita held her breath. She craned her neck to see if Chandani would touch Pundit Anand's feet respectfully, slip him the customary rolled-up dollar bills as payment for his holy service. The moment seemed to stretch on forever, with Chandani hinged at the hips like a broken doll and Pundit Anand Govind staring down at her bowed head, a mixture of great expectation and worry writ in the lines and folds of his face. Sangita laced her fingers together to keep from poking Chandani from her daze and glanced back at the dozens of villagers winding to the rear of the mandir, waiting their turn. But as her keen eyes fell on the last three men in the line, her stomach pitched and she paled.

At once she whirled back and grasped Chandani's sharp elbow in her soft hands. "Let we go, Chand," she whispered, her back to the congregation.

Chandani tried to wrench free. "Sangita, wait your turn! I ain't finish here yet."

Sangita tightened her grip and brought her mouth close to Chandani's ear. "Your husband is holding a kitten at the rear of the mandir."

Chandani screwed her face up and her thick eyebrows joined at the centre of her forehead.

"He's with Puncheon, Chandani."

Chandani darkened. Squaring her shoulders, she turned and marched away from the altar without so much as a cursory glance at Pundit Anand Govind.

Sangita coaxed her pretty mouth into an innocent smile for the priest, bowed deeply to the palana and flew after Chandani. She kicked the pearl-encrusted pleats of her sari in staccato

steps as she swept by the line, conscious—even in her haste—
of enchanting the world around her.

Chandani sneered at the men as she barrelled down the
aisle. They watched her like frightened children, holding
their wriggling kittens to their chests and bunching close.
"Outside." Her voice was so steady it sent shivers rippling up
Sangita's spine. The men shuffled around, bumping into one
another, until finally Chandani and Sangita herded them like
daft sheep into the darkness.

The Stormy Alliance

Thunder rolled through the churning, nebulous clouds. Sea surf surged skyward and broke furiously on the bay as the coastline pitched itself farther and farther across the beach. On either side of the cove, the mountains loomed against the black sky like the shadows of beasts, and sheets of silver rain pelted downward, threatening to plunge the island into the sea.

Faizal gripped Minty and Vimla by the wrists and dragged them from the shore. They hurtled toward the headlights with their heads down. Faizal flung open the rear car door and Minty and Vimla clambered in. "Mangoes! This is a real paranormal rain," he yelled, sliding into the driver's seat and slamming the door shut. He spun round to glare at Minty and Vimla. "Allyuh listen: when we get back to Chance, I ain't want to have anything to do with you little witches." He pointed into the darkness, "Especially that one there!"

Vimla looked out her window. Through the rills of rain streaming down her glass, she saw Chalisa spinning with her arms outstretched; a whorl of white twisting across a menacing bay. Vimla felt dizzy watching her; she felt dizzy thinking about her, too. Just before the rain, Chalisa had said that she didn't love Krishna. How could that be? Vimla ached for him; her spirit was withering away in his absence, and Chalisa Shankar couldn't even bring herself to *like* him. *And how does he feel about you?* Vimla had wanted to ask. But her puffed-up pride had lodged itself in her throat, so that she could only stare dumbly at the gypsy who was to marry Krishna. *Her* Krishna.

Minty slithered across the back seat and leaned against Vimla, shivering. "What she doing?"

Chalisa breezed through the rain toward Faizal's car and rapped the window with her knuckles. Faizal spun around in his seat. "Keep she out of my car. I have my hands full with allyuh as it is."

Vimla felt for the handle in the dark and rolled the glass down a few inches, inviting the storm inside.

Faizal sucked his teeth. "These harden children go kill me." He ran his hands through his wet hair and let his head fall against the headrest.

"I wouldn't marry Krishna!" Chalisa shouted. She snaked a hand into the car and gripped Vimla's shoulder. "We go have to work together, Vimla!"

Chalisa's driver came up behind her and cupped her elbow in his hand. His face, Vimla noticed, was that of a young man who had only recently bidden his boyhood goodbye. There was a devotion in his eyes that deepened the aching in Vimla's heart, and yet, as he stood guarding Chalisa with the storm at his back, Vimla knew he was the type of man who hid his intensity in silence. "Gavin?" Chalisa said, as if surprised to find him there at all. Gavin said something that was lost in the wind and then gathered Chalisa under his arm and guided her to the car. They sickened Vimla for reasons she only partly understood, but still she couldn't look away, no matter how she tried.

Faizal cranked the key in the ignition and the car purred to life. "You know why you does get into so much trouble, Vimla?" Vimla winced at his surly frown reflected in the rear-view mirror. "Is because you real stupid. Don't you mix yourself up with she, you hear? If the two allyuh is trouble"—he looked from Minty to Vimla—"then Chalisa Shankar is the devil self."

Vimla watched silently as the wipers lashed against the downpour and the car trundled onto the road, not because she was too drained to argue but because she thought Faizal might be right. The car coiled slowly down the precarious mountain and she gripped the door handle. They swung around sharp bends, just skimming the edge of plummeting cliffs, climbing uphill and sailing down slopes, constantly juddering against the backs of their seats. It went on like this for ten minutes, until the hail of rain tapered into a drizzle and grey mist settled in the rustling trees lining either side of the dark road. Vimla shivered in her damp clothes.

"I think Chalisa Shankar does do witchcrafts," Faizal muttered.

Minty peeled her sodden skirt off her thighs, straightened it and let it fall back again. "Chalisa ain't a witch, Faizal. She just . . ."

"Dotish? Wayward?"

"Free."

"Ha!" Faizal slapped his steering wheel. "I never see a girl behave so wild in my life. Chance people think Vimla hot? Whey, sir! Wait till they see this one! Chalisa Shankar ain't free—she slack too bad!" He laughed. "Is no wonder she Nanny coming quite Chance to find she a husband." He swerved around a tight corner. "I want to know how she manage to come and frolic at the beach on Krishna Janamashtami. Ain't she should be in the temple?"

Vimla let her head loll against Minty's shoulder. She had wondered the same thing, but then, Minty and Vimla had found a way to escape. Minty had said she needed to review her calculus, and Vimla had said she was too embarrassed to go to the mandir and see Pundit Anand Govind. It had worked. Sangita and Rajesh wanted Minty to be the top student in Chance come September, and Om and Chandani were happy to leave Vimla hidden away from the entire village for the night. As long as their parents stayed in the mandir until at least midnight, Vimla and Minty were safe.

Faizal rolled his window down and a burst of crisp air rushed into the car. He was quiet for a moment and then a groan so mournful escaped his lips that Vimla sat up and leaned forward to see. "Oh mangoes!" he wailed, shaking his head. "We turning back." He slowed the car; it swerved over a blanket of slick leaves.

"What you mean? You can't stop here!" Vimla looked behind them; Gavin and Chalisa were twenty feet away, their headlights two unblinking eyes in the night.

Faizal pulled his car to the side of the road, alongside a mesh of dishevelled branches and dripping leaves. "I left my Qur'an on the beach . . . and my prayer mat!"

"But, Faizal, your Qur'an will be soaked and ruined. You go have to get a next one."

"A next one?" His eyes bulged in horror. "You Hindus have 10,001 different scriptures. Allyuh don't understand the significance or sacred-ity of the Qur'an." He gripped the steering wheel. "And that mat is special!"

"But you does sell prayer mats in your store, Faizal. You have plenty to choose from!"

Faizal held the girls' gazes in the rear-view mirror again. "Sangita embroidered that mat for me. I does say my best, most holiest, most religious prayers on that mat."

The car fell silent. Vimla felt Minty tense at her side.

Gavin pulled up beside Faizal then. "Everything all right?"

"I going back to get my Qur'an and mat!" Faizal yelled.

The rear driver's-side door flung open and Chalisa spilled out like a wave. She had swept her wet ringlets into a bun on top of her head. She looked neat and regal; Vimla felt like a bedraggled dog, watching her. Chalisa's eyes flashed as she rounded Faizal's car and banged her fist on the hood.

"What wrong with you, girl?" Faizal demanded.

"You want to dead?"

"What?" Faizal turned to Gavin for an explanation, but Gavin was already striding after Chalisa and laying a hand on her shoulder. His fingers could have been raindrops; she showed no indication of feeling them.

"Allyuh go dead driving on this road so," Chalisa said. Vimla thought she saw terror in Chalisa's face, but everything was muted beneath layers of shadow, and she couldn't be sure. "The weather bad. The road narrow. And that drop there—" she pointed to the cliff's edge "—is a drop to allyuh death."

Faizal Mohammed sucked his teeth. "Eh, Miss Lady. If it wasn't for me, the three allyuh would still be playing fairy-maid in the water." He scowled deeply. "And allyuh would have drown, too! You wasn't thinking about death then!" He twisted his neck out of the car and glared at her. "Ain't it was you who wanted to come here in the night?"

Chalisa scowled.

"Now, move. I turning back."

Gavin lowered to Faizal's eye level. "If you turning back, I could drop the girls home." Vimla heard his voice this time; it was husky, barely used.

She held her breath. She didn't want to ride with Chalisa all the way home. She was uncomfortable enough sitting in wet clothes in the back of Faizal's car, trying to decipher Chalisa's intentions, and hoping she and Minty would be in bed before their parents. She didn't need the additional anxiety of sitting next to Chalisa Shankar when she was busy wilting and worrying in the darkness.

"Oh for fuck sakes. Never mind." Faizal rolled the window up and peeled away, leaving Chalisa and her driver staring after them by the side of the road.

For a few moments nobody said a word. Faizal jerked the car left and right and pressed his foot heavier on the gas. The car slewed over muddy puddles. Twigs and vines slapped the windshield. The tires trembled over ruts in the road.

"Faizal . . . Faizal!" Minty grasped his shoulder with her pudgy hand.

"Blasted mangoes! What you want from me?"

"Slow down!"

Faizal sucked his teeth, but he pumped the brakes.

"Why you ain't make we go back to the beach? Or ride with Chalisa?"

"Is one thing if I loss Sangita's prayer mat—is another thing if I loss she daughter." Faizal turned the radio on, signalling the end of the conversation.

Minty and Vimla snuggled against each other for warmth as the sweet voice of Indian superstar songstress Lata Mangeshkar filled the car. Vimla closed her eyes and curled her legs under her. She felt empty, like someone had scooped all the hope out of her soul. The more Lata sang of love, the more Vimla understood that it had slipped away.

Bhang! II

Chandani looked over her shoulder at the mandir in the distance. It was only a minute glimmer of light now, but the devotional bhajans and rhythmic drumming seemed to dance up the dark road behind her, beckoning her back. She grew increasingly bitter with every step she took toward home, tightening her claw-like grip on Om's arm. "Oh Lawd, what I do to deserve this sufferation in my life?"

Puncheon zigzagged in between the couple and fell flat on the ground, ripping Chandani's fingernails from Om's flesh. "Om, I dizzy, man. I real dizzy. Just leave me here and let me dead by the side of the road." He lay on his belly with his arms splayed on either side of him, the side of his face pressed into the mud.

Om stared down at Puncheon, dazed, stroking the tiny orange-and-white head of his kitten with a fat thumb.

Chandani shook him. "Pick him up, Om!" Om blinked back at her. Chandani looked around for Rajesh and found him crouched in a sprawl of wild bushes, whimpering, a black kitten nestled in the crook of his arm. Sangita stood by his side, rubbing his back and warning him not to soil her sari.

Chandani grimaced. They were at least a fifteen-minute walk from home. She could go back to the mandir and ask for help, but what would she say? That her husband and his friends were high and stranded in the dark on Krishna Janamashtami? She knew neighbours would be eager to help and they would mean well, too, but tomorrow those very same neighbours would peddle Chandani's misfortune to anyone willing to listen. She couldn't have that. *Everyone* was willing to listen in Chance and Chandani had already endured a lifetime of embarrassment in the past weeks.

She thought of Vimla then, with her big bold eyes and the mischievous twist of her shapely lips. She used to plait Vimla's long, unruly mane with such care, making a wish for her daughter every time she folded one black lock over the next; it was like weaving dreams into her hair. But by the end of each day, stray, rebellious curls always managed to fly free, and Chandani would sigh, soak Vimla's hair in coconut oil and do it all over again before bed. This is what she remembered when Om brought Vimla home from the ravine that night and Vimla's hair was loose and flowing wildly over her shoulders. The sight made Chandani feel like her daughter had unravelled every wish she'd ever made for her and flung it away for a boy. That's what had hurt Chandani most—that it was all for a boy.

Sangita shimmied over, smelling of sweet sandalwood. "Raj

think a soucouyant go suck he blood." She looked down at Puncheon and then up into Om's black, glassy eyes. "What we go do?"

Chandani's gaze swished over Sangita. She frowned at her sensual mouth and skintight sari blouse, wondering why of all the women in Chance she had to get tangled up in this predicament with Sangita Gopalsingh. "We have to walk."

"Walk?" Sangita's slanted eyes glowed like a cat's. "Look at them, Chandani!" She gestured to Puncheon, who had rolled onto his side and pulled his knees up to his chest as he sang Trinidad's national anthem. "Maybe I should get Faizal. He could pick we up in his car."

Chandani narrowed her gaze at Sangita. She had seen Sangita and Faizal Mohammed interacting in the market; they bantered with a familiarity that was almost intimate. Chandani had always wondered whether there was more to their neighbourly friendship than Rajesh knew. "Sangita, you can't walk home alone dressed like that." She circled her index finger around Sangita's exposed cleavage. "And you can't leave me alone with these fools neither. We have to walk. All of we. Together. Now!"

Sangita pouted, and Chandani was unsure if the woman was insulted about her blouse or disappointed about Faizal. She didn't care either way. "Get Rajesh. Let we go."

Rajesh moaned and Sangita, Chandani and Om turned to look. He was staring at the mandir in the distance, shaking his head slowly, his eyes bulging from their sockets like twin moons as he backed away. Sangita touched his broad shoulder. He jumped, dropping his kitten, which bolted into the underbrush. He shielded his face with his hands.

Chandani stomped her foot, sending sludge splattering into Puncheon's hair. "Lawd Father, give me strength not to kill this fool on Shri Krishna's birthday." She stalked up to Rajesh and wrenched his flesh in a painful pinch. "Cut this nonsense, you hear me?"

Rajesh whelped. "The soucouyant is coming for me." He pointed a shaky finger at the lights of the mandir. "Look, she flying in the air like a fireball to suck my blood!"

Chandani rose on her tiptoes, grabbed Rajesh's big square face in her hands and forced him to look down at her. "Rajesh, it ain't have no vampire living in Chance, but it have me, and I worse!" she said through clenched teeth. "If you don't haul your ass home, I go do worse to you than a shitting soucouyant!"

Rajesh winced, then he reached for Sangita's hand and lumbered with leaden feet to stand beside Om, who still hadn't moved.

Chandani sighed. "Good." She placed her balled-up hands on her narrow waist and leaned over so she could shriek directly into Puncheon's ear. "Stop singing!"

"Oh gosh, Chandani, leave me in peace, nuh? I don't know why Om didn't beat you when I tell him to."

Chandani sucked her teeth and nudged him with her sandal. "Puncheon, you look like a half-dead manicou bounced down by a car. Get up! Let we go!"

Puncheon pinched his features together so that he really did resemble a wild opossum. Grumbling, he pulled himself up on all fours and teetered to his feet, bracing on Om's solid shoulder for balance.

Chandani nodded, pleased, although it was impossible to

tell by the severe line of her mouth or the dark swoop of her angry eyebrows. "March!"

The men shuffled at an excruciatingly slow pace; Om concentrated hard to place one foot in front of the other; Rajesh trod with caution, constantly looking over his massive shoulder; and Puncheon staggered, griping with each step. Chandani and Sangita walked behind them in silence, making sure they didn't wander into the middle of the road or the dark undergrowth. They trekked on like this for seven minutes, until Puncheon began to gag.

"Oh God, Puncheon, please don't." Sangita reached for her sari phaloo and held it over her nose and mouth, turning away and then looking, turning away and then looking.

Puncheon sank to his knees. "Oh gosh, I go dead. I go dead here tonight."

Rajesh glanced around wildly. "Is the soucouyant," he whispered.

Chandani glared at him. "Is not the soucouyant. Is the blasted marijuana all you stupidies drink!"

Om's red, glazed eyes fixated on Chandani, but he couldn't bring himself to articulate any of the thoughts streaming through his mind. He gave her a placid smile and nuzzled the head of his kitten. She scowled back at him.

Puncheon crawled away from the group and hung his head in the bushes, where dozens of mosquitoes could devour his face. He groaned and gagged again, his entire body convulsing.

"I fed up, Chandani. I going to fetch Faizal." Sangita released Rajesh's arm and whisked away before Chandani could protest, half walking and half running up the road with her glittering phaloo fluttering behind her.

The Race Home

It was eleven o'clock when Faizal arrived in Chance, more than enough time to rid himself of Minty and Vimla before their parents came home. "Praise Allah," he muttered, thinking of the storm that had driven them from Maracas Bay. He glanced in the rear-view mirror at the girls; they were still nestled together like sleeping puppies. They looked innocent, cuddled up that way; hard to believe these girls had blackmailed him to take them to Maracas Bay in the first place. Faizal thought about his beloved Qur'an and prayer mat lying abandoned and sopped on the beach. He sighed tiredly, vowing to have nothing to do with Minty and Vimla once they returned his chain and he delivered them home.

"Eh! Allyuh wake up. We almost reach."

The girls stirred, sleepy eyed, as Chance unfolded in the darkness before them. They squinted at the old homes, cloaked in shadows and foliage, sheltered behind iron gates. The eyes of scrawny vagabond dogs glowed in the headlights as they watched Faizal's car putter by on the otherwise deserted dirt road.

"I said wake up, not sit up. Allyuh want somebody to see you in the car?"

Vimla and Minty looked at each other and then shrank against their seats, stealing glances out the window in their excitement.

"Look at the mandir, Vimi. It packed. People overflowing onto the road!"

Faizal gripped the steering wheel. "Duck!"

The girls swooped down as they whizzed by the mandir.

"I think we did it, Vimla. We really did it!" Minty's eyes shone.

Faizal smiled despite himself. "Allyuh ain't do one blasted thing except play the fool at the beach and ride around in my car like the queen and duchess of Trinidad and Tobago. *I* did it. Thank me."

"Thank you, Faizal," the girls chorused.

"Now, give me back my damn chain and leave me the hell alone."

Minty nodded and was about to slip the chain off from around her neck, when Faizal yelled, "Mangoes! Duck!"

Minty and Vimla dropped to the floor this time and lay as still as they could, their bodies overlapping like rag dolls.

Faizal motored up the rolling main road slowly. He blinked, shook his head, blinked again. Sangita was sailing toward the car, twenty feet away, holding the delicate pleats of her sari out of the mud as she came. The material wrapped around her torso had slackened, revealing her skimpy bejewelled blouse and soft, flat belly, glowing luminous in his headlights. Faizal moaned. "Forgive me, Sangita." He peeled off over the pitted road then lurched to a stop before his front gate. He scrambled from the car, unlocked the gate and pushed it open, so that it scraped and screeched against the asphalt of his front court-yard. He glided the car under the house.

Vimla and Minty were frantically untangling themselves in the back of the car, preparing to scurry out of the vehicle and bolt to Faizal's garden. From there they would go their separate ways, creeping through trees, around chicken coups and cow pens, until they could slip into their respective homes.

"Allyuh stop moving." Faizal's voice betrayed his unease and the girls fell still again, their eyes wide in the blackness.

He heard the jingle of her anklets as she drew nearer. "Sangita coming. Don't move and don't talk until I tell—"

"Faizal? Fai-zal!" Her voice floated from the road.

Faizal licked his lips and ran his hands through his hair, mumbling a combination of curse and prayer before step-ping from the car. "Good night, Sangita." He put his hands in his pockets and strolled toward her as if a visit after mid-night from Sangita dressed in a luscious sari was a common-place occurrence.

Sangita flounced into the courtyard, her hands on her shapely hips. "Faizal Mohammed, you ain't see me walking up the road?" She gave him a withering stare and then stopped short as he drew nearer. "Oh! What happened to you?"

He stared back at her wearily. His hair was windswept, his shirt crushed and hanging loosely from his dirty trousers.

"I had a rough night liming in Port of Spain with the boys."
He shrugged.

She peered into his face and arched an eyebrow at him.
"You think I born big so? You think I don't know that you
was out romping around with some misses?! Look at your
ramfle-up shirt. Look at your condition, Faizal!"

He grinned wickedly. "Look at yours."

Sangita cut her eye at him, pulling the silk over her visible
cleavage with a huff, but not before Faizal had a chance to
admire the plunging neckline of her blouse, noting with
approval the subtle pearls and peacock-blue and silver sequins
stitched in perfect rows across the seams at her neck, arms and
midriff. They glinted, sketching a sparkling silhouette against
the night.

"I need your help. I need a drop." Sangita raised her chin
and bustled past him to the car, throwing her sari phaloo over
her shoulder.

Faizal snatched the jewelled fabric and gently reeled her
toward him, a technique he'd learned from the popular love
scenes of Indian cinema. "Why you always in a rush?" He
leaned against his trunk and held Sangita, wrapped in her
ornamental silk, to his chest, filling his lungs with her intoxi-
cating scent.

She wriggled away. "Don't hold me up with your nasty
hands. Move from me. I don't know who you kiss with that
mouth tonight." She scrunched up her striking features to
embellish her disgust. "I ain't come here for you to feel me up
with your dirty self. I come for help. Chandani send me!"
Sangita narrowed her gaze at him. "Faizal, is that sand?" She
jabbed a finger at his chest.

Faizal's hand flew to the black wires springing from his partly exposed chest, feeling the grit of sand sprinkled in the tangles. He buttoned his shirt up to the collar and folded his arms in front of him. "No."

Sangita bored her piercing eyes into his guilty ones. "Well, Faizal, I real sorry to trouble you at this hour for help, especially after you spend the evening rolling around in the sand with some jammette from Port of Spain, but Puncheon, Rajesh and Om find themselves in some trouble and they need you."

Faizal cleared his throat. "Me? What they need *me* for?"

"Faizal Mohammed, you really acting strange tonight, you know that? Usually you is the first person on the scene when things go wrong, and the first person to broadcast it to the district the next day. Your mouth is like the *Trinidad Express* self!" She leaned closer to him, studying his face. "So tell me, what happened? You sick? Your jammette jam you too hard? What?"

"Eh, you want to stand up here and make noise, or you want my help?" Faizal scowled. "Tell me what happened."

"Humph!" Sangita gave him a disapproving once-over. "Puncheon, Om and Rajesh decide to drink bhang tonight."

Faizal's eyes widened. "Really?"

"And they show up in the mandir tight . . . holding kittens!"

"Oh mangoes!" He slapped his knee, doubling over with laughter. "Kittens!"

"Yes, kittens. And so me and Chandani started to walk the boys home, but Puncheon get sick and Rajesh afraid a soucouyant go drink he blood, so they idling by the side of the road waiting for *you* to pick them up in your car."

"My car?" Faizal sobered. He remembered Vimla and Minty huddled in back, waiting for an opportune moment to escape. They had come so far—all three of them—to be found out now. He knew that if they were discovered, he would be implicated in the ruse, and he was not built to endure the inevitable thrashing from Rajesh or Om. Of course, if the girls were caught, then Minty might not return his chain, or worse, she might show her father. And if that happened—

"Faizal!"

Faizal looked up from his feet into Sangita's suspicious face. "Yes?"

"Let we go!" She made for the passenger side of his car again, but he barred her way with a lean arm.

"We can't take my car."

"Why not?"

"Because is too small to fit everyone." He thought quickly. "And what if the motion of the car make Puncheon more sick?"

Sangita bit her lip, considering this, and Faizal grew more confident. "They go feel better if they walk. Fresh air is the best thing." He thought of burly Om standing with a kitten in the night, of Rajesh cowering like a child from vampires. "Let we fetch them together, nuh? I go help out the fellas if they need it." Faizal straightened to his full six feet and took giant, purposeful strides toward his open gate, hoping Sangita would follow without a fuss.

"Faiz—" she rushed after him "—if you going to get them, then I could go home." She fluttered her thick fringe of lashes. "I already walk all the way from the mandir, boy, and my foot tired."

Faizal shifted his gaze to the car and then back to Sangita. "No, you go have to help Rajesh get into the house. You think he could operate a key and a lock in that state of stupidness right now? You go help Raj, I go help Puncheon, and Chandani go help Om . . . and the kittens!" His mouth split into a wide grin. "Oh mangoes, I can't wait to see this!"

Sangita pouted, fiddling with the drape of her sari.

Faizal wrapped an arm around her slender shoulders in a reassuring squeeze. "Besides, you looking so radiant tonight I want to walk down the road with the prettiest woman in the district before she husband get back sober." He winked at her.

Sangita's full lips turned up in a playful smile. She swished past Faizal through the gate and onto the road, rocking her hips and twinkling with all the modesty of a peacock.

Mastana Bahar

Early the next morning Chalisa Shankar smoothed creamy coral lipstick on her Cupid's-bow lips and studied her reflection in the mirror. She turned her face to the left and then to the right, puckering and glancing sideways at herself. She tried a smile with all lips, a half-smile and a full-out beam that showed off her even white teeth and accentuated her prominent cheekbones. She gathered her lips in a pout, a pucker and frown. She bit her bottom lip as if contemplating something significant. She formed an O of surprise. And for the finale, she breathed in through her nose and exhaled slowly through her mouth to create a look of sensual breathlessness.

Chalisa clapped her hands and spun around in front of her mother's vanity, giggling.

"Your face go look squingy like Nanny's own one day."

She stopped short and glanced around the bedroom. Avinash stood in the doorway of the ensuite washroom. He fixed her with his serious black eyes, round and glowing with the wisdom of a worldly old man. His unusually small mouth was pursed and his hook nose twitched and flared in solemn thought. He blew a tuft of feathery hair from his eyes and folded his arms over his small chest. Chalisa smiled at him; he reminded her of a young spectacled owl.

"Why you does always sneak up on me, Avi?"

Avinash shrugged. He crossed the room and climbed onto the vanity chair, wriggling his bottom close enough to the edge so he could swing his legs.

"Do you really think I go look like Nanny when I get old?" Chalisa thought of her grandmother's papery skin, lined and weathered like an old road map to nowhere. She shuddered and sought the contours of her supple face with the tips of her fingers.

Avinash blinked his earnest eyes and nodded. "Unless you press your face with the iron."

"Avi! You cannot press a person's skin—it go burn!"

Avinash gripped the sides of the chair and swung harder. "Oh."

Chalisa stood beside the vanity and trailed her fingers with tenderness over her mother's lipsticks and blushes, the black eye kajal and fancy barrettes set on white crocheted doilies. She examined the perfume bottles one by one, spraying a mist of her favourite into the air and bounding through it.

Avinash watched her, crinkling his beakish nose at the floral fragrance. "Nanny vexed with you."

Chalisa went back to the vanity and pinched the kajal in

between two fingers. "I think Nanny vexed with the whole of Trinidad." She wondered if Nanny knew she had snuck out again last night, but the worry floated through her mind like a cloud and drifted away. If Nanny knew then Avinash knew, and he would have blurted it out by now. She glanced at her brother, who looked back at her with his penetrating gaze. She smiled, and taking a slow, deep breath to summon concentration, Chalisa drew close to the mirror and began to outline her gold-brown eyes with a steady, practised hand.

"I think you go get licks."

Chalisa looked at Avinash in the mirror. "I too old for licks, Avi." She swung a rope of black curls over her shoulder and resumed her work on her eyes. She was careful to start at the inner corner just above her soft fringe of lashes with a precise fine line that gradually thickened across her eyelid and finished in an upward sweep. Every Indian film Chalisa had ever watched featured a doe-eyed beauty with the same dramatic eyes. She had spent months duplicating the effect and this morning she stepped back pleased with her efforts.

Avinash strolled to the door and paused, wrapping his little hand around the knob. "You look like a manicou." He pulled the door open and marched into the hallway. "It's eight thirty, Chalisa. Breakfast ready."

Chalisa peeked at her reflection from beneath her lashes and smiled. "Manicou, my big toe," she whispered, flying after Avinash.

Chalisa hummed down the hall, twirling her wrists and swaying into the kitchen, but the song died on her lips and she hid her hands behind her back when she found herself staring into Nanny's severe face. She groaned inwardly. Avinash hadn't mentioned Nanny would be joining them for breakfast this morning. She looked at her brother, who lowered his gaze and climbed into his chair.

"Have a seat, Miss Mastana Bahar." Nanny glared at Chalisa through cataract eyes and pointed a veiny finger at the chair adjacent hers.

Chalisa swallowed hard. Two weeks ago she had auditioned in secret for *Mastana Bahar*, Trinidad's popular talent competition on televsion. It had been an incredible experience, a moment plucked from her dreams and made real. Every day she recalled the thrill of walking out in front of the judges and erupting into song and dance. She had felt so alive. Something inside her had awakened. Best of all, Chalisa had impressed the judges. They couldn't believe she'd never had any formal training, that her voice was so sweet and her movements so graceful. She was more than just pretty—she was glamorous. She was meant for the stage. She was born for Indian cinema. They told Chalisa what she always knew in her heart: she was going to be a star. And of course she was invited back for rehearsals and a final taping for the show.

Nanny brought her face close to Chalisa's and scrutinized her granddaughter's features. "Humph." She swiped her wrinkly thumb across Chalisa's full lips and smeared the coral glob to her own dry mouth. "How do I look, Avinash? Like Chalisa?" Nanny puckered at the boy and twirled her old, brittle wrists. Avinash stared back at her, stunned.

Nanny leaned across the table and pricked Delores, the cooking lady, with her poisonous stare. "Is really no wonder Chalisa want to sing and fling up she self for all of Trinidad

to see when you does let she eat breakfast with three pound of
makeup on she face."

Delores's red-rimmed eyes burned with years of unspoken
retorts, but she kept her lips squeezed tight and withdrew to
attend to the pot of Milo warming on the stove.

"Is a shame she parents didn't send she to live with me earlier.
I would have beat this flim-star stupidness right out of she!"

Under the table, Chalisa dug a fingernail into the palm of
her hand and twisted. It was how she distracted herself from
crying. She did this every time Nanny spoke of her parents like
they were just in the other room instead of dead. Burned to
ashes. Floating in a river somewhere.

"But let we get on with the business here," Nanny continued. "I ain't have time to sit and blame this body and that
body, when we all know who body fault this is." She looked
pointedly at Chalisa.

Delores brought the pot of steaming Milo to the table and
one by one filled the mugs to the rim. Nanny placed her lined
hand over the mouth of her mug. "Tea, Delores, with a splash
of milk and two spoon of sugar."

Delores sniffed and retreated again.

Nanny sat up straight and balanced her bony elbows on the
table, so that the sleeves of her pale-green sateen dress slipped
downward and revealed a dozen matching green veins rising
from her translucent skin. "Now, let we talk business, nuh?
Miss Mastana Bahar, I firing Gavin today. Did you know?"

Chalisa's eyes widened. She set her mug of Milo down and
stared into the creases marking angry Xs all over Nanny's face.

"You think you could tell me why?" Nanny held her empty
mug out to Delores, who filled it with tea.

Chalisa shook her head no, but that was a lie; she could think of several reasons Nanny might want to fire Gavin.

Nanny pivoted on her bony bottom and peered down at her grandson. "Avinash? You know why Nanny firing Gavin today?"

Avinash opened his mouth to answer and then clamped it shut again, seeing Chalisa's warning look across the table. He shrugged.

"Is because Chalisa bat up she eyelash at poor Gavin and make him take she to the *Mastana Bahar* auditions."

Nanny filled her small chest with air and yelled, "Gavin, come and take your leave, boy!"

Chalisa gasped.

Gavin shuffled into the kitchen with his head down. He was dressed in a white-and-brown checked shirt and a pair of brown dress pants. His hair was coiffed in a black poof at the front, and the rest was plastered to his scalp with Brylcreem. Chalisa's heart turned over in her chest.

Nanny waved her bony hand at Gavin. "Goodbye to you, Gavin. I hope you could find a next job in a next family home with a less wayward girl who wouldn't take advantage of you like my lovely and wonderful Miss Mastana Bahar." She blew on her tea and then rattled her mug against the saucer without taking a sip.

Gavin swallowed and nodded. He looked at Delores, whose bottom lip trembled, touched Nanny's feet respectfully and ruffled Avinash's plumy hair before heading to the door. He didn't dare glance back at Chalisa, but Chalisa followed him with her eyes until he disappeared and she heard the back door swing shut. Avinash burst into tears, covering his face with his hands. "Gavin was my best partner!"

Nanny gave Avinash a cursory glance before continuing. "I hope you is real happy and glad that Gavin is gone, Chalisa. As you can see, the rest of the family feeling real joyous and jubilant about it." She reached for her mug and brought it to her pale lips, slurping noisily while everyone waited. "Now, let we continue discussing even jollier matters—let we talk about your wedding." Nanny helped herself to the freshly baked currants rolls Delores placed in the middle of the table. "Let we start at the beginning, nuh? Chalisa, you went to the *Mastana Bahar* auditions without my permission. Ain't that so?" Nanny chomped the end of the roll and chewed like a grazing cow.

Chalisa nodded, her eyes flitting from Delores to Avinash. This wasn't news. Why was Nanny bringing this up again?

Nanny spoke, displaying the masticated contents in her mouth. "And you went to the taping of Mastana Bahar, too. Ain't that so?"

Chalisa wanted to scream. Yes! She had gone to the taping. She had kissed Gavin on the cheek to persuade him to take her. It was because she had gone to the taping, and Nanny had found out, that the hasty marriage arrangement with the Govinds in Chance had been made.

Nanny reached for her mug and stopped. She squinted across the table at Chalisa. "When that episode of you shaking up go air across Trinidad? October, ain't?"

Nanny wanted her married before the show was aired and the entire country saw Chalisa "singing and dancing like some slack no-where-ian vagrant child who never had parents to lick she tail with bamboo and keep she ass in line." Those had been her exact words.

Chalisa dropped her gaze to her empty plate. "September."

Avinash peeked through his fingers across the table at Chalisa. His owl eyes flashed with unasked questions.

"September when?" Nanny asked.

Chalisa shrugged, wrapped a ringlet round her finger.

"No problem." Nanny's smile was sly. "I go set the wedding for September first, soon in the morning."

"Yes—" Nanny whipped a green handkerchief from her bosom and waved it in Chalisa's face "—cry, beti, you have much to cry and bawl about, because by the time the episode of you shaking up your bamsee air all over the country, you go already married to that Krishna Govind boy." Nanny belched. "Delores, pass me another currants roll, nuh, gyul."

Chalisa stared, stupefied, at her grandmother. "But, Nanny, that too soon! It go be September first in two weeks!"

Nanny paused with her second fat currant roll in front of her lips. "Yes, not to worry. Your Nanny have it all figure out." She shoved the flaky pastry into her mouth and chewed off a giant piece with all the decorum of an agouti.

Avinash raised his head and propped his chin in his palm. "But why Chalisa have to marry now?"

"Avi." Nanny lowered her face to her grandson's. "Which respectable family go want their son to marry Chalisa after she twirl up all over *Mastana Bahar*'s stage? If I ain't marry she to Krishna now, no good boy go ever take she. I can't mind she here forever. I know I still looking pretty, but I's a old woman now."

Avinash averted his gaze.

Chalisa dug her fingernail into her palm again. That no one else would take her wasn't true. She knew for a fact that Gavin would marry her this minute if he could. Who wouldn't want to marry a star? Chalisa fixed her big, pleading eyes on Nanny. "But why must I marry Krishna? I ain't want to marry a pundit's son and live in the bush!"

"Eh! I ain't have time for your melodrama!" Nanny slapped her hand against the table, sending Milo and tea sloshing over the sides of the mugs. She furrowed her brow, creating creases upon creases on her forehead. "Stop answering me back, you hear? Nanny done talk, and when Nanny done talk, she done talk." Nanny brushed the crumbs from the lace of her dress and folded her bony arms.

A single black tear rolled down Chalisa's cheek. When she wiped it away, she left a smear of kajal in its place. Nanny looked at her. "Eh, Miss Mastana Bahar, you ain't looking like a *flim-star* to me, you know. Go and pretty up yourself. We going Chance to change the wedding date to September first."

Avinash brightened with interest. "Where is Chance, Nanny?"

"In the bush." Nanny sprang to her feet. "Behind God's back."

The Officious
and Auspicious

....

CHANCE, TRINIDAD

A nand Govind sat cross-legged on his bed, studying the wads of crumpled bills lying in his outstretched palms. He closed his eyes and raised and lowered his palms like scales. Anand sighed. He didn't have to count the pile of money to know that it was less than last year's Krishna Janamashtami earnings. He could feel the weight of loss in his hands. His shoulders slumped and the loose fleshy folds on his face drooped heavily in defeat. He brought his hands together, nestling the bills between them, and bowed so that his forehead rested on the tips of his fingers. Anand thought of praying, but he was too full of anguish for that. Instead he allowed his uncertainties about Krishna to seep from the dams of denial he'd constructed in his mind and swamp his thoughts.

Krishna was handsome, tall and well built. He was studi-
ous, too, absorbing the Ramayana, Bhagavad Gita and Vedas
with a zealousness comparable to Anand's as a youth. But
Krishna was no pundit. He was too much of a rascal to devote
his own life to God, never mind lead others along a righteous
path. Anand grimaced as he thought of Krishna's roguish episode with Vimla Narine for the hundredth time that day. The
ripple effect of Krishna's indiscretion was far-reaching; so
much so it had affected Anand's reputation in the village,
diminishing his popularity with the people and by extension
decreasing his earnings. Now there was this wedding to put
together, a desperate attempt to rescue the Govind name from
the mouths of the scandalmongers. "Give them a wedding to
dance at, and they go forget all about Vimla Narine." Anand
had reassured Maya. But the impending wedding expenses
gave him chest pains at night.

Anand fanned the money out in one hand and inhaled its
gritty scent deep into his lungs. Then he snapped the bills
one by one from the fan between a moistened thumb and
forefinger and tenderly arranged the bills into neat colour-
coded piles on the bed. When he had counted each pile twice
and totalled their sums in his head, he heaped the piles
together and cradled the substantial mound to his chest like
a sleeping baby.

"Anand."

Anand looked up to see Maya standing in the doorway,
holding a tall glass of water in her hands. A sheepish expression crossed her brown face when she noted the money clasped
to her husband's heart. Mouthing an apology, Maya padded
across the room and set the sweating glass down on the

bedside table. Then she took a seat on the edge of the bed, watching and waiting.

Anand lingered for a moment, appearing wistful and doting at once, before placing the bundle of money back on the bed. With a hairy hooked finger, he pulled out the bottom drawer of his bedside table and retrieved a shiny green metal box with a fat brass lock. He reached into his loose cotton shirt and scooped out the key that hung around his neck on a gold chain hidden behind a grotesque *aum* pendant. With careful hands he fitted the key into the lock and held his breath for the quiet *click*. He opened the lid so that it fell back on its hinges and he stared with a father's affection at the bundles of money tightly packed into the rectangular box.

"Anand!" Maya whispered, leaning close. The pair of gold bangles at her right wrist jingled with the movement.

Anand raised his silver eyebrows; she knew better than to interrupt him now. She was watching him with wide shiny eyes, near ready to burst with something to say. Anand sighed, crammed the new bundle of money into the box with the others, closed the lid, clicked the lock shut and deposited the box back in the drawer. He would count the bundle again before bed. He would count all the bundles again before bed. "Yes, Maya?"

"The Shankars is coming!"

Anand interlaced his fingers. "What Krishna do now?" He began to twiddle his thumbs in his lap. "They find out about Vimla Narine?"

Maya waved the worry away, tinkling her bangles an inch from Anand's bulbous nose. "No, no, nothing like that. The Shankars want to change the wedding date. They want the wedding sooner!"

"Sooner than September 17?" Anand reached for his glass of water and took a series of sips as he turned the idea over in his mind.

"Yes." Maya leaned forward and slapped the bed with her hand. "*Sooner.* They coming this afternoon self. What we go do?"

Anand returned the glass to the side table and resumed twiddling. "Do?"

Maya shook her head at him, impatient. "Anand, we can't have the wedding any sooner. It have too much to prepare. Even with Sangita help, this wedding go can't happen before next Saturday."

Anand's fingers paused mid-twiddle and he raised his eyebrows so high they nearly merged with his silver hairline. "Sangita?" He reclined against the headboard as a vision of Sangita Gopalsingh materialized in his mind. She had bowed deeply to him the night before, the soft mounds of her bosom nearly spilling out of her too-tight blouse and falling sinfully into baby Sri Krishna's innocent face. Anand's forehead furrowed.

"Anand!" Maya folded her arms. "You hearing me?"

The vision of Sangita dissolved. Anand cleared his throat and studied his wife. As always, Maya's hair was pulled back into a loose plait that started at her nape and wound down her back to her waist. Silver fly-aways sprang from her hairline, framing her dark oval face like a scanty lion's mane. Her black eyes were still luminous, but now dark shadows were permanently smudged beneath them, and when she smiled, her eyes crinkled to half the size they once were. Anand couldn't remember if this had happened before or after Krishna's recklessness.

"Yes, yes, Maya. Of course we go listen to what the Shankars have to say before we make a decision, but you right—it go be difficult to plan a wedding any sooner than September 17."

"Impossible, not difficult, Anand!"

Anand patted his wife's hand. "Nothing impossible with Mother Lakshmi's grace. Have faith." Anand said this so matter-of-factly he almost believed it himself.

"You think God have time to come down here and help prepare for Krishna's maticoor night and such? Ask she, nuh, the next time you talk to she." Maya pouted and folded her arms.

Anand's expression was serious, but his eyes danced with amusement. "Maya, you could ask she, too. When was the last time you had a nice conversation with Mother Lakshmi?"

Maya sniffed and raised her chin. "Is a terrible fate for a pundit's wife," she said, standing up, "who does have to hear steady preaching in she ears whole day and night."

Anand stroked his silvery-grey moustache to hide his twitching lips.

Maya heaved a dramatic sigh on her way to the door. "Even when I dead, my poor soul go have to listen to my pundit-husband's mantras until it safely reach heaven." She rounded the corner out of sight, heading down the hallway. "Oh Bhagwan," Maya cried, "what kind of immoral being was I in my past life to deserve these endless lectures? . . . *You hear that, Anand? I talking to God!*"

And then there was silence, and Anand knew Maya had crushed her fingers against her pursed lips.

That afternoon Anand stood on his veranda in a loose cotton shirt and a new cream dhoti that ballooned and fluttered about his legs in the afternoon breeze. He looked out onto the main road, waiting for the Shankars' shiny blue Datsun Skyline to appear. Anand frowned at the gaping potholes staring back at him like hollow eyes and prayed the Skyline wouldn't plunge into any of them. Behind him Maya flitted like a humming-bird about the veranda, laying out saucers and teacups, glasses and napkins on their wicker table.

Soon Anand saw a glint of white sunlight flash off the roof of the Skyline as it wrapped around the sharp bend and accel-erated onto Kiskadee Trace. "Maya, they reach." Maya darted to Anand's side, but neither of them spoke as the Shankars glided through the open gates and made their entrance at the Govind residence.

Nanny pushed the car door open and swung her legs around so that her dangling feet created two egg-shaped shadows in the dirt. She hopped to the ground, grunting, "*Jai* Shiva Shankar!" Glory to Lord Shiva, and then adjusted her mango-coloured sari pleats with her green-veined hands.

The new driver toddled on his squat legs around the front of the car, puffing and sweating. "Careful, Nanny." He mopped his fat neck with an already damp handkerchief. "I coming to help you." He took hold of Nanny's reedy arm and guided her away from the car, air whistling through his flaring nostrils.

Nanny wrenched her arm free. "You looking like you need more help than me, Driver." She shook her grey bun and jabbed his belly with her finger. "Less roti, less rice, just dhal, you hear me? Drink it like soup. Dhal soup." She cupped her lined hands to her mouth and made slurping noises. The driver looked away, embarrassed. "Eh! Look at me. Watch my figure!" Nanny placed her balled-up hands on her bony hips and wiggled them side to side like a dancing skeleton. "Would you believe I am sixty-six? Is dhal soup have me looking so sexy at sixty-six, Driver." She raised a finger just between his beady eyes. "But expect gas, Driver. Expect it day and night."

Anand cleared his throat loudly and pressed his palms together. "Sita-Ram! Welcome."

Nanny stopped short, and the driver scuttled away and stuffed himself back behind the steering wheel. Delores, Chalisa and Avinash filed from the car and stood behind their tiny leader like tin soldiers.

When they were all seated on the veranda, Anand folded his hands in his lap and began to twiddle his thumbs again. He was unsure how to start this spontaneous meeting without sounding harassed or leery, although he certainly felt both. He hadn't mentioned it to Maya, but suspicions like fat leeches had slithered into his gut the moment he learned the Shankars wanted the wedding date moved forward, and now they were feeding on his confidence in this wedding. It seemed hasty, desperate almost.

Anand stole a glance at his daughter-in-law-to-be. Chalisa was sitting in between Delores and Nanny, staring down at her hands. Her profuse inky hair was wrung into a single spiral that she had swept forward over her right shoulder and let cascade into her lap. Anand thought it looked like a sleeping serpent, but still she was lovely—there was no denying that.

Nanny tapped her foot against the white and burgundy veranda tiles, so that her petite frame vibrated with impatience. "Thank you for having us at such late notice." She smiled, but there was nothing tender in it. "I really ain't want to take up too much of allyuh time." She looked at Anand. "I know

it have plenty wedding preparations to see about. Hmm?"
She reached for a piece of pink sugar cake, still warm from
the oven.

Anand stopped twiddling. He had hoped for more formal-
ities to help ease him into the wedding talk. He shifted under
Nanny's incisive stare, trying to coax a smile from behind his
moustache while he thought of something fitting to say.

Nanny licked the pink sugar crystals from her chapped lips.
She eyed Maya. "And where is our Krishna?"

Anand felt Maya bristle at his side. "Visiting with relatives
to concentrate on his studies," she said quickly. Too quickly.

Nanny arched a sparse eyebrow.

"But he go be real heartbroken when he know he miss
Chalisa," Anand added.

Chalisa looked up at the sound of her name. She tilted her
head to the side and held Anand in her gaze. Her striking eyes
were filled with disappointment so profound they were almost
sorrowful. Anand wondered if she had truly taken a liking to
his son.

"Well, no matter, they have the rest of they lives to see each
other." Nanny slid to the edge of her chair. It was the closest
she could come to Anand and Maya without knocking over
the table that divided them. "I come to request the wedding be
moved to September first."

Anand nodded. He began processing the idea all over again.
For a few long moments he let the request hang between them
as he brought a glass of cold mauby to his lips and took a big
swallow. "Like the mauby, son?" He smiled at Avinash, lowering his glass.

Avinash shook his head. "Bitter, Pundit-ji."

"Pundit?" Nanny eyed him.

"Yes, yes, the wedding date. September first." Anand set the sweating glass down on the table. "We go have to check the book, Nanny. The wedding must take place on a auspicious day." Anand heard the authority creep into his voice and he sat up taller. "September seventeenth at 4:40 p.m. is the absolute best time for Krishna and Chalisa to marry." He shrugged.

Nanny frowned. "But it must have another *better* best day, Pundit. Look at my Chalisa." Anand and Maya looked. "You know why she pretty face long so? Is because she pining away for Krishna."

Chalisa raised her gaze halfway. Tears glistened like crystals on her dark lashes.

Nanny stroked Chalisa's arm with her arthritic fingers. "It possible to check the book again, Baba?" she asked.

Anand smiled his favourite priestly smile. "Of course, of course, Nanny." It suddenly dawned on him that he could proclaim September first the most ill-fated day of the year for Chalisa and Krishna to marry if that was his desire, and Nanny wouldn't know the difference. "Maya, fetch my book." Anand, buoyed by his power, rocked back and forth and sang a bhajan while he waited.

"Excuse me, Baba." Avinash fixed him with his owl stare.

The chorus died on Anand's lips. "Hmm?"

"What you looking for in the book?"

"Good question!" Anand's eyes brightened. He fancied himself a superb teacher. "First I take Chalisa's and Krishna's dates of birth, times of birth and places of birth and draw up their astrological charts." He made big sweeping gestures in the air. "Then I match these charts together to see if Chalisa and Krishna go have a long, loving marriage." He brought his palms together at his heart.

Avinash considered this. "Will they?"

"Yes." Anand raised a finger and his expression grew serious. "But then I have to select a favourable day for them to marry. The trouble is that there is only a few of these to choose from based on their dates, times and places of birth. If Krishna and Chalisa marry on an ominous date, they marriage go be cursed with mother-in-law quarrels and burn-up roti." Anand winked at Avinash.

Avinash blinked back at him. His mother was dead.

Nanny pinched her grandson. "That's enough, Avi. Let the pundit do his work." She watched as Maya returned and placed the time-worn text in Anand's outstretched arms.

Anand mumbled a prayer over the holy book before opening the cover. The loose spine crackled then splayed easily across Anand's lap. He turned the pages with care, tracing a finger beneath the Sanskrit script with a gradualness he was sure would exasperate Nanny. He furrowed his brow and murmured to himself. He stroked his moustache and sighed. He shook his head and looked pensive, doubtful.

Nanny reached across the table and touched Maya's knee. "Maya, would you believe last night I dream Krishna run away with someone else before the wedding and left my Chalisa heartbroken?"

Maya gasped and pressed her fingertips to her mouth.

"I wake up sweating and crying and poor Delores had to squeeze my head with Limacol in the middle of the night." Nanny shrugged. "Dream's real strange, ain't?"

Maya nodded. Delores looked down at her hands.

"You know, I does only sleep restless these days, Maya. Is all the worries I have dancing up like jumbies in my head." Nanny sighed and hunched over so that she appeared smaller and more frail than she actually was. "Ever since my son and he wife dead, is me alone who does have to look after the Shankar orange estate. Every man I hire is a cheat and crook who only trying to take advantage of a old lady and she money. Would you believe only this morning I had to fire and terminate a next man for he trickery and treachery?"

Chalisa looked away from Nanny's theatrics. Avinash's serious eyes grew rounder and glowed.

"Oh!" Maya reached across the table and grasped Nanny's veiny hands in hers. "Is such a shame, Nanny, I real sorry for—"

Nanny raised her voice over Maya's fussing. "But I ain't have long to worry and fret again because I know Krishna go manage my affairs when he marry Chalisa." She snatched up another sugar cake and deposited it in her mouth. "In fact," she said between chews, "I go just sign the whole thing over to Krishna when the wedding done. What a old lady like me worrying about money for? Let the young people see to it. Just think, Krishna go be known as The Great Orange Pundit!"

Maya's glass of mauby stopped inches from her lips. She gazed at Anand, whose focus remained on his scriptures but whose head—or ear, rather—was tilted toward the conversation. He sat perfectly still.

"So, Baba?" Nanny looked at Anand, too, as she crossed her ankles casually. "How the dates looking? September first good?"

Pundit Anand smiled and closed the book. "Very auspicious."

Sunday School

K rishna reclined in Auntie Kay's netted rainbow hammock, one leg flung over the side. A text lay open on his belly, its gilded pages turning themselves in the breeze as he scratched a swelling mosquito bite shaped like a banana leaf on his forearm. The itch became a burn. He abandoned it for a luxurious stretch and nestled deeper into his cocoon, watching wisps of almost-clouds drift across the sky.

"Studying hard?"

A dreadlock fell into view, slicing the perfect sky in two. It swung above Krishna's nose like a pendulum. Dutchie's grinning upside-down face appeared next. His eyes danced with their usual mirth.

"Auntie Kay!" Dutchie's voice boomed across the small courtyard. "Every time I come here your nephew does be dreaming. You see him read a page in that book yet?"

Krishna shut the book and shoved it aside before pulling himself into a seated position. He watched, amused, as Auntie Kay set her laundry down and was enveloped in Dutchie's embrace. Already petite, Auntie Kay appeared like a doll in Dutchie's arms with her black bob and yellow headband. She wore a polka dot dress this morning, pink and white with a sash she'd sewn herself, and slippers she could have shared with a child if she'd had any.

"Dutchie-boy, what I go tell you? He does lie in that hammock with a book on he belly, but is only the birds and sky and flowers and trees he studying." Auntie Kay tried an admonishing look, but it dissolved into a beam as quickly as it began.

Dutchie picked up a pair of Krishna's wet shorts and clipped them to the clothesline. "You think he lazy, Auntie?"

Auntie Kay considered this, shaking out a yellow sundress and hanging it next to the shorts. "Lazy? No."

"Stupid, then. Only a stupid man would have plenty-plenty books and never read one." Dutchie two-stepped around Auntie Kay, light on his feet, adding a T-shirt to the line.

"Stupid? No."

"Well, then the boy must have real *tabanca*, Auntie." Dutchie swept a few locks from his face and secured them behind his head with two clothespins. "It ain't have no other explanation for that." He tipped his chin at Krishna.

"Yes! Heartache!" Auntie Kay giggled, fastening a skirt to the line.

Krishna collapsed back into the hammock. "Allyuh laugh! Laugh, nuh! My life is one big joke." He hid his smile behind the hammock's edge and kicked off the ground with one foot until he was rocking.

Dutchie sauntered back to his friend. He gripped the hammock ropes and swung Krishna high. The ropes slackened as the hammock soared to the house beams and grew taut again as it descended. Krishna's stomach followed a millisecond behind. The wind whistled in his ears.

"So what we doing today, Boss?" Dutchie asked.

Krishna splayed his arms and legs out as he flew. Auntie Kay's pink and orange bougainvillea eddied with the sky and the palms, the concrete and the clothes hanging on the line.

"Before allyuh go knock about Tobago, do your Auntie Kay a favour, nuh?"

Krishna slowed the hammock, using his feet as brakes. "Anything." And he meant it. Auntie Kay had doted on him from the moment he'd arrived in Tobago. She'd taken one look at his suitcases bulging with Hinduism and pulled him into her home, defiance flickering in her black eyes. She wanted to know just why her brother had sent Krishna away; what Hindu law forbade love? She pitied Vimla even more than she did Krishna, often wishing she could send for her. She made Krishna tell her their story again and again until she grew morose or furious, or a peculiar combination of both. And when she'd heard enough, she curled up in her rainbow hammock and woke with the sunny disposition of a child without a care in the world. After that Auntie Kay only spoke of Krishna's plight when he brought it up. She never pried; she never asked questions; she never passed judgment.

Dutchie and Auntie Kay were fast friends, too. He came by one morning to take Krishna to the wharf, a bushel of fresh dasheen bhajee in his arms. Auntie Kay was tickled by his thoughtfulness and couldn't be more pleased that someone

like Dutchie—"a free spirit," she called him—had taken
Krishna under his wing while he was in Tobago. When the
neighbour inquired about the "tall dark fella with the long
dreadlocks to he backside" hanging around the place, Auntie
Kay told him that was her nephew, Dutchie.

"I feeling to eat a caimite." Auntie Kay squinted up at one
of her trees laden with the purple fruit. "Allyuh mind?"

A boyish grin lit Krishna's face. "Say no more." In an instant
he was out of the hammock and around the back of the house
in search of something long enough to prize the ripe fruit
from its branches. He returned with a piece of bamboo.

Dutchie nodded his approval. "That is the correct thing to
chook a caimite."

Without a word, Dutchie and Krishna positioned themselves under the great tree with all the seriousness of two
professional cricketers. Krishna prodded the branches with the
bamboo and Dutchie caught the falling fruit, somersaulting
and diving in the grass when he didn't need to.

Auntie Kay giggled. "Is like I have two young children for
the first time," she said.

Krishna waited while Dutchie deposited the fruit in his
pocket. "You try, Auntie Kay!" he said.

She didn't need to be asked twice. Auntie Kay kicked off her
slippers and bounded onto the grass. Krishna skipped around
the tree, shaking the branches with more force and with greater
speed so that Dutchie and Auntie Kay had to dart this way
and that to catch the raining caimites. Auntie Kay squealed
with delight, whirling around with outstretched arms. Most of
the caimites ended up on the ground, always a few inches shy
of her grasp.

In the end the trio scored nine. They gathered below the house to cool off while Dutchie halved the fruit. The caimites yielded easily to the knife. They fell open, revealing soft purple flesh glistening with juice.

"When last you sit and eat a caimite like this?" Dutchie asked, propping his feet up on a footstool and sinking into his fruit. Droplets dribbled over his chin and sprinkled his tank top.

Krishna spat three slippery seeds into his palm and shrugged. Over the last couple years, he had done little in the way of relaxing in Trinidad. He spent most of his time shadowing his father during pujas. Every time a baby was born or a couple was married, Krishna was there. Every time someone fell sick or was plagued by bad luck, Krishna was there. He sat through puja after puja, muttering mantras in unison with his father, handing him flowers or incense or lit diyas, eating bag after bag of prasad. His days began early and ended late and he always came home miserable with soot in his nostrils. It was only recently, when he and Vimla began meeting in secret, that Krishna remembered what joy felt like, and strangely, all the wonderful things Trinidad had to offer.

A frown settled on his brow. He had only ever told this to Vimla. It seemed immoral for a pundit's son—for a pundit-in-training—to loathe his work the way he did. His father said it was his *dharma*, his duty, to become a spiritual leader, but Krishna felt like a pretender. Worse, a pretender to God.

"What happened, Krish?" Auntie Kay smoothed his brow with her finger, sticky with caimite juice.

Dutchie slapped Krishna on the back. "I tell you the man have tabanca. He thinking of Miss Vimla Narine steady." Dutchie's smile was wicked.

Krishna dropped the skin of his caimite on the table, having cleaned the flesh right out. "I was just thinking how nice it is to have a day to do nothing. To just lime under the house with good people, with no one waiting on you and no particular place to be."

Dutchie wiped his mouth with his hand. "But we *do* have a particular place to be tonight, my friend," he said, winking.

Auntie Kay, always curious about their adventures, inclined her head in Dutchie's direction. "What allyuh boys up to tonight?"

"We going to Sunday School in Buccoo Reef." He got up and dropped a kiss on Auntie Kay's head. "And you going, too, Auntie."

Auntie Kay waved her hand. "Oh no. You boys have your fun. I too old for late-night liming."

Dutchie produced an unconvincing sulk. "You ain't want to go fishing. You ain't want to go snorkelling." He gestured in the air, feigning exasperation. "You does twist up your mouth every time I ask you to play cricket. Like you vexed with me or what?"

Auntie Kay swatted Dutchie's arm. "You expect me to fish and snorkel? What wrong with you, boy?" She smoothed her polka dot dress over her knees, embarrassed by the thought of it.

Dutchie and Krishna chuckled. "Well, tonight we dancing, Auntie Kay, and I know you could do that." He turned to Krishna and ruffled his hair. "I coming by at ten. Fix yourself up a little, nuh? You looking like a vagrant."

Krishna glanced down at his old shorts and his rumpled T-shirt and decided not to argue.

———

Krishna knew Tobago's Sunday School had nothing to do with Bible studies, but he wasn't expecting an open street party. The Buccoo Beach he'd seen was quiet but for tourists getting on and off tour boats and the odd vendor who sold Tobago bottle openers and magnets, sunhats and sarongs.

Dutchie nudged Krishna. "You recognize this place?"

"Hardly."

The quiet bars with the unhurried wait staff were draped in Christmas lights that twinkled white against the cobalt sky; patrons overflowed onto the street now. There were people everywhere, holding drinks or hands or waists. They moved in waves past each other, clinking their drinks against friends' and strangers' drinks, saying "Good night, good night" and smiling the breeziest smiles Krishna had ever seen.

The harmony of a steel pan band played in the background. Dutchie led Krishna and Auntie Kay through the crowd until they could see the panmen in their matching red shirts, managing two or three steelpans each and hitting every perfect note in time. The pannists danced as they played, like the rhythm of their song started in their feet instead of the other way around. There was an easiness about them that reminded Krishna of Dutchie.

The street was lined with food vendors and their Caribbean fare wafted in the night. Krishna saw enormous pots of corn soup and fish broth bubbling on firecrackers. An older woman sat beside her pot and cut chunks of sweet potato into the corn soup, tapping her foot to the music. There was barbecue, too. Chicken sizzled on the grill and drew crowds of people, who waited patiently in line for a fat thigh or a breast. Krishna's stomach turned at the sight of the meat lying on the plate. On the other side of the street there was a doubles stand. He smiled to himself, remembering Vimla and Minty in the market.

"You want a doubles?" Dutchie asked above the music.

"Nah. Let we get some roast corn."

Dutchie wrapped an arm around Auntie Kay's shoulders as she bobbed at his side to the music. "So how you going, Miss Auntie?" he said. "What you think about Sunday School?"

"Your Auntie Kay could get used to this kind of church!" she said, allowing Dutchie to guide her in the direction of a corn stand.

Dutchie hailed a man sitting with four coolers while Krishna purchased the roasted corn. "What you have tonight, Ernest?" Dutchie asked.

Ernest made a production of rolling his white linen sleeves to his elbows before lifting all four lids. "Rum. Rum. Beer. Sweet drink. What you want?"

Auntie Kay danced over with her corn in hand. "I go take a Carib, please, mister." Krishna's eyes bulged. "But put it in a cup for me, nuh? A lady doesn't drink from beer bottle so."

Dutchie laughed. "I go have the same."

"And a cup for you, too, sweetheart?" Ernest asked Dutchie.

Dutchie grabbed the beer from Ernest's outstretched hand. "Don't play the ass, nuh, man."

"And you." Ernest nodded his chin at Krishna. "You go take one, Boss?"

Krishna shoved his hands in his pocket. "Nothing for me, thanks."

Ernest shrugged, unrolled his sleeves and dropped the lids of his coolers one by one. Krishna wondered how many times he would do that tonight.

Auntie Kay took a sip of her beer. Her hips rocked as she drank.

"Auntie Kay, since when you does drink? Does my father know?"

"Why he have to know? I's a big woman. I living in my own house and paying my own bills." She nibbled at her corn. "Your father doesn't mind me—I does mind myself."

"Lucky you," Krishna said. He pictured Anand then, trembling in rage, blaming Auntie Kay for costing him a fortune, as he'd stuffed Krishna's belongings into a bag. Krishna was about to ask Auntie Kay what his father had meant by that, when she flashed him a disarming smile and he decided he didn't care. An impromptu dance floor was opening up in the middle of the street. Somewhere, a speaker was blaring The Mighty Sparrow's latest hit, "We Pass That Stage." Waists swivelled and bumped up against neighbours'. Krishna watched the revellers with interest. Some were youthful; some were bent and creased with age; there were even some pink-faced tourists with cameras around their necks, making merry with the locals.

"This is how Carnival in Trinidad does be?" Krishna asked.

Dutchie looked at Krishna, disbelieving. "This? You mad or what? Man, Tobago's Sunday School is really like Sunday School compared to Trinidad's Carnival. Where you from?"

"How you mean?" Krishna felt foolish not knowing, especially since he had lived his entire life in Trinidad. He almost explained that Chance was just a small town nestled in the southernmost tip of the island, far way from Port of Spain. He almost mentioned that he was Pundit Anand Govind's only son and that there was no place for carnival in his life.

Dutchie inched closer to his friend. "You see that pretty girl watching you? The one in the corner with she two friends? Not that one!" Dutchie turned Krishna's head to the right. *"She."*

Krishna swallowed and nodded.

"Now, imagine that sugar plum with sequins and feathers covering all she goodies and nothing else. Imagine she prancing in Port of Spain with a glittery headdress and face paint to match. That's Carnival."

"Oh."

"Now, look over there. You see that young couple dancing with each other? Tasteful, ain't?"

His father might not have thought so, but Krishna did. "Yeah."

"Well, imagine that couple grinding up on each other, unbridled wickedness on display for everyone to see. That's Carnival."

Krishna blushed in the darkness.

Dutchie gestured to the panmen who were taking a break at a bar. "They good, right? Yeah, I think so, too. But them is only half the party. Carnival must have pan *and* a handful of good calypsonians to keep the fete alive. No calypsonians here tonight. Just the speaker box playing they hits."

Krishna considered this.

Dutchie drained the last of his beer. "Sunday School in Buccoo Reef is a weekly fete with an easygoing vibe." He gyrated his waist slow and seductive. "Not a wild bacchanal vibe." He thrust his pelvis back and forth in quick, raunchy succession. A local woman pinched his cheek as she passed. A tourist tittered behind her hand, scandalized.

"Thanks for the demonstration." Krishna crossed his arms over his chest. He was embarrassed by his own naïveté. He had never been to any kind of fete like this before, let alone Carnival. The closest he ever got to festivity was at the weddings his father dragged him to. But even then, he knew everyone contained the celebrating until the pundit and his family left. The real excitement erupted when Krishna was behind the Govind gates again, listening to his father sing bhajans in his scratchy voice. Nobody had ever done anything remotely similar to what Dutchie had just done in Krishna's presence.

His resentment must have shown on his face, because Auntie Kay looped her arm through his and said, "Never mind him. Enjoy yourself, son. Is not every day you come to Tobago. And is not every day you get to fete with your Auntie Kay!" She leaned her head against his arm.

Dutchie was just about to tell Auntie Kay how grateful he was for her, when he thought he spotted a familiar face in the sea of dancing people. As she turned, the woman's fiery hair blazed bright under the Christmas lights and Krishna knew for certain who she was. He made to nudge Dutchie, but Dutchie was two steps ahead of him, dancing his way into the crowd, an extra drink in his hand.

"Oh gosh! Who is that lady Dutchie sweet-talking?" Auntie Kay asked. She stood on her tiptoes for a better look.

They watched Dutchie brush the woman's freckled face with his lips and hand her a drink.

"What colour she hair is, Krish? Copper?" Auntie Kay inched forward and Krishna pulled her back.

"Where you think Dutchie meet a white woman like that? She so pale. She make my Dutchie look blacker than he is."

Auntie Kay squinted at the pair. "Oh gosh, Krish, he teaching she to dance! Watch! Watch!"

Krishna draped an arm around Auntie Kay and spun her. "Come on, let we get a drink."

Auntie Kay went reluctantly, stealing glances over her shoulder. When she could no longer make Dutchie out in the crowd, she looked up at Krishna. "How about a sweet drink? You used to like red Solo when you was small." She reached up and grabbed his chin in her hand.

It was true, Solo had been his favourite—it still was, really. But he wasn't small anymore and he wasn't in Chance either. He pushed his shoulders back and sauntered to Ernest the way Dutchie had, dragging Auntie Kay on his arm. "I go take a rum and Coke, please. More rum. Less Coke. No ice. Thanks." He needed to catch up.

Auntie Kay placed a hand on her hip and Krishna thought she might make him cancel that order. "What about me?" she asked instead.

He surveyed her: flushed cheeks, restless feet, swaying hips. "And one more," he told Ernest. "Less rum. More Coke. Plenty ice."

Liquid bravado had Krishna twirling Auntie Kay on the dance floor in minutes. She giggled like a girl, telling Krishna she hadn't been to Sunday School since Bas left. Bas? Krishna thought he remembered his parents whispering about Bas and Auntie Kay a long time ago. He pushed the thought from his mind. He didn't want to know about Bas now, and he didn't think Auntie Kay really wanted to talk about him either, the way she was tilting her head back and laughing as she spun.

"Eh-eh! What is this!" Dutchie's voice sounded over the music. His grinned, dancing around Auntie Kay and Krishna with the easy rhythm of a true islander.

The rum made Krishna feel warm and light. It loosened his limbs so that he moved easily; it loosened his waist so that he fell into a wine that caught the attention of the attractive girl who'd been watching him earlier.

Dutchie raised an eyebrow at his friend. "Careful, Boss," he said. "A wine like that does draw women like flies to shit."

Auntie Kay poked Dutchie's chest and gestured to the red-head ogling him from the bar. "You should know, Mr. Captain Man!"

Krishna laughed the way people do when they forget they're supposed to be sad: a burst of unexpected delight. As Dutchie's arm draped over his shoulder and Auntie Kay's arm slipped around his waist, Krishna felt a part of himself unknot and fall away.

Bacolet Bay

K rishna stood knee-deep in the water at Bacolet Bay,
watching the morning sun glitter off the wavelets racing
to shore. The water splashed against his chins, playful, inviting. He stooped and trailed his fingers in the froth, a promise
that he would return, and then headed on his way. As he
trudged across the beach, sandals hooked on his index finger,
Krishna hummed to himself.

Dutchie's house was tucked away amid a flourish of green-
ery on a hill overlooking the secluded bay. It was humble, a
small two-bedroom structure invisible to the world until
Dutchie painted it red. Now it sat like a splash of sorrel in the
trees. At night Dutchie reclined on his front porch and
watched the sun set over Bacolet Bay. He once said nothing
was prettier, nothing felt sweeter, than having the Tobago sun
bid you goodnight. Krishna couldn't blame Dutchie for

thinking so; he had never had the pleasure of Vimla's good-night kiss.

Krishna jogged up the thirty-four steps that led to Dutchie's front door. The seashell wind chimes dangling from the porch clinked against each other. The pot of white bougainvillea from Auntie Kay sat on the top step, its blossoms cascading over the sides. Last night's shorts were flung over the railing. They billowed, threatening to blow away. Krishna suspected Dutchie had discarded them there after a late-night swim before bed.

He let himself in as he always did. "Dutchie!" he called. "Your head bad from last night?" They had spent the evening at Castara Bay in the company of fishermen who insisted they join them for fried fish and a few bottles of rum punch on the beach. Krishna passed on the fish—he still couldn't bear the smell of meat—but he did have a few drinks. Dutchie had had a few more.

Dutchie's bedroom door was wide open. He sat on the edge of the bed, grinning, his elbows resting on his knees. "Morning, Pundit!"

Krishna laughed. "Yeah, right."

Something moved in the twist of white sheets behind Dutchie. Krishna raised an eyebrow at his friend just as a blaze of red hair, an alabaster forehead, piercing green eyes peeked over Dutchie's shoulder. "Morning," the woman said.

Krishna stood, dumbstruck, and raked his fingers through his hair. Dutchie tilted his head back and let his rich laughter fill the small room. "Krishna, this is Tatiana. You remember she from—"

"*The Reverie?*"

"Don't stand up there like you see a ghost!" Dutchie said. Although in truth, Tatiana was so pale, her hair so red, there *was* something otherworldly about her. "How about some grapefruit juice, Krishna? The tree in the back laden."

Krishna realized this was a cue, that he still hadn't moved and Tatiana was probably naked under the sheets. He took a step backward, bumped into the door frame. "Coming up." But just as Krishna made to pull the door closed, ears burning, Tatiana called, "I'll do it!"

She wrapped the sheets around her and slid off the other side of the bed. As she passed in front of the window, sunlight set her curls aflame, and Krishna's eyes grew wider still. He watched her expertly secure the white bedsheet around her voluptuous body in seconds and cross the room as elegantly as if she were wearing a gown. "Excuse me, Krishna," she crooned, brushing past him into the hallway. Her eyes were laughing. She smelled of talcum and cinnamon.

Dutchie's lips twitched before they broke into his signature grin.

Krishna shrugged. "Well, how I supposed to know Miss Lady from the boat go end up in your bed?"

Dutchie looped a dreadlock in the air like a lasso and reined in something invisible. "Is only a matter of time before the sexy ones fall into my bed, Pundit," he said.

Krishna rolled his eyes. "You didn't even have to try with she. She nearly pounce you on the boat self."

Dutchie sauntered to the mirror hanging on the wall. A jagged crack sliced down the centre. "Well, if I handsome, I handsome," he said, rolling his dreadlocks into a thick knot. "Can't do nothing about that."

"Ain't she have a child? The little boy with the binoculars is she own."

"Anthony."

"And where is our little Anthony?" Krishna asked.

Dutchie stretched and yawned. "With he grandfather. Tatiana's father, Charles, own a resort in Pigeon Point."

"How convenient for Tatiana," Krishna said.

"How convenient for Captain Dutchie!"

"So what we doing today?"

Dutchie swaggered down the hall to the washroom. "Let we lime right here by the bay today, nuh? For some reason, I feeling real tired this morning."

Tatiana lay across the sand, her legs stretching on forever. She wore a wide-brimmed hat and dark shades. Both seemed bigger, somehow, than the pink bikini fastened around her body with strings. A book lay at her side, but she rarely picked it up. Instead she turned herself in the sun every fifteen minutes. "To tan evenly but to avoid burning," she had explained to Dutchie. Now and again she waved at Krishna and Dutchie drifting along on their body boards. The slow part of her pink lips as they curved into a smile made Krishna feel like his swim trunks had been whisked away with a wave.

Dutchie paddled closer to Krishna. "Pundit, when you going home?"

Krishna didn't look up. His cheek was pressed against the board. "What happen? You want me leave?"

"Yeah. I want you go home and marry your girl," Dutchie said.

"Which one?"

"I find you real smart today, Pundit," Dutchie answered.

Krishna slid off his board and stood in the water. He stacked his fists on the board and rested his chin on top. "My father call Auntie Kay last night. He want me back this Friday night." Krishna sighed. "I find myself in a real mess, Dutchie. My father done set the date for my wedding to Chalisa Shankar."

"When?"

"September first."

"But what kind of bacchanal is this?" Dutchie said, paddling himself in a circle. "Hear, nuh, tell your old man this: 'Pops, you see this marriage you fix up with that Chalisa? Cancel it one-time. Me ain't like she and she ain't like me. I marrying Vimla.'" He lifted his hands from the water and twirled in the cyclone he'd created.

Dutchie made it seem so simple. "I would like to see you tell my father that. Besides"—Krishna kicked his feet off the sandy ground into a float, holding the body board at arm's length—"Vimla probably so vexed with me she ain't go want to marry me neither."

Dutchie laughed. "Serves you right."

"What?"

"The least you could have done is tell the girl something before you leap the island so." He turned serious, a rarity that made Krishna pay attention. "You have she suffering in oblivion in Trinidad. You just take off and leave she there to wonder."

Krishna knew Dutchie was right, but it had been impossible to see Vimla after they were found out.

"Let we send she a message, nuh?" Dutchie said. He flipped onto his back now and gazed at the sky.

"With who? No. It wouldn't work. You can't keep secrets in Chance. I go only get she in more trouble."

Dutchie sucked his teeth. "Man, you fell I's like you? I know how to romance a girl good and I know how to keep it a secret." He winked at his friend. "Just think of what you want to say and leave the rest to Captain Dutchie."

Krishna was doubtful, but he didn't protest. Dutchie had a way of reeling you in and making you feel like everything was going to be just fine. He wondered when he went back to Trinidad if he would ever see Dutchie again. He wondered if he could even go back to his old life at all.

Bacolet Bay remained deserted throughout the afternoon. The trio lounged in the sun, swimming, drinking and eating mangoes from the tree. The day drifted by in a haze and for once Krishna stopped thinking of time.

Tatiana sat behind Dutchie with her legs wrapped around his waist. She trailed her fingers through his dreadlocks. "How about a French braid, Captain?" she asked, nipping his ear between her teeth.

Dutchie took a swig of his Stout and deposited it back in the hole he'd dug in the sand. "Mmm-hmm." Nothing cured a hangover like a cold Stout. Krishna learned that first-hand after their night at Sunday School.

He gave the couple a sideways glance. He'd tried several times to go for a walk, to go for a swim, but every time Krishna made to leave, one of them engaged him in conversation again. It wasn't that he didn't enjoy their company; he just wished Tatiana would nuzzle, nibble and stroke Dutchie less in his presence.

"I hear you're in love, Krishna," she said, lacing a handful of Dutchie's dreadlocks over another.

A pair of birds hopped and tittered in the trees behind them.

Krishna threw Dutchie an exasperated look, which Dutchie pretended not to see.

"It's nice to be in love, isn't it?" she said, more to herself than to him.

Krishna picked up a piece of driftwood and drew a crab in the sand. "Is not all that nice." He wasn't in the mood for this conversation—especially with a woman he'd only just met. His stomach rumbled; he longed for dinner.

Tatiana wrinkled her nose at him. Krishna noticed she was browner now, her freckles less startling. "Hmm." She bit her lip as she wove Dutchie's dreadlocks into a neat French braid. When she finished, she trailed a finger over the ridges thoughtfully. "I wish I had love, Krishna."

Krishna hated to admit it, even to himself, but he liked the way Tatiana said his name. He didn't understand her longing, though. Wasn't she falling in love with Dutchie before his eyes?

Tatiana wrapped her arms around Dutchie's neck and laughed. There was nothing innocent or ladylike about her laugh. It was full of life and knowing and something else Krishna couldn't quite place. "This isn't love!" she exclaimed, reading Krishna's bewilderment. Tatiana kissed Dutchie's hair, paused for a moment inhaling the sea that was a part of him.

Krishna searched Dutchie's face for hurt, but there was none.

Tatiana reached out and stroked Krishna's cheek. Condescending and sensual at once. Her fingers were soft, but it was the flash of her wedding ring that captured his attention.

"This is lust, darling. Passion. Abandon." She winked a green eye at him. "Tobago."

Tatiana's fingers fell away, but the burn lingered on his skin. Tobago was none of those things to Krishna, but he nodded as if he understood. Shortly after, Krishna excused himself and climbed the steps to Dutchie's house. When he glanced down at the beach again, Dutchie and Tatiana were devouring each other, their bodies twisting, insatiable, in the sand.

The Plan

Wednesday August 21, 1974

....

BACOLET BAY, TOBAGO

They sat on Dutchie's porch, watching the orange ember burn its way round a mosquito coil until there was nothing. "The thing cheap," Dutchie said. He sat on the floor, his back pressed against his red front door. But the mosquito coil wasn't cheap. And it was the same kind of coil they sat around every night to keep the mosquitoes away. It just seemed to fail them now because Krishna was leaving and in some strange way the withering mosquito coil was an indication of time passing too quickly.

Auntie Kay curled herself up in the dark like a shrimp, her pink dress draped neatly over her legs. "You pack everything? You forget anything?"

Krishna smiled, nodded, then shook his head. He glanced at the suitcase abandoned in the sand at the bottom of the steps. It bulged in all the wrong places like a woman in an ill-fitting dress. Even in the shadows they could make out the outline of scriptures and balled-up clothing stuffed across every square inch with equal neglect.

The seashell wind chime jangled in the moonlight. The white bougainvillea stirred in its pot and settled again. Below, rowdy waves flung themselves on top of one another like noisy schoolchildren at play. Bacolet Bay was the same tonight as it always had been, except it wasn't. Krishna was leaving.

Dutchie hooked his arms around his knees and clasped his hands. "Man, you holding your head like you have worries," he said.

But Krishna sensed he wasn't the only apprehensive one. Nervous energy crackled between them and it troubled him to think that he had drawn the two most light-hearted people he knew into his torment. Yet he was touched that they cared enough to be emotionally invested, and that they felt they needed to hide it from him. Krishna raised his head from the cradle of his palms and asked the question gnawing at his mind: "What if the plan ain't work?"

"How you mean? The plan go work, Pundit. Ain't I help devise it?"

Krishna nodded.

Dutchie flashed a reassuring smile. "Right," he said, as if his contribution to the plan guaranteed its success. And Krishna knew that in a very big way it did.

Dutchie narrowed his gaze at Krishna. "Stick to the plan, you hear? Don't improvise. Don't add frills. Don't complicate it. The plan is not carnival. The plan is the plan. And the plan is simple."

Krishna swallowed, nodded.

"Right. By tomorrow afternoon, the message go done deliver to Vimla. Allyuh go meet in she father cane field. You know the place, right?"

Of course Krishna knew the place. He could picture Vimla standing amid the tall stalks now, impatience and hope in her brown face.

"And when you meet she, you go apologize for being a jackass and deserting she. Fall on your knees and beg if you have to." Dutchie's eyes twinkled as he said this and Krishna knew he hoped Krishna would have to do just that. "Then tell she the plan."

Krishna tried to imagine what Vimla would say when he told her he wouldn't marry Chalisa, that he knew a way for Vimla and him to be together. He wondered if this would be the moment that rendered Vimla speechless.

"But what if—"

"Don't worry yourself with anything else. Just do like I tell you and I go take care of the rest." He grinned. "Everything fix up nice."

Auntie Kay sighed and nuzzled into her crooked arm. "I had a husband once," she said, her voice small. "His name was Bas." She looked at Krishna. "Your father didn't like him. He used to call him 'Bas the Ass.'"

Krishna dropped his head back into his hands as if he were somehow responsible for his father's insolence.

"What was wrong with Bas?" Dutchie asked.

Krishna held his breath. Auntie Kay had mentioned his name a few times since he'd been in Tobago, but always in passing, never in a moment charged with so much tension.

"What *wasn't* wrong with Bas?" Auntie Kay's girlish voice danced between them. "For one, the man was too tall for me. Krishna's father used to say I would break my neck trying to kiss his beef-eating mouth."

"Beef-eating?" Krishna said.

"Bas was a Christian."

"*Bas?* A Christian?"

"Sebastian was he correct name."

"Oh."

"So what happen to Bas, Auntie Kay?" Dutchie asked.

"Anand make we life together miserable. He used to come Tobago, sit down on my veranda and sing bhajans early in the morning to wake Bas up. For Christmas he send we a dry black cake and the Ramayana. On Easter he pretend he was dying to prevent we going to church."

Krishna shook his head.

Dutchie smiled. "Allyuh didn't find it funny? You have to laugh at people like that."

"I did, but Bas didn't. Anand used to quarrel with Bas. He would say he piece and then as soon as Bas open he mouth to argue, Anand would close he eyes and chant mantras loud-loud. It get so bad, one time Anand even ring he bell and blow he conch as soon as Bas walk into the room. That is when we marriage really start to fall apart."

"So what happen?"

"Bas left me. He went Venezuela and pick up some young Spanish thing." She tucked a lock of her short black hair behind her ear. "Anand was right. The man was really a ass, but Anand was the bigger ass out of the two."

Dutchie snorted. "It sound so."

Auntie Kay tittered in the darkness. "Bas's Spanish girl used to send me letters threatening to come Tobago and take my house and land. After she done take my husband she want *my* house and land? Imagine that! I tell she try."

Krishna sat up. "She ever try?" He saw worry flit across Dutchie's face.

"Never."

Krishna slapped at the mosquito on his leg. Auntie Kay looked so small, and for the first time vulnerable, lying curled up in the shadows that way. Krishna knew she was naïve to think that Bas and his Spanish girlfriend wouldn't one day follow through on that threat. If the property truly belonged to Bas, then what would stop them from ousting Auntie Kay on a whim? And suddenly Krishna remembered Gloria Ramnath, sweating and gushing on about her loyalty to Anand and what? That the gossips claimed he'd been sending money to Venezuela? Krishna shook his head in wonderment. Could his father be—?

"You better off without him, Auntie," Dutchie said.

"Probably." Auntie Kay shrugged. "Your father is not a easy man, Krishna. I know that first-hand." She gave him a weak smile and he realized how much it pained her to speak so openly of her past. "But you and you alone know who and what go make you happy."

Krishna heaved a sigh. He knew what was going on: they thought he might desert the plan, that his nerves would not hold up when the time came to set his life right again. He could tell by the way Dutchie trivialized the enormity of Krishna's undertaking, and by Auntie Kay's timely sharing of her unsuccessful marriage to Bas. It hurt that they still doubted his resolve even after the hours they'd spent spinning the minutest details of the plan together. But Krishna knew he couldn't really blame them. They recognized—as he did—that he had never once stood in his truth.

He grumbled at his father's heels after every long, smoky puja, feeling fatigued and fraudulent, but he had never once said, "Pa, this is not for me." Instead he'd invited resentment to take up residence in his heart, nursed his anguish until it was bigger than his desire to begin something new. Krishna's anger had been misdirected. All this time he should have blamed himself.

And then there was Vimla. His fight for her had been pitiable at best. What defence had he offered against his father's slanders? Later he told himself he'd been distracted by his exile to Tobago, but the fact was Krishna hadn't had the courage to challenge his father's wishes. His exile had really been his escape.

Life in Tobago with Dutchie and Auntie Kay helped show him where he had gone wrong. Now, after basking in their light for nearly two weeks, Krishna knew what it meant to love and laugh without apology, to leap into a day with the greatest expectations and have them all fulfilled. Auntie Kay and Dutchie had taught him how to live life with integrity and he wanted to prove to them—as much as he did to himself and Vimla—that he could cut his own path in the world despite anyone else's misgivings.

As he thought this, Krishna's mood lightened. He felt the mellow glow of hope in his belly burgeon into optimism.

"Eh." Dutchie's velvet voice filled the silence. "Let we make a move. Allyuh ready?"

Auntie Kay straightened. "Aye-aye, Captain," she said. Her eyes were wide with excitement.

Krishna rose, stretched his arms and arched his back. "Is about time. I thought allyuh sleep away," he said. He galloped down the steps. "I was going to sail out on *The Reverie* without you!" He grabbed hold of his suitcase and lugged it onto the beach, the music of Dutchie and Auntie Kay's cheering drifting behind him.

Krishna breathed in the sea and catapulted himself into the air with a whoop. He wouldn't let Vimla down again. This time he would get it right.

A Message

Vimla whisked her tumultuous mane into one hand and threaded it through a wide elastic band held in the other. She wound the elastic band around her ponytail once, twice, three times, until it could stretch no more. Vimla paused. Three times? She wrapped her fist around the base of her ponytail and found that her thumb overlapped the rest of her fingers by more than an inch. Slowly she slid her grasp down her hair. It was coarse with whorls and waves as usual, but it felt lighter, thinner somehow.

She flew to the oval mirror hanging on the wall, tugged the elastic from her hair, and shook out her mane so that it flowed over her shoulders and down her back. With frantic fingers Vimla divided her hair on either side of her head and brought her face close to the mirror. The part gleamed back at her like a fat, jagged scar cutting through her scalp. Gasping, Vimla looked away and noticed the discarded elastic band lying on the floor, strangling in her thick black hairs. When had this happened? She shoved her laundry aside and fell across her bed, feeling the familiar dig of the old springs in her ribs. Rolling onto one side, Vimla gathered her knees to her chest and stared, unseeing, at the yellow gauze curtains fluttering at her window.

Pitch Lake at La Brea. That's where Krishna had taken her the first Sunday he had picked her up when her parents were at Chaguanas Market. She had never been curious about the Pitch Lake, but she would have followed Krishna anywhere then. And if the Pitch Lake didn't excite her, the danger of their furtive meeting did. She remembered staring at the gold *aum* swinging like a pendulum from the rear-view mirror as the car rattled over the rutted road leading to the Pitch Lake. The car belonged, of course, to Pundit Anand, and she had wondered how he might react if he saw her and Krishna there together, holding hands in his car.

They left their slippers behind and crept hand in hand across the baking asphalt that stretched on for a hundred acres. It was dull and desolate grey lingering on forever until it collided with the blue sky on the horizon where the oil refinery stood. Bountiful green guava, breadfruit and palm trees bordered the jagged periphery of the Pitch Lake like a fetching frame for a plain picture. Vimla stopped walking and stared at the vast emptiness.

"So what you think?" Krishna squinted against the dazzling sun.

"I think it real ugly."

Krishna nodded as if he'd been expecting that. "Well, let we explore this ugly place, nuh? Come on."

Vimla looked down at her toes and wriggled them against the warm tar. "Krishna, I sinking!" She skipped away from the spot in which she had been standing and peered, agape, at the faint imprints she'd left behind.

Krishna smiled and tugged at her hand. "When the pitch get warm, it does shift. Is alive." Vimla allowed herself to be guided away from her footprints. She and Krishna padded over the furrowed pitch until their path was unexpectedly severed by a watercourse. From there they could see arteries of water, broad and narrow, cutting through the expansive Pitch Lake for acres. Some opened up into pools of clear water; others led to marshy ponds overflowing with sky-reaching reeds and pink and purple water lilies gazing into the sun. Vimla pressed her toes into the pitch again. "I never see anything like this before," she murmured, admiring the layers of velvety pink petals.

"The flower?"

Vimla inched forward so that her toes lined up with the asphalt's edge. "The flower in the middle of this wasteland." She gestured to their surroundings. "I never would have expect to find something so beautiful growing in a place like this."

Krishna watched a black corbeau circling slowly overhead. "That is why I bring you here. If I did bring you to the botanical gardens in Port of Spain, you would have get bored, you would have tell me your father have the same flowers growing in he garden. Only unusual things does interest you." He followed the corbeau as it looped its way in wide circles down to the Pitch Lake and thrust its beak into a nearby puddle.

Vimla smiled. "Are you unusual?"

"I must be if you spending so much time with me." He nodded toward the shallow pool. "Go on, dip your toe in."

Vimla took in the vast emptiness of the place again, trying to ignore the corbeau, which had her fixed in its black, glassy gaze now. "In *that* water?"

"How you mean? This is the clearest, cleanest water in Trinidad, girl." Krishna crouched down and grazed the quiet pond with his fingertips then sat back on his haunches to watch the ripples. "People does say it have healing properties. Is good for your hair and your skin." He rolled up his pant legs and stepped into the water, nudging the lily pads with his knees.

Vimla studied him for a moment. There was something about Krishna that made her trust him. It was in the way he stood with his hands in the pockets of his trousers and his head just tilted to the side when he looked at her, as if he was discovering her for the first time all over again. It was his smile, too. Each one seemed to start in his soul and make its way to his eyes before lighting up his face. His smiles were warm and sincere, and he lavished her with them. He dispelled the loneliness of the place with his presence, filled Vimla with a hope and devotion she'd never before known.

She gripped Krishna's shoulders and skipped into the shallow water with a splash. The water was warm, and when she peered between the lily pads, she could see her toes overlapping his through the clear water. Vimla closed her eyes and lifted her face to the sky as Krishna fished a lily out of the water and threaded it into her hair. Droplets trickled down the back of her neck and the length of her spine. She quivered at the gentle thrill.

Vimla rolled over and squeezed her eyes closed, damming her tears behind wrinkled eyelids. Now, with Krishna gone, her heart was a grey landscape of emptiness; nothing to discover except loss and maybe regret. She hadn't decided yet.

"Fish make a nice dish! Fish make a sweet dish!"

Vimla sat up. A bedspring pierced her tailbone. It was Sookhoo, the fish man, and he was on Kiskadee Trace! Vimla shoved her feet in her slippers and dashed down the stairs just as Sookhoo's white pickup truck rolled toward the house. The speakers mounted on the truck's roof blared, "Want fresh kingfish, red snapper and cascadoo? Come to the truck and buy from Big Sookhoo!"

Sookhoo saw Vimla coming and put his truck into park. "Vimla, how you going?" He had faded brown eyes, purple smoker's lips and weathered skin the colour of old coffee grounds. When he smiled at her, the scar on his cheek stretched into the salt-and-pepper stubble at his chin. His cropped hair was hidden behind a white cap worn backward.

"The red snapper fresh?"

"You ever know me not to have fresh fish, girl?" He sucked his teeth, but his question was good-natured. "See for yourself and tell me if I lie."

Vimla followed him to the back of the pickup, where five large Styrofoam coolers were lined up. Sookhoo took the lid off the second cooler and Vimla rose on her tiptoes to peek inside at the dozens of bright-red fish lying on beds of ice. The smell of the sea filled her lungs.

"What I tell you, Vimla? Ain't the fish looking fresh to you?" He scooped one up and held it in his palm for her to inspect. Fishy droplets seeped between his fingers and onto the road.

Vimla nodded. "Give me three red snapper."

Sookhoo grabbed a clear bag. "Take four, nuh?"

"Three good. Thanks."

Sookhoo turned his face away and busied himself with scooping the fish from the cooler and dropping them into the bag. "Take four and I go give you a message from Krishna." His voice was low when he spoke. He wrapped a dark hand around the belly of a particularly big red snapper and waited.

"And how I know you ain't lying to make a sale?"

Sookhoo frowned. "If you think I lying, don't buy the fish." He made to drop the red snapper. "And I wouldn't tell you the message."

Vimla studied his face. "How I know you ain't going straight to the rum shop after you take my money and tell everybody that Krishna send a message for me?"

Sookhoo fitted the lid back on the cooler. "You see me? I is a big man. I don't have time for this love-story shit, and I not in the business of selling gossip." He pointed to the side of his truck. "What that say? BIG SOOKHOO'S FISH." He jabbed his broad chest with his thumb. "That's me. Big Sookhoo. The fish man. I sell fish, and on the occasion, I deliver a message or two—if I like the message. If you ain't want to know the message, that's fine. And if you want to know, well, that's finer."

Vimla studied Sookhoo, who wore the look of a slighted child on his weathered face. His frown reduced his scar to the size of a baby smelt. "Okay, give me a next fish and tell me the message."

Sookhoo removed the cooler lid and plucked the fish by the tail in one smooth motion, his spirits lifted again. "Your lovah-boy coming back Chance for the wedding. He want to see you before."

Vimla felt sick. She put a hand over her face to block out

the fishy smell and hide her trembling chin. "When is the wedding?"

"September first."

Vimla gasped. "When he coming to see me?"

"Tonight self." Sookhoo placed the bag of four fish on his scale, which was nestled between two of the coolers.

She gave him the crumpled bills, moist from her hand. "When Krishna tell you that?"

Sookhoo climbed back into his truck and peered down at her through the open space that should have been a window. "I was liming in Tobago with my partner, Dutchie, yesterday. Krishna does work with he now." Sookhoo shifted into drive and brought his megaphone to his lips again. "Get fresh fish from Big Sookhoo—shrimps, kingfish and tilapia, too!" The truck inched forward.

"Wait!" Vimla trotted alongside the window, her heart hammering. "Where to meet him? What time?"

Sookhoo winked at her. "Relax, nuh, girl! Tell your father I coming back this afternoon to buy two drake. I go give you the details then."

Panic swept through her. What if he didn't come back? "Tell me now, Sookhoo. Please." Her voice cracked, but she was too frightened to be embarrassed.

Sookhoo shook his head. "Krishna write you a note with details and thing in it. I left it home, but I go bring it later." He took up the megaphone again. "Tell your father is two fat drake I want. I coming back half two."

He waved to Vimla and was gone.

Sookhoo's Duck

Vimla stood at the kitchen sink washing wares for the third time that day. She rinsed the soapy suds off a pot with her gaze fixed out the window. A rooster darted by and she smiled despite herself. She had grown up with these fowls, seen them every day of her life, and still a running rooster amused her. She could appreciate their pompous strut around the backyard as if they owned it, the clamour of their talons on the rooftops and their incessant crowing throughout the day; it was the springiness of their run she found comical. Another, bigger, rooster took off after the first, green chest thrust forward, brown plumy tail dancing behind him as he skipped through the dirt. She heard the cry and she knew: a cockfight. But before Vimla could finish wiping her hands dry on a dishtowel, Chandani was zipping past the window with a stick in her hand. "Allyuh want to fight?"

Vimla giggled and she was startled by the foreignness of the sound.

The smaller rooster flapped its way onto the galvanized-steel roofing of the chicken coup and turned his back on his pursuer and Chandani as if they were no more significant than sandflies.

Chandani stood with her fists on her straight hips, looking around the backyard, daring one of the four roosters to pick a fight under her watch. The roosters scratched and pecked at the earth as if she wasn't there, and she smiled a triumphant smile. "I thought so."

A genuine smile! Vimla was relieved. She had suffered silently through the stages of her mother's disappointment over the past weeks. There had been the days of withdrawal when Chandani spent hours on end in her bedroom mourning the loss of the Narines' reputation. There had been the days of outrage when stinging reprisals spewed from her mouth and fell on Om's and Vimla's heads without mercy. And then there had been the quiet days, when Chandani had moved about the house in eerie silence, busying herself with the cooking and washing and tending to her fowl in deep thought. Now she was returning to her old self, Vimla thought: firm and dictatorial with a hint of humour. Vimla sighed. She had missed her mother.

As Chandani disappeared from view, Vimla noticed the two fat green barbadines dangling from a tree a few feet from the chicken coop. With a quick shuffle of her feet, she exchanged her below-the-house slippers for her outside-slippers and walked around to the rear of the house. She pulled the barbadines off their vine and cradled them in her arms back to the kitchen. She would make barbadine punch for her mother.

That would keep her busy until Sookhoo came with Krishna's message.

Vimla felt her spirits lift higher than they had in a long time. Her mother was happier, and if all went well, Vimla would see Krishna tonight. Krishna, after three weeks! Krishna. She turned the name over in her head, saw his smile in her mind's eye. Her stomach flipped in anticipation.

Vimla sliced open the barbadines and extracted the seeds from the soft white flesh. *Krishna would admit that he loved her, call off his wedding with Chalisa Shankar.*

She whisked and mashed the barbadine fruit and watched the pulp become a lumpy liquid. *Krishna would ask Om for Vimla's hand in marriage.*

She strained the lumpy liquid into an empty jug. *Vimla and Krishna would have a grand wedding and all of Chance would be sorry for what they had said about her.*

She poured a full can of condensed milk into the jug and stirred. *Headmaster Roop G. Kapil would ask Vimla to teach at Saraswati Hindu School again.*

She spooned sugar into the jug and stirred. *Vimla's reputation would be restored—improved, even—by her new teaching job—*she added more sugar to the mixture—*and marriage to Pundit Krishna Govind.*

Vimla poured herself a glass of the barbadine punch and tasted the sweetness of her future. The creamy rich drink left a white froth on her upper lip like a lingering kiss and sent her taste buds dancing.

Sunshine dripped in through the window. Vimla fitted the jug into the icebox and reclined against the counter in a pool of warmth. She saw that two roosters were on the chicken coup now, parading over the dozens of ducks and chickens pecking their way through the dirt. Vimla closed her eyes and allowed one dangerous moment of peace to fill her soul.

The ducks sensed their peril the moment Om pulled on his tall rubber boots and began creeping toward them with long, deliberate strides. They flocked together, a sea of pure white, shuffling in one direction and then the next. At first their panic was quiet and contained, but as Om drew nearer and the dogs began to bark excitedly at his heels, the ducks' anxiety increased. They honked and waddled faster, their wings brushing up against their neighbours', until they found themselves driven straight into the duck pen. Om pulled the pen gate closed behind him, locking the ducks in and the dogs out. The dogs went wild, baying and leaping up on their hind legs, their hunting instincts roused. The ducks cowered in the farthest corner of the pen and watched Om with their terrified red eyes. Om reached his arms forward and lunged at one of the ducks that had the misfortune of being at the back of the flock going into the pen and was now at the front of the flock inside the pen. The duck darted away, chest first, white wings spanned wide. Then the other ducks began to break rank and shuffle in different directions. Om charged left and then right. He whirled then brought his hands down on a *whoosh* of air and a few lost feathers. He righted himself and tried again, cursing under his breath.

"Vimla!"

Vimla groaned inwardly from beneath the caimite tree where she stood beside Sookhoo, watching. She didn't like helping her father catch ducks. She didn't like the look in their eyes just before they were plunged into the darkness of the empty feed bag. It was always a mixture of dread and blame. And it was too quiet. The ducks' fight—if they even bothered—was pitiful. They would tussle in the bag for a second and then retreat into shock, quietly resigned to their deaths. There was that, and she needed a minute to talk to Sookhoo. "Yes, Pa?" she asked, trying to keep the irritation out of her voice.

"Hold the dogs!" Om yelled over the barking.

Vimla left the shade of the caimite tree and managed to pull Blackie, Brownie and Scratch away from the duck pen. She ushered them toward their kennel, stamping menacingly in the dirt to show she meant business. Blackie and Scratch slunk to the kennel with their tails between their legs, but Brownie got away. He bounded past Vimla around the other side of the pen, nipping the ducks' tail feathers through a gap in the wood. Brownie howled, frustrated and excited at once.

Sookhoo leaned against the caimite tree. "Fishing doesn't be frantic so," he told Vimla when she returned from locking the kennel door.

Vimla thought of the information Soohoo had for her. Her heart flip-flopped behind her rib cage like a captured tilapia and she knew that fishing was just as frantic. *Tell me about Krishna!* she wanted to scream.

"You blasted web-foot, ugly-mouth, white-backside, little—" Om's mutterings stole Sookhoo's attention. "You think you fast, ain't?" Om turned to Vimla and Sookhoo holding a drake up by its wings, its orange feet piercing the air like arrows. "Vims, bring me a feed bag!" Sweat glistened on his brown face.

Vimla swiped an empty feed bag made of jute off the table

and hurried to the pen. She held it open and turned her face away as Om lowered the drake inside. The bag felt heavier than she had expected. *The weight of fear,* she told herself.

Om nodded to Sookhoo beneath the caimite tree. "Is two drake you want?"

"Yeah. Give me a next fat one like that again." Sookhoo pointed to the bulging bag in Vimla's hands.

Vimla hoisted the bag high as Brownie came flying around the duck pen and barrelled into her leg. The dog sprang up and balanced his paws on Vimla's belly, barking and scratching at the bag. "Down, Brownie!" she scolded. Brownie backed away and then trotted at Vimla's heels again as she set the bag on the table that was pushed up against the back wall of the house.

Chandani came out of the kitchen and craned her skinny neck to see how Om was faring. "Vimla, why you don't go and help your father." It was a statement rather than a question.

Vimla hesitated. She glanced at the bag behind her, imagining the bird suffocating in its own feathers and fear. "Brownie go throw down this duck as soon as I leave it."

Chandani sucked her teeth. "Brownie!" she said to the dog pacing back and forth at Vimla's feet. "Get and go on! Move your tail from there!" The dog watched her, panting. Chandani slapped Brownie's rump. "In the kennel," she said. Brownie took off toward Om, who whistled for their attention: he was holding the second drake. Vimla wasn't sure why it mattered, but it pleased her to see the drake flail in her father's grip for a moment. She hoped that its courage would endure the dark unknowing of the feed bag and the glint of the cutlass before the weapon came swinging toward its neck later.

Chandani scooped the first bagged duck off the table and carried it like a fat baby in her arms to the scale. Reluctantly Vimla held another feed bag open for her father and conjured gladness. She thought of her sweet barbadine punch cooling in the icebox, of Krishna coming to profess his love. She thought of laughing with Minty in the cane fields, of Chalisa Shankar's face disfigured and covered in pock marks. Vimla didn't even realize when the drake sank to the bottom of the bag and her father took it from her hands. She watched, relieved, as Om clomped toward the scale in his rubber boots, now marred with duck excrement and mud.

Brownie trotted after Om, his tail wagging. Vimla was about to call him back when an idea came to her. As Om and Chandani busied themselves weighing the first duck, Vimla slunk away and released the latch on the kennel door. In an instant Blackie and Scratch hurtled toward the scale and pounced on the drake in the bag.

Om and Chandani pushed the dogs away, but the animals could smell blood and longed to sink their teeth into warm flesh. The hullabaloo interrupted the weighing and caused enough distraction for Vimla and Sookhoo to exchange a few hurried words unheard. Vimla grabbed a coconut broom and dragged the bristles across the concrete at Sookhoo's feet.

He smiled and the scar in his cheek stretched and shone across his dark skin. Then, instead of muttering the message, Sookhoo fished into his pocket and pulled out a scrap of paper, which he let fall from his fingers in front of Vimla's broom before moving to join her parents. Vimla fell to her knees and plucked the note from the dust. Quickly she folded the scrap and tucked it into the breast pocket of her brown dress. She imagined she could feel the weight of Krishna's words, like a captured drake in a jute bag, against her heart.

Sookhoo slapped some bills into Om's palm in a handshake and swung the two bags over his shoulder and out of the dogs' reaches. Chandani and Om walked Sookhoo to the front gate with the dogs at their heels.

"I going back Tobago for a week, but I go see allyuh for the wedding," Sookhoo said.

Vimla drew near, turning the paper round and round in her pocket with her fingers. She waited for her parents to make some excuse for not attending the wedding, or to brush the comment away. Instead Om said, "We go lash out a bottle of Puncheon that day, boy! Tell the old lady I say hello."

And then Sookhoo was gone.

The barbadine punch was cool now. Chandani sat with her back erect and the sharp points of her elbows digging into the table, her hand wrapped around a tall glass. "What you swell up for now? Every time I turn around, your mouth swell up for something else. What happen? I starving you here? Your father does give you licks?" She sipped the punch. "Children these days too blasted ungrateful. Nothing good enough. Sometimes I does feel to just slap that look out your face, Vimla," Chandani said. A stiff smile appeared and vanished again.

Vimla ignored her mother's attempt at humour. "Allyuh get invitation to the wedding?" Her voice trembled; the tilapia convulsed.

"How you mean? Of course we get invitation, Vimla!" Chandani exclaimed, as if there had ever been a doubt. "The

Govinds live over the road! How they wouldn't invite we?"

"Ma!" She glared at her mother, recalling Chandani's recent temper over the matter. "So allyuh going to the wedding?"

Chandani straightened the straight tablecloth. "How it go look if we ain't go?"

Vimla clenched her hands. "How it go look if allyuh *go*?"

"If people ain't see we, they go wonder why. Then they go remember my daughter decide to take up man. Then they go remember which man she decide to take up. Then they go remember Krishna. And they go see how Krishna marrying a nice girl and left you in Chance to milk cow. And then you know what go happen?"

Vimla sighed.

"They go laugh. Everybody go laugh at we again." Chandani took a swallow of her punch. "You think I keep a clean house and cook for my husband and mind child to the best of my abilities for people to laugh at me?"

For a moment, Vimla regarded Chandani, with the ring of white froth around her mouth. Then she pushed her chair back and headed for the door.

"Vimla, it only have one woman and one man living in this house and that is me and your father," Chandani said to her back. "If you feel you too big for we, pack your bags and go, nuh?"

Vimla had heard this line all her life, but this time, as she stomped up the stairs to her bedroom with the sickening feeling of betrayal in her stomach, she considered the suggestion.

Stitch by Stitch

Thursday August 22, 1974

....

CHANCE, TRINIDAD

Sangita leaned on the windowpane in her sewing room and stared out at the cricketers gathering across the road. There was not a better view in Chance, she thought with a secret smile. Joe, the young man Om hired to cut his cane in cane season, stood to the side working on his batting form. Sangita imagined his back muscles contracting and releasing beneath his shirt. She knew every sinew and ripple, had committed them to memory during last cane season as Joe swung his cutlass bareback in the fields.

Often she had thought how nice it would be to bring him a cup of water, but she didn't dare, not while he toiled in the neighbours' field. She shook her head and laughed, her earrings springing against her neck. What silliness! Joe was but a child. No more than twenty, surely. She was lonely; that was all.

Sangita spotted the giant of a man Rajesh had hired to work in their fields, as the fellow was strapping on shin pads. He was ridiculously powerful and always remained a quarter of an acre ahead of Joe, but his gut was generous and hair sprang from the dark recesses of his ears. Sangita found him appalling, even more so when he bared his rotting teeth to smile. She wished Rajesh had hired Joe instead. At least then she would have had something—someone—to please her during the day, even if from afar.

Faizal Mohammed strode onto the field then, as if to remind her who really owned her heart. He balanced a new bat on his shoulder, looking sharp in startling white clothes, while the other men wore grungy shirts and shorts meant for the mud. Sangita tapped her lips with her fingers. Faizal was a superb batsman and was delicious in his success. Her stomach fluttered whenever he hit a six and it took all her self-control not to cheer him on from the window. That would be dangerous, especially since Rajesh played with the men, too.

Sangita found Rajesh. He was setting up the wickets, bawling orders to the others, picking men for his team. He wouldn't choose Faizal Mohammed, no matter how strong a batsman he was. He never did. Sangita wondered just how deep Rajesh's suspicions ran.

"Mammy?"

Sangita jumped, drew the curtains across the window.

"What you watching?" Minty eyed her as she picked across the fabric-strewn floor.

"Your father. He playing cricket."

It was partially true, but Minty's eyes filled with doubt anyway. Sangita brushed past her and returned to the unfinished pillowcase pinned beneath her sewing machine's needle. She tapped the pedal under the table and the machine whirred to life. "You studying or you looking for something to do?" Sangita eased the fabric away from her, the bangles at her wrists tinkling, and watched the needle bob. She never lifted her eyes from her work.

Minty sighed the sigh of a woman fatigued. She cleared the wooden bench of fabrics and sat. "I tired studying calculus."

Sangita lifted her foot off the pedal and let her hands fall into her lap. "Well, pick up the geography book then!" she said.

Minty pouted, and the dimple in her chin deepened. She rubbed her eyes with the back of her hand. Sangita saw the shadows, like crescent moons turned on their bellies, beneath her daughter's eyes. Her milky skin was splotched with red, a sure sign that she was worried.

"If you tired, Mints, go and take a rest. I go wake you in a hour."

Minty picked up the roll of white lace Sangita used for Gloria Ramnath's curtains. She draped it over her blue dress and glimpsed her reflection in the mirror. "Mammy," she began, "I go try my best, but I wouldn't make as high as Vimla."

Sangita examined her stitch—although she knew it was flawless—so she wouldn't glimpse the defeat in Minty's face. "How you mean? You have one more year again, Minty! It ain't have a girl brighter than you." She held up the pillowcase cover. It was the vibrant shade of a scarlet ibis. "You like this?"

Minty dropped the lace. "Vimla brighter than me, Mammy." It was a simple statement, untarnished by even the faintest hint of jealousy. "I wouldn't score as high as she."

Sangita wished Minty had more fire in her soul. Competition was healthy—necessary these days. "Vimla Narine?" She rose from her seat and moved to the iron she'd heated with coals earlier. "Minty, it seem to me Miss Vimla have she head everywhere except on she future these days. Maybe she pass all she subjects, but she's a duncy-head in my books. Better she stay home and learn to cook a proper roti. A soft roti that swells. Not that burn-up thing she feed she father when Chandani gone on strike." Sangita laughed.

Minty looked hurt on her friend's behalf. Sangita shook out the pillowcase and smoothed it on the table with her hand. "Mints, don't study Vimla. You have your own future to make."

Minty looked away. She discovered a scrap of pink satin and brushed it against her cheek. "I could sew like you."

Pride lit Sangita's face for a moment. She cleaned the iron of soot with an old rag, turned the pillowcase inside out and pressed it with the iron. "Yes, but what about university?"

Minty looked doubtful and Sangita knew what she was thinking. It was almost impossible to get into university. It took brilliance and good fortune. Was Vimla even going? Sangita flipped the pillowcase over and pressed the crinkles out on that side. "You know, in the meantime, after you sit for the A Levels, you could teach at Saraswati Hindu School." She was pleased with how casual she sounded.

Minty gasped. "Vimla's position?"

Sangita huffed. "No." She set the iron down with a *clunk* and forced patience into her voice. "Pundit Anand and Headmaster Roop G. Kapil done take that job away from Vimla, Mints. You know that. Vimla ain't right for the school. It does take more than a little smarts to teach primary school."

Minty's face crumpled in worry and Sangita felt herself flinch. "Ma, I don't want to teach at that school. I don't want to teach anywhere. I want to sew," Minty said.

Sangita flicked her wrist at her daughter. "Humph! Minty, is an honour to teach—especially for Saraswati Hindu School! Teachers well respected. Is the right thing for you to do."

"Seamstresses important, too," Minty said.

Sangita looked across her tiny sewing room at the fabrics and ribbons, the spools of coloured thread. Bulldog's pants hung on a wire hanger, waiting to be hemmed. Gloria Ramnath's sari needed to be stitched into a skirt and blouse. Maya's dress had to be taken in—she had lost so much weight since Sangita had discovered Krishna's escapade with Vimla. Scraps from drapes and pillowcases cascaded over chairs and littered the floor. Yes, she was important in this district, indeed. She had sewn for nearly every family in Chance. A smile bloomed on her face as she reversed the pillowcase once more and gave it a shake.

"Chance done have a seamstress, sweetie," Sangita said. "And anyhow"—she placed the pillowcase on an identical one lying on her sewing table—"everything done fix up. Once you pass the A Levels, you go teach at Saraswati Hindu School."

Minty stood from the bench. It creaked again. Sangita caught a spark of anger in her daughter's eyes. "Who say?" Minty asked.

"I say." Sangita turned her back to Minty. She slid Bulldog's pants from the hanger. "And Pundit Anand say, too."

She flipped open her case of threads and selected the brown. She snipped a generous piece and wet the end in her mouth. The room went quiet. Minty's hands were still; there was no rustling of fabric now. Sangita wondered how long Minty could stifle her reaction in silence. She extracted a needle from the spool of red thread and waited. She would have to speak sometime. Sangita squinted one eye and, with careful precision, threaded the needle on her first attempt. She got partway through hemming Bulldog's pants, when she could bare the silence no longer. "Minty? Say something, nuh, girl."

No answer.

Sangita looked over her shoulder and found the bench empty.

"Minty!" she called, setting Bulldog's pants down.

She started to the door, a lesson on good manners poised at the tip of her tongue, and that's when she saw it: a gold chain, unclasped, snaking across the bench in a very purposeful *F.M.*

Sangita gasped, swiping the chain off the bench. Her heart somersaulted in her chest and plummeted into her belly. She had turned the rooms upside down looking for this. Where had Minty found it, and more important, where were the gold initials that had been attached?

Lal's Surprise

F aizal Mohammed strolled toward Lal's Rum Shop snapping his fingers and whistling the theme song from *Bonanza*. Sam skittered back and forth across his shoulder, bobbing his head and falling in tune with Faizal when the moment seized him. They were a dashing pair that evening, Faizal in his new red, flared trousers, yellow disco shirt and two-inch brown platform shoes, and Sam with his blue and yellow feathers fresh and fluffy with afternoon rain.

Faizal glanced down Kiskadee Trace, lined on either side by tall mangrove trees and shallow drains of murky green sludge. It had been a stifling day and he was grateful for the shadows cast by the retreating sun. He smiled into the breeze created by the briskness of his movements. As dusk descended on Chance, Faizal recalled his latest sweet encounter with Sangita Gopalsingh. "Man, just the other night me and Sangita was walking up this road together. That woman light up the whole district for we to see—is so much sequin and thing she had all over she bosom." The memory delighted him; it also sent a feeling he could not define rippling through him. "You think she go be at Lal's tonight, Sam?"

Sam adjusted the feathers on his back and took up *Bonanza*'s theme song on his own.

Faizal undid a button and loosened his collar as he walked toward the rum shop's open entrance. "Nah, you right. She wouldn't be there. She probably sewing she clothes for the big wedding coming up." He stroked Sam's head with his finger. "Now, *that* is a woman who know she fashion." Faizal turned up Lal's driveway and paused in the doorway for a moment, squinting against the fluorescent lighting. "Good night, every-one," he said, when he could see clearly again. The rum shop fell silent as Faizal coaxed Sam onto his index finger and strut-ted across the room on his brown platform shoes. Om, Gloria, Lal and Puncheon followed his jaunty, long strides, a blend of bemusement and hilarity tugging at their features.

Faizal ignored them, hooking the toe of his shoe around a chair leg and sliding the chair out from beneath the round table in one easy motion. He placed his finger at the table's edge and allowed Sam to march across it before lowering himself into his seat and drawing his left ankle onto his right knee, as blasé as could be. He looked up at his gaping neighbours and said, "What happened? Allyuh never see a man with style before?"

Gloria gave Faizal a lingering once-over, pulling idly at her earlobe with her ringed fingers. "You is a real star-boy, Faizal."

Faizal patted his hair with a smile, careful not to flatten the puff he'd coiffed at the front.

Puncheon leaned over a round table and rested his chin on his stacked fists. His eyes were bloodshot and heavy lidded, his cheeks sunken and splotched with premature age spots. Faizal thought even his lopsided smile looked drunk. "Eh, Boss, mind your crotch burn up in them fire pants," Puncheon said.

Om's hearty laughter filled the bar. Gloria's body shook in quiet amusement, a tear trapping itself in the crinkle of one eye.

Faizal jiggled his ankle, miffed, but the weight of his new shoes pleased him and he quickly recovered. As he relaxed, he took in his surroundings, thinking it had been a long time since he'd visited the rum shop. He noted the posters of scantily clad women gazing back at him from the Caribbean-blue walls, the Carib and Stag Lager Beer banners hanging from the bar and tacked on the washroom door. He noted the familiar picture of Lord Shiva high up on the wall behind the bar, forever smiling his dreamy smile; the same splintery chairs and stools tucked beneath the tables that wobbled. He counted the regular customers who filled Lal's Rum Shop and noted Lal himself, who looked as he always did, with his crisp white shirt rolled neatly to his elbows and his placid smile turned to the world.

Faizal pulled in a breath and his lungs filled with a fusion of liquor and spicy curry, sweat and sweet Vaseline. Outside, from a house hidden in the thick of vegetation, a woman sang a Hindi film song and then forgot the words to the chorus. A mosquito danced across the cracked plaster of the wall. A string of ants snaked over the concrete floor and disappeared under the drapes of Gloria's dress. Faizal sighed, feeling the pandemonium of the other night slip from his mind. He nodded to Lal.

Lal leaned back on the counter behind the bar and folded his arms. His kind eyes twinkled with mirth. "Faizal, don't let that parrot shit up my bar again. Keep it right there on your shoulder." He reached for a glass. "You drinking tonight?"

Faizal waved his hand at Lal. "Nah, Boss. Allyuh heathens drink up, nuh? I go take a ginger beer."

Rajesh lumbered out of the washroom then, a closet-sized rectangle with a dingy urinal, toilet and standpipe. He shook the water from his hands as he made his way to the bar. "Eh, Faizal, take a real drink, nuh, man. Allah done know about all your debauchery already."

Faizal sucked his teeth and reached for the ginger beer that Lal had brought to his table on a Carib coaster. "You talking to me about debauchery?" Faizal grinned. "You forget about Krishna Janamashtami when you get high and stupid and I had to leave my bed in the middle of the night to save you from the soucouyant?"

Gloria slapped the table. "Allyuh men real dotish." A tear spilled down her plump cheek, which was pink from the heat.

Om, who was shovelling pieces of spicy curried goat into his mouth, spun around on his bar stool. "We dotish? You is the one who announce Pundit Anand's death the same afternoon I see him taking a stroll to Headmaster's house. You calling Pundit Anand the living dead?"

Gloria's grin dissolved. She puffed herself up and folded her arms over her ample chest. "Well, who could blame me for thinking the man just lie down and dead in the temple after what your daughter and Krishna do?" She raised her three chins. "Ever since she give me talks in the market, I know Vimla was trouble," Gloria told the room.

Faizal's jaw fell. Gloria's comment didn't qualify as good-natured rum-shop shit-talk. If she had been a man, if Om had had enough to drink, that remark could have earned Gloria a cuff in the mouth. Instead Om stared back at her, stony faced, and said, "Krishna and Vimla ain't do nothing you didn't used to do yourself when you was less fat and less ugly."

Puncheon sidled up to Gloria. "Is that so, Ms. Glory!" He planted a wet kiss on her cheek. She scowled and jabbed him with her dimpled elbow. Puncheon fell back into a chair, holding a hand to his ribs, his loose tongue stumbling through a sequence of curses.

"Pundit Anand far from dead—the man planning big wedding for Krishna," Rajesh said. "Is a nice girl he find for he son. Chalisa Shankar she name."

Faizal sat up tall, his interest pricked. "You meet she?" Out of the corner of his eye he saw hurt flit across Om's face, and remembered seeing the same expression reflected in his rear-view mirror a few nights ago.

Rajesh nodded. "Yeah, man. When she come with she Nanny to meet Anand and Maya on Sunday, Sangita insist we drop by to see if Maya need she help with the wedding."

Gloria snorted. "Sangita is one frontish woman."

Rajesh shot Gloria a warning look and she clamped her mouth shut, fearful of inviting another biting insult. "Chalisa timid," Rajesh continued. "The girl sit with she hands fold up in she lap and she eyes watching down whole time."

Faizal sprayed a mouthful of ginger beer across the table, which Sam dodged just in time. "You say she timid? Chalisa Shankar?" He caught the rag Lal threw at him and began wiping up his mess. Chalisa Shankar? Timid? He thought of the girl who strode, fully clothed, into the chilly sea and lolled across the water like it was a bed of down; of the girl who had twirled with abandon through a storm like a flash of lightning. He remembered how she'd demanded he drive slower down the mountain, her eyes sparkling like hot flints. She must not want to get married, he thought.

Rajesh gave Faizal a curious look. "Yeah. Why? What you hear?"

Faizal shoved the bottle against his lips again and began to chug his ginger beer. The fizz burned his throat. He couldn't tell them she was a witch without implicating himself somehow. They would want to know how he knew Chalisa, and his secrets would inevitably unravel with hers. When Faizal had drained the last drop from the bottle, he shrugged and set it down with a belch. "I ain't hear nothing."

"Krishna wasn't there?" Gloria asked. "I haven't seen that handsome boy around since he get into trouble with Vimla. How Pundit Anand and Maya arrange the marriage without Krishna meeting Chalisa?"

"I hear Krishna gone Tobago," Lal said.

"Tobago!" Gloria swatted the table with her pudgy hand, sending it rocking. "Lawd Father, what he doing in Tobago?" she exclaimed.

Nobody could say. They sat in silent speculation for a moment until Headmaster Roop G. Kapil walked through the door with a pen tucked behind his ear and a small notebook shoved in his back pocket. He stopped in his tracks and looked around. "How this place so quiet? Allyuh think Pundit Anand dead again?" He chuckled, finding a spot next to Om. "Scotch on the rocks, Lal. Thanks."

"Headmaster, what you know about the big wedding coming up?" Gloria asked.

Headmaster brushed his salt-and-pepper hair out of his face and shoved his glasses up on his nose with an ink-stained finger. "I ain't know nothing allyuh ain't know," he said, swirling the ice in his glass.

Om turned to him and sat up tall so as to show the width of his chest and the bulk of his arms. "Who getting the teaching job at Saraswati Hindu School next year? You know that at least?"

Headmaster glanced away and shrugged his lean shoulders. "Not yet."

Om sucked his teeth. "This headmaster ain't know he ass from he elbow, if you ask me. Lal, bring me a next beer, man."

Headmaster looked appalled, but he had neither the wit nor vulgarity to sling jibes with this group. He cupped his hands around his cold scotch and stared mutely into the amber liquid as if the answer to Om's question lay somewhere among the ice cubes.

Lal waved his arms in the air. "Allyuh take a break from gossiping and troubling one another for a minute, nuh." The rum shop fell quiet and all eyes turned to Lal. "I have a surprise for allyuh." Nervous excitement played on his face.

Faizal jiggled his ankle again and sighed. A surprise? Lal's last surprise was Daisy, the dark-skinned beauty holding a sweating Carib to her red lips, pinned up behind Gloria's head. Faizal was not interested in another racy poster, or a new packet of coasters, or even one of Lal's pots of fresh curry, however good. He wanted to know the details of Krishna and Chalisa's wedding. He was also curious about this new tension between Om and Headmaster. Surely it had something to do with Vimla. Suddenly he laughed at himself, shaking the puff on his head. How had the affairs of silly children come to consume him this way?

Rajesh cast Faizal a sidelong glance that said he was crazy and then turned back to the bar, strumming his fingers on the table, waiting for Lal to return with his surprise.

Faizal scowled at the back of Rajesh's head. He asked himself for the umpteenth time what Sangita had ever seen in Rajesh, with his loud mouth and oxen-like features. Yes, Rajesh was an esteemed member of the district, he owned more acres of land than most, he treated Sangita with respect. But there was so much more that Rajesh was not. He was not funny or fashionable; he was not curious or daring. He was not worthy of Sangita because he was not Faizal Mohammed. And that was that.

A vision of Sangita pouty and bejewelled, clinging to his arm as they walked up Kiskadee Trace, materialized in Faizal's mind. He wet his lips and smiled to himself.

Sam nipped at Faizal's finger, and Faizal reached idly into his shirt pocket and retrieved a handful of unshelled peanuts. When he scattered them on the table, Sam grasped a shell in his black claw. He brought the shell to his beak and worked away at it until the nut was free. Faizal stroked Sam's head with his finger. "Nice boy," he murmured absent-mindedly.

Lal returned then, hugging a box draped in an old pink curtain to his chest. He set the box down on the bar and, checking to make sure all eyes were on him, whipped the curtain off like a magician.

Puncheon shoved his chair back and stood, upsetting his

drink and wobbling dangerously close to Gloria's lap. Rajesh manoeuvred around Faizal and Gloria and took a seat closer to the bar. Om and Headmaster pivoted on their bar stools in unison to face the unveiled object.

Faizal gasped quietly. His face fell ashen.

"Eh, boy." Om whistled. "That television nice. It working?"

Lal ran his hand over the twelve-inch television, beaming like a child with a new toy. When he plugged it in and turned it on, the screen crackled to life in a whirr of silver static.

"Adjust the antenna!" Gloria cried.

"To the left," Headmaster said.

"Move it one inch so," Rajesh said, gesturing to the right with his hand.

"Bring the right one down and leave the left one up," Om said.

"Hold up! Hold up!" Puncheon exclaimed as Lucille Ball and Desi Arnaz appeared on the screen.

Gloria clapped, and then pressed her hands to her chest, beaming. "*I Love Lucy!* I does watch this show when I visit my son in Port of Spain," she told the room. "He have two television. My son own a jewellery store, you know."

Nobody answered her. They all leaned in and admired what they thought was the first black-and-white television in the district.

"Where you get this, Lal?" Om asked.

"Port of Spain." Lal dusted an invisible speck of dust off the television.

"How much channels you could catch?" Rajesh asked.

"Two."

"What you could see?" Om asked.

"*Panorama News. I Love Lucy. Bonanza. Teen Dance Party. Mastana Bahar*—"

"*Mastana Bahar!* Eh, boy, I does always hear about that talent show on the radio, but I never see it yet," Rajesh said.

"Shh! I can't hear!" Gloria waved her hand with impatience.

Puncheon and Om signalled silently for another round of drinks and propped their chins in their hands at the bar. Gloria lifted her swollen ankles onto a stool and arranged her floral dress over her knees before settling against the hard back of her chair. Rajesh slouched in his seat and interlaced his fingers behind his head, so that his brawny arms were partially flexed and jutted out to the side like wings. Headmaster glanced back and forth from the television screen to his notebook, scribbling with haste. There would be no more gossiping tonight. No more digs.

Faizal looked away from his neighbours. He seethed with jealousy. It was too late now to tell them that he had purchased a television a month ago. If they believed him, they would want to know why he hadn't told anyone, why he had kept it all to himself. They would accuse him of selfishness. But selfishness had never been his motive for secrecy. Sangita had. He had wanted to show her his new television first. Except the opportunity hadn't presented itself and now Lal had ruined everything.

Faizal's face twisted into a profound sulk. He pushed Sam's empty peanut shells around the table with a finger. He was thinking how unfair life could be, when something occurred to him and he froze: Rajesh wouldn't be home for hours now. Faizal grinned. Suddenly he was scraping the unshelled peanuts off the table and depositing them back in his pocket. He held out his finger for Sam, who stepped nimbly on and crept up to Faizal's shoulder again. In an instant Faizal Mohammed was tiptoeing behind the turned backs of his neighbours and slipping out the door. As he disappeared into the night, Sam began to whistle.

Black Water River

Friday August 23, 1974

....

CHANCE, TRINIDAD

"I like a woman with broad hips and a big, fat, round bamsee. When she dance, she bamsee must roll." Puncheon gyrated his narrow hips, puckering his lips at Raj. "When she walk, she bamsee must swing." He sashayed along the riverbank, wagging his scrawny bottom from right to left.

Rajesh shook his head. "Man, behave yourself! If I see a woman move like that, I go bust I down the road in the opposite direction.".0

Puncheon pulled his T-shirt over his head and his smile disappeared momentarily. He revealed a chest permanently scorched by the sun. Silver threads stretched against his pectorals with coconut oil. "How this looking, Raj?" He reached for his crab net, a long stick with a scrap of wire mesh fastened to the end. "Nice?"

Rajesh nodded. "Nice." He lay back in the grass, enjoying

the familiar prickle against his hardened heels and the backs of his calves. It was a cloudless day and the sun blazed in the sky. "I think is a woman like Gloria Ramnath you want," Rajesh said, crossing one ankle over the other and lacing his fingers behind his head.

"Gloria?" Puncheon sucked his teeth as he settled onto his belly and propped his chin in his hands. "I tell you I like a woman with curves, man, not a lumpy pillow with two hand and two foot."

"How about Leela, then?"

"That mosquito? She too skinny-minny for me. Nothing to pinch on that body except she big nose." Puncheon twirled the net in his fingers, scanning the river bottom for crabs.

Rajesh raised his head and squinted at Puncheon with one eye. "I find you too picky, man. You go pick and pick until you pick shit."

"Who said I picking? Nah, man. I go stay a bachelor for life. I just saying, I like a woman with broad hips and a big, fat, round bamsee. That is all."

"But why you never marry? It have plenty gyul like that in Trinidad."

"Marry?" Puncheon looked at Rajesh, incredulous. "It mark *stupid* on my forehead?" He leaned in close to Rajesh's face, tapping the spot just between his eyebrows. "Marriage is only one set of problems."

Rajesh palmed Puncheon's gaunt face and pushed it away. "How you mean?"

"When I liming in the rum shop, ain't you think my wife go get lonely? Ain't you think she go look for a man-friend to keep she company?" Puncheon shook his finger in Rajesh's face like a windshield wiper. "Uh-uh. No, sir. Marriage ain't for me. If I find a next man with my woman, I go surely end up in jail. And, Raj"—Puncheon looked sombre—"jail ain't have rum, so I go surely dead." He deposited his chin back in his palm. "So you see, marriage go kill me."

Rajesh grunted a laugh. "Rum go kill you first."

"I rather dead from too much rum than none at all," Puncheon said, his gaze trained on the rippling water again. And then: "Man, it look like all the crab hiding today. They must be see your ugly face and hole up in the mud, Raj."

"Shut your ass and do fast. I ain't have all day to lime by the river and catch crab. I have garden work to see about."

Puncheon extended the net so that it hovered over the water, ready to dip it in at the first sight of a crab shell. "You have to hurry home to make sure nobody ain't running Sangita down for a kiss!" He flashed a wicked smile.

Rajesh sucked his teeth, but a familiar uneasiness wormed its way into his brain.

"If you wasn't so big like a bison, I would be waiting by she gates, too. Everybody need some Puncheon in they life—even Sangita Gopalsingh."

Rajesh's face was stony. "Puncheon, you is a real motherfu—"

"Relax, nuh, man. Is a joke," Puncheon said. He plucked a blade of grass and tickled the bottom of Rajesh's foot.

Rajesh delivered a swift kick to Puncheon's hand, and Puncheon crowed with mischievous delight before turning back to his fishing.

Rajesh thought of Sangita. Was she lonely? It was true: he was away from her a lot, tending to his land, liming in the rum shop or by the river, playing cards. He scratched the scruff at his neck, itchy with sweat. Would Sangita seek out a "man-friend"? For a moment, the doubt dithered and he almost laughed at the absurdity of heeding Puncheon's reservations about marriage. Puncheon, who had collapsed everywhere in Chance, from the ditch by his house to a stranger's plate of curried duck. Puncheon, who for a time was banned from all weddings after he arrived at one intoxicated, dressed like a pundit, and tried to officiate a ceremony. Puncheon, who stole clean shorts from his neighbours' clothesline when his were dirty. This was not a man you took seriously, and yet, the more Rajesh scorned his outrageous ideas about marriage, the louder Puncheon's words rang true in his heart.

Sangita Gopalsingh was a busy woman, but she was not lonely. His wife—a tentative smile softened his expression—was a businesswoman, after all, too busy to seek companionship outside their marriage. In fact, Rajesh thought, Sangita was always bustling about the neighbourhood, taking measurements for someone, sewing this dress and that blouse. When would she find the time? The smile faltered on his lips as he realized he was working hard to convince himself.

He had heard whispers about Sangita. She was too showy, too forward, too free. But those were the words of envious women. Women like Gloria Ramnath and Chandani Narine, who had no beauty to speak of and no skill beyond the kitchen to set them apart from the other women in the district. Their words were nothing but idle gossip steeped in insecurity, Rajesh told himself.

He shielded his face from the pelting sun, as if to hide his growing suspicions behind his forearms. "Punch, who you think go be interested in Sangita?" He tried to sound casual, but Rajesh heard the insecurity in his own voice.

Puncheon abandoned his net and rolled onto his back, laughing and hugging his knees to his chest. He laughed until tears streamed down his face and fell into the parched grass. "Who?" He gazed, unbelieving, at Rajesh. "Me. Om. Lal. Pundit Anand. Krishna. Kapil. Bulldog. Dr. Mohan. Faizal Mohammed. Pudding." He began to count on his toes. "The dreadlock vagrant. Headmaster—"

Rajesh growled. "I ain't ask you to list all the damn men in the district, jackass."

"Eh—you just now figure out you have a pretty wife and you calling *me* a jackass?"

Rajesh sat up and glared at Puncheon. His old friend just grinned back, drunken merriment dancing in his watery brown eyes.

Something rustled in the grass across the river. Rajesh saw a pair of orange ears twitch and heard a familiar purr. Flambeaux stalked into the open and sat on the other side of the riverbank, staring at Rajesh and Puncheon in his haughty way.

"Watch Flambeaux, Puncheon."

"But how Sangita does let she cat run free all over the place?"

"Get home, Flambeaux," Rajesh said.

Flambeaux squinted at Rajesh, flicked his tail and walked away.

Puncheon nudged Rajesh with the handle of his net. He had spotted the crimson shell of a crab through the shallow water. It glistened in the sunlight, a jewel free for the taking. "Eh, sweetie-sweetie," Puncheon said as if cooing to an infant.

He inched closer to the riverbank. "Come to Punch, my dahling." In one quick motion, Puncheon scooped the crab and a blob of sludge from the river bottom and flung the crab through the air. It landed a foot from where Rajesh sat.

Puncheon began to leap and whoop.

"Catch the damn thing before it run away," Rajesh said.

Puncheon dropped the net in the grass and fell to his hands and knees. "Don't talk to me as if I never catch crab, Raj. I catching crab by this riverbank since I was two years old." He called to the crab as it scuttled away. "When I was two years old, I used to say to myself, 'Self, why you don't go and catch a crab for your mother?' And so I did, with my bare hand and my eyes close." Puncheon pounced on the crab, his bony bottom thrust in the air. "Got you, dahling!"

As he stood, the crab twisted in Puncheon's hand and fastened its claw around his thumb.

"You blasted motherfucking crab!" Puncheon held his hand away from his body and shook, but the crab held on.

Rajesh watched, amused, as Puncheon danced around in the grass with the crab dangling from his thumb. He didn't notice the blood at first, mistaking it, in the whir of Puncheon's movements, for the crab itself. But when Rajesh saw red trickle down the length of Puncheon's skinny arm and drip away at his elbow, he sighed and lumbered to his feet. Puncheon cussed and stomped while Rajesh pried the crab's claw open and freed his thumb.

Rajesh tossed the crab. It went cartwheeling through the air, claws snapping in vain, until it landed with a splash in the pail of water sitting on the bank. "I thought you was catching crab by this riverbank since you was two years old?"

he said, sauntering away. He plunged his feet into the water, stirring up swirls of brown and green sediment.

Puncheon examined his bloody thumb and scowled. "Who catch the damn thing—you or me?" He dunked his hand in the river and then wrapped it in the shirt he'd discarded earlier. "Next time go be better."

"Next time? I ready to leave, man."

"Raj, I can't make a pot of callaloo with one crab, who look half sick at that. I need at least three crab." He sighed, and his shoulders slumped. "I already pick the dasheen bhaji from Headmaster's yard, and t'ief three coconut from Bulldog. Is only the crab I missing! This is your fault. If only you ask your greedy cousin Pudding to lend me two crab, you wouldn't have to wait with me."

Rajesh didn't respond. His gaze was fixed on Krishna Govind, marching up the riverbank, trailing a bulging suitcase through the bush. "But wait, what the ass is this?" he muttered.

The Last Acre

K rishna was on his way.

Vimla squared her shoulders, fixed her gaze forward and ducked between two rows of sugar cane. She parted a path through the leaves and vowed she would not allow her guilty conscience to drag her back home. She would not go all this way to be heartbroken. And this time, she would not be discovered by a ragtag search party. Vimla wanted a victory as much as she wanted Krishna and she would come home with both.

The leaves grazed the light cotton of her sleeves and brushed the top of her head as she went, welcoming her back and then closing in again behind her, possessive. Vimla was no stranger to this last acre of sugar cane.

She picked through the field and touched the ribbons of coloured cloth tied in a bow around every tenth cane stalk.

Pink, orange, yellow, burgundy. This was the rainbow that marked her way. It had been Minty's idea to use scraps from her mother's sewing basket as markers, and she'd filched them herself, choosing the brightest and prettiest fabric available.

Vimla listened to the steady breath of the sugar cane. It inhaled and exhaled in the wind, as much alive as the creatures hiding in its green skirts. She heard the flap and rustle of wings against underbrush. The whir of birds landing and taking flight. The crunch of her footsteps, quick and light with anticipation, measured with deliberateness.

Vimla pumped her arms and strode with more vigour than she needed to. A trick to occupy her mind. Fifteen minutes into her walk and already her cotton blouse clung to her back with perspiration and her hair had gone rogue in the humidity. She lifted the locks off her neck and dropped them over her shoulder knowing it was useless to try to comb through the damp tangles now. She ignored the fine strands that remained twined in her fingers. Droplets pooled on her upper lip and glistened on her nose. Even her knees were wet. Still she pushed against the solid walls of heat so they didn't close in around her.

Vimla reached into her pocket and retrieved Krishna's folded note again. The message had blurred with her constant handling, Krishna's confident pen strokes trailing off into indistinct smudges. But she knew the message as well as she knew his laugh. The paper, damp and wrinkled, was merely proof she wasn't dreaming:

Red. 5 p.m.
With love,
K.G.

The red marker was twenty stalks away. Vimla knew it well. It was organza with two matching red sequins that hung precariously from loose threads of gold. Her heart quickened and she laboured on.

White. Green. Gold. She touched the markers as she passed, recalling the stories Minty had told her about each one. The white cotton came from a widow's sari blouse. The green silk, from a Muslim bride's *lengha*. The gold, from the false flowers in a *bharatnatyam* dancer's hair. Vimla imagined the spirits of these women cheering her on her course. She fancied them women of passion and courage, women like her and Minty.

Minty. A smile loosened the hard line of Vimla's mouth. At one time their mischief had been as harmless as stealing oranges from Headmaster Roop G. Kapil's tree or playing tricks on Puncheon in the market; now they were plotting against the district, undoing a wedding, deceiving a pundit. Vimla knew she had entwined Minty in her mess. As she swatted away a blade reaching for her face, she wondered how far Minty would follow her before it became too much.

Vimla peeled her blouse off her chest and let air filter over the rivers of perspiration. She told herself that it didn't matter anymore; this dangerous game they were planning was nearly over. After all, Krishna was trudging his way through the cane field from the opposite end and at five o'clock he would meet her at the red marker. Vimla imagined what Krishna would say: Chalisa Shankar might be beautiful, with her dimples and her grace and her spotless reputation, but that wasn't enough for him. The farther she walked the surer she became of this. Why else would Krishna initiate a risky meeting with her when his wedding to Chalisa was less than two weeks away? Why else would he sign his note "with love"?

With love.

Buoyed by her reasoning, Vimla reached into her pocket and exchanged Krishna's note for Faizal Mohammed's gold watch. She laughed out loud, startling a family of roosting doves, startling herself. How he must have cursed when Minty blackmailed him for this! Vimla turned the heavy timepiece over in her hand so that the round face stared back at her. Four fifty-seven. Her stomach pitched like a tidal wave. Teal. Turquoise. Silver.

Twenty minutes later Vimla sat on the ground beneath the red marker, having discarded her misgivings about soiling her skirt. For a while she had watched the second hand tick around the clock, but that only made her cross-eyed and crazy. Now she huddled like a wounded animal in a state of numbed shock, hugging her knees to her chest and sniffling into the wrinkles in her skirt.

Krishna was not coming.

She forced air into her lungs.

Krishna was not coming.

How embarrassed her mother would be if she could see her now. Chandani, severe face, haunting eyes, would be furious at Vimla for sneaking away, for being the fool again. Vimla groaned and traded her mother's face for her father's in her mind's eye. If this failed attempt at snagging Krishna became news—as most things in the district did—Om would not say much. He would endure Chandani's tirades and fill his glass more frequently at Lal's. He would have no harsh words for Vimla, only sad eyes that stung more than licks or a berating ever could.

Vimla gathered the ends of her skirt and wiped her face, leaving smears of dirt and sweat behind.

She wondered why Krishna had changed his mind about seeing her. The thought opened the floodgates for a dozen suppositions, each one more distressing than the one before. They darted like a school of smelt. She squeezed her eyes shut and pressed her hands against her temples until the whirl slowed to a steady current of truths: Krishna Govind had sullied her reputation, deserted her for Tobago, detached himself from their disgrace by choosing Chalisa Shankar for a bride. Krishna Govind was a crook.

Vimla pressed her hands more firmly into the sides of her head as if she would squash the blasphemy within. A crook? No. She shook her head. Those were Chandani's charges, not hers. But the more Vimla thought about it, the less she was sure what she believed of Krishna and what she didn't.

Suddenly the heat was unbearable. Vimla dragged the back of her hand across her forehead. She needed water or she would faint. Already delirium skirted the edge of her mind, coaxing her to lay her head in the dirt and die. She had lost Krishna. She had lost her teaching post. She had lost her reputation. Failure licked her insides like flames on a funeral pyre.

And then it happened.

Vimla felt fangs sink into her left ankle and at once her lethargy was overpowered by raw terror. She cried out, tripping over herself as she scrambled to her feet. Pain exploded up her right leg, but she forced herself to leap from the rustling bush. When she dared to look over her shoulder, she found herself held in the opaque stare of a macajuel snake, its brown body stretching on forever across the earth. Vimla's heart pounded. Panic sent her flying. She grit her teeth and clawed wildly at the leaves. They swung back at her, slashing her arms with their razor edges, marring her skin with crimson stripes. The heat grew thicker and she had to double her efforts to move, to breathe, to stay vertical. Sweat and tears stung her eyes and blurred her vision, but the snake's cold stare remained tattooed to her mind.

Vimla ran for what seemed like an eternity, chasing her breath until her heart nearly burst. Finally, when she thought she could go no farther, the cane opened up into a field of savannah grass. Relief shuddered through her as she slowed to a stagger. She sapped the last of her energy in a heart-wrenching cry and collapsed in a heap, letting the wind rush over her.

Vimla didn't hear the shuffle of slippers in the grass or see the shadow fall across her crumpled body, but as she lay panting, she knew instinctively that someone was there.

A Hero

Faizal Mohammed took one look at Vimla crying in his field and cursed. Every time he thought he was finally through with Minty and Vimla, one of them showed up to spoil his day. It wasn't enough that they had his gold chain, initial pendant and his watch; they wanted his sanity, too, it seemed. His lips twisted in disgust. Minty and Vimla couldn't control him if Sangita would leave Rajesh and marry him once and for all. Then the blackmailing would stop. Then they would see who was the boss of who. Witches!

Vimla sniffled. Faizal took a step backward. He thought about turning around and heading home. She was not his responsibility. Not this time. Faizal was almost certain Vimla's unsightly display of grief had something to do with that Krishna Govind. He folded his arms over his chest, staring down at her with as much pity as he'd shown Puncheon when

Puncheon had capsized into the drain on Christmas. What mischief had Vimla got herself into this time? He looked over his shoulder then scanned the open field. And where the hell was Minty?

The crying was subsiding. Good. Faizal felt relief creep through him. The thought of comforting Vimla made him edgy. He took another retreating step, as stealthy as Flambeaux, willing Vimla to peel herself off his property and go home. Faizal thought of the cup of cocoa tea he planned to make, of *Bonanza*, which would begin in just minutes. He licked his lips and wiggled his toes in anticipation.

She uncurled from the knot she'd balled herself into, stretching her arms first, then her legs from beneath her skirt. That's when Faizal saw the scrapes on Vimla's arms and the bloody mess that was her ankle. "Mangoes!" he yelled, leaping back yet another foot.

His outburst startled Vimla. She scrambled to sit up, and when her eyes found his face, Faizal saw hope dissolve into disappointment.

She groaned. "What you doing here, Faizal?"

"What *I* doing here? This is my land! What *you* doing here?" He pointed a long, accusing finger at Vimla, annoyed by her cheek. "And what the hell happened to your foot?"

Vimla peered down at her ankle, wincing as she tried to move it. "A snake" was all she could manage.

Faizal ran his hands through his hair and left them there, holding his head. He glanced at the Narine residence, only a hundred metres away, and felt his heart drop into his belly: they weren't home. He knew they weren't home because he had been spying out the window at them when they bustled onto Kiskadee

Trace an hour and a half ago. Om had lumbered off to Bulldog's house with a jar of pepper sauce under his arm and Chandani had gone in the direction of the mandir—probably to pray for Vimla's soul. Faizal cursed them both beneath his breath.

"Get up, get up!" He crouched low and draped her arm around his shoulder. "We going to the hospital."

Vimla moaned. "No hospital." Her breath was ragged. She looked like she'd torn through a war zone.

Faizal lifted her into his arms. "No hospital? You mad or what?" He headed toward his home. "If I ain't take you to the hospital, that crazy mother of yours go cuss me upside down. No, sir! We going San Fernando General now for now!"

Vimla let her head loll against Faizal's shoulder. "It was only a macajuel," she muttered.

"Only a macajuel?"

"Not poisonous." She grimaced with the jostling. "Careful."

"How you know it was a macajuel, Vimla?" Faizal couldn't believe that even after a snake had sunk its fangs into her ankle, Vimla had the strength to argue.

"I see it." She shuddered. "Them ain't poisonous, just mean and ugly. A macajuel bite my father once. It was hiding in a pile of cane trash that he tried to pick up." She closed her eyes.

Faizal hurried on with Vimla in his arms. He couldn't take her to the hospital on his own. A vulnerable young girl under the care of a dashing bachelor like himself? It wouldn't look good. Besides, someone had to keep Vimla conscious while he drove. Sangita would have to ride along. He just hoped that big bison Rajesh was visiting Bulldog with Om.

Faizal was just nearing the Gopalsinghs' backyard when Minty came flying out of the house and intercepted him.

"What happen to she?" Minty rubbed Vimla's arm. "Vimi! Wake up." Her gaze darted back and forth from Vimla to the cane field.

"A macajuel bite she," he snapped.

Minty gasped.

Faizal manoeuvred around her.

"Where you going?"

He heard the panic in Minty's voice as she scurried after him.

"Go get your mother. We going San Fernando General," Faizal said.

Minty's eyes grew wide. "No, no. We can take care of the snake bite home. Macajuels ain't poisonous." She glanced over his shoulder into the distance.

Faizal frowned. How did they know so much about snakes? They were such a suspicious pair. Of course they were hiding something. Minty had demanded his watch earlier that day and Vimla had obviously been alone in her father's cane field when she was bitten by the snake. But why? The mystery gnawed at Faizal. He longed to know and yet to know would be to conspire alongside them.

Vimla whimpered.

"Get your mother!" he yelled at Minty. He would not indulge them this time. He was eager to be rid of Vimla. He wanted her to be someone else's problem. And when she was, when he had detached himself from their confusion again, he would find out just what their confusion was all about.

Minty's face hardened and Faizal thought she might object. Her gaze slid to Vimla, lying limp in his arms. She hesitated;

he could tell she didn't like having to make this decision without Vimla.

"Okay, Faizal." She wrung her braid, not unlike her mother. "Okay, but remember . . ." And then Minty did the unspeakable. She dropped her hair and burrowed into her pocket. When she uncurled her fingers, Faizal saw his initial pendant glistening in the palm of her chubby hand. "The snake bite Vimla when she was seeing about the bull and the cow. You notice she in the savannah grass outside she house."

Faizal wanted to cuff her. "Where the hell is my blasted chain and watch?"

Minty shrugged.

Faizal stormed past her into the Gopalsinghs' backyard and yelled for Sangita.

Faizal Mohammed climbed into bed with his cup of cocoa tea and his parrot. "Don't vex with me, Sam," he cooed. Sam stepped off Faizal's finger, turned his back and toddled across the coverlet to Faizal's feet. Sam was in a sour mood after having spent the evening alone in the dark.

Faizal crossed one ankle over the other and looked out the window. "Is Minty and Vimla's fault. They trap me in their web again." Sam nipped Faizal's little toe, but Faizal was distracted by Sangita's silhouette shimmying out of her nightie behind drawn curtains next door. He told himself her bedroom curtains were sheer for a reason and took a sip of his cocoa tea to enhance the sweetness of the moment.

Sam climbed onto Faizal's leg and screeched like someone was plucking his feathers out one by one.

Sangita disappeared and Faizal scratched the parrot's head. "I miss *Bonanza* today, too, Sam. Not you alone." Sam closed his eyes and hummed his satisfaction.

"Ah, Sam. You should have see how Sangita romance me today, boy! The whole time I was driving home from San Fernando General, she was making eyes at me from the back seat in the rear-view mirror. Is a miracle I ain't run off the road!"

Sam cocked his head.

Rajesh's bulky silhouette filled the window frame and Faizal slouched against his pillows, spilling cocoa tea on Sam's wing.

"A hero. That's what she call me, Sam. A hero!" A dreamy smile played on Faizal's lips. "And the best part was that Vimla was asleep in Sangita's lap and Minty was sitting beside me like she mother sew up she mouth. Not a sound! Not a peep from the witches! Can you believe that, Sam?" He took a big gulp then and smacked his lips.

Sam spread his wings as he made his way up Faizal's chest and settled on his shoulder.

"But you know what was real peculiar? After we carry Vimla home, I drop Minty and Sangita by them gates and guess who was waiting for them? Rajesh. He look vexed to see me, Sam. He give me one piece of nasty cut-eye and ain't even bother to invite me in for a cup of water self. Not that I want to drink anything with him, but can you believe that, Sam? Is like the man forget he manners."

"Jackass," Sam said.

"Yes. You right. Rajesh is a real jackass." Faizal put his cup down on the bedside table and stretched. "He usher Sangita and Minty into the house like two little goats. I wonder what could have happen to make he vexed so?"

"Motherfu—"

"If you ask me, Sam, the people in Chance behaving stranger and stranger these days." Faizal wriggled under the coverlet and laid his head on his pillow. Sam's wings brushed against his face. "Back in your cage, Sam." He yawned and pulled the covers to his chin.

In the darkness, Faizal said, "You know, Sam, I think I love Sangita Gopalsingh."

Sam lifted his tail feathers and shit in Faizal's hair.

Chalisa's Bangles

A vinash arranged the emerald sari over his head and glided around the bedroom.

"What a pretty ghost you are, Avi," Chalisa said. She was lying on her belly on what used to be her parents' bed, her chin propped in her palm. The sari Avinash was playing ghost in was one of twenty-two draped over the chairs and the bed-head and lying in opulent piles on the floor. Nanny was trying to bury her in wedding clothes.

Avinash lifted the gold edge off his toes and peeked out at her. "I like this one, Chalisa." Chalisa shook her head. "Nanny said you have to choose one," Avinash reminded her, shrouding himself in the sari again.

The door suddenly swung open. "And when Nanny done talk—" Nanny sang, barrelling into the room. Delores trailed behind her, looking upset as always.

"She done talk!" Avinash finished.

Nanny's skeleton fingers found her hips as she looked around the room. "What happened? None of these saris pretty enough for Miss Mastana Bahar?" She swept a burgundy sari encrusted with silver jewels off the floor and tossed it at Delores. "I could have take you shopping, but your mouth so long these days." She wet her chapped lips. "Is embarrassing. People go feel I forcing you to marry." She pushed a mountain of red, yellow and pink saris to the side and propped herself on the edge of the bed. The white dress she wore made the veins snaking up her arm all the bluer.

"You *are* forcing me to marry."

Nanny pretended not to hear. It was her favourite elder trick, that and faking heart attacks.

"Chalisa, when you become a pundit's wife, you go can't dress up like this again. You go have to learn to be humble." Nanny gave her granddaughter a skeptical once-over. "Just make believe you playing the part of a pundit's wife in a flim." An ironic smile creased her face further. "Only, the flim goes on forever." Nanny tossed the pink sari at Delores, who had just finished folding the burgundy one and setting it on the dresser.

Chalisa closed her eyes, shutting Nanny out. She thought of her mother instead. Her easy laughter. Her perfect smile. Rosewater in her hair and cloves on her breath. Her mother would never allow this loveless marriage to happen. Chalisa wondered for the millionth time if her mother had thought of her and Avinash as she'd tumbled off the cliff to her death. A tremor of loss rippled through her. She dug her fingernail into her palm and twisted.

Nanny tapped Chalisa's forehead. "Eh, Miss Mastana Bahar! Wake up!"

Chalisa didn't want to wake up. She realized that her chance at freedom hinged on Vimla and Krishna running away together. A far-fetched fantasy at best. Vimla wasn't as courageous as she would have Chalisa think. All that haughty bravado at the beach had been a performance to intimidate Chalisa, to veil her terror of losing Krishna. Minty had thought they could all be friends, that Chalisa could persuade Vimla to pursue Krishna despite the pandemonium their tryst had unleashed in her world. Minty had been wrong on both counts. Now they would all lose.

Chalisa wondered vaguely how this story might play out on the silver screen. She saw herself dangling from an orange tree, her noose a rainbow of knotted wedding saris.

"Chalisa, I ain't have time for this." Nanny was gesturing at the mess. "You lucky I ain't make Delores sew two sequins on a tarpaulin and wrap you up in that for the wedding."

Avinash giggled beneath the sari.

"Now, here." Nanny pulled out the drawer from the bedside table and extracted a velvet case from the very back. When she opened the case, two gold bangles etched with intricate design gleamed in the sunshine pouring in through the window. They clinked when she picked them up. "This was mine. I give them to your mother when she married my son. Now they yours."

Delores watched the exchange out the corner of one eye, pulling the sari off Avinash's head and then folding the six-foot-long fabric with mechanical movements.

Chalisa slipped the bangles onto her wrist one at a time.

They were too big. She could have slid them past her elbow and worn them as an armband if she'd wanted to. A silence tumbled into the room as she turned them round and round, searching for the right words to say. But there were no right words. These bangles should have been gifted to her by her mother. They should have come with blessings for a sweet marriage. Instead they were noisy reminders of all that she had lost and all that she was about to lose.

Nanny cleared the phlegm from her throat. "If you and Mr. Holy and Religious ever have a daughter, you go pass these on to she. If not, pass them on to your daughter-in-law. Keep it in the family. Is good gold."

Chalisa wanted to stuff the bangles back into the box and shut the lid. This is not what her parents would have wanted for her.

Nanny folded her arms and looked crossly at Chalisa.

Avinash climbed onto the mound of saris between the two. "Say thank you!" he whispered to Chalisa through cupped hands, his knees crushing the silky fabric.

Nanny barked a laugh. "Thank you? Avninash——" She took her grandson's pointy chin in her hand. "Nanny does only get swell-up mouth and twist-up mouth and long-mouth from this one." She nodded her chin at Chalisa, who looked as if someone had handed her a box with a scorpion inside. "I hope when you grow up you is more grateful and thankful than she."

Avinash's eye grew round. He nodded with all the seriousness of an old man. "I hope so, too, Nanny," he said.

Nanny's bony fingers fell away from his face. "Delores!" she screeched.

Delores jumped.

"Where is that girl?"

Avinash pointed behind Nanny. Delores dropped the sari she was caressing her cheek with. "Yes, Nanny?"

Nanny narrowed her gaze at the woman. "My throat feeling dry." She stroked the loose flesh at her neck. "Bring a shot of Puncheon. And you—" Nanny turned to Avinash. "Bring that picture." She pointed to a row of picture frames lining the giant teak armoire in the corner of the room. "Not the picture of you, Avinash, the one next to it, with me and that ugly man."

"Grandpa?"

"That's the one. Bring it come."

Nanny held the gilt frame in her hands, studying the black-and-white couple trapped inside. "Come here, Chalisa. Let me show you something."

Chalisa inched closer. Nanny was a bouquet of Limacol, Bengay and coconut oil.

"See your grandfather here?" She poked the man in the face. "I married he when I was thirteen years old."

Grandpa looked twenty, maybe twenty-five. He was wearing a suit and a sulk, one foot forward like he was preparing to walk away, one hand raised like he was trying to stop the picture. From afar it might have seemed he was waving, but there was something in his eyes, upon closer examination, that said posing for the camera had disrupted his day in a big way. A young girl in a dress with too many frills stood at his shoulder. Nanny. Her eyes were big and serious, like Avinash's. They stared into the camera. Nanny neither smiled nor frowned. Her expression was neutral, ready for her new husband to paint her emotions. The odd pair stood on either side of an orange tree that was even younger than Nanny.

Chalisa thought the girl in the photograph should be afraid, but she was unconvinced Nanny could register fear, even as a child.

"Your grandfather—Mr. Deo Shankar—was one miserable man. His face always appear vexy-vexy so." She tapped her nail on his nose now.

Chalisa tried to remember Grandpa. He barely spoke to anyone, just rode his bike hunched over the handles until one day he died and stopped riding.

"I used to cook roti three times a day for him, and massage he feet when he come home from the orange estate. In those days, your grandfather used to pick orange with he men." Nanny had a far-off look in her eyes as she handed Chalisa the photograph. "He used to drink, too, and lash hard when he drink."

Avinash climbed onto the bed and cozied up next to Chalisa.

"And he mother!" Nanny snorted. "That woman was one nasty thing. She used to make me wash back she clothes three times before she wear them. Three times." Nanny looked at Chalisa. "I was thirteen then. By the time I make your father, I was fifteen."

Chalisa wondered what Nanny was like before she married Grandpa, if Nanny remembered what she was like.

"Count your blessings you ain't marrying a man like Grandpa." There was no sarcasm and Chalisa found the absence of it oddly unsettling. Nanny was right: Krishna wasn't like Grandpa. He was a fool and a bore, yes, but he was no tyrant. Chalisa felt pity for the young bride who was Nanny, but that didn't make her any more eager to marry Krishna Govind.

"I was a innocent little girl in that picture. And through my marriage, Grandpa and he kiss-me-ass mother nearly drive me mad." Nanny's face was wistful and Chalisa almost reached out and squeezed her bony hand. "But I learn to cook and wash. I learn to avoid Grandpa's tirades. I learn to mind a child. I learn to take care of the orange estate and grow the business. Eventually them two fools couldn't do a damn thing without me." Nanny grinned. "And look at me now!"

Delores reappeared with a glass wrapped in a napkin.

"Is about time, Delores. You get loss or what?"

Delores handed Nanny the glass. "I had to go by the shop and pick up a next bottle."

Nanny tipped the seventy-five-proof fire down her throat and winked a cataract eye at Chalisa. "And I learn to drink, too."

All Fours

The old almond tree's leaves stirred in the mid-morning air. A toucan sat in its uppermost branches, lording over the card players below. He scratched his rainbow throat with his claw and squawked.

Faizal pointed. "Watch a toucan," he said to the others.

The men twisted in their chairs and craned their necks. Faizal slid a card from his hand into the deck and extracted another. Ace of hearts. Trump. He grinned. The toucan bobbed, showing off the yellow stripe down the centre of his beak.

"The bird watching my card!" Puncheon exclaimed, laying his hand flat on the table.

The toucan took flight. A leaf helicoptered from its branch and landed on the table. Everyone turned back to the game.

"Nobody ain't watching your card, Puncheon. You ain't have nothing to watch except that deuce." Rajesh jiggled his eyebrows.

Puncheon glowered back at him. "Eh. Keep your eyes on your own hand when you playing with a champion," he said. Puncheon took All Fours seriously. He was a shrewd player who could read the hands around the table better than anyone else. It amazed Faizal that the same man who rode Om's ram goat for sport down Kiskadee Trace in the rain won one All Fours tournament after another across the country. Puncheon's aptitude for the game was enough to redeem him from all his larks in the district. The people forgave him his midnight serenades and for upsetting their produce in the market because Puncheon gave his card-playing partners boasting rights wherever they went.

Puncheon and Faizal exchanged glances.

Puncheon leaned back in his chair and scratched a mosquito bite on his nose. "I ain't have nothing, eh? You save that jack for me, Raj. I go take care of it real good for you!" he said. His watery eyes danced with merriment.

Faizal held his hand close. "Who to play?" he asked, although he knew it was Rajesh's turn.

Rajesh studied his hand before choosing a card from the middle. Puncheon whistled a tune and followed suit with a casual indifference that made Om second-guess his own play and glance to Rajesh for reassurance. When it was Faizal's turn, Puncheon signalled to him to play a low card and Faizal knew Puncheon wanted Rajesh to win the hand. The next two rounds passed in this way, until each player remained with one card in his possession. Rajesh looked around the table and smirked.

Faizal's lips twitched. For once he anticipated the showy exhibition that would follow Rajesh's jack.

Rajesh lifted his arm high, bent his elbow in the air and whipped the card onto the table. It spiralled in the centre, a whir of red and white. "Take that!" he cried. "Save your deuce, Puncheon! You feel you could hang my jack? I is not them children you does be playing with in those small people tournament, you know! I is a big man, with a big jack of hearts, running, like that!" They watched as the jack of hearts slowed to a stop and stared up at them.

Om slammed his hand on the table. "Whey, sir!" He grinned at Rajesh.

Puncheon shrugged and twirled his deuce onto the table. Om followed with a ten of spades.

"Like we go get Gamble, too," Rajesh boasted. "Allyuh take a point for your lowness."

"The game ain't done yet, man," Puncheon warned. He nodded at Faizal. "Play, Boss."

Faizal cupped his card, a look of defeat on his gaunt face.

"What happen, Faizal? You tired get your ass bust?" Rajesh asked. He leaned back in his chair and laced his fingers behind his head. That is five games in a row for we."

"Wait, nuh! A man could play he last card?" Faizal sprang to his feet, sending his chair tumbling back into the grass. He took his ace of hearts in his right hand and Rajesh's jack of hearts in his left hand and slowly, purposefully, sliced the ace across the neck of the jack. "Take that!" he yelled, mocking Rajesh's earlier taunting.

Puncheon whooped. "Whey, sir! Faizal hang your jack, boy!" He jumped up, swiped the jack off the table and stamped it to his forehead. "Allyuh take licks on all side! High, Low, Hang-Jack, Gamble; six days!" His hips jutted in a circle as he called out his points. "And that give we fourteen to go! Who taking cut-ass now?"

Rajesh stood up and knocked his chair over. "Allyuh cheat!"

Faizal gave Rajesh a taciturn look, noting how anger made him all the uglier. "Take the cut-ass like a man," he said.

Om pried the winning hand from Puncheon, added it to the others and shuffled the deck. "Is okay. They get licks whole afternoon—let them have this one."

"Nah!" Rajesh narrowed his gaze at Faizal and then Puncheon. "I ain't wasting my time playing with cheaters."

Puncheon stood up and hiked his shorts high. "What you think? The All Fours trophies in Lal's Rum Shop walk there from all over Trinidad?" He grinned. "I win them with my own two hand and my one big brain," he said, knocking his forehead with a knuckle. "I's a man who don't cheat."

Nobody reminded Puncheon that he played with a partner and that his accolades, however respected, were shared. No one reminded him, because Puncheon could play with the most inexperienced partner and still finish victorious. Puncheon told people Lady Luck was his lover and rum was his best friend, and he took them both to each competition. And to bed.

"Eh. Haul your ass, nuh, man!" Rajesh said to Puncheon. "I ain't talking to you—I talking to *he*." Rajesh pointed a finger in Faizal Mohammed's face.

Faizal was a full head taller than Rajesh, but he was spindly and Rajesh could snap him like a string of bodi if he wanted to. He locked eyes with Rajesh anyway and gritted his teeth for good measure. Eventually Sangita would hear about this. Faizal had to be brave no matter how much he wanted to spit in Rajesh's eyes and take off down the road.

Om tapped the deck against the table so that the edges of the cards lined up. "Relax, Raj. Sit down." He looked wary. He dovetailed the cards, his eyes trained on Rajesh.

Rajesh ignored him. "Where you get that ace, Faizal? You didn't have that ace before, or you would have play it."

Faizal shrugged. Better to say nothing, he told himself. Let Rajesh rile himself up. Let him behave like a jackass for everyone to see. All Faizal had to do was maintain his composure and enjoy the show.

"Check the hands, Om," Rajesh said.

Om paused mid-shuffle. "The card done mix up."

Rajesh sucked his teeth.

Faizal's eyes twinkled at Puncheon, but his expression remained serious. He wondered why Rajesh was on edge today. It was true they had been neighbours for ten years and had never fostered any kind of friendship, but still, they were acquaintances and they always behaved civilly in each other's company. Faizal told himself Rajesh was just a sore loser, that the dander in his gaze had nothing to do with Sangita and him.

Puncheon grasped a lower branch on the almond tree and swung himself, his knees tucked to his chest. "You know," he said, "practice is what you need, Raj. And focus."

Rajesh snorted. "Eh! Practise shutting your ass, nuh?" He surveyed Faizal from his toes to his black puff of hair. His voice was low, almost eerie, when he continued. "I know the game, and I know this man's game, too." He leaned in close to Faizal. An intimidation tactic. "He's a trickster. A scamp. Always watching my card and watching my wife."

Puncheon released his grasp on the branch and fell with a *thud*. "Humph! Is no wonder allyuh never win a competition yet. You too busy fighting like women to play card like men."

Om's chair creaked as he rose. "Raj, you gone too far. Come, let we pack up and go." He began to fold the chairs, glancing over his shoulder to see if Rajesh followed.

Faizal's heart fluttered against his rib cage like a humming-bird's wings. He thought about turning to leave, but he couldn't tear his gaze from Rajesh's square face, his thick neck, the nasty twist of his mouth. He shuddered to think that this was the first thing Sangita's eyes fell on in the morning. Faizal stood a little taller, feeling superior somehow, with his clean-shaven face and his freshly laundered shirt. Rajesh was a bully, he told himself, but *he* was a man, dashing and stylish. And beyond all that, Sangita adored him. Sometimes.

"Who say I watching your wife, Raj?" Faizal asked.

Om shook his head as if to suggest Faizal should have run when he'd had the Chance. Faizal didn't care. He had spent years flirting with Sangita from the other side of the fence; years stealing glances in the market, and more recently, forbidden embraces under the most bizarre circumstances. It was a game. Their game. But lately Faizal found himself frustrated, restless with longing. He could not play at romance with Sangita for-ever. Perhaps this would mark the end of all that. Faizal thought about telling Rajesh how Sangita had left his kitchen breathless only days ago, how he had held her in his arms on Krishna Janamashtami while Rajesh whimpered over soucouy-ants and other simi-dimi foolishness along the side of the road. But Sangita would be livid, and worse, she would deny it. Faizal bit his tongue, feeling trapped.

Rajesh's laugh was bitter. "You like a fly, always buzzing around my wife." He spat in the grass. "What a woman like *she* go do with a man like *you*? Eh, Mr. Disco Dancer?" Rajesh flipped the collar on Faizal's orange shirt. "Go home and hug up your parrot!"

Faizal turned his collar back down and scowled. If there had been any fear, it was dissolved in his enmity now. "Rajesh, tell the boys you ain't really vexed about the game, nuh?" His lips curled cruelly. "Tell them how you frighten your wife go run away with me." Faizal could hear his heart thumping in his ears. This is how men must feel before they fight, he told himself. He clenched his hands and braced himself for the first blow.

Faizal felt a *whoosh* of air and it struck like thunder across his cheek. Then, the soft prickle of grass on his eyelids and in his nostrils. There was a moment of numbness, coppery blood on his tongue before the pain came. Faizal groaned, dragged breath back into his lungs as the pain ebbed to a persistent throb. He gathered himself and clambered back to his feet.

Om was yelling, but Faizal couldn't make out his words through the ringing in his ears. Faizal staggered and then lunged at Rajesh, noting with satisfaction the surprise on Rajesh's face before they both went down.

Chandani's Pone

Chandani knelt at her humble altar with her hands clasped, mumbling a mantra she'd learned as a girl. The mantra came out hurried, so she started again from the beginning, trying to take breaths at the end of each line. She did this nine times before it felt right, nine times, until her hands stopped shaking and her heart fell into its regular rhythm.

Chandani sat back on her heels and dropped her hands into her lap. The floorboards beneath her knees creaked. Her gaze flitted from the blazing diya sitting at Lakshmi Devi's feet to Vimla's closed bedroom door. Chandani hoped she hadn't woken Vimla. It was a silly fear, she knew. Vimla had slept through Om's snoring and the cocks' crowing for years. A creaky floorboard wouldn't disturb her now, not when she was fighting a fever hotter than Om's peppers. But Chandani worried about it anyway. She couldn't help herself. Her daughter had been bitten by a snake; what else was a mother to do?

Before she began her prayers, Chandani had deliberated over which of Bhagwan's incarnations she should appeal to. Lord Shiva had come to mind first. After all, unlike the other deities, who wore flowers around their necks, Lord Shiva's garland was a snake. Chandani had lit the diya in front of her picture of Lord Shiva and begun to pray. The prayers went well until she snuck a glimpse of the snake coiled around his neck. It seemed to glare back at her, a hint of wicked mocking in its eyes. Startled, Chandani slid the diya with her finger across the floor in front of Lakshmi Devi's picture, feeling safer under the soft gaze of the ever-smiling goddess. Now that she was finished, she hoped she had made the right decision.

Chandani rose from the altar, leaving the diya burning. She turned the handle to Vimla's door and pushed it open just wide enough for her to slip through. A splotch of grey and mauve drifted on the horizon, casting the room in early-morning shadows. The air was stale; the place felt muggy and smelled of suffering. Chandani tied the ends of both drapes into knots to allow more air to circulate through the room then sank into the worn chair by Vimla's bedside.

Vimla was lying on her back, the coverlet tangled in her limbs like she'd fought it through the night. Her bandaged ankle lay propped on a pillow, her other leg bent at a forty-five-degree angle. As always, Vimla's hair was a mess of waves. It splayed across the pillow and clung to the sides of her face, damp from a night of sweating. She moaned. Chandani froze, held her breath. Vimla flung her arm to the side, just missing Chandani's knee, and then settled into the mattress again. Exhaling,

Chandani reached over to brush the hair from her daughter's face, then stopped herself. She knew the next few days would be wretched for Vimla; better not to disturb her sleep, however fitful.

Chandani picked an old copybook off Vimla's desk and fanned herself. As the air blew across her sticky skin, she let last night's ruminations drag themselves to the forefront of her mind. After Vimla had fallen asleep, Chandani had spent the quiet hours considering the implications of the snake bite. Everyone would have a prediction after hearing of it, and nobody would be shy about sharing it. Chandani sighed, already wary of the expert analyses that would come her way. She only hoped the wedding would overshadow Vimla's incident. Certainly Faizal Mohammed had made it clear he thought Vimla was cursed; he prayed Allah would protect him from any residual misfortune he might experience through proximity alone. Chandani had wanted to stand on a footstool and slap him, but then, that would have been ungrateful, considering he'd taken Vimla to the hospital. She knew Faizal wouldn't be the only one in the district to think Vimla's encounter with the macajuel was portentous. Hadn't she lost her reputation and her teaching post in a day and a night? Vimla was like a star that kept falling. But Chandani clung— as any mother would—to the hope that Vimla's snake bite was some deranged signal from Lord Shiva that she was under his care, a suggestion maybe of a turning of events. Chandani nodded, as if to congratulate herself on the theory. She settled into her chair and shut her eyes, chanting the name of Lord Shiva under her breath until eventually her fanning slowed, her recitation trailed off and she was pulled into a deep sleep.

———

Two hours later Chandani rattled around in her kitchen, trying to expend some of her nervous energy. Vimla was awake now, but she was still weak with fever.

"Chand." Om lumbered through the door, setting a basket of bird peppers on the kitchen counter. "What you doing?"

Chandani hated being jerked from her thoughts. "Why I always have to be *doing* something?" she asked, removing the grater from the cupboard.

Om's eyebrows flew skyward. "You don't, but I can see that you doing something," he said, sitting down. "I only asking what it is." He shrugged and swatted at a fly buzzing around his head.

"Om, what I could possibly be doing in the kitchen?" She grasped the grater in one hand and a cassava in the other. "I partying!" she said, awkwardly twisting her narrow torso, a scowl on her lips.

Om made a face. "You need practice. You go can't dance at the wedding like *that*."

Chandani sucked her teeth. "It have any ripe pumpkin in the vine? Go and cut one for me, nuh? I making pone."

Om brightened. "Anything for you, my sweet sapodilla." He whistled as he lumbered out of the kitchen and around the back of the house. "Chand," he called to her through the open window. "How you think Vimla get bite by that snake?"

Chandani froze mid-grate with the cassava in her hand. She pursed her lips tightly over her answer.

Om appeared in the window, holding a pumpkin in the palm of one hand and his cutlass in the other. "Is strange for a macajuel to come into the open savannah grass, ain't?" He blinked at Chandani, waiting for her to agree.

Chandani grated faster, saying nothing.

Om shrugged. He spread a piece of newsprint on the ground and set the pumpkin down. Grunting as he squatted, Om raised the cutlass high. Chandani saw the blade flash in the sunlight and slice through the thick air. It struck the pumpkin with a crack and the gourd fell open and displayed its guts. "Chand, you want me grate this up outside?"

"Well, it wouldn't grate itself, Om." As soon as Chandani said it she was sorry; she didn't want him to come back in the kitchen and talk to her of Vimla. Chandani handed Om her grater through the window and turned her back on him to search for another.

"A plate, too," Om said.

"You think you marry a coolie labourer here? I busy. Come and get what you need."

"If that's the case, I could have just grate the pumpkin inside," he said.

Chandani bit back the sharp remark ready on her tongue and handed him a plate. She resumed her grating—head down.

"So, Chand, Faizal said he find Vimla in the savannah grass. He said the snake bite she as she was bringing home the bull and the cow."

Chandani ground the cassava, now small, against the grater until she nearly cut her finger. "But you know, I remember I bring the cow and the bull in before I leave yesterday," Om said.

Chandani realized she was groaning. She cleared her throat and tried for impassivity.

"And the bull and the cow was tie up exactly how I leave them. The rope was not loose and in a halfway knot how Vimla does tie it." Om looked up at Chandani now, having finished grating half the pumpkin. He passed the plate to her through the window, fanning it with his other hand to keep the flies off.

Chandani regarded him warily. "So what you saying, Om?" She turned her back, making ceremony out of placing the grated pumpkin on the countertop and covering it with a dishtowel. She knew what he was saying. It had taken him all this time to realize what she had gathered the moment she'd laid eyes on the scratches on Vimla's arms and face, on her soiled clothes and muddy slippers.

Om folded his arms over his chest and shrugged. "I think Vimla get bite by the macajuel in the cane. But what she gone there for?" He was talking to himself now, trying to unravel the mystery aloud.

Chandani rolled her eyes. She emptied the grated cassava and pumpkin into a mixing bowl.

Om popped his head through the window. "You want some coconut for that, Chand? Gloria Ramnath does make she pone with grate coconut and that thing does taste sweet and nice." He smacked his lips.

Chandani bristled. "Why you don't go and live by Gloria Ramnath and eat she coconut pone whole day and night?"

Om reached his hand through the window and grabbed his wife's chin playfully. "Don't jealous, Chand!" he said.

Chandani slapped his hand away and reached for the sugar.

The crash of glass against concrete distracted Om. "Blackie! Scratch!" he yelled, turning away from the window. Chandani was grateful when he took off after his dogs. She knew they had barrelled into his pepper sauce jars sitting in the sun again. "You mother's ass!" she heard Om holler, his slippers slapping across the ground. The dogs howled.

"Om!" she yelled. "Light the coals in the barrel for me, nuh!" She waited for him to grunt a response and then let her thoughts travel back to Vimla—they always came back to Vimla. Of course she hadn't been bitten when she was seeing about the cow and bull. There were so many gaping holes in that story even Om had figured that out.

Chandani added a lump of butter, evaporated milk, cinnamon and vanilla extract to the cassava and pumpkin. She folded them all together until they were a sweet mess.

There was only one explanation for Vimla sneaking through the cane field alone and it sent a muddle of pain and fury bubbling in Chandani's blood.

She tilted her mixing bowl over a baking pan and used the back of her spoon to evenly spread the batter.

Chandani had wanted to scream when she figured it out, to shake Vimla and demand why she would even attempt such a thing. But Vimla was barely lucid and Chandani found her rage quickly quelled by her daughter's suffering. This only added to Chandani's exasperation. She did not like having to control her anger. It meant that she had to go about her chores with all her curses and questions stuffed inside her soul. They couldn't stay there long. It was only a matter of time.

Chandani took her pan outside to the metal barrel. She used the dishtowel slung over her shoulder to remove the hot lid. A haze of heat and coal smoke rose up to greet her from the bottom. Chandani lowered the pan onto a rack balanced in the middle of the barrel on two pipes. Then she returned the cover and lit the coals on the bottom with the book of matches Om had left her on the ground. She stepped away from the barrel, feeling uncomfortable now that her hands were idle, and sighed.

As the pone baked, Chandani cast her gaze across Om's cane fields. The cane was tall, profuse with leaves. Someone who didn't know the land could easily get lost in the heart of it all. Someone who did know the land could use it to shroud all sorts of clandestine adventures from the rest of the world. Chandani looked farther, squinting against the sun. Om's last acre bordered Faizal Mohammed's land, and just at the edge of their plots, a private road opened up and led right out of the district. She was sure the macajuel had bitten Vimla somewhere there and that she had headed in the direction of home immediately after. That explained how Faizal had discovered her.

What Chandani couldn't fathom was why Vimla wanted to run away from home and where the ass she was planning to go.

Chalisa's Maticoor

Chalisa tiptoed outside, away from the bedee where the puja had taken place, leaving the smells of dahlias, incense and ghee behind. Nanny had told her to wait inside until they returned, but the house was stifling and lonesome without Avinash and Delores. She crept into the tent erected for her maticoor and took long, luxurious breaths. The tent trembled and snapped in the night air. She looked up and squinted at the dazzling lights one of Nanny's minions had wired throughout the tent. Enormous moths fluttered under the canopy, their gossamer wings like windows. The sheets spread across the floorboards lay askew now, upset by the shifting of bottoms and traffic of excited feet as they'd hurried away. It occurred to her that she would never be alone again before the wedding. Now was the time to run.

She snorted, not unlike Nanny, looking beyond the tent.

The men hadn't gone to the river with the women. They had slipped into the darkness, chatting idly with one another on the driveway and along the periphery of Nanny's lime trees. Surely they would see Chalisa in her saffron sari tiptoeing through the shadows. And even if by some miracle they missed her, where would she go? Chalisa thought of Gavin. Had he heard that she would be married in just two days? Would he watch her on *Mastana Bahar* tonight and remember that her dream had cost him his job?

Her heart spasmed. *Mastana Bahar*. She turned the talent show's name over and over in her mind like the name of a lost lover. Something had happened to her the day of the auditions. She had come alive, felt an energy raw and pure surge through her as she burst into song for the judges. It had been more than just adrenaline. It had been an awakening, a knowing that she had found her place in the world. A feeling that she belonged somewhere. Nanny couldn't fathom how song and dance breathed life into that part of her that had perished with her parents. If she did, maybe she wouldn't have ripped Chalisa's dreams from her grasp the way she had.

Nanny's punishment was an emotional flogging to her spirit. A knot formed in Chalisa's stomach as she thought of people across the island who would watch her perform on *Mastana Bahar* while she sat captive on Nanny's estate. To deny her the joy of seeing herself on television then to usher her into a marriage with a pundit's son from the country was beyond callous. Chalisa willed breath into her lungs, brushing away an angry tear trapped in her lower lashes. She would not let Nanny wring more from her than she already had. She raised her chin and played the brave heroine, however fragile she felt inside.

Tonight Chalisa was dressed in the simplest sari from the collection Nanny had brought. Her hair was pulled into a bun stabbed with too many pins. Delores had draped the sari's dupatha over her hair so that even the tiny kiss curls Chalisa had fashioned at her temples were hidden. Her wrists were bare of her favourite ruby bangles, her face scrubbed clean of kajal and blush. Nothing about Chalisa sparkled tonight; she was dismal from the inside out.

The drumming of the tassa group rolled in the distance. Despite her bitterness, Chalisa's eyes lit up. The women were returning in a procession, having made homage to the earth for her fertility. They would spill into the tent dancing now, just for tonight losing themselves in a ritual that belonged solely to women. Chalisa crushed her right foot with her left to stop it from tapping, remembering Nanny's warning. She rubbed her knuckles together, wrung her hands, fiddled with her dupatha, bit her nail. Anything to suppress her innate desire to move with the drums. The tassa grew faster, louder, as it neared the house. Chalisa squinted into the darkness that wrapped around the tent. No one was watching. She chewed her lip, jiggled her knees up and down, buried her head momentarily in her lap. The drumming stopped and she held her breath waiting for it to break into a livelier beat. When it did, desire triumphed over duty and Chalisa succumbed to the pulse.

The tassa pulsed through her body and pulled her off the *peerha*. Blood rushed through her numb legs. She hiked up her sari, discarding the manners of a demure bride, and dashed to the edge of the tent where the drumming was the loudest. Her heart pounded and she smiled knowing this was bold and reckless and all wrong. In an instant, her wrists twirled and her hips swayed. She was a starlet enraptured by her stolen freedom.

Somewhere a woman whooped and another cackled.

The tassa grew rowdier, the bass more insistent.

Chalisa pulled her dupatha free of her hair and spun so that it caught an air current and ballooned around her. She fancied herself the sun ablaze in a night sky, singular in her beauty.

The drumming reverberated off the walls of the house. Chalisa forced herself to stop twirling, but the tent did not. It orbited around her, lights flashing in all directions as she wove back to the peerha. By the time she'd pinned her dupatha in place and assembled her sari pleats over her toes again, the women came barrelling into the yard cheering and laughing, their hands spiralling overhead. Chalisa peeked at their antics from beneath her lashes and caught Nanny eyeing her flushed cheeks with suspicion.

The women had grown boisterous since Pundit Panday had packed up his puja things and gone. Now they were eager for a long night of song and ceremony. Chalisa's wedding celebrations were officially underway; it was a shame she would be only a spectator to all the exciting parts.

The tassa group was made up of four men with heavy drums hanging like yokes from their necks, a young boy with cymbals. The five stood in a circle, playing their instruments with impassive faces. Sweat dribbled down their temples as they shifted their weight into one foot and then the other. They switched the rhythm of their drumming in perfect unison without so much as a nod from the leader to indicate the change. In this way, they set the pace of the women's hips and were an integral component to Chalisa's maticoor night.

Chalisa looked on with envy as the women made their way back into the tent. Some were as old as Nanny. They did the typical grandmother dance: bobbing on their toes and clapping. The other women were the age Chalisa's mother would have been had she lived to see this day. There was mischief in their movements, which were at times deliciously obscene as they illustrated Chalisa's carnal duties after marriage. Then there were the young girls who giggled at their mothers behind their hands and twirled in their dresses until they grew dizzy and fell to the tent floor. Chalisa spotted Avinash in the mix. He was jumping up and down like a monkey, having lost his seriousness in the revelry, too. She smiled fondly at him and he waved at her.

A circle formed around Nanny for the finale. She put one hand in the air and one hand on her hip and began to wine like a woman whose bones didn't ache for Bengay at night. A cheer went up and dissolved into laughter. The drumming stopped and Nanny bowed. Chalisa darkened at the injustice.

The tassa players wiped their sweat with the backs of their hands and retreated into the darkness. Chalisa knew they would find the husbands and fathers of these women and share a shot or two of rum to end the night. How easy to be a man, she mused, shifting on her seat again.

The women greeted Chalisa with smiles before they arranged themselves on the tent floor in a circle. Nanny brought Auntie Dotty a dholak and Auntie Kamala an empty bottle with two spoons. That's when Auntie Ahaliya, Nanny's closest friend, began to sing. She had the voice of an old soul and she crooned wedding songs their ancestors had stowed away in their hearts on journeys here from India. Nanny's eyes grew misty and Chalisa dropped her gaze. What was Nanny remembering? Her son's marriage, her own?

Fortunately Chalisa's attention was stolen by some new activity. Delores was gathering five young girls around Chalisa and giving them instruction on the next ritual. The girls were to pinch rice grains and doop grass in their little hands and touch Chalisa at her toes, knees and shoulders before sweeping the materials over her head and then dropping them at her feet again. Each girl did this five times and then dipped her fingers into a bowl of *haldi* and smeared it on Chalisa's face and arms. Chalisa scrunched her face up the first time, startled by how cold the yellow paste was.

Delores tutted. "Chalisa! Sit still. This go make your skin glow Sunday. You go be the prettiest bride in Trinidad." She smudged a dot of haldi onto Chalisa's cheek and kissed her forhead.

Chalisa looked doubtful. "What this paste make with?"

Delores steered the next girl in line toward Chalisa, who flashed Chalisa a toothy grin before she began. "Coconut oil and turmeric." Delores nodded her approval as the girl completed her task without error. "The coconut oil go make your skin smooth and soft. The turmeric go make it glow."

"True?" Chalisa eyed the bowl of haldi, wondering why she hadn't been introduced to this beauty aid before.

Delores straightened Chalisa's crooked dupatha. "You go look like a real goddess at Krishna's side, Chalisa," she murmured, letting her fingers trail over the soft material and then fall into her lap.

Chalisa's heart sank at the sound of his name. Somewhere in Chance, Krishna was being coated in haldi, too. She wondered fleetingly if, unlike her, he had friends to bolster his spirits tonight.

Nanny joined them, her knees cracking as she crouched at Chalisa's feet. "Ah. This haldi." She picked up the bowl with the remaining mixture. "I does use it every night on my skin and see how smooth my face looking!" Nanny grinned at the little girls and the wrinkles in her face quadrupled. She scraped the rest of the haldi into her palm. "Come, my pretty little Miss Mastana Bahar!" Nanny said, coating every inch of Chalisa's exposed skin with it. She massaged it gently on her face and vigorously on her arms and feet, dropping globs on Chalisa's sari as she worked.

Chalisa's mouth fell open.

"No, no, Chalisa." Nanny wagged her finger at her granddaughter. "This is not to eat."

The little girls erupted into giggles, hopping up and down and asking for another turn.

The mood of the singing was changing. Chalisa peeked around the girls, who had closed in around her to witness Nanny's shenanigans. Auntie Ahaliya was singing something more uptempo. Auntie Dotty had her eyes closed and her lips puckered as she beat the dholak with surprising rhythm. Auntie Kamala had given a spoon to her neighbour and they each tapped one side of the bottle. The other women beat time on their knees and swayed so that their shoulders touched and fell away from one another's. Although the Bhojpuri was lost on Chalisa, she could almost read the meaning on Auntie Ahaliya's face. A blush spread across her cheeks and Chalisa was grateful the haldi masked her embarrassment.

Nanny wiped her hands on a towel and piloted Delores into the circle. Delores tried to wiggle out of Nanny's bony grip, but the ladies clapped, encouraging her to dance, and she was caught. For a moment Delores stood still, but when Avinash tapped her from behind and broke into a comical gyration of his little hips, she shuffled her feet to the beat, too.

Chalisa laughed and the drying haldi cracked around her mouth. For the first time since the women had returned, she stopped hoping the tent would come tumbling down on them all. She would miss Avinash when she was married.

Krishna's Maticoor

"The only man missing here tonight is Gloria Ramnath!" Puncheon observed, swivelling in his stool so he could survey the rum shop.

A placid smile stretched slow and deliberate across Lal's face. Word had spread about his black-and-white television. Now people were showing up in droves to follow the adventures of Ben Cartwright and his sons over a flash of rum and a plate of cutters. Om was glad for all the activity. It helped take his mind off Vimla and Chandani.

"It have more people here tonight than last Friday," Lal said to himself. He was watching, amused, as Bulldog stole curious glances at *Teen Dance Party* and shuffled a deck of cards.

Om withdrew the Broadway tucked behind his ear. "Is Krishna's maticoor night," he said. Rajesh scratched a match against its book and Om leaned into the flame with the cigarette between his lips now. He took a luxurious puff and exhaled through his nostrils. "All the ladies gone to the wedding house, so all the men break away tonight."

All the women except Chandani, that is, Om thought. She had stayed behind to look after Vimla, scowling after Sangita as she flounced by the gates on her way to the Govinds'. Poor Chandani. Vimla's accident had shaken her. When he left for Lal's, she had been polishing Vimla's photographs with a cloth, round and round across her face as if she could clean the smut from Vimla's dubious reputation. Om wondered if Chandani suspected Vimla had been in the cane when she was bitten, as he did. Chandani hadn't agreed with his theory, but neither had she disagreed. Instead, she'd kept her head down and grated the cassava furiously, as if everything depended on the perfection of her pone.

Rajesh sipped his White Oak. "It have people here I never see in the rum shop before. Lal—" Rajesh tipped his chin at a man with a string of beads around his neck and a shock of white hair down his centre part. The man was staring, glassy eyed, at the flaking blue paint. "You know he?"

Lal studied Rajesh for a moment. He opened his mouth to answer and then closed it again.

Rajesh arched an eyebrow. "Eh. Like you have friends too good for we, or what?" He sipped his drink and observed the man, intrigued now more than ever.

Puncheon slapped Rajesh on the back. "Who is 'we'? You have mice in your pocket?" He pulled his sagging shorts up and pushed his shoulders back. "I know that man."

Rajesh dismissed the claim with a wave of his hand, sending ribbons of smoke curling into Puncheon's face. "Puncheon, you ain't know anybody I ain't know." He tapped the ash from his cigarette into an ashtray.

Puncheon coughed and blinked his smarting eyes, flapping the smoke away with his hands. When he recovered, he tucked his T-shirt into his shorts, smoothed his salt-and-pepper hair down and swaggered toward the stranger. Puncheon touched the stranger's shoulder and the distant look in the man's eyes dissolved into warmth. Puncheon pumped the stranger's hand with too much vigour. He smiled wider than usual. He tilted his head back and held his belly when he laughed. He made sweeping gestures with his hands. He nodded and widened his eyes when it was the stranger's turn to talk. Then, when Puncheon had put on a grand enough show for his audience, he clasped the stranger in an embrace, throwing Rajesh a smug smile before he let go and swaggered back to the bar.

Rajesh grunted his annoyance. "Okay, so what your partner's name, Puncheon? I never see he in the district before."

Lal's teenaged son, pimple-faced and frantic, dragged Lal away to adjust the television antennas.

Puncheon leaned against the bar. "Everything have a price," he said. "The name of that fella go cost you a flash of rum."

Rajesh scowled. "Everything have a price, but I never see you pay for a damn thing, Puncheon."

Puncheon shrugged and hopped back onto his stool. He strummed his fingers on the bar and pretended to whistle along with the *Teen Dance Party* music, but he didn't know the tune and it was obvious.

"No matter. I go ask Lal," Rajesh said, shrugging. He crushed his cigarette into the ashtray.

Puncheon nodded to Lal, who was holding the antennas in

place so his patrons could watch the rest of the program. "You go have to wait, then," Puncheon said with a grin.

Rajesh sucked his teeth. He motioned Lal's son over. "Bring a nip of White Oak for this t'ief, Shiv."

Puncheon whooped. He wrapped his hands protectively around the bottle when it came and leaned in toward Om and Rajesh. "He name Ramdeo. He is a seer man from Jaipur Village."

Rajesh's eyes bulged and his glass stopped midway to his lips. "What a seer man doing here?" He shifted on his seat and peeped around Om's bulk at the man.

Om clinked the cubes in his empty glass, trying to suppress his laughter. He remembered the night Rajesh's terrible apparitions had pursued him down Kiskadee Trace. Rajesh had whimpered like a child all the way home and vowed never to touch bhang again. The only thing Rajesh feared was magic and the men and women who made it.

Puncheon poured himself a generous drink, ignoring Om's and Rajesh's empty glasses. "Don't worry, nuh, man!" he said. "Ramdeo is a good fella. A healer. He does give me hangover herbs once a month."

Rajesh reached, wary-eyed, for Puncheon's flash of White Oak.

"What the hell is 'hangover herbs,' man?" Om asked. He was enjoying watching Puncheon exasperate Rajesh this way.

"If I knew, I would mix them myself."

Rajesh, Puncheon and Om finished a bottle and a half of White Oak among them and joined the crowd gathering around Lal's television. Everything felt liquid to Om now. He braced himself on Rajesh's shoulder and slid into a chair. "What you said is the name of this show?"

Nobody answered. The screen crackled and went blank and there was a moment of quiet before the room erupted into groans. Lal swung the antennas to the right and the screen came alive again. The men rejoiced and leaned in a little closer, arms resting on neighbours' shoulders, chins propped in hands. "Don't move, Lall-y!" someone called out.

"I love you, Lall-y," Puncheon slurred. He was lying face down at a nearby table. When he hiccuped, his frame convulsed like a dying bird. Om reached to pat his back, but the table was too far and his hand fell to his side.

"Anyone can take Punch home?" Lal asked.

Silence. Everyone was watching with anticipation as the first contestant made his way onto the *Mastana Bahar* stage. He was a short man named Rasheed, with a moustache that curled at the ends. He sang "Aur Nahin Bas Aur Nahin," but he arched his eyebrows and stood on his tiptoes every time he reached for a high note. It made his performance comical when it wasn't meant to be. Lal's patrons snickered through Rasheed's performance and heckled him as he walked off the stage. Someone mimicked his singing with exaggerated eyebrow movements and the men exploded into laughter again. Om thought he sounded like Scratch and Blackie when they howled. When the next contestant walked onto the stage, someone had to stop Om's mirth with a slap to the back.

Om quieted down, but his thoughts drifted from the television to Vimla. She would like this *Mastana Bahar* show. He wondered if she knew of it. They had no radio at home, and when was the last time Vimla had left the house? Om hiccuped. Except to go to the cane field, a voice reminded him. He wondered not for the first time what Vimla had been doing in the cane when she was bitten by the snake. It dawned on him now that he had never asked. Om hiccuped again. Yes, he would just ask Vimla. She would tell him. And then he felt the hurt he'd buried surge to the surface. He remembered Krishna, and hiccuped. Or maybe she wouldn't tell him after all.

Rajesh was shaking his arm. "Om! Om!"

Om turned his head slowly to face Rajesh; a blur of lights followed. A strange silence loomed in the rum shop. Om wondered if he'd said anything aloud. "What happened? Punch vomit?"

Rajesh looked horrified. "Oh Lawd, Om, watch the television, nuh, man!"

The television came slowly into focus. Om squinted at the screen and made out a young woman standing in the centre of the stage, regaling Trinidad in the sweetest voice. The camera zoomed in on her face and the men in the rum shop found themselves staring into a pair of sultry eyes, made up with thick sweeps of kajal. Her fanned eyelashes lowered like a veil and then lifted again slowly. Someone whistled. A smile crept across her full mouth as if in response. Dimples appeared then vanished. She rocked her waist and beat time on her thigh as she sang.

Somebody in the room sighed longingly. Om hoped it wasn't him.

When the woman's song came to an end, she half bowed, her eyes locked on the camera.

"Thank you, Miss Chalisa Shankar!" the host said.

The woman looked over her shoulder and winked.

Rajesh's eyes bulged in his square face.

Lal released the antennas as if he'd been burned. The screen scrambled again. Nobody protested.

Puncheon clapped. "She better than Rasheed," he said.

Rajesh stood up, wiping his hand over his face. "Allyuh fellas know who is that girl? Puncheon, you know who you clapping for?"

Puncheon mumbled something and laid his head back down.

"Chalisa Shankar," someone said.

Rajesh nodded. "Krishna's bride."

Om stood, fell back in his chair and stood again. "You think Pundit Anand know he future daughter-in-law do *that* on *Mastana Bahar*?" He couldn't help himself grinning.

Rajesh shook his head. "Not a damn chance, Boss."

Carrying News

"**M**other of mangoes!" Faizal yelped. He bounded down the stairs two at a time. He had to tell Sangita what he had seen. Adrenaline pumped through his veins and his heart hammered against his ribs. News did this to him, made him giddy with excitement, made him forget the danger.

Sam screeched to be included in the fuss, but Faizal ignored him, leaving him to watch the rest of *Mastana Bahar* alone. He switched the lights on downstairs and peered over at the Gopalsinghs' home. Darkness. That rum sucker Rajesh was definitely at Lal's tonight. He touched the bruise on his cheek and cursed; it was still tender. Sangita was at Krishna's maticoor, he realized. Faizal clasped his hands behind his back and paced back and forth next to the fence, thinking.

He couldn't show up at Pundit Anand's home on Krishna's maticoor night to speak to Sangita. So few men would be there as it was, and it would seem odd for Faizal Mohammed of all people to attend. Not only that, if Faizal sought Sangita out of the crowd of women and whispered in her ear what he'd seen, well, that would look suspicious. Speaking to Sangita had grown more challenging since his scuffle with Rajesh. People were always watching. Faizal sighed. He missed her sandalwood scent, but the last thing he needed was Rajesh Gopalsingh charging into his home wielding a cutlass in his face. Isn't that what he had threatened to do if he ever found Faizal too close to Sangita again? Faizal winced. He was too handsome to be marred by a brute like Rajesh.

Faizal heard muttering. He turned toward the Narine home and cocked his head like Sam. It was Chandani. He knew by the clipped words. Faizal crossed his courtyard in seven steps and climbed onto one of his empty Coca-Cola crates. He peered over the fence, the puff of his hair and his eyes barely visible in the night.

"How it taste, Roopy?" Chandani was saying, probing Headmaster Roop G. Kapil with her severe gaze.

Faizal gasped and then ducked, covering his mouth with his hands. What was Headmaster doing at the Narines' at this hour? He straightened again slowly when Headmaster responded.

"Yes, yes. Good. Sweet." Headmaster chewed, crossing and uncrossing his legs, averting his gaze from Chandani's. "Coconut, right?"

Chandani pursed her lips and tucked a strand of limp hair behind her ear. "Roopy, thank you for visiting Vimla." She sat in a chair, her back erect, fingers knotted in her lap.

Headmaster pushed his glasses up on his nose and looked around the place, wary of the dogs, which lay on their bellies, watching him. "Well, thanks for inviting me to come and see she."

Faizal nearly stumbled off the crate. Chandani *invited* Headmaster to her house when Om was out? At this hour? With pone? This was not the prudish Chandani he so detested. A smile sprang to his lips. What an eventful night this was turning out to be.

Chandani wrung her hands. Once. Twice. Then she stopped and took a breath, plucking courage from somewhere deep. "Roopy, Vimla has had some bad luck." She smoothed an invisible wrinkle on her skirt.

Headmaster nodded.

Bad luck? Faizal thought. Vimla was too slack. That was the problem.

"I hear you ain't fill the teaching position at Saraswati Hindu School as yet," Chandani went on.

A heavy silence hung between them. Headmaster looked unsure if he should continue eating or not. Chandani seemed to be waiting for him to say something. "Consider Vimla again, nuh, Roopy? You know she bright," Chandani finally said.

Faizal's mouth fell open. He had never heard Chandani cajole anyone before.

Headmaster put the piece of pone travelling to his mouth back on the plate. "Yes. Bright. My best student. Most promising. But, Chand, as you know, Pundit Anand busy these days." He gestured to the darkness, where the tassa was rolling. "I cannot make that decision on my own."

Chandani tried to soften the line of her mouth into an understanding smile. The effect was unfortunate, ugly even.

Faizal flinched behind the fence. "Well, Roop, I asking you as a old friend to consider Vimla again."

Old friend? Faizal wiggled his toes. He was near bursting with interest now.

"We both know," Chandani continued, the edge creeping back into her voice, "that Pundit Anand already forget Vimla's . . . error. He done move on! Krishna done move on!" The tassa from the wedding house seemed to grow louder, emphasizing her point.

Headmaster rose now and set the plate on the chair. He took Chandani's hand clumsily, wetting his lips. Faizal thought he might kiss her hand, but then Headmaster said, "I go talk to Pundit Anand, Chand. I go try my best for you." He cleared his throat. "Vimla."

Faizal watched, amazed, as the stiffness melted from Chandani's shoulders and she almost smiled. "Thanks." She withdrew her hand from his like she'd been burned. Headmaster stepped away, embarrassed, and hooked his fingers behind his back. The dogs sat up and took notice at the shift between them.

"Okay, then," he said, backing away. "Thanks for the pone. It was moist and nice." He was trying to fill the silence between them as Chandani walked him to the gate. "You grate the coconut so fine I almost ain't know it was there self. Delicious. Perfect."

Chandani opened the gate. "Good night, Headmaster Roop G. Kapil," she said, formal and crisp all over again.

Faizal shook his head from behind the fence. He would never understand that woman. She disappeared into the kitchen, and he stepped off the crate feeling giddy over the turn of events.

Sam squawked from upstairs.

Sangita. He needed to talk to Sangita. He wondered if she would be pleasantly scandalized by what he'd seen on television tonight, or if she would be outraged that the Govinds were giving their good name to a flirtatious songstress. Faizal laughed. Haughty, too, but she hadn't shown that face to the camera.

And what about Chandani, begging Headmaster for Vimla's teaching position? What would Sangita think of that? He knew, deep down, Sangita wanted that job to fall into Minty's hands. She hadn't said as much, but nobody read her body language or the messages tucked behind her words the way Faizal Mohammed did.

Faizal slipped out of his front gate and disappeared into the darkness. He didn't know how he would speak to Sangita once he got there, but he knew he had to go to the Govinds'. He couldn't sleep with his brain swimming with all he'd witnessed tonight and Sangita would be vexed with him if she knew he'd kept it all from her. He smiled, remembering the hungry way she'd eyed him in his rear-view mirror on the way home from San Fernando General. As he neared the Govind residence, Faizal played her possible reactions over in his mind like a film.

Rajesh and Om stood outside the Govind gates, making small talk with the Hibiscus Tassa Group when Faizal arrived. "Hello. Good night." Faizal was curt but not impolite. What were they doing here? He shuffled his feet, wondering if he should make some excuse and return home.

"Hello. Good night, Faizal," Om said. He grinned like a child.

Rajesh regarded Faizal warily. He muttered a greeting that was lost in a half-grunt. "Where you coming from?"

The question sounded more like an accusation. Mind your damn business, Faizal thought. He pushed his irritation aside and tried to look natural. "Home. Going for a stroll," he said.

One of the tassa men pulled his drum strap over his head and lowered the drum to the ground. "So late?" He threw Faizal a knowing smile. "Strolling home from some woman's bed is more like it." He fished a pack of Broadways from his pocket. "Any allyuh have a light?"

Faizal gave the customary chuckle, all the while wondering how he would see Sangita now with her big lout of a husband lingering outside the gates. Rajesh tossed his matchbook to the man. The members of the Hibiscus Tassa Group each slid a cigarette from the pack and leaned one by one into the flame held by the leader. Faizal watched their faces illuminate and fall dark again.

"Faizal, you miss a good show tonight, boy," Om said, folding his arms across his chest and swaying.

Rajesh sighed and rubbed his head, looking to the Govind home behind the gates with dismay. His body leaned toward the home, as if he would swing the gates open and walk through, but his feet stayed planted where they were.

Faizal lowered his voice. "*Mastana Bahar*?" He saw the surprise on Rajesh's face and was pleased. This was as good a time as any to let them know that Lal wasn't the only man in the district with a television. "I was watching it home." He made his face grim and shook his head, enjoying Rajesh's irritation. "I wonder how Pundit Anand go react to the news."

"I ain't know, but I go have to tell him," Rajesh said flatly.

The Hibiscus Tassa Group puffed silently by the ixora bush, the orange embers of their cigarettes the only indication that they were there.

"Now?" Faizal heard the urgency in his voice.

Rajesh shrugged. "When then? Next year? The wedding Sunday, Faizal." Faizal resented the condescension in Rajesh's tone. He was glad Rajesh felt burdened by the responsibility of telling Pundit Anand that he had been made a fool by the Shankars. He wished it would kill Rajesh dead.

"So what? You think Pundit Anand go cancel the wedding?" Om asked, rocking on his heels now.

A tassa player choked on his inhale. "The wedding *cancel?*" He coughed. "Then Pundit Anand better pay we tonight self."

"No. No." Rajesh sucked his teeth. "The wedding ain't cancel." He glared at Om, who glared back just for the sake of it.

Chatter circled from around the house and drifted to the front gates. A group of ladies filed toward them. "Everything wrap up now," a tassa man said.

Rajesh opened the gates for the women. He nodded and smiled something terse. "Hello. Good night."

"Sangita, look—your husband come to escort you home!" Leela announced to the trail of ladies. "Where Sangita gone now, Glory?"

Sangita appeared at the gates, anklets and bangles tinkling. "Rajesh?" She took his arm. "What happened?"

Faizal's heart burned with envy. He craved that simple intimacy.

Rajesh clenched his jaw. "Nothing, nothing. I have to talk to Pundit Anand."

The ladies paraded past them in twos and threes, waving goodbye. As they set out down the main road, Faizal heard someone say: "Glory, you don't have shame? The pundit was watching how you roll your bamsee up to the tassa tonight." Laughter ensued. Someone else said, "Allyuh notice how Krishna swell up he mouth whole night? Is like he ain't want to marry." And then: "Allyuh hush, nuh? You want Pundit Anand to hear we?"

Their voices grew smaller and smaller until they were swallowed by the cicadas and were gone. That's when Sangita noticed Faizal. "Liming in the rum shop with these boys tonight?" she asked, inclining her head toward Rajesh and Om. Her tone was indifferent, but he caught the fire in her eyes and could almost feel the heat of her curiosity emanating from her core.

Rajesh didn't wait for Faizal to answer. His voice was gruff. "Where Pundit Anand, Sangita? I need to talk to he." He pushed past her, leaving Om, Sangita and Faizal staring after him.

Sangita's eyes widened. "Oh gosh! Raj look vexed." She fidgeted with her braid. "What happened?" Her magnetic gaze flicked to Om. "Please, Om, go with Raj. Don't let him embarrass me here tonight! How much he drink?" She touched Om's arm with her fingertips and Faizal could almost see the jolt of energy crackle through him.

Om stumbled through the gates after Rajesh, calling to his friend as he weaved a crooked path across the Govinds' front yard.

Faizal wanted to gather Sangita up in his arms. Clever and beautiful. She made his blood rush. There was no time for that, though, and the Hibiscus Tassa group was still lingering by the gates, pretending not to listen but listening all the same.

"What going on Faizal?" Sangita whispered, clipping her lower lip between her teeth.

Faizal pulled his eyes away from her mouth. "All of Trinidad and Tobago see Chalisa Shankar perform on *Mastana Bahar* tonight."

Sangita looked let down. She dropped her braid, a fast pout settling on her mouth. He wanted to devour that mouth. "I hear she does sing sweet bhajans. She Nanny tell Maya so," Sangita said.

"Bhajans?" Faizal gripped her elbow and pulled her an inch closer. "Sangita, that girl ain't sing anything for God's ears."

Her eyes widened and glowed like Flambeaux's.

"And never mind that—she can well work up she waist, too," Faizal hissed.

Sangita gasped and exhaled. Her breath smelled of kurma. Sugary sweet.

"And Chandani—"

A yell fractured their exchange. Sangita jumped back. A startled tassa man cursed, his cigarette falling and creating diminutive orange fireworks at their feet.

"Who yelling so, Faizal?" Sangita asked. She shrank against the bush close to the tassa group and peered at the house from her cover.

"Pundit Anand for sure."

Suddenly Om and Rajesh were walking back toward them. They hurried like chastised children who had just narrowly avoided licks. Pundit Anand gazed down on them from his veranda, his expression cloaked in darkness.

Vimla's Recovery

The snake coils on a rock. Vimla knows it is dangerous, but she draws near anyway. There is something about it, the way its rainbow scales glisten under the noon-hour sun like it has polished itself for her. There are bangles around its body, bands of gold with gems that flash white in the sunlight. She reaches out to touch one and the snake springs up, its bangles clinking against one another. Vimla jumps back, her scream trapped in her throat. The snake hisses and fans its hood, displaying an intricate mehndi pattern. Vimla freezes in its icy gaze. The snake lunges at her heart—

"Vimla!" Chandani shook her. "Wake up, nuh, gyul."

Vimla's thrashing grew wilder under Chandani's grip. The back of her hand cracked against her mother's nose as she tried to wrench the snake free from her heart.

"Vim-*la!*"

Vimla felt someone pin her against the softening earth. She screamed herself into wakefulness and found Chandani straddling her, the palms of her hands pressing into Vimla's shoulders.

"Ma?"

Tendrils of hair had come loose from Chandani's bun. They fell in corkscrew curls about her sweaty face. She was panting. Blood dribbled from her right nostril. "Vimla. What the hell is wrong with you?" She climbed off her daughter, embarrassed, pulling out the handkerchief tucked in her bra strap to dab away the blood. "You nearly kill me." Chandani released her slack bun, combed her hair through with her fingers and twisted it into a knot so tight her eyes lifted at the corners. "You know how long I trying to wake you?" She stabbed the knot with two pins and patted it twice with her fingers.

"Sorry," Vimla mumbled, squirming into a seated position. She let her head fall back against the wall and her lids drop over her eyes. What day was it? Was he married now?

Chandani sighed and touched her cheek. "Fever." The bed creaked as Chandani shifted her weight. "How your foot feeling?"

"Fine." Vimla watched kaleidoscopic light dance behind her eyelids. "But I feeling weak and my head hurting." *And my heart.* It seemed like an eternity since she'd been any place besides this bedroom. No matter how wide her mother opened the window, how often she knotted the drapes or swept them onto the chair, there was never enough air in the room. She longed to run, feel the wind playing in her hair. She missed sunlight on her skin. Vimla wanted freedom. And Krishna.

Chandani folded the coverlet over Vimla's lap. "Your foot looking better," she said, gathering Vimla's hair to one side. "I wonder when this fever go break."

Even through the fog, Vimla detected the undercurrent of concern in her mother's admonishment. She thought about smiling to show she was all right, but she didn't because she wasn't.

Chandani reached for the Limacol sitting on Vimla's desk. She tipped the yellow liquid directly onto Vimla's scalp and knelt on the bed so that she could apply pressure with her hands. As Chandani massaged the lemony liquid into Vimla's hair, coolness spread through Vimla and she felt the throbbing in her head ebb. She sighed a thank-you. Tears blurred the lights behind her eyelids.

"Vimla, how your hair get so scanty?" Chandani's fingers threaded through Vimla's damp waves.

Her hair had been the first part of her to come undone when Krishna left Trinidad. It tangled itself in her comb, remained on her pillow when she woke in the morning. The strands fell away with her faith, but lingered on her clothes and gathered in the corners of her room to remind her of her many losses, her inferior beauty since Chalisa Shankar came into her life.

Vimla shrugged a response. The room was quiet but for the creak of bedsprings beneath Chandani's knees and the squelchy sound of her palms suctioning Vimla's scalp. Vimla knew Chandani's lips were pursed against an inventory of her faults that had caused her hair to shed. In that moment, she was grateful for the exhaustion that sealed her eyes shut.

"Dr. Mohan coming this afternoon," Chandani finally said,

her hands falling away from Vimla's hair. "Maybe he go give we something to break this fever."

Vimla managed a nod. She wondered how much her father would have to pay Dr. Mohan to come to the house. Most people did without doctors if they could, relying on concoctions mixed with ingredients from the earth. When Vimla thought of doctors, she thought mostly of babies coming into the world or elders exiting it. Was she one of the unfortunate few in between? Maybe she was sicker than she thought.

"Minty coming to visit, too." Chandani stood up, screwing the blue cap back on the Limacol bottle.

Vimla's eyes opened halfway. "When?"

Chandani faltered and then shrouded her hurt in a scowl. "Soon," she said, closing the bedroom door behind her. As she stomped down the stairs louder than should be possible for such a tiny woman, Vimla heard her say, "No matter what you do for your children, they does always cuff you in your nose in the end. Humph! One of these days, I go strike again—I go really strike again!" Vimla heard her scrape the coconut broom across the concrete. "And look at this jackass here, lying like lead in the hammock. Om!" she hollered. "Don't go by Lal's next time, boy. Stay home and I go bathe you in rum. You go like that, ain't?"

Vimla rolled onto her side so that she could see out the window. The last time she'd spoken to Minty alone was just before she'd ducked into her father's cane to meet Krishna. Minty had dropped Faizal Mohammed's watch into her palm and closed her fingers over it. "So you know when he coming," she'd said.

He never came. A familiar wave of grief rose in Vimla's stomach, but this time it broke into a hundred furious wavelets.

Vimla darkened now when she remembered how she'd languished in the humidity, waiting for Krishna to follow through on his own design. She had gambled a great deal to meet him. She always had. Now, as she lay limp with fever, her snake-bitten ankle still propped on pillows, Vimla realized what her daring had cost her. Again. Suddenly it felt like Krishna always slipped free and she was left behind to detangle herself from the shame of her blunders. She had a dozen questions for him and it vexed her to know she would never have the opportunity to ask them now.

The door whined open. Vimla turned her head as Minty crept gingerly over the floorboards. "I waking, Mints," Vimla said.

Minty looked up and brightened. She flung her arms around Vimla's neck and squeezed too hard. "You bathe in Limacol today?" she asked, pulling away, her nose crinkling.

"My head hurting me steady, Mints. Limacol the only thing that works." Vimla curled into a ball, watching her friend.

Minty frowned and flopped into Vimla's desk chair. "Vims, my mother here, too. We go have to talk fast."

Vimla rolled her eyes. Of course Sangita was here. How else would the status of Vimla's snake bite reach the village? "Quickly, then," she said.

Minty nodded. She didn't need prompting. "He sorry, Vims."

Vimla wasn't sure how she had expected the conversation to begin, but it wasn't like this. She had just finished stoking her ire. She wasn't ready for Minty to douse it with news of Krishna's regret. "He say so?" she asked, despite herself.

Minty nodded. "Up, Vimla. Let we exercise while we talk."

Vimla groaned, but Minty threw off the coverlet and

draped Vimla's arm over her shoulder. There was no sense arguing—there was no time anyway. "Yeah, he was upset at he maticoor. I think is guilt had him so, Vimi. He tell me he feel real bad he couldn't reach you in the cane."

Vimla dropped her good foot over the side of the bed and lowered the other with care until her toes just touched the floorboards. "So what happen? He know how long I wait for he? He hear about the snake?" Her voice rose with each question. She was riling herself up again and she was glad. Better anger than grief.

Minty wrapped her arm around Vimla's waist, pinching her flesh through her shirt. "Shh! The window open, Vimla." She hoisted Vimla to a standing position. "Shift your weight on me." Vimla did as she was told, filled her lungs with air and took a cautious step forward. "Good," Minty said. "It wasn't he fault, really," she continued. "My father and Puncheon see he walking along the river and they stop Krishna to catch crab with them. They wanted to hear about Tobago. You know none of we ever see Tobago before, Vimi."

Vimla frowned. While she was flying from the macajuel, Krishna had been fishing for crab. Minty read the expression on her face. "Well, he couldn't tell them he was coming to see *you*, Vims," she said. She tightened her grip and pulled Vimla along. "Another step. Come on."

Vimla hobbled forward, feeling blood rush into her legs. "So what he wanted to meet me for when everything done fix up for he to marry Chalisa Shankar?"

"To tell you he sorry—"

Vimla sucked her teeth long and hard. "How much things Krishna sorry for?" she said, resisting the thawing in her heart.

"I nearly dead in the cane for him to tell me he *sorry?*" She grunted with the effort of her next step, but she was building momentum now.

"You ain't nearly dead, Vimla," Minty said, although they both knew that if she'd encountered a venomous snake, they might not be having this conversation now. "Let me finish what I have to tell you, nuh?"

Vimla clamped her mouth shut. They reached the window and she leaned on the sill to rest. Downstairs Sangita was making small talk with Chandani and Chandani was eyeing Sangita's flimsy white blouse with disapproval.

"He wanted to tell you is only you he was studying in Tobago. He cannot stand Chalisa Shankar. Not at all."

"Why?" she murmured. The room tilted on an angle.

Minty giggled. "'Too much style in she backside for me.'"

Vimla raised an eyebrow. A smile tugged at her lips. "Krishna say that?"

"And he love you, Vims."

"He say that, too?"

Minty nodded. "And he ain't marrieding Chalisa again. He go come for you tonight and allyuh go sail to Tobago to live. His partner, Dutchie, have a boat. He say his Auntie Kay cannot wait to meet you."

Vimla's knees went weak and Minty had to tighten her grip so she didn't fall.

"Let we go back to the bed," Minty said.

Vimla shook her head. "Let go. I want to try for myself." Vimla uncurled her arm from around Minty's neck and limped to the bed on her own. She fell across it and rolled onto her back. "Krishna really coming for me?" she asked Minty, breathless.

"Yes! What I go lie for, Vimi?" Minty smiled and collapsed on the bed beside Vimla. Together they stared at the silver galvanized roof. "Vimla."

"Mmm?" Vimla's mind was far away now. She was falling into Krishna's arms, sailing on a boat, running along a beach, feeling freer than she ever had.

"It have more to the story."

Vimla turned her head so she was staring at Minty's milky face. What more could there be?

"Remember I tell you about *Mastana Bahar*? Chalisa Shankar sing on the show last night."

Vimla raised her head. "You story."

"Is true."

"So?"

"So Pundit Anand vex like you wouldn't believe. We hear him bawling in the mandir this morning."

Vimla propped herself up on her elbows. "Why? Ain't he happy to have a daughter-in-law who could sing in the mandir when he son saying prayers? Pundit Anand like nothing better than to put on a good show." She giggled. He would be livid when he discovered Krishna gone on the morning of the wedding.

"But it was a film song, Vims, and Chalisa's performance was . . . *sexy*." Minty's fair complexion coloured.

"Who say?"

"My father."

"Who know?"

"Nearly everybody."

Vimla's head fell against the bed again. She chewed her lip, trying to ignore the fluttering in her belly. Vimla knew what

Minty was thinking; she herself was thinking the same thing. But what were the chances that after all this preparation to marry Chalisa and Krishna, Pundit Anand would call off the wedding?

Headmaster's Appeal

K rishna retreated to the veranda to drink his morning Ovaltine in peace. He swung his feet onto the railing and crossed one ankle over the other, ignoring the angry incantations rising from the prayer room. His father's madness swung like a pendulum, one minute petitioning God to curse the Shankars, the other cursing the Shankars and their money-making oranges of his own volition. It had gone on in this way through the night and Krishna couldn't bear to listen any longer.

The plan had gone awry and he could think of nothing else. Dutchie had warned him not to deviate from their design in any way, but how could Krishna have known that Om and Puncheon would be liming by the river, that he would be intercepted, held back for an hour while Vimla waited for him in the cane field? Krishna sighed. A niggling voice told him

Dutchie would have known how to fend off their questions and carry on his way without arousing suspicion. Krishna cursed himself. He wondered if Vimla could ever forgive him.

Vimla flounced into his mind, fire in her eyes, and vehemently shook her head no.

Krishna stared into his Ovaltine. He wished he could talk to her now. She was a mere seven minutes away—three if he ran—but the distance made no difference: she was just as inaccessible now as she had been from Tobago. Still, it was worse here somehow. At least in Tobago, Dutchie and Auntie Kay had bolstered his black moods with their laughter and antics. Here, at home, he was subject to constant orders: *Read this. Study that. Sit here. Marry she. Smile—Bhagwan is watching. Pray— Bhagwan is listening.* Now his father was delirious, his mother weepy, and Vimla had probably tumbled so far out of love with him there was no point in even hoping anymore.

And yet he did. He hoped that Minty would deliver his regrets, his adoration, his proposal to Vimla in time. If she managed this, maybe they would end up together after all.

"Sita-Ram and good morning, Pundit!"

Krishna started. *Good morning?* Who would be so foolish as to bid his father good morning today of all days? He swung his legs from the railing and peered down at the road. Headmaster Roop G. Kapil stood before the house, admiring the profuse orange ixora stuffing themselves through the gates. He looked up and caught Krishna's eye. "Sita-Ram, son." His blazer lifted and winged to the side when he waved, exposing, nestled beneath his armpit, a sweat stain the shape of a hummingbird's wing.

Krishna set his Ovaltine on the wicker table and trotted

down the stairs to unlatch the gates. "Sita-Ram, Headmaster."
He didn't know how to tell the headmaster he had chosen
the worst time to call, that his father was busy imploding
in the prayer room. "Come in."

Headmaster strolled in. He looked taller than Krishna
remembered. And there was a spring in his step that was new.
"Nice to have you back from Tobago, son. I hope your Auntie
Kay is well." He patted him on the back as they made their
way to a table and four chairs below the house. Headmaster
took a seat and rested his elbows on the table. "Where the old
man this morning?" He glanced at his watch. "I wouldn't
keep he long. I know he have a little wrinkle to iron out."
Headmaster tried an apologetic look, but it was lost in his
unusual cheerfulness.

Krishna hesitated. His father would have little patience for
Headmaster Roop G. Kapil in this state of joy, especially when
it was clear he'd already heard of Chalisa's indiscretions. "You
go take some coffee? Tea?"

Headmaster waved the offer away just as Anand yelled,
"Chalisa Shankar gone on *Mastana Bahar* and make a ass out of
we family! Does that old Nanny think I is a fool? Does she
think she can dump she slack granddaughter on my family and
we go open we arms like stupidies for she?"

"Anand, shh. Somebody downstairs," Maya said.

"You think the neighbours ain't already know?" Anand
asked, but he lowered his voice anyway because even in crisis
his reputation was to be swathed in piety. "It only have one
television in Chance, but somehow every man, woman and
child done hear about Chalisa Shankar's"—there was a pause
and Krishna imagined his father grasping at the air for the

right word—"spectacle! The people in this district does spend too much time talking to each other and not enough time talking to Bhagwan, Maya."

Maya murmured for him to breathe deeply, to mind his heart, to attend to the visitor who was waiting.

"Krishna! Who come here so early?" Anand called. "I ain't doing no pujas for a week!"

Headmaster's smile faltered. Krishna looked away, embarrassed. "Is Headmaster Roop G. Kapil, Pa," he said.

They heard him grumble something. The floorboards creaked. Maya coaxed. Then there was silence.

Krishna shrugged. "He coming, Headmaster." Krishna would let his father make his own excuses for his rancid mood. After all—and Krishna felt smug here—his father had been smitten by the Shankar family up until last night. This was his predicament to solve. His disgrace to explain away.

They heard Anand's heavy footfalls above. He appeared at the top of the stairs, dark puffs beneath his red-rimmed eyes. His cheeks sagged and pulled the corners of his mouth into a profound frown. For a moment, he loomed above Krishna and Headmaster as if he would snuff them out like diyas in the breeze.

Headmaster cleared his throat and looked uncertain, but Anand's face softened with each step. He unforrowed his brow and forced humanity into his gaze. He turned his lips the other way and straightened his shoulders. By the time he reached the bottom step, his hands were joined together at his heart. "Sita-Ram. Sita-Ram. Nice to see you, Roop," Annad said.

Krishna shook his head, amazed. This was the same man

who had marched to the mandir before sunrise and hurled his disappointment at Bhagwan before throwing himself onto the floor and howling. Krishnna and Maya had had to bring him home and put him to bed, but he only rose again and locked himself in his puja room.

Headmaster exhaled the breath he'd been holding.

Maya flew past them to the kitchen. "Three sugars, Headmaster?" she called from behind the beaded curtain.

Headmaster cleared his throat. "Nothing for me this morning, Maya. Thanks. I wouldn't stay long."

Anand held Headmaster's shoulder. "Take some coffee, nuh? Every guest to my home is like the Lord himself come to visit." His smile didn't touch his eyes.

Krishna fell into the hammock, where he was close enough to listen but far enough away not to be dragged into conversation. He hoped his father would manage to keep himself together until Headmaster left.

Anand rubbed his tired eyes with the heel of one hand. "How you keeping, Roop?"

"Good. Fine. Yes." Headmaster pushed his glasses up on his nose. He opened his mouth and closed it, tilted his head as if to examine Anand from a different angle. "And you, my friend? How you keeping?"

Anand rolled his shoulders back, grunted with satisfaction when something released and cracked. "Nice. Is a happy time for me, Roop. My only son getting married." He adjusted the mala around his neck and then hastily dropped his hands into his lap as if it had burned him for his lie.

Anand noticed Krishna in the hammock then. "Go and bring the coffee, nuh, boy."

"It ain't ready," Krishna heard himself say. He had grown lazy in Tobago, spoiled under Auntie Kay's doting.

Anand arched an eyebrow, wiry grey, pointed directly at him. "Then go and watch the water boil."

Krishna found his mother staring at the rising steam, tears glistening in the corners of her eyes. "Ma." He put his hand on her shoulder and noticed how delicate, how frail, it felt. "What happened?"

Maya's chin trembled. She shook her head, silver fly-aways quivering. "Is your father, Krishna. He so old and everybody only breaking he heart steady." She gazed up at him, imploring and snappish as if Krishna could set it right if only he wanted to.

"What we go do? How we could marry you to Chalisa Shankar now? People go say she slack."

They had said the same of Vimla once. Maybe they still did. Krishna couldn't be sure.

"Your father work hard to be a good pundit to these people. He work hard to keep the Govind name clean."

The Govind name. It always came down to that. Status. Pride.

"And allyuh only dutty-ing it up!" Maya raised her voice to a harsh whisper. "Shamelessness all over the place!"

Krishna's hand fell from her shoulder. She was blaming him. He stared at her, bewildered. Had she thought this of him all along? Krishna wanted to remind his mother that the disgrace hovering over the Govind family was not his doing. Not this time.

A tear escaped the others and slid down Maya's cheek. "Your father want to see you marry a nice girl before he dead,

Krishna. He asking too much?" She brushed the tear away and clasped her fingers around the mug handles. "He want to see you become a successful pundit. Why you doesn't study hard and be grateful for the man's guidance?"

She lifted the mugs off the counter. Krishna stepped away to let her pass. He didn't ask when they would consider what *he* wanted. He realized now that had never been their concern. Krishna's sole purpose was to carry on the Govind name and safeguard its integrity. Beyond that, he had no value.

"You see, Baba . . ." Headmaster started cautiously; he tiptoed with his words. "I still ain't have a teacher for Saraswati Hindu School."

Krishna saw his father's eye twitch, the green vein beneath his left eye throb. Maya set the mugs down on the table and retreated, throwing Krishna a worried look.

Headmaster coughed. He started to lift the coffee to his lips, but the mug wavered in his hand under Anand's stare and he set it down again. "Is important—as you know—to give the novice teachers time to prepare and already the new school year is upon us."

Anand fell quiet. Krishna stole a glance at him from the hammock. Maya sat outside the kitchen door and broke bodi into a bowl on her lap for today's lunch. The beans snapped between her fingers like nervous heartbeats.

When Anand said nothing, Headmaster went on. "It ain't have a better person for the job than Vimla Narine."

Krishna brought his foot down and the hammock skidded to a halt. Maya brought her hand to her lips.

Headmaster's gaze flitted like a bird from Anand's dark stare. It landed on the table, on his hands, on Maya, and then curiously, travelled up Kiskadee Trace like he was searching for someone. He returned to the conversation and this time his voice quaked less, although Krishna couldn't imagine why. "She is the brightest. We must think of the students . . ." He trailed off at Anand's sharp intake of breath.

"The students?" It came out in a hoarse whisper. Anand leaned forward with his palms together as if he were beseeching Headmaster not to be a fool. "You come here to talk about the students and Saraswati Hindu School, when I planning my son wedding to a hoity-toity—"

"Anand!" Maya interjected. She put the bowl down and hurried to his side just as Anand bolted out of his chair and sent it toppling.

Headmaster shrivelled. He mopped his face with his yellow handkerchief and for a moment pressed the fabric behind his lenses and over his eyelids.

Krishna was on his feet now, ready to restrain his father should madness bait him into doing something foolish.

Maya's fingers found Anand's. She murmured to him with tenderness, the way a mother would a small child. The pulsing beneath his eye slowed until it was no more. His shoulders slackened. "Roop, I ain't have time for this nonsense now," he said. He kneaded his forehead.

Headmaster shook his head and swallowed. "Baba—" His voice was pleading, persistent. "You forget Vimla is one of the top-scoring students in the country. She go raise Saraswati Hindu School standing in the south."

Anand studied Headmaster. Krishna could tell by the way

his father trailed his fingers along the bristles of his moustache that what Headmaster had said pleased him. "True. It go be good for the school."

"And, Baba," Headmaster said, "if we don't offer Vimla a position at we school, she go surely go elsewhere. To another school. Attend university, maybe."

Anand's fingers strummed his moustache now. "Surely," he repeated.

"Saraswati Hindu School go lose the brightest student we ever had, and maybe the best teacher." Headmaster's voice grew louder, more urgent now. "We must keep she so she could draw more students, more prestige, to the school!"

"But, Roop." Anand sounded old, tired. "You forget that Miss Vimla Narine ain't have the purist reputation in the district. She is a sound student, yes, but she character?" The question hung in the air between them for a moment.

Headmaster pushed his glasses up on his nose. "Baba, it was a moment of indiscretion." His smile was reassuring. "And can we really blame she?" He gestured to Krishna, standing stunned by the hammock. "Look at your fine son! He is the spitting image of Bhagwan Shri Krishna self. And we know, Baba," Headmaster said with a wink, "how our Bhagwan Shri Krishna tempted the fair milk-maids into the night with only his charm and the song of his flute!"

Anand's eyes misted. "Jai Shri Krishna," he murmured. Glory to Lord Krishna. He glanced at his son. Pride coaxed his lips into a half-smile.

"We know that aside from this unfortunate error, Vimla Narine is a wonderful girl."

Anand sighed and folded his arms across his chest, but he did not disagree.

Headmaster shifted to the edge of his seat and leaned forward. "She was my brightest scholar. And look, Baba, at her parents. Is there a more devout woman in the district than Chandani Narine?"

Anand's chin dipped. A nod? "But Om Narine is a rum sucker." He shuddered. "Remember Krishna Janamashtami? Disgraceful."

"He does work hard at least."

Anand's fingers found his moustache again. "Roop, will she uphold the school's values? Can I trust she?"

Headmaster folded his hands on the table and looked his old friend square in the eyes. "Anand, your compassion is infinite like Bhagwan's. If you could forgive the Shankars for their awful misstep and accept Chalisa as your daughter-in-law, surely you could forgive Vimla. She was once the district's darling."

And she is still mine, Krishna thought.

Anand's back went rigid and Krishna feared all Headmaster's convincing would come to nothing now. He braced himself, waiting for his father's temper to spark yet again, but instead Anand's attention fell on a blue emperor butterfly circling the air between him and Headmaster Roop G. Kapil. It flitted close to his face, brushing his forehead. "Jai Shri Krishna," Anand said, smiling. The butterfly danced away and he turned back to Headmaster, his face animated with an excitement indicative of a bright idea. "Roop—" He extended his hand. "Tell Chandani, Om and Vimla to come and see me this afternoon self."

Headmaster took Anand's hand in his own and beamed. "Sita-Ram, Baba. Sita-Ram." He bobbed a bow and was gone before Anand could change his mind.

The Seer Man

Om pulled the car to the side of the narrow road and honked his horn. The seer man's house was painted salmon and Om wondered if there was some magical significance to the colour or if the seer man just preferred salmon to, say, the ever-popular Caribbean-blue or sea green. Inside the gates, Om spotted a dozen dinner-plate hibiscus flowers in bloom. The petals of the enormous red flowers reminded him of ruffles on a lady's dress—nothing, of course, that Chandani would wear. They fluttered in the wind, doubling over and falling out again with grace.

"Whey! Watch them hibiscus, Om. One of them flowers could hold a nip of Johnny Walker." He craned his neck to get a better view. "Remind me to pick one when I leaving. I go try it when I get home."

"Puncheon, don't you touch the seer man's garden, you

hear? Next thing you know, we wake up tomorrow with flowers blooming out we ass!" Rajesh said. He was sitting in the back seat, sweaty palms pressed against his knees. He'd barely said a word from Chance to Jaipur Village, and now that they were parked in front of the seer man's house, he looked ill.

"He coming there," Om said. The seer man appeared from under the house wearing a kurtha and a pair of beige pants. His hair was plastered to the sides of his head; under the sun the white part down the middle shone with Brylcreem. He raised his arm in greeting then drew open the gates.

In the rear-view mirror, Om saw Rajesh close his eyes and mutter a prayer. He chuckled and manoeuvred the car into the dirt next to the seer man's bicycle and turned off the ignition.

Puncheon bounded from the car and clasped the seer man in a hug. The seer man smiled at Puncheon's boyish display of affection. Om looked for a hint of wickedness in that smile, but there was none. "Glad to see you, Parmeshwar," the seer man said.

Puncheon seemed to humble under the man's touch. His grin softened into a reverent smile and some of the mischief melted from his eyes. Om took note. Perhaps the magic was in the name. The next time Puncheon went wild, Om would call him Parmeshwar and hope for this same transformation.

The seer man nodded at Om. When he smiled, his cheeks kissed the pockets of flesh beneath his eyes. "*Bhai*, brother, your friend sick?"

Om followed the seer man's gaze. Rajesh had opened the car door, but he remained in the back seat. Despite the shade, Rajesh's whole face shone with sweat and seemed to grow shinier by the second. His eyes shifted back and forth from the seer man to his surroundings, no doubt looking for signs of evil.

The seer man bowed to Rajesh, his palms pressed together at his heart. Then he murmured to Puncheon, "I go wait in the room. Bring your friends when they ready." His eyes twinkled with amusement.

He disappeared into a room behind a curtain of beads and took Puncheon's good behaviour with him. Puncheon marched to the car and reached in for Rajesh's shirt collar. "What happen to you? You wasting the man time."

Rajesh wiped his hand down the front of his face from his forehead to his chin and droplets fell onto Puncheon's hand. "Let we go home, nuh, man. I change my mind," he said.

Puncheon tugged at Rajesh's shirt collar. "Too late for that. We done reach."

Om could see where this was going, and as much as he relished a showdown between Rajesh and Puncheon, he didn't think the seer man's home was the appropriate place. He pushed Puncheon out of the way and stuck his head in the car. "Raj, we done drive all this way. Let we stay for ten minutes and hear what the man have to say."

Puncheon jammed his head in under Om's arm. "You forget we come here for *you?*"

The room was a cramped square, with lattice windows that invited plenty of sunshine but not nearly enough air for four men. The windows cast an intricate labyrinth pattern on the opposite wall. Om, Rajesh and Puncheon passed in front of it, caught momentarily in the design, before they lowered themselves into the upholstered chairs. A pungent odour drifted from the unlabelled jars of dried herbs and other indistinguishable powders stacked on a shelf behind the seer man. The smell permeated the rug, the chairs, the pores of their skin.

The seer man crooked one knee over the other and rested his palms on top. "So, Rajesh," he finally said, fingering the fat beads around his neck. "Tell me how I could help you."

Puncheon leaned forward in his chair so he could see Rajesh around Om. They all waited for him to answer. He opened his mouth, but instead of words, air whistled through his lips. He seemed to be entranced by the man's beads. Om nudged him, but that only startled Rajesh and tongue-tied him further. Rajesh leaned back into his chair and sweated.

The seer man tucked his beads inside his shirt and tried again. "I think, Rajesh Gopalsingh, your wife giving you trouble." He said it as casually as if he were commenting on the price of flour.

Puncheon clucked his tongue like a woman in the market. The seer man touched his shoulder without looking and he stopped.

Rajesh avoided the seer man's deep-set eyes, but Om could tell he was studying the other peculiarities of the man's face: his sparse eyebrows, the uneven line of his lips, the black stubble at his chin that profoundly contrasted with the white stripe in his hair.

"What kind of trouble it is?" the seer man asked, probing yet patient.

Puncheon sprang an inch off his chair. "Cheatery!"

The seer man's eyes widened at Puncheon's outburst. He tapped his lips with his fingers. "Cheatery, Parmeshwar?"

Om bit back his laughter.

Rajesh growled to life. He sat straighter and shot Puncheon a murderous stare over Om's head.

Puncheon ignored the caution, gesturing as he clarified. "Infidelity, unfaithfulness, disloy—"

The seer man held his hand up and Puncheon closed his mouth. Om looked on, impressed.

"Rajesh?" the seer man said.

Rajesh cleared his throat. "Sangita ain't any of those things, Mr. Seer Man." He scratched his square jaw. "But is a possibility other men might try and seduce *she*." His shoulders slumped.

The seer man nodded as if he knew all about it. "Sangita," he said. "She beautiful, ain't?"

Rajesh swallowed. "Yes, of course."

"Real nice, Mr. Seer Man. Sweet like a ripe—"

The seer man closed his eyes for what seemed like an eternity and Om wondered if he had conjured a vision of Sangita without ever having met her. They watched him in silence. Neither of them dared to look away for fear they would miss some great display of magic that could change their lives, or else make for an interesting story one day.

Om hoped Chandani never learned about this visit. It wasn't that she didn't believe in the power of a seer man; it was the darkness of their art that frightened her. She sided with the mandir-goers and the pundits of the world—the people who prayed for blessings, not the ones who manipulated lives through black simi-dimi. Om might as well have been running through Chance naked, being here. If she found out, Chandani would fall on her knees and ask Bhagwan what she ever did to deserve a dotish husband like Om, and if she was feeling generous, she might even ask Bhagwan to forgive him, but Om doubted that.

To the seer man's credit, there were no snakes or dead chickens littering the room; nobody was sipping blood or tearing out their hair in madness. That's what Rajesh had thought he'd find here, and by the way he sat barely breathing, he still expected a creature to barrel into the room and hypnotize him with her red eyes at any moment. Om did not take the seer man as seriously as did Chandani, Rajesh or Puncheon. Curiosity brought him here and he would leave satisfied, without any real desire to return.

The seer man's eyes fluttered open. In seconds his glazed look sharpened. "Rajesh Gopalsingh—" He stood, and Rajesh shrank in his chair. "You must bathe every morning at five o'clock for fifteen days."

Om saw Puncheon whip a sheet of creased paper and pen from his pocket and begin scribbling. It dawned on Om that he had never seen Puncheon write anything before. In fact, he had assumed years ago that Puncheon just didn't know how.

"As you bathe, think about washing away your doubt for your wife."

"I don't doubt my wife," Rajesh blurted. It sounded as flimsy as the dinner-plate hibiscus dancing in the wind outside.

The seer man stroked the black stubble at his chin, tapped his fingers against his lips again. "You do. You doubt she. If you didn't doubt she, you wouldn't be here." He spread his arms as if the oppressive square room with the jars and the upholstered chairs was a palace.

Rajesh hung his head. Om looked at his hands. Puncheon tucked his pen and paper back in his pocket and jiggled his knees.

"When you done bathe," the seer man continued, "pick a flowers." He turned his head at an angle and regarded Rajesh. "You have flowers in your yard?"

Rajesh nodded.

"Good. Pick a flowers and put it where your wife go see it." The seer man stood and turned to his shelf of jars.

Om tapped Rajesh on the knee and gestured to the car outside. "Let we go." He didn't think it was fair to subject his friend to this foolishness any longer. But Rajesh shook his head no.

The seer man trailed a finger across the front of the jars. When he found one he liked, he tapped it. The clink of nail against glass was the only noise in the room. One by one, the seer man pulled jars from the shelf and set them on a ledge by the window. He unscrewed the covers and brought the jars to his nose and smiled. Om suspected smelling the ingredients was not part of the man's work but an act that pleased him. The seer man dropped a pinch of each powder into an empty jar and gave it a shake.

"Rajesh, put this in hot water and drink it like tea. If your situation ain't improve in three weeks, come back and see me."

Rajesh accepted the jar and Om noticed his hand only trembled a little. "Mr. Seer Man, what about something for Sangita?"

"To make she less pretty, maybe," Puncheon suggested.

The seer man shook his head at Puncheon. "The problem is you, Rajesh Gopalsingh," he said. "You ain't paying attention when you should. There is something preventing you from engaging in love."

Om knew Rajesh wanted to protest, but he didn't.

"And anyway, ain't you said she faithful?" The question created an awkward silence. When the seer man realized Rajesh was not going to answer, he smiled and said, "It have a man who fall in love with your wife, Rajesh Gopalsingh. You must do as I say: bathe at five, pick a flowers for your wife, drink the tea and pay attention. If you do as I say, the evil separating you and she go disappear." He snapped his fingers.

Some of Rajesh's gruffness worked its way to the surface now. "Who fall in love with my wife?"

"Rajesh Gopalsingh, I will not encourage quarreling among neighbours. Fix yourself."

Om felt he might as well have named Faizal Mohammed.

The seer man rummaged around in a woven basket filled with bags of herbs and handed one to Puncheon. "Your hangover medicine." Then he flopped in his chair and closed his eyes—a dismissal of sorts—and Om, Rajesh and Puncheon filed out of the room.

Faizal's Chain

Saturday August 31, 1974

....

CHANCE, TRINIDAD

Faizal meandered through his frangipani trees with his hands clasped behind his back. He was thinking of adding televisions to his shop inventory. After last night, Faizal realized Trinidadians wanted more than just radio; they wanted to see the world—and themselves. They needed television, and he would give it to them.

"Is a good plan, Sam. What you think?" Faizal said. Sam was perched in the frangipani tree with the pink blossoms. He took two steps to the right, one to the left and finished with a small bob. Faizal grinned. "Sweet, sweet parrot," he cooed.

"Faizal, that parrot does get more attention than me!"

Faizal glanced over his shoulder. Sangita was fingering the soft white petals on another tree. She smiled at him, secret and suggestive. "Well, stay with me, nuh, and you go get more attention," Faizal replied. He wondered if she knew he was only half joking.

Sangita crossed the yard. Her hips swayed with each step. Her blouse rippled over the curves beneath it. Faizal's breath caught in his throat. "An unexpected visit from Mrs. Gopalsingh, Sam. How lucky we are," he said, hoping to cover his pleasure in dryness.

She drew near, arching an eyebrow. "I only come to see how you keeping, Faizal." She stared at his cheek where the purple bruise had paled into something dirty and grey. She touched the bruise so lightly it could have been the wind.

Sangita never came just to see how he was keeping. She was a hungry cat always stalking something; sometimes it was gossip, other times company and always, always affection. Faizal never minded. He gave her everything willingly. Perhaps that's why he could not hold her.

"Mr. Gopalsingh is suspicious, Mrs. Gopalsingh. Is that why you come? So he could come here and break my ass?"

Sangita pouted. "He gone somewhere with Om, Faizal."

Faizal shook his head. "The two of them is like a pair of anti-man," he muttered as Sam stepped onto his extended finger. Sangita gasped, but she did not storm away. A good sign. "I ain't know why they doesn't just build a shack and live together."

"Faizal Mohammed!" Sangita exclaimed. She swatted his arm.

His heart danced. She was even more luscious in a huff. "And Minty? Where she gone?"

"By Vimla."

Faizal paused, distracted by the rise and fall of Sangita's chest as she sighed. "What happen to Vimla? She still stick?" he asked. He forced the worry away, irritated with himself.

"She foot better. Is the fever that have she still lock up in she room." Sangita's blouse whispered against Faizal's arm as they strolled. "I doesn't wish people bad, Faizal." She lowered her voice. "But I think is better Vimla remain in she room for a while. The girl does behave so wild! How she *really* get bite by a macajuel? That is what *I* want to know."

They rounded the orange hibiscus. Sam squawked. Faizal set him on his shoulder and said nothing.

"I does feel sorry for Chandani sometimes. That woman straight like a needle and she daughter come out like a fireworks."

A tendril of hair escaped her plait and dangled alongside her face. Faizal resisted the urge to tuck it away. He shoved his hands in his pockets.

"Could you imagine Vimla teaching at Saraswati Hindu School?"

Faizal did not particularly care for Vimla, but he thought the young children of the district might. There was no denying her spark. She would make the classroom come alive in ways the older, more conservative teachers couldn't. He held his tongue and veered closer to Sangita so that her shoulder grazed his biceps.

"Is a good thing I talk to Pundit Anand about Minty," Sangita mused.

"Minty?"

"Of course!" The high pitch of Sangita's voice vexed Sam. He squawked back at her and inched toward Faizal's ear. "Minty go teach at Saraswati Hindu School instead of Vimla."

Faizal didn't know why this made him uncomfortable. "But Minty ain't write she exams yet. Pundit Anand wouldn't just put any and anybody in the school. And neither Headmaster," he added as an afterthought.

Sangita waved her hand. The bangles at her wrist slid to her elbow and clinked. Her cheeks were flushed with excitement. "A minor detail!"

"And so how you manage to convince Pundit Anand and Headmaster?"

She stopped and turned to him, tilting her face to the sun as she laughed. "Oh, Faizal! Ain't you know me and Maya is good friends?" Sangita trailed a finger across his bruise again. "Besides, people doesn't tell me no."

Sangita and Maya's unlikely friendship had sprung from the ruins of Vimla's reputation. Faizal never knew what Sangita had suddenly found in common with Pundit Anand's worrisome wife, but now he understood. She had been spilling Minty's good merits into Maya's ear, priming her to speak to Anand on her behalf for the coveted teaching position at Saraswati Hindu School. He wondered if in the process Sangita had sullied Vimla's name into the ground to ensure she fell out of the running for good. He wondered why he even cared.

Faizal caught Sangita's fingers in his. Her feline eyes glowed before she hid them behind a fringe of dark lashes. He pressed her fingers to his lips.

"Faizal!" she said, but she made no effort to pull her fingers away. "Minty go be home soon." And then her face changed as if she'd remembered something horrible.

"What happened?"

Sangita reclaimed her fingers and fished into her skirt pocket. "Look what I find." She dropped the gold chain into

Faizal's hand with a clink. He saw her open her mouth to say something more and decide against it.

Faizal fastened the chain around his neck. "I guess you ain't find the pendant," he said. His face remained impassive, but he knew it was impossible for Sangita to suddenly *find* his chain. Minty was not a careless girl and his chain had been in her safekeeping for weeks. What was Sangita not telling him?

Her lips twitched with another lie. She looked away under his watchful eye. "No. I ain't know how the pendant fall out, Faizal," Sangita said. Her words dripped with sweetness. "I go look again."

Faizal nodded, amused. "Where you find it?"

"In my sewing room!" Sangita smiled now. "I have so much fabric and clothes lying all over the place is no wonder it loss for so long." She touched the chain and her fingers brushed his skin, feverish with longing. "You know, Faizal, I think that pendant hook up on a piece of cloth somewhere."

Faizal suppressed his laughter. He slipped his arm around Sangita's waist and began to walk, linking the pieces together in his mind. He believed Sangita when she said she discovered the chain in her sewing room. That's precisely the place Minty would leave it if she wanted to startle—even threaten—her mother. And of course, Minty had kept the pendant. She had shown him it the day Vimla was bit by the snake. It was the key to her blackmailing him, and it would keep Sangita in check, too. He smiled despite himself. Minty was cunning— he gave her that much. But what had upset Minty so much to make her leave the chain for Sangita to find? Faizal looked down at the woman by his side and knew that he would not find out from her.

"Faizal?" She leaned into him as they walked. "What you was going to tell me last night? About Chandani?" She was fishing for something to quell her own anxiety. This was the reason she was here.

They arrived at the edge of his lot where a mango tree slouched with unpicked fruit. Faizal twisted one from its branch. The leaves rustled as the branch bounced back like a slingshot. He handed the mango to Sangita. "Chandani? I can't remember."

She frowned. "But you looked excited, like it was something important. How you mean you can't remember?"

Faizal lifted her chin and daringly lowered his face toward hers. "Because," he murmured, "you does make me forget everything else."

It was only a half-truth. Sangita would be livid if she knew Chandani had charmed Headmaster into appealing Anand's decision. No doubt she would retaliate. Faizal didn't like the idea of it. It was unfair to pit two friends—sisters, really—against one another for nothing more than a teaching post. He placed his hands on either side of Sangita's face and wondered when he had become the witches' advocate.

Sangita sighed, breathless with impatience. "Kiss me, nuh, Faizal. I have to go home!"

Faizal crushed his lips against hers and she melted into his arms.

Changing Winds

Saturday August 31, 1974

....

CHANCE, TRINIDAD

V imla sat cross-legged on her bed, staring at the globe her father had purchased in Port of Spain. She found Trinidad and Tobago, sisters who promised to always stay near, floating off the coast of Venezuela. She touched the islands and they disappeared beneath her finger.

Her ankle was better. The snake bite had healed nicely and Dr. Mohan assured her the scars would eventually fade. She spun the globe so that the land and great bodies of water blurred into one, then with a finger she stopped the globe at random. She smiled. North America. Canada. They wore boots in Canada. Nobody would see her scarred ankle if ever she moved there.

"Vim-*la!*"

Hurried footsteps filled the hallway outside her room. Heavy and laboured, light and frantic. Vimla's door swung open with a crash and she wondered how her mother expected her to get well with all the noise. Chandani panted in the doorway. Her face was more animated than Vimla had seen it in weeks—months even. Om hopped in behind her, pulling his best pants over a pair of shorts. He grinned.

Vimla twisted so that she was facing her parents. Something had happened.

"Vimla," Chandani breathed, "get dressed." She scurried into the room and began dragging open drawers. "Pundit Anand want to see we right away."

The globe toppled sideways onto the bed. "Why?" Although it didn't matter why: Vimla would stand before Pundit Anand to be chastised if it meant catching a glimpse, exchanging a glance, a quick word, with Krishna.

Chandani threw a few dresses at Vimla. "I ain't know *why*. It ain't matter *why*. He want to talk to we and we going!"

Of course Chandani had an inkling why. She wouldn't be so enthusiastic if she didn't. Chandani and Pundit Anand, once respected friends, had been at a standoff the past few weeks over Vimla and Krishna's relationship. It was unlikely Chandani would anticipate any kind of interaction with him unless she was certain she would benefit from it. Even Om, who had never trusted Pundit Anand, seemed pleased. "Do fast, Vimi," he said.

"Ma, my hair need to wash." Vimla felt the residue left behind by the Limacol.

Chandani stopped sifting through Vimla's clothes and straightened. For a moment she looked worried about keeping Pundit Anand waiting. Then she set her jaw, let her lips settle into their usual hard line and said, "Don't sit there and watch

me like a manicoo in a headlights, Vimla. Get up! I go help
you wash out your hair."

Vimla sat in an old dress on a stool behind the house while her
mother filled a bucket of water from the standpipe. "Vimla,
how you feeling? You feeling good? You feeling like you go
faint?" Chandani asked.

Chandani was anxious, and Vimla knew her mother was
harbouring great expectations in her heart about this meeting with Pundit Anand. For the first time Vimla felt sorry
for Chandani. This unease, this desperation was the result of
her own carelessness. "I feeling okay, Ma," Vimla answered,
although her gut was twisting with similar emotions.

Chandani dumped half the bucket of water over Vimla's
head and Vimla squealed. "Humph! Just like when you was
a child, Vimla. Sit still."

Vimla did as she was told, feeling very much like a small
child indeed. Chandani squirted shampoo into her palm and
applied it to Vimla's scalp. She lathered and scrubbed, creating
a rope of bubbles down the length of Vimla's back. "Vimla,"
she said, "your hair feeling so fine-fine."

Vimla bit her lip and said nothing. She felt the scrubbing
soften to a gentle kneading, heard the squish of suds through
her mother's fingers. She closed her eyes and relished the
extraordinary tenderness of this moment. She had missed this.

Without warning another *whoosh* came and water cascaded
onto her head. Vimla yelped like a puppy. The soapy water
swirled across the concrete. Rainbow bubbles shone in the
sunlight before they disappeared down the drain. Vimla felt a

towel warmed by the sun fall across her head. She wondered if Chandani would comb out the tangles, too. And then she decided she didn't want her mother to see just how much of her hair remained in the comb when the task was done.

They arrived at the Govinds' residence an hour later. Chandani marched behind Om and in front of Vimla with her back straight and her chin tilted. The gates had been left open. They were expected.

Vimla's palms sweated; her stomach roiled with nerves. Minty's words danced through her brain: *He sorry, Vims. He love you, too. He go come for you tonight and allyuh go sail to Tobago to live.* They collided with her deepest insecurities: And what if he changed his mind? What if he didn't come? She felt utterly lost.

Pundit Anand ushered them up to his veranda, where Maya was already sitting. Her smile was not cold, but it was false and that was worse. They all sat on the edge of their seats except Pundit Anand, who cozied into his cushioned chair as if he were a king, and Vimla realized that he was, in his own right. His silver moustache lifted and revealed a smile. "Water? Coffee? Cane juice? Mauby?" He listed the options quickly, setting the pace for the meeting.

Chandani wanted water, Om cane juice. Vimla's stomach would pitch them all onto Pundit Anand's lovely wicker table, so she declined as politely as she could. Chandani bristled at her side.

But Pundit Anand didn't seem to mind. He called his drinks down to the help in the kitchen, rested his left ankle on his right knee and with two hands clasped the place where they joined. "You know," he began, his voice rising, "Bhagwan does see what we cannot. And everything that happen, does happen to teach we lessons. Ain't so, Vimla?"

Vimla nodded mechanically. Usually she loathed Pundit Anand's long, preachy discourses, but this time she found herself hanging on every word.

"I am a humble man," he continued. "A man who can admit an error when an error is made. And I must, mustn't I, Vimla?"

Vimla didn't know, but she nodded again anyway.

"Because a pundit's duty is to set examples for the people." He sighed, as if the burden of his station fatigued him, as if his pockets did not bulge after every Hindu celebration. "And so today, Chandani, Om"—he nodded to them both—"Vimla"—he smiled at her—"I called you here to declare that I judged you wrong."

Vimla's breath caught in her chest. She wanted to look at Chandani, but she didn't dare, not when Pundit Anand was gazing at her so intently.

"Vimla, you have made Chance proud with your scholarly achievements. I must congratulate you."

"Thank you, Baba," Vimla said. She wished she sounded shyer, more modest.

"So after much thought, I am hoping that once again you will accept the teaching post at Saraswati Hindu School," Pundit Anand finished. Of course, this wasn't a request; it was an indulgence, a privilege that the Narines would snatch from his hands like thieves. And he knew it.

"Baba, this is an honour," Om said.

"What a surprise." Chandani actually beamed, although she didn't look surprised at all.

They all turned to Vimla. She pressed her hands together as she knew she should and smiled. "I go make you and Headmaster proud, Baba." She felt a tingling at the bridge of her nose, a telltale sign that tears were near. The teaching post was more than just an esteemed position; it signified the renaissance of her reputation, the key to her freedom. She could travel beyond her home now with her head held high, knowing that she was in Pundit Anand's good graces again. Vimla couldn't wait to share her news with Minty. And then she wondered what could have changed Pundit Anand's mind—especially now, the day before Krishna's wedding, the day after Chalisa Shankar's sultry performance on *Mastana Bahar*. He had more urgent affairs to attend to, did he not?

Vimla noted the shadowy pouches beneath Pundit Anand's eyes, the extra crinkles when he smiled. She saw the way Maya avoided eye contact, the hunch in her shoulders like she'd suffered some great defeat. Vimla realized beneath this facade of hospitality and repentance lingered shame. These parents were not celebrating their son's wedding to Chalisa any more than Vimla was.

The clink of glasses nudging each other interrupted her thoughts. Her throat felt parched now and she wished she had asked for some water after all.

"Oh!" Chandani exclaimed.

Vimla looked up and found herself gazing into Krishna's smiling face. He was holding the tray of drinks with unsteady hands. The liquids splashed over the rims into the other glasses. "Sita-Ram, Auntie. Sita-Ram, Uncle." He set the tray down then shook Om's hand and kissed Chandani's cheek.

Vimla's heart thudded. She tangled her fingers in her lap and reminded herself to breathe. Krishna stole a glance at her before he sat next to his father. The bridge of Vimla's nose tingled again and she glanced away. She hadn't prepared herself for this.

"My son is back from studying in Tobago. A little wiser. A little darker." Anand laughed, determined to dispel the tension that had stiffened Maya's and Chandani's spines. Nobody responded. What could they say when they all knew the truth: that Krishna had been sent away because of Vimla?

Anand looked like he might launch into another meandering homily. He sat up tall, lifted his hand to gesture, untucked his priestly smile from the bristles of his moustache and leaned forward. But Maya touched his knee—a discreet brush of her fingertips across his cotton dhoti—and he seemed to change his mind. There was urgency in that touch; whatever Anand had prepared to say next, Maya wanted said quickly.

Anand smiled, his eyes crinkled. "Last night, after the maticoor, Krishna tell me he in love with your daughter."

Vimla gasped before she could stop herself, but only Maya appeared to notice. The others stared, stunned at Pundit Anand as if he'd just denounced his faith.

Pundit Anand put his hand to his heart. "I am not a cruel man," he said. "I know my son go be miserable without Vimla in he life. He didn't have to tell me so—I could read it in he face." Everyone looked at Krishna's face to see if they could read it, too. Krishna's eyes were wide with disbelief.

Vimla's chin trembled. Her eyes pooled with tears. She thought of their many secret encounters in the cane field, of the night they were discovered. She remembered the lonesome days when Krishna was in Tobago, the moment she lost her teaching post. She recalled the first time she heard Chalisa Shankar's name, the news of the wedding, Maracas Bay, the macajuel snake, her terrible nights of fever and heartache. Tears spilled over Vimla's lashes and fell freely into her lap. She released the clenching in her stomach and allowed herself a luxurious sob.

Chandani did not pat Vimla's back. For the first time in her life, she was tongue-tied.

"And so," Pundit Anand continued, "Krishna is requesting Vimla's hand in marriage." He raised his voice so there was no mistaking his words. "Tomorrow. September first."

An Uncertain Future

Delores stood in the middle of the kitchen, wringing her apron in her hands.

Breakfast was already laid out: hot roti, fried baigan, slices of ripe avocado and mounds of homemade guava jelly for Avinash to slather on his roti. The kettle whistled on the stove. Nanny's teacup gleamed, empty.

"*Delores*—the kettle!" Nanny screeched.

Delores jumped when she was called and removed the kettle from the stove.

"Delores, what happen to you this morning? You dance till you can't work?" Nanny asked. She snapped the newspaper open in front of her face so that Delores didn't have a chance to answer.

Chalisa threw Delores a nervous look, but Delores turned away as if she hadn't seen and busied herself with fixing Nanny's first cup of tea of the day.

Avinash helped himself to a quarter slice of roti. "I dance so much last night I could hardly *walk* today!" He broke a piece of roti and dipped it into the jelly. Delores took the roti from his hands, opened it up and spread the jelly in the hot fold like a sandwich. She handed it back to him and returned to the stove.

Nanny turned the page. "Avi, why you don't ask your big sister how she does manage to dance whole night and walk the next day. Your sister is a professional, you know."

Chalisa made a face at Nanny from the other side of the newspaper. She pushed her breakfast around her plate with her fingers.

Avinash opened his mouth to ask, but Delores tapped him on the head and shook her head no. Avinash cupped his hands and leaned toward Chalisa so that he could ask her in a whisper. Delores made to take Avinash's breakfast away, and his hands fell to his plate as he forgot all about his question.

Delores filled Nanny's teacup with sugary tea and retreated with a sigh.

"Delores," Nanny said from behind her paper, "this is a wedding house, not a funeral home. Stop sighing and walking around like someone capsized and dead." She turned the page and shook out the folds. "You starting to remind me of Miss Mastana Ba—"

Nanny fell suddenly silent.

Chalisa and Avinash stared at the wall of news blocking Nanny's face. Delores cowered in the farthest corner of the kitchen. Waiting.

It began with a groan, a guttural sound an animal might make in labour or in death. The newspaper trembled, then the words at the paper's edges crumpled in Nanny's hands. Then she let go and the paper fell across the breakfast spread with a *whoosh*. Avinash's wispy hair fluttered.

Nanny looked like her orange estates had gone up in flames. She pushed her chair back, the legs scraping the floor. Her gaze fell on Chalisa, murderous and fearful at once. "Lying wretch!" She wheeled around. "Delores! Call driver!"

Delores shrank against the stove "Driver quit."

"Quit?" Nanny's eyes bulged from her shrivelled face. She paced with one hand on her hip and the other holding the side of her grey head. She muttered, "The man just start working for me! . . . Who to call?" She closed her eyes. "Who to call?"

Chalisa could think of a dozen workers who would drive Nanny where she needed to go, but none that would keep the reason for Nanny's hysterics confidential, no matter how much she paid them.

"Gavin!" Nanny snapped her fingers. "Call that boy now for now."

Chalisa looked at the polished teak, deadpan. Avinash kicked his feet excitedly under the table.

Delores swallowed. "You fire Gavin, Nanny."

Nanny sucked her teeth. "That boy go run come if he know he could see Chalisa." Nanny waved her hand in Chalisa's direction as if loving her was a weakness.

"Where you going, Nanny?" Avinash asked.

But Nanny didn't answer. She was climbing on a chair, reaching to remove the false cupboard door that hid her safe.

———

Unbeknownst to Nanny, *Mastana Bahar* had aired the night before and now Chalisa was mentioned in the *Trinidad Guardian* as "a rising star with talent and finesse." Talent and finesse!

A multitude of emotions rattled around in Chalisa's heart like Avinash's jacks. She had changed her fortune with a single lie. She wasn't sorry either. Nanny had to be stopped from resigning her to a monotonous life alongside a pundit and spoiling Chalisa's chance at fame. She smiled out the window. Now that her waywardness had made national television, Nanny was petrified Pundit Anand would call off the wedding. As the car trundled along, she hoped Pundit Anand was just as appalled by her passion for performance as Nanny; she hoped he thought his son too good for her; she hoped he snipped her from his plan and let her fly free.

And here was Gavin, taking her to meet her fate. Chalisa thought he'd never forgive her for causing him to lose his job and she certainly never thought she'd see him again. Gavin, with his Elvis hair and deep, adoring eyes, had never failed her. Chalisa was sorry now that she'd laughed all his proposals away.

It took just under two hours to get to Chance. The gates were flung open when they arrived, but not for them; the Govinds had company, it seemed. Another family lingered in the entrance as the Govinds bade them goodbye, essentially barring Gavin from pulling the car into their lot. As Gavin let the car idle at an awkward angle, partly on the road, partly on the driveway, the Govinds and their guests turned their heads to see who had come. That's when Chalisa knew that Nanny hadn't phoned before visiting, that they were unexpected—worse, unwanted—visitors.

Chalisa's eyes met Vimla's first. She had forgotten how much they were like oceans of cocoa tea, how her private thoughts swam naked to the surface. Something passed between them before Nanny ordered Chalisa out of the car: an understanding that while they were not friends, they were allies in the same cause. The glitter of triumph in Vimla's eyes told Chalisa they were winning. She nodded, a movement almost imperceptible, and followed Nanny.

"Good morning and Sita-Ram." Nanny's smile twinkled with innocence. "And Krishna! Welcome home, my son." The group stared, dumbfounded, as she walked toward them. Chalisa hung her head and played the disgraced grand-daughter, which helped to hide her embarrassment.

Krishna mumbled a greeting and managed a weak smile. Chalisa could tell that he did not know how to play this game.

Pundit Anand's silver eyebrows gathered in the centre; his moustache drooped on either side of his down-turned mouth. He hesitated as if he were searching for a response then filtering it with care. It came out civil, but it was not warm. "Nanny. We wasn't expecting to see you—or Chalisa today."

Maya pressed her fingers to her lips and said nothing. She had looked no happier standing in the Narines' company than she did now that Nanny and Chalisa had arrived. Perhaps no girl was good enough for her son.

Vimla's mother started at the sound of Chalisa's name. She inspected Chalisa like a mango, looking expressly for blem-ishes. The scrutiny took but two seconds before she flicked her gaze away as if Chalisa were yet unripe and sour. The slight chafed Chalisa's ego. Who was this plain, country-dwelling woman to dismiss her like a piece of market fruit? She hid her irritation behind a veil of lashes.

Nanny disregarded the Narines altogether. She spoke directly to Pundit Anand as though they were already relatives, as though she took precedence over neighbours calling on a Saturday morning. "Baba, I come to speak with you about a important matter." Her panic slipped into the cracks in her face so that she appeared calm, merry even. She edged closer to him, turned her face from the others and said in a loud whisper, "Regarding the wedding tomorrow, nuh."

Pundit Anand shook his head with wonder, exchanged a glance with Chandani and Om over Nanny's head. "We go talk in a minute, Nanny," he said. "I just walking we friends out." He patted Om on the shoulder and Om grew half an inch with self-importance.

Friends.

Chalisa looked from Vimla to Krishna and back. They gawked openly at one another like they'd been granted permission. Chalisa didn't want Krishna for herself, but still, she felt worse than small in their company—she felt invisible.

Nanny wasn't faring well either. She endured the Govinds' cool reception, the Narines' victorious air, with a brilliant mixture of patience and feigned oblivion, but Chalisa knew inside she was hot with rage. She supposed this time Nanny's anger was justified; it was plain Pundit Anand had replaced them with the Narines. Chalisa shrugged. Let Krishna and Vimla marry. Let Nanny burn. She wanted out of the blistering sun and back in the car, where she could make things right with Gavin.

"Don't go as yet." Nanny put her arm out just as Chandani edged closer to the gates. "Allyuh don't leave because of we."

She turned to Pundit Anand and Maya, one creased hand lying like a handcuff on Chandani's wrist. "We ain't staying long. We only come to show something to Krishna. He was in Tobago the last time I visit, you see." Nanny rummaged around in her handbag now, a sheepish expression on her face. "I doesn't remember good again. Is old age have me so."

They all stared at her—even Vimla and Krishna—and in that moment as the winds changed direction again, Chalisa knew there was no woman in all of Trinidad as clever and wily as Nanny.

Nanny pulled a piece of paper from her handbag. "Here. I find it!" She flattened it to her stomach and smoothed it with her other hand. "Come, *beta*." She crooked a finger at Krishna.

Krishna hesitated. He looked for guidance to Pundit Anand, who shrugged his concession. Chalisa caught the glint of avarice in Pundit Anand's eyes, but it was the peculiar way Krishna lingered on his father's face, as if he were understanding something about him for the first time, that told Chalisa something was shifting in Krishna. But what? It vexed her not to know. Chalisa scowled openly, but no one was paying attention to her; they were all following Krishna's eyes across the paper in his hands now.

"What's that?" Pundit Anand asked.

Chandani folded her arms across her flat chest. She was irritated by his interest, or perhaps, Chalisa thought, irritated by her own.

"A deed," said Krishna.

Nanny wiggled her way into the centre of the circle that had formed around Krishna. "Is a deed, yes. Is the deed to we orchard in Carapichaima on Orange Field Road. Is the biggest and largest one in the Shankar estate." She peeled her lips back into a saccharine smile and extracted the worn square of paper from Krishna's fingers again.

Pundit Anand gasped and then attempted to cover his delight in a spell of false coughs.

"What a special boy you are. I know you go take good care of my gem!" As everyone followed her gaze to Chalisa, Nanny stuffed the deed back into her purse.

Chalisa found she was amused at how easily Nanny poured her lies at Pundit Anand's feet. The orchard on Orange Field Road belonged to she and Avinash. This deed—if it really was an authentic deed—could only be for her last and smallest orchard, a significant piece of property in Quinam, but nowhere near as formidable as the others. And Chalisa knew she couldn't just *give* the deed away; she had to legally transfer the land into Krishna's name if she wanted him to have it.

But what really amazed Chalisa was the way Krishna remained locked in silence as Pundit Anand and Nanny clasped one another's hands and his fate was irrevocably warped. This was no bridal dowry—this was a bribe; and for all that he looked torn, Krishna had allowed it to happen.

Chalisa saw her own defeat reflected in Vimla's eyes before she flicked her hair over her shoulder and made her way back to the car.

Chandani's Tirade

O m poured a generous shot of Old Oak into Chandani's glass.

She scowled. "Pour, nuh, man. Ain't you is a expert at this?"

Om poured until her glass was a quarter full. She downed the rum in one gulp and then scrunched her face and shook herself like a fowl cock in the rain. "Whey, sir!"

They were sitting under the house, having just returned from the Govinds'. Chandani had brought out the bottle of Old Oak, and she was lashing drink after drink like the cane cutters on payday. Om sighed; she would be drunk in minutes if she didn't stop. He was grateful Vimla had walked over to Minty's house.

"Well, I never see more!" Chandani began. "That kiss-me-ass lady drive all the way from St. Joseph to Chance to give

Krishna a deed?" Chandani stood up and pointed in the direction of the Govind home. "She feel I born big so. She feel she real smart." Chandani stood over Om, yelled in his face and stomped. "That old woman is a *naaasty* crook!"

Om nodded, poured himself a drink. Out of the corner of his eye, he saw the dogs retreat to the kennel with their tails between their legs.

"You know, I have one mind to go back there and wring the smile from that wretch's mouth." She gestured the assault in the air. "Just wring it out!"

"Is Pundit Anand who accept the estate deed, Chand. Is he to blame," Om said. He sat hunched over with his head in his hands.

Chandani paced. She kicked her empty glass over in the process and Om set it right. "That man greedy. Lawd Father, he greedy." Chandani weaved back to Om and lowered her face to his. "Tell me, nuh? Tell me what the ass Anand go do with a field of orange?" She cackled. "You think Maya go pick orange in the hot sun? She backside lazy too bad!"

Chandani was bordering on hysteria. Om wondered if he should take her upstairs, let her vent in their bedroom, where he could close the windows. But then, there was a part of him that thought the neighbours needed to hear the truth about Pundit Anand. When word began spreading, he wanted it to be Chandani's. He let her rage on. She deserved this much at least.

"And if Pundit Anand think I go put *my* daughter in *he* school to teach, he have a next thing coming!" The veins in Chandani's skinny neck grew taut.

Om watched the enmity on her face and pitied her. He knew when it sputtered out, the embarrassment of today would remain like a film on her heart. And yet he was powerless to help her. If only he could have made Pundit Anand a counter-offer—a better dowry. Then they wouldn't have had to hang their heads and return home worse off than when they left.

"Let he give the job to he new daughter-in-law. She could teach the children to dance and prance and wine up they waist all over Trinidad!" Chandani exclaimed.

"And as for Krishna. It ain't matter how much he pray, how much he read them scriptures—Bhagwan would never bless him with a happy marriage. Not after he dutty my daughter good name and throw she away like a mango seed. What a nasty man. He come out just like he miserly father!"

Chandani bent to pick her glass up off the ground and nearly toppled forward. Om caught her around the waist and she steadied herself against his solid frame for a moment, her head resting on his. "Om." Her voice was smaller now. "Pundit Anand real shit we up, boy," she said.

Om pulled her onto his lap like a rag doll and took the empty glass from her hands. "Yeah, but what we go do? Is no point railing up, Chand. Them corrupt too bad. I ain't a pundit like Anand, and I ain't have plenty land and estate like Nanny, but I am a honest fella." Even as he said it, Om felt hollow inside, like being honest suddenly counted for nothing.

Chandani looked like she might argue, but the effort was too much. Instead she draped an arm around Om's thick neck and slurred, "Pour, nuh?"

He did not have the heart to refuse her. Om wrapped his arm around Chandani, the bottle of Old Oak in his hand, and poured a splash into her glass.

Chandani's face crumpled and she began to cry.

A Dream in a Cow Pen

Vimla and Minty sat on two overturned buckets under the shed where the cow and the calf were tied and eavesdropped on Chandani's tirade. Minty's eyes widened and her mouth dropped open at the mention of the deed. "She story!" Minty whispered.

Vimla shook her head. She was ringing the hem of her skirt in her hands. "Is true."

The calf nosed its way under her mother's belly and suckled. The cow stepped to the side as if she would free her teat from her baby's tug and then resigned herself to her duty with a moan, swishing her tail against the flies.

When Chandani fell quiet, Minty wrapped an arm around Vimla's slight shoulders. "So what happen? Pundit Anand take back the wedding offer?"

Vimla shrugged. "If you see how he face light up when he

see that deed, Minty! All of a sudden, me and my mother and my father come like strangers. He act like he ain't invite we to come by he self, like we was just passing by the gates and drop in unexpected."

Minty gasped.

"After that ugly crapaud-mouth Nanny show up with she big handbag and she big deed, Pundit Anand pretend like he ain't ask for me to marry Krishna! What we could do? If we did mention it again, it would have look like we begging. He already embarrass we, Mints, and by the way he get real friendly with Nanny we done know he wouldn't keep he word."

"So what you do?"

Vimla shrugged and then let her shoulders slump forward again. "We come away fast-fast. What else we could do?"

The cow lowed and tried to nudge her calf away.

Minty rose and flipped the bucket right side up. She gestured for Vimla to pass her the yellow bucket of molasses shoved into a corner. "And what about Mr. Man?" she asked dryly.

Vimla pivoted on her bottom to face Minty. "Krishna? He just stand up there like a fool." It pained her to say it, but it was the truth. She could forgive him his other negligence—Tobago, the meeting in the cane field—but this she could not forgive; this humiliation, this public rejection, was branded on her heart forever.

"He ain't say nothing?"

"He almost say something. Almost. I could see he wanted to stop Pundit Anand and that nasty old Nanny, but when he watch he father's face, he just freeze up, Mints."

Minty folded her arms. "You think is the money Krishna after?"

Vimla dropped her chin into the palms of her hands and studied the scar on her ankle. "I really don't know."

Minty disappeared around the side of the shed with the empty bucket. Vimla heard her dip it into the rain barrel. She returned lugging the bucket from its wire handle as water spilled onto her feet. Vimla could tell by the red splotches on her otherwise fair skin that Minty was biting back angry words. "Open the molasses, nuh?"

Vimla peeled the cover off the molasses bucket. The cow lumbered near and lowered her great head so that her velvet nose brushed Vimla's hand.

"Get back, Swishy!" Minty scolded. Gently she pushed the cow's head away and scooped molasses into the bucket of water. She regarded Vimla warily as she mixed the two. "I know that look, Vims," she said. A sheen of sweat dotted her hairline. The cow stretched her tongue into the bucket and stole a lick. Minty nudged her away.

Vimla stood up, her eyes steely. Now, when Krishna had finally slipped through her fingers, she could not cry. She did not want to. Instead she summoned her loss and humiliation and let it morph into anger and rise in her chest like a white-capped wave. She had let her fate fall prey to the whims of the Govinds and the Shankars for weeks now, and in the end, they gave her false hope then hurled her lower than she'd ever been. She gathered her pride and vowed to succeed at something new. Something grander than *Mastana Bahar* or the glorious line of Govind pundits.

Minty slid the bucket of molasses in front of the cow. "Vimla, what going on in your head?"

"Mints, I leaving."

"Home? Your mother tight—she ain't looking for you. I sure you father putting she to bed now." Minty smiled. "Stay, nuh? We does hardly see each other again."

"No, no. I leaving Chance, Mints." Vimla's eyes were huge with adventure. She took hold of Minty's shoulders, gave them a little shake. "I going foreign."

"What?" Minty gawked at Vimla like she'd gone mad. "Foreign? Where?"

"Canada." It slipped from her lips the way Krishna's name once had. Fluid. Dangerous. "I leaving this place." She released Minty's shoulders and stared across the dancing cane. "I leaving." The words were a whisper this time.

Minty put her hands on either side of Vimla's head and turned it to face her. "You ain't need to run, Vimla. Canada is a far place to run to."

"Run?" Vimla scowled. "I ain't running from anybody, but what I staying here for, Mints?" She leaned on the wooden post the cow and calf were tied to. "It ain't have nothing here for me again."

Minty brushed the perspiration from her hairline to hide her hurt. "What it have in Canada except ice and the Niagara Escarpment?"

Vimla arched an eyebrow, impressed. Minty had been studying her geography over the summer. "I want to go to school there."

The cow upset the bucket of molasses, lifted her head and mooed.

A silence fell between Vimla and Minty. They knew of two people from a neighbouring village who had gone abroad to study—one to England, the other to Canada—and neither of them had returned. Minty let her hands drop to her sides and looked away. "You can't just pack your bags and leave. Your mother wouldn't allow you to go over alone."

Vimla heard the challenge in Minty's voice and softened her approach. "I ain't think my mother go mind if I leave here to go over—especially after Anand embarrass she today, Minty. Think how much satisfaction she go get telling people in the market that she daughter gone Canada to study!"

Minty averted her gaze from Vimla's mischievous smile.

The calf ducked under her mother's sagging udders and stuck her entire face in the molasses bucket. She lapped greedily, pushing the bucket along the ground until the rope grew taut and she could go no farther. Minty picked up the bucket and held it for the calf, her back to Vimla. "What about Krishna? He make plans to take you Tobago to live. He promise to meet you tonight, remember?"

Vimla threw her head back and laughed, madly and uninhibitedly. The wind danced in the cane. "When last Krishna follow through on he word?"

"How you go pay for the ticket?" Minty asked.

Vimla could tell by the way she straightened her spine and stood with her feet planted firmly apart that Minty thought she had trumped her.

"I know you go help me, Mints," Vimla said.

"Me? I can't help you this time. I ain't have no money. Not a red cent."

This wasn't the first time Vimla had assuaged her hurt with the idea of leaving Trinidad and she had an idea. "Ain't you still have Faizal Mohammed's jewellery?"

A flock of black birds volleyed out of the cane into the sky in a cacophony of twitters. They glided right and then swept into the opposite direction like a lost cloud chasing a storm.

The Suitcase

Chandani woke with a thudding in the back of her head. She propped herself up on her elbows. The thudding rolled to her temples and intensified. A sliver of late-afternoon sun cut through an opening in the curtains and pierced her eyes. Chandani moaned, lowered herself back onto her pillow and shielded her eyes with her hand. Her tongue felt pasty, sour. She peeled it from the roof of her mouth and croaked Om's name.

"He gone to play card."

She turned her head. Vimla was kneeling in the shadows, her palms pressed to the top of an old blue suitcase someone had given Om years ago.

"Vimla?" She struggled to a seated position, winced as her stomach churned and then settled.

Vimla pointed to the glass of water she'd left on Chandani's bedside table. Chandani guzzled it noisily as if someone might take it from her. As the last drop rolled into her parched mouth, she vowed never to touch Om's Old Oak again. "What you doing there?" she asked, setting the glass down.

"Since when you does drink so, Ma?" Vimla asked, mirth in her eyes.

For a moment Chandani saw a little girl at play again, a girl full of tricks and mischief, a girl who used to fall asleep in her arms smiling. She glanced at the framed pictures hung at an angle above Vimla's head and saw that nothing in that face had changed, really, but everything had grown stronger: the tenacious lift of her chin, the brightness of her eyes, the unpredictability of her giggles and glowers. Chandani sucked her teeth. "Is your father fault. He hand heavy. He does throw big-big drink for me." She smoothed her hair and twiddled her thumbs in her lap. The movement of her fingers helped take her mind from the queasiness in her belly.

"That's not what Pa tell me," Vimla said. Something clicked and the latches on the suitcase flew open.

Chandani pulled the coverlet over her legs and busied herself with creating a perfect fold. "Humph! Your father could well carry news!" This morning's events trolled through the fog to the forefront of her brain. "And anyhow, I earn my drink after Pundit Anand . . ." Her outburst trailed off and disappeared. A lump formed in her throat. She traced the rose pattern on the coverlet again and again with her finger until the urge to cry subsided.

Vimla walked around the suitcase and sat cross-legged on the bed at Chandani's feet. She felt Chandani's toes through the coverlet and gave them a wiggle. "Ma, forget he, nuh? He too money hungry for we and he does lie too bad for one pundit. I ain't want to teach in he school and I ain't want to marry he son neither."

For once Chandani let Vimla's impertinence pass. "You mean to tell me you ain't like that boy again?" She snorted. "Ain't just the other day you meet Krishna in the cane field?"

Vimla froze.

Chandani smiled a mother's knowing smile. "Ain't that where your foot got bit-up?"

"Today is the first time I see Krishna since Pundit Anand send he Tobago."

Chandani shrugged as if it didn't matter. She watched relief soften the furrow on her daughter's brow. "So how come you ain't bawling down the place like I expect? Instead *I* gone and play the ass and drink till my head get bad." She laughed, but it sounded more like she was clearing her throat.

"Ma? You all right?"

Chandani forced herself to sit up straighter. "What you think—is the first time I ever take a drink?" She longed for another glass of water and the luxury of uninterrupted sleep.

Vimla laughed. "I think is the first time you ever drink the whole bottle."

Chandani scowled and lay down again. "I wish I could have rip that moustache out Pundit Anand's mouth," she said. "He make we lose everything." She banged her tiny fist into the spring of the bed. "Imagine how shame your father feel now."

Vimla swung her legs over the side of the bed. "Ma, Saraswati Hindu School and Krishna Govind ain't everything." She knelt in front of the suitcase again and this time flung it open.

Chandani knew she couldn't really feel that way, but still, Vimla's resilience was admirable. "Girl, what you doing with that old thing?"

A musty smell filled the room. Chandani sneezed three times, coughed once and glared at Vimla.

"I taking it with me when I go Canada."

The resolve in Vimla's voice sent a jolt of dread through Chandani's chest. "Canada?" She pulled the coverlet over her nose so only her eyes were visible. "Who say you going Canada? Put away that suitcase and go and boil some rice for dinner."

Vimla stared, unmoving, into the belly of the suitcase as if she were filling it with things in her mind.

"Vimla! You hear me? Put it away. That thing smelling stink!"

The curtains at the window fluttered and a wash of sunlight filled the suitcase. Chandani saw the way Vimla looked longingly at it, and wished she had thrown it out long ago. They had no use for a suitcase. They weren't going anywhere.

Vimla's fingers whispered over the beige lining, still pristine. "I could leave Chance and go over to study. Then it wouldn't matter to we who marry Krishna and who teach in the stupid school."

Chandani blinked at her daughter like she was speaking some unknown tongue.

"I go study to become a teacher or a nurse. And when I done school, I go come back."

She looked up at Chandani and Chandani looked away. Vimla was right, of course. She would rise above her disgrace the moment she left for a place people in Chance only dreamed of. The elusiveness of life in Canada, where snow fell in the winter and apples blossomed in the spring, would garner their respect, their adoration and secret envy all over again.

But she was only a girl. What did Vimla know about a place as vast and remote as Canada? What did Chandani and Om know? A thousand misfortunes could befall Vimla in Canada and Chandani and Om would be powerless to help. Chandani let her imagination conjure the worst of them: Vimla lost in a big city; Vimla frozen into an ice block; Vimla forced to dine on beef and pork; Vimla romanced and impregnated by a man of indistinct race and questionable intentions; Vimla deciding never to come home.

"Ma! You hearing me?" Vimla asked.

Chandani regarded her in silence. Suddenly Vimla was not a naughty girl or a prize pupil; she was a young woman who from the nadirs of her grief had found fresh optimism and greater ambition than Chandani had ever imagined for her.

Chandani faked a cough and pulled the coverlet over her head to hide her grown daughter from her eyes. If she said yes, if she allowed Vimla to leap beyond this small village, she would lose her, send away the person she loved more than anyone else in the world.

"Ma! What you think?"

From beneath the coverlet she said, "I think you should put away that damn suitcase and air out the room before you kill me. And boil the rice like I ask you."

"And?"

"And bring me a next glass of water. My throat get scratchy from all the dust that suitcase let go." She sucked her teeth for good measure.

"And what about Canada?"

Chandani pressed her fingers to her temples. Her headache was worsening. "Vimla, is no wonder you does always end up in trouble—you does look for it steady! Krishna and Chalisa ain't even marry yet, school ain't even open back yet, and you already looking for some next shit to land up in." She worked saliva into her mouth and let it sit for a second on her dry tongue before swallowing. "And how you could ask me so boldface to go and knock about in Canada after I see how wild you behave right here at home? Humph! You must be mad!" Chandani listened for an answer, and when there was none, she said, "Bring a tablet with the water when you coming." She held her breath and waited. When the door slammed, it rattled the door frame and her aching head. Chandani buried her face in her pillow and cursed until she needed air.

That night, Om and Chandani listened to the constant click and snap of the suitcase latches and the sporadic creak of floorboards as Vimla paced in her room across the hall. Chandani stretched like a pipe over the bed, inflexible and silvered by the moon. "I thought I tell you to bust up that suitcase and throw it away?" she said.

Om filled his lungs and let the air whistle softly through his nostrils. They flared and he sneezed. "I try, but she watch me like she go dead if I take it."

Chandani sucked her teeth, but she had made no attempt to do the deed herself. In the darkest recess of her mind—the place where she dared to glance inward—Chandani wondered why she was afraid to yank the suitcase from Vimla's grasp.

She had no problem forbidding her going to Canada, criticizing the very absurdity of the idea, but the suitcase she could not take from Vimla. Tears slid from her half-shut eyes into the pillow as she realized that a part of her—a small, yet significant part—hoped Vimla found some way to disobey her.

An hour before dawn, when faint stars were still visible against the colourless sky, Chandani heard Vimla creep from her room. She sat up and nudged Om. "Wake up." But she knew he wasn't sleeping—he hadn't snored all night.

Om caught Chandani's hand. "Don't quarrel with she," he said. His voice was flat, as if he'd already resigned himself to letting his daughter go.

Chandani tugged her hand away. "Ge up, nuh? I ain't make Vimla by myself." As she bustled to the door, she realized her heart was pounding.

Vimla was not upstairs. Chandani and Om dashed out to the veranda. It was empty. Chandani was about to scream when she saw Vimla downstairs, standing at the open gates, the suitcase at her feet. Her hair was twisted into a neat plait that dangled down her straight back. She wore a dress that once belonged to Chandani, only it looked different on Vimla somehow, more elegant, less like a flour sack. From this distance Vimla could have been any woman with a plan. But she wasn't; she was their daughter.

A car rolled through the gloom and idled outside the Narine gates with the headlights off. Chandani gasped and flew down the stairs just as Krishna stepped out and gathered Vimla in an embrace that warmed Chandani's heart in spite of herself.

She opened her mouth to question Krishna's intentions, but something in the way Vimla said "So you reach at last" made her hang back in the shadows and watch.

Krishna's gallant smile faltered. His hands slid down Vimla's arms, lingered at her fingertips and fell away at his sides. He stumbled through an apology that grew so long-winded and pleading in Vimla's silence even Chandani pitied him. But more than that, Chandani took secret delight in the way Vimla stood with her shoulders pushed back and her chin tilted just so, listening to Krishna promise himself to her yet again. When he finished—or rather, exhausted—all the ways he could convince Vimla of his loyalty, Krishna said, "Let we go now," and held out his hand to her.

Om made to charge toward them, but Chandani grabbed his bicep and clung there.

Vimla inclined her head to the side as if she were seeing Krishna for the first time. "To?"

"Tobago." He gestured to the suitcase sitting at her feet. "I send a message with Minty!"

Vimla's smile was wistful. "Yes. And you send a message with Sookhoo to meet you in the cane field, too."

Chandani scowled in the darkness. So Sookhoo was a fish-monger and a news carrier. She would fix him the next time she saw him.

"Here." Vimla knelt beside the suitcase. The silver latches gleamed in the moonlight. They clicked under the gentle pressure of her fingers and the suitcase fell open like a yawn-ing mouth.

A conch shell of pearl and pink shimmered against the beige lining. Vimla took it in her hands and cradled it like an object long treasured before offering it to Krishna. "Take it back."

Something shifted in the twilight. The cicadas held their breath. The palm fronds arcing over the pair rose and fell in a sigh. Flambeaux, who sat watching them from the fence, flicked his tail and stalked away.

"You ain't coming with me?" Krishna dragged his fingers through his hair and sank to his knees.

"No."

Chandani closed her eyes. Om wrapped an arm around her spindly shoulders and drew her near.

"But Dutchie and Auntie Kay waiting."

Vimla shook her head. "Who?"

Krishna took the conch from her outstretched hand and held it to her ear. "Listen. Hear that freedom? Hear that energy?" He had a far-off look in his eyes. "I have a friend called Dutchie . . ."

The Sweetness of Tobago

Saturday, August 31, 1974

....

BACOLET BAY, TOBAGO

Dutchie and Krishna looped their way over the narrow road on old bicycles that *click-clacked* as they pedalled. Branches studded with leaves still wet from last night's rain slapped the bare chests of the cyclists in greeting. Krishna turned his face to the sky and caught sight of a blue-crowned motmot high in the trees, swinging its long tail feathers like a pendulum.

Dutchie glanced over his shoulder. "You good, Mr. Pundit? We going up a small hill just now."

"I good, I good," Krishna said. Sweat streamed down the sides of his body and soaked the elastic waistband of his shorts.

"You sure? I know you does spend whole day praying in Trinidad. Pundit work is real laziness," Dutchie said.

A driver popped his horn and Dutchie and Krishna veered to the side of the road to let him pass. "Good morning, boys!" Auntie Kay called, waving a yellow handkerchief out the window.

"I could ask that man to give you a drop by my parents' house, too, you know," Dutchie said, just as the car coughed around a bend in a haze of exhaust fumes. "Don't feel shame to ride with the lady."

Krishna pedalled past Dutchie. "I find you have all kind of big talks this morning, Captain. You must be forget how I bowl you out yesterday. Like allyuh doesn't know how to play cricket in Tobago, or what?"

Dutchie sailed past Krishna, steering with his knees as he styled his dreadlocks into an elaborate knot.

"Very Parisian," Krishna said.

"Hush your ass."

Krishna knew the house as soon as he saw it. The bungalow, painted sunset orange with a white wraparound veranda, sat tucked among a riot of blooming poui, flaming immortelle and bougainvillea trees. Pink climbing roses and vines of purple clematis wrapped the home in an embrace. And just outside the front door, throwing its bumpy leaves skyward in a perpetual expression of celebration, grew four fat aloe vera plants.

"We reach," Dutchie said, dropping his bicycle in the grass. "This is home." He jaunted across the lawn and ducked under a trellis of meandering vines and yellow roses. "Well, don't just stand up there like you lost. Come, Pundit!" And then he vanished around the back of the house.

Krishna's heart pinched with a strange mixture of wonderment and envy. Even as a boy, he couldn't ever remember feeling this eager to be in his parents' company. He lingered before the wooden signs standing proudly by the roadside: THE ICE CREAM MAN AND SOUP LADY LIVE HERE. WELCOME! A tortoise planter squatted at the foot of the sign, blue hydrangeas spilling out of its shell; seashell wind chimes tinkled on the porch; a baby goat curled up on the cushioned bench, dozing in the shade.

And certainly, Krishna thought, his home never held this much magic.

"Pundit!"

Krishna strode across the lawn and ducked under the trellis, where he found Dutchie stirring an enormous pot of soup. The soup bubbled and sent up the warm, rich aroma of broth that had cooked slowly, purposefully, for hours. "What kind of soup is it?"

"Provisions soup, my love."

Krishna glanced up and there stood Dutchie's mother in the doorway, holding a knife in one hand and a bowl of whole plantains in the other. She smiled at him and her eyes crinkled at the corners the way Dutchie's did. Krishna looked for dreadlocks hidden somewhere beneath the green bandana tied around her head, but he found hair like soft silver wool instead.

"My name is Iris, my love, but everybody does call me The Soup Lady, or Auntie Soup Lady, or Mama." She smiled, as if this last name was a particular favourite. "Welcome to my little Tobago haven." Iris sat on a chair before the pot and began to cut fat chunks of plantain directly into the soup. Her hands worked quickly, but her gaze remained trained on Krishna's face. "Do you like soup, son?"

He didn't really, but she glowed with such enthusiasm Krishna knew he'd be a fool to refuse anything Iris had to offer. "Yes."

Iris reached for another plantain and held it for a moment over the soup. "Not as much as my little Dutchie, I gather." The plantain tumbled into the soup and sank beneath the surface. "He does show up here every Sunday morning with the sun for the first bowl of the day." She tugged a dreadlock loose from his knot. "Nothing does cure a hangover like my soup, ain't, Dutchie?"

Dutchie threw his head back and laughed. "What you put in the soup so far, Mama? It nearly done cook?"

Iris took the long-handled spoon from Dutchie's hand and stirred. Her whole body swayed with the movement. A soft breeze lifted and dropped the green triangle of her bandana. "Cassava, eddoes, green fig, carrots, ochroe, sweet potato—"

"Hello. Good morning, Ms. Soup Lady!"

Iris stopped mid-stir and glanced over her shoulder. There stood a man and his daughter in their Sunday church clothes, grinning at her.

Iris placed a hand on her doughy hip. "Well, good morning, Clyde, and good morning, Jillian."

"The soup ready?" Clyde asked, craning his neck to peek into the pot.

"Almost. I ain't make the dumplings as yet, Clyde. Pass by on your way back from church, nuh?"

Clyde averted his gaze. "We ain't going to church today, Auntie Ms. Soup Lady!" Jillian exclaimed. The pink baubles in her hair bounced with her. "Daddy say God go forgive we if we miss a day of church to eat ice cream."

Iris smothered her laugh with a hand.

"And what your mommy say, Jillian?" Dutchie asked.

"Mommy ain't say anything because Mommy in Trinidad visiting Auntie Pat."

Clyde looked embarrassed. He lifted his daughter into his arms. "Jones in the back, Iris?"

"As usual," Iris said with a wink. She inclined her head to Krishna then. "Your sweet Auntie Kay has been taste-testing for the past twenty minutes."

Auntie Kay drifted back and forth on a swing suspended from a guava tree, a plastic spoon clamped in her mouth.

"What you think of my classic coconut, Kay?" Dutchie's father, Jones, asked. He poured a milky mixture into the metal drum of his ice cream maker. "People from all over the island does come just for that."

"Delicious, Jones," Auntie Kay said, licking the spoon clean. "Better than the guava, not as good as the soursop, equal to the star fruit."

Jones was packing the space between the drum and the outer barrel with ice. He stopped, brow furrowed. "True? The soursop better?" He poured salt overtop the ice to keep it from melting, deposited the cover and turned the ice cream maker's handle round.

"And the mango?"

Kay looked at him wide eyed. "I forget how the mango taste!"

Jones chuckled. "Well, better taste it again, then." He

nodded to the barrels lined up on a table covered with wet cloths. "Is the one in the centre."

Kay slipped off the swing and hummed her way to the ice creams. She helped herself to an extra spoonful of each.

Jillian skipped through the grass with the goat, mimicking his bleating sounds and squealing with delight. "Mr. Uncle Jones, you have any chocolate ice cream for me and the goat?"

Jones stopped his cranking. "Chocolate ice cream?" He crouched in the grass. "Ms. Jillian, you ever know me to make chocolate ice cream?"

The girl shrugged. "You could start."

"What about sapodilla?"

Krishna made a face behind Jones and Jillian copied it. Jones stood up and brushed the grass off his knees. "Dutchie!" He snapped his fingers at his son, who lay sprawled in the grass, staring at the sky. "Turn that ice cream there. I going to introduce the wonders of sapodilla ice cream to little Jillian."

It turned out Dutchie could churn a pale of ice cream as well as his father did. He wound the handle round and round, until sweat gathered at his temples. Jones nodded approvingly and then took Jillian by the hand and led her to a tree laden with sapodillas. "Look here." Jones plucked the brown fruit from a branch and turned it in his hands. "This ain't good. It half ripe." He pelted it at Dutchie, who ducked just in time, and Jillian laughed. "But you see this one?" Jones twisted another from the same branch. "This one get nice and full on the tree. This is a sweet sapodilla good enough for Uncle Jones's ice cream."

Jillian looked at Jones askance.

"Dutchie, scoop out some ice cream from that pail for me, boy."

Dutchie lifted the cover off the barrel and shovelled a generous serving of ice cream into an enamel cup for Jillian. She flicked her tongue over the ice cream, pensive. "This is sapodilla?" she asked.

Jones nodded, his brow furrowed again. "What you think?"

"I think you pick force-ripe sapodillas for this batch, Uncle Jones." The goat nosed her belly and she let him gobble her ice cream up. "Why you don't try and make barbadine ice cream instead?"

Jones scratched his head. "Barbadine?" A far-off look crept into his eyes and Krishna knew he was tasting barbadine ice cream in his mind for the first time. "Now, there's an idea, Jillian!" he said, and gathered her into his arms.

Vimla listened intently to Krishna's account of his stay in Tobago. He heard the enthusiasm in his own voice, became aware of his gesturing to help give shape to this other life he'd lived with Dutchie and Auntie Kay. Vimla laughed and grew pensive in all the right places—she even looked like she might be imagining herself in Tobago with Krishna. But when he was finished, Vimla swung the end of her plait back and forth and asked, "But what Tobago have for me?"

Krishna stared, dumbfounded, as if Vimla hadn't heard him at all. He thought of telling her another story—there were so many to tell. Perhaps he hadn't described his experience in enough colour, or maybe he'd told the jokes wrong. Even if that were true, certainly Vimla could see how much joy

Tobago had brought him. Couldn't she? "Me," Krishna said. "You will be in Tobago with me."

The silence that followed said everything. Vimla brushed a tear away, climbed to her feet and lifted the empty suitcase off the ground.

"I ain't going without you," Krishna said.

Vimla gave him a half-smile as if maybe she didn't believe him. "Well, then I guess I go see you at the wedding in a few hours." She backed away and pushed her weight against one of the gates and Krishna had no choice but to edge onto the road alone. They stared through the diamond pattern at one another—an eternity in a minute—until Vimla broke the spell, slipping a piece of paper to him without touching his fingers. Only after she'd turned away did Krishna read the note, climb back into his car and disappear.

Eye for an Eye

Faizal Mohammed threw a towel over one shoulder and set Sam on the other. "Allahu Akbar," they exclaimed in unison. On his way to his rain barrel, Faizal whistled and tossed a new bar of soap in his hands. Sam whistled back, bobbing his head. "The wedding today, Sam," Faizal said. "I telling you from now: you go have to stay home. Don't let me come home in the evening and find you vexed."

Sam whistled.

"Good parrot. Nice parrot."

Faizal sauntered into his bathroom and checked the rain barrel for floating blossoms. A frown creased his brow. "Not one, Sam" he said gravely. "Something bad does always happen when the barrel have nothing." He mumbled a prayer as he shuffled out of his slippers and flung his towel over the slab of corrugated iron that served as a wall. That's when he heard the crash next door.

"Mangoes! Sam—you hear that?" Sam cocked his head in the direction of the Gopalsinghs' residence. Faizal crept around the wall and squinted into the gloom.

"Who the hell put this bicycle here?" a voice growled.

Faizal darkened. Rajesh Gopalsingh. He felt cheated that Rajesh should sully his sacred bathing time with his wakefulness. Why was he up so early? This was Faizal's hour!

Faizal heard the distinct twist of a pipe and the fall of water in a bucket. His ears burned.

"Sam, what the hell Rajesh think he doing?" He folded his arms and stood for the duration of Rajesh's shamelessly short bath, relishing his groans of displeasure under the cascade of chilly water. When he was sure Rajesh had gone, Faizal stomped barefoot into his washroom and let Sam waddle off his finger onto the floor. He muttered while he stripped off his shorts and hoisted himself into the massive rain barrel. As the water rose to his chest and then his chin, Faizal let some of his irascible mood dissolve. But only some.

He vigorously lathered until clouds of silver-blue bubbles shimmered and rolled over the barrel's edge, all the while hating Rajesh for stealing Sangita Gopalsingh and his bath hour, too. Sam strutted about with importance, catching lathers on his outstretched wings.

"Hello. Good morning, Faizal Mohammed."

Faizal froze with the bar of soap in his armpit hair as Minty Gopalsingh rounded the corner into his bathroom. "Mangoes!" He dropped the soap into the water with a *plunk* and sank as low as he could into his barrel.

Minty took in the corrugated-iron walls, the large rain barrel, the soap holder, the frangipani awning, Sam waddling in the wet. And when her eyes fell on Faizal's shorts and towel, she took them down one at a time. Faizal folded his arms in the bubbles and scowled so deeply his face hurt with the effort. "What the ass you doing here?"

Minty raised an eyebrow, not unlike Sangita. "Visiting."

Faizal's eyes bulged at her flippant air. "You are not welcome here. At this hour. *In my bathroom!*" he hissed.

"Is my mother?" Minty draped the towel over her shoulder and folded Faizal's shorts into a neat rectangle, then again, into a square.

He flinched. "No." He shifted uncomfortably in the barrel. "What you want from me now?"

"Vimla going away," Minty said, tucking Faizal's folded shorts beneath her arm.

"Good. Where she going?"

"Canada." Minty folded the towel now, slow and precise.

Faizal looked genuinely surprised. Curiosity softened his grimace. "For what? She mother sending she away? That stupid ass Krishna know?"

Minty shook her head. "Faizal, you think I come here to stand up and talk to you in your barrel?" she said.

Faizal's ears reddened. "So what the hell you want from me, then? I can't drive she Canada if that what you come here for."

"She need money for the plane ticket."

Faizal sucked his teeth. "Tell she ask she father."

Minty hugged Faizal's shorts and towel to her chest, ignoring the suggestion altogether. "I see my mother give you back your chain."

He felt the rope at his neck and shrugged.

"How much you think we could get for that chain and the pendant and the watch? Enough for a ticket?"

Faizal's eyes narrowed to slits. "You ain't getting this chain back, girl. And don't you dare sell my pendant and my watch. I want them back!"

Minty shrugged. "Well then, buy Vimla a ticket then."

"I look like the bank to you?"

Minty began to inch away. "Okay, Faizal."

"'Okay, Faizal,'" he mocked, his lips an ugly twist. But then he realized she was walking away with his shorts and towel.

"Eh! You t'ief! Where you going with that?"

She kept her back turned to him, but he could hear the smile in her tone. "I going to put your shorts where my father could find them. He bedroom. Maybe inside he drawer. I think when he pull out these shorts he go know they ain't his. Look how narrow the waist is." She glanced over her shoulder at him and held them up for him to see. "What you think, Faizal?"

Faizal's fist splashed the water, soaking Sam in an unexpected shower. "Shut up! Shut up!" Sam cried.

"Eh, girl. What happen to you? Don't make joke." Faizal gripped the sides of the barrel and leaned toward Minty. "Rajesh go break my ass in two!"

Minty shrugged and made to leave again.

"Okay. All right. I go give you the money for the damn ticket. The farther away Vimla go, the better for me. Why you don't go and all?" he said.

Minty whirled on him. "Because somebody have to stay here and watch you, Faizal." She smiled. "I go see you at the wedding later." She flung his belongings into the frangipani tree and was gone.

The Power of
Periwinkles

Sunday September 1, 1974

....

CHANCE, TRINIDAD

Rajesh ambled naked through the house, dripping water onto the floor. "Sangita, where my towel?" He followed the ring of her anklets and found her gliding around the sewing room in a plum nightgown as translucent as a jellyfish.

Sangita spun around, her damp hair following a millisecond after. "Look how you wetting up the floor!" The dreaminess faded from her slanted eyes. "Check the cupboard, Raj."

He stayed rooted in the doorway. "I did. It ain't there."

The strap of Sangita's nightgown slid off her shoulder and she restored it with an impatient flip of her thumb. "I find you up early this morning," she said, crossing the room to the teak armoire in the corner. *Tink! Tink! Tink!* She yanked open the doors, bangles rattling at her wrists, and stopped.

"Raj?"

Rajesh wished he'd pulled on a pair of shorts at least. "Is a bunch of periwinkle flowers," he said gruffly.

"Of course it is. I know that." She tickled her nose with the miniature bouquet. "But in the cupboard?"

Rajesh tried to read the unusual set of Sangita's lips. Was she angry? He puffed out his broad chest and crossed his arms over it, filling the entire doorway. "Is a surprise for you," he said.

Sangita arched an eyebrow at him. "For me? A surprise for me, Raj?" She rose onto her toes so that she could look him in the eye. "In eighteen years, you never once surprise me." She narrowed her cat eyes at him. "Not once. So—"

"What about that extra piece of land I buy in the back there?" Rajesh jutted his thumb over his shoulder. "You was real surprise to see how much crop bare on that land."

"Crop?" Sangita turned the flowers round in her hands.

"And the pen for the cows. That pen didn't build itself. I build it in the hot sun for you."

"For me?"

"For your cows."

"My cows?" She tapped her honey décolletage with a finger.

"Well—*we* cows."

"Hmm." Sangita peered closer into Rajesh's face. "You up to something, Raj."

The floorboards groaned under Rajesh's shifting weight. He had played this scene over in his mind a dozen times through the night and a dozen more during this morning's chilly shower, and in none of those versions did Sangita accuse him of being "up to something." In fact, in one of his more liberal imaginings, he and Sangita had ended up making love in the hammock amid a scattering of periwinkles.

"Are you blushing?" Sangita asked.

Rajesh did not blush; at least, he didn't think so. "Sangita, throw me a towel, nuh! You don't see I standing up here naked?"

She swished back to the armoire and Rajesh sighed. It was those damn eyes of hers. Startlingly tawny. Soul penetrating. Animal eyes. They undid him every time, made him play the ass when he wanted very much to show her how much he cherished her.

Perhaps the periwinkles had been a mistake. Perhaps— Rajesh darkened—the seer man was full of shit.

"Shut up! Shut up! Shut up!"

Rajesh glanced out the window. There was Faizal Mohammed's kiss-me-ass parrot flapping his wings as he strutted along the fence. "The Love Boat!" the parrot squawked. Rajesh cringed. He wanted to wring its neck as much as he wanted to wring Faizal Mohammed's, but that would only vex Sangita. She had quarrelled with him the day he'd cuffed Faizal, as if—what? She cared for him? Rajesh scowled just as a towel arced through the air and smacked him in the face.

"Surprise!" Sangita's laughter was like the peal of bells.

Rajesh's expression softened; a hesitant smile spread its way across his face. He wrapped the towel snugly around his waist and decided to try again.

"The flowers is like your sari," Rajesh said, gesturing casually to the sari she'd pressed the night before. It was draped over a chair by the window. The intricate beadwork caught the early-morning sunshine and threw playful designs on the whitewashed wall. It was gold and periwinkle blue.

Sangita looked from the flowers in her hand to the sari and back again. She fingered the delicate petals of a single blossom one by one as if she'd never seen a periwinkle before.

"Ain't it matching?" Raj lifted the sari off the chair and held it in the light pouring through the window. "Is the same blue, I think." His forehead crinkled. "Deepa at Deepa Textiles say it is the same blue."

Sangita's lips just barely curved at the corners. "Deepa Textiles?"

Rajesh sucked his teeth to hide his embarrassment. "Never mind that!"

She hid her mouth behind the spray of flowers, but her eyes shimmered with amusement. "Deepa was right, Raj," she said.

Rajesh cleared his throat. "Good. You're welcome." He stood awkwardly in the middle of the room, not knowing where to look or what to do next, and so he said, "Where my shirt and pants for the wedding? Everything done press?" Although he could see his clothes hanging neatly from a hanger in the open closet. He noticed Sangita had embroidered his shirt collar and cuffs with gold threading, and replaced the plain white buttons with pearly fastens instead. She had been busy. Should he thank her?

Sangita laid her flowers next to her sewing machine and handed Rajesh his suit of clothes. "Raj?"

"What?" He sounded surly, but only because she had interrupted his thoughts.

"What you want me to do with the flowers? Hold them? Put them in a vase?"

Rajesh regarded her as if she'd asked him to sell all his land or, worse, take up house with that panty-man Faizal Mohammed. "Sangita, they for your hair, girl."

She blinked her mysterious eyes at him.

He sucked his teeth again, flustered. "Never mind. Meet me in the garden when you done dress," he said, striding out the door. "And bring the flowers with you. I going to finish my tea."

"Tea!" Sangita dissolved into girlish giggles as he rounded the corner down the hallway. "Since when you does drink tea? Rajesh Gopalsingh, you wake up real crazy this morning!"

He shrugged. Maybe she was right, but he was certain Sangita hadn't laughed that way with him in years.

He waited for her under the shady mango tree, his back pressed against the steady trunk. A warm breeze whispered in the branches and set the leaves a-quiver. Rajesh inhaled the sweet scent of ripe mangoes and felt his nerves drift away.

He checked to make sure he'd remembered everything. There was the stool for Sangita to sit on, and there, just next to it, a makeshift table of cardboard where her hairpins were laid out. Beside the pins, a cup of coffee with sugar and cream sat steaming in the already hot day.

Rajesh inclined his head to the ringing of Sangita's footfalls, accompanied this time by a song. He closed his eyes and listened. It was an old wedding song, and not just any: it was his, or rather, *theirs*. Buoyed, Rajesh welcomed Sangita under the mango tree with an uncharacteristic flourish of his arm.

Her sari was lovely, yes, but it was her body curving beneath the drapes and folds of the ethereal fabric, and the flecks of light dancing through her curious eyes that made Sangita so achingly beautiful in that moment. Her very movements made music: bells at her feet, bangles at her wrists, gold hangers jingling from her lobes. When had Rajesh stopped noticing this? She cast him a coy look and something stirred deep in his heart.

"Sit," he said, guiding her toward the stool.

She obliged but swivelled to face him, the flowers in her lap. "I just waiting for my hair to dry before I plait it and weave the periwinkles through," she said.

Rajesh laughed. "A plait? No." He circled the stool so that he stood behind Sangita again and in one motion swept the heavy mass of her inky hair off her neck.

"Rajesh! What you—?"

"Wait, nuh, girl!" Rajesh began to coil Sangita's hair, twisting the long rope of it again and again against the back of her head until he'd fashioned a bun.

"Rajesh Gopalsingh, you gone mad. You really gone mad!"

"Sangita, you want your bun to come out loose and lopsided? You want to look like a one-horned ram goat? Wait!"

Rajesh fumbled with the dainty hairpins. Some were lost in the grass, others contorted under the pressure of his thick fingers. But the pins he salvaged he jammed in and around Sangita's bun to secure it in place.

"Rajesh, those hairpins chooking like nails!" Sangita winced.

"Sorry, sorry!"

"Hear, boy: you could cut cane, and you could mind animal, and you could own plenty land, but you is no hairdresser!"

Rajesh could hear her smiling. He reached over her shoulder and extracted the bouquet from her fingers. And then, with the hands that so capably wielded a cutlass in the cane field, Rajesh pinned each periwinkle flower into Sangita's bun until the entire twist was covered in blue blossoms.

"Miss Lady," he teased, "maybe I look like a big dotish ass, but I had eight sisters, and if is one thing I could do, is dress a woman's bun with flowers."

Sangita tilted her head back and laughed, and seeing this as his chance, Rajesh placed his big hands on either side of her face, leaned forward and kissed his wife.

From next door, Rajesh heard the unmistakable *thwack* of a coconut broom pelted against the fence. "Motherfucking mangoes, Sam. You see that?"

Rajesh closed his eyes and smiled into the soft peaks of Sangita's lips.

Unexpected
Wedding Guests

"Oh Bhagwan, give me strength." Anand staggered backward in a haze of sandalwood smoke. Maya extracted the incense sticks from his fingers and Krishna lowered him gently into a chair on the veranda. "Kaywattie pick up a creole man in Tobago and bring him *here? Now?*" he said.

Maya's eyes were round with panic. "Don't watch, Anand," she pleaded. "You go send up your pressure." She smoothed the hair back around her face, but it only sprang up again.

Krishna saw his father grip the sides of his chair, noted the tremor in his loose, fleshy jowls and knew it was too late for that. "She couldn't put on something better than that for the wedding?" he said. "Short-short hair, short-short skirt! And don't talk about that dreadlock fella with the captain's hat." He hid his hands in his face and groaned.

Krishna shuffled uncomfortably at Anand's side. Auntie Kay and Dutchie hadn't come to Trinidad for a wedding; they had come to whisk Vimla and Krishna away to Tobago on the *The Reverie*. But early that morning, when Krishna had arrived at the designated meeting spot behind Lal's Rum Shop, alone and heartbroken, he had set their plans terribly awry.

"What you mean, she ain't want to live in Tobago?" Dutchie had asked, incredulous.

"Oh, dahlin." Auntie Kay had stroked the side of Krishna's drawn face, her own eyes gleaming with tears. "Let we set sail for home."

But Krishna wouldn't go. If Vimla refused to run away to Tobago with him, then he would stay in Trinidad, marry Chalisa Shankar, do right by his father and . . .

"Anand, you see how your sister behaving like she ain't have morals?" Maya said, jarring Krishna from his thoughts.

"I thought you tell me don't watch!" Anand snapped, although Krishna could see his father peeking through splayed fingers at the spectacle below.

Auntie Kay turned here and there, rising onto her toes and throwing herself into various open arms. She wore every colour on her dress in a print both mesmerizing and maddening to the eyes. The twirl of her skirt was like peering through a kaleidoscope and each person she smiled at lit up like a diya. Dutchie followed close behind. He doffed his white captain's hat at everyone who enveloped Auntie Kay and bowed gallantly to the children who scampered after him to touch his red-brown dreadlocks. In a matter of minutes Auntie Kay and

Dutchie were at the very heart of the wedding chaos and everyone rotated around them as if they were twin suns.

Auntie Kay capered through the churn of activity as if life
were like this every day. She nodded to the Hummingbird
Tassa Group heating their drums by the fireside and the men
stirring enormous, bubbling pots on firecrackers. Carefully
she picked her way around the guests bent over fresh, green
sohari leaves brimming with mounds of food, and the revellers who rolled their waists to music booming from a speaker
box in the kitchen. As she mounted the first step to the
veranda, Bulldog, drinking respectfully outside the Govind
gates on Kiskadee Trace, called, "Kay, you coming back
Trinidad to live?"

She waved at him. "Not likely, dahlin."

He raised his cup to her. "We miss you, that is all."

"You too sweet, Bulldog," Auntie Kay said, but she didn't
say she missed them back. "And where is the good pundit?"
Her eyes twinkled with mischief.

Bulldog nodded at the second storey and Auntie Kay trotted up the staircase, with Dutchie taking two steps at a time
by her side.

Anand was already abusing the air with angry gestures when
Auntie Kay planted her small, slippered feet on the veranda.
"Of all the days, Kaywattie!" he exclaimed.

Auntie Kay rolled her eyes, one hand resting on her slender
hip.

"Sita-Ram, Pundit-ji. The name is Captain Dutchie."
Dutchie clasped his hands and bowed.

Anand stopped waving and winced. "A Hindu creole?" he mumbled.

Dutchie tossed his dreadlocks back and laughed from deep in his belly. "Not really. My church is in my heart."

Anand scowled at him. "Stupidness."

Krishna sighed. "Dutchie is a good friend, Pa."

Anand glanced at Krishna, who was standing behind him in no shirt and a pair of old pants. "I didn't send you Tobago to make friends," he shot back. "Go and dress for the wedding."

But Krishna lingered. Auntie Kay had perched on the edge of a chair adjacent to Anand and now she said, "I hear you marrieding your son to a stranger."

The very frankness of her remark made Anand's eyes bulge red and veiny from his face. Like a mean fish, Krishna thought.

"And so you come Trinidad to see?" Anand spat. "Well, if I knew a wedding would bring you home, I would have find Krishna a bride sooner! How long I ain't see you?" He stroked his moustache. "Ten, twelve years?"

Auntie Kay folded her arms and narrowed her eyes at her brother. "Four," she said.

Anand shrugged. "Four. Excuse me. I miscount."

She laughed in his brooding face. "Anand, you never miscount a thing in your life. Counting is your expertise." She turned to Krishna. "Did you know your father had his own currency using rocks when he was a child?" She giggled despite herself. "He would collect he dollar rocks, count them throughout the day and then bury them under the guava tree in the back every evening."

Anand stood up, the lovely silk drapes of his cream dhoti billowing in the breeze. "Excuse me, Kaywattie . . ."

The smile vanished from her face.

"I have guests to greet, Krishna have to dress and we leaving for St. Joseph very soon. Is there something I can do for you and your *friend*?"

Krishna found himself wondering the same thing. He hadn't expected to see Auntie Kay and Dutchie again for some time, let alone on the morning of his wedding in the presence of his deeply indignant father. But still, he was glad to share this small square of space with them, if only for a few minutes before Anand sent them away. Auntie Kay and Dutchie radiated the very qualities Krishna did not have, hope and courage, and most of all the two of them were vivacious in all they did. While he did not believe that Auntie Kay and Dutchie could sail into the Govind residence and successfully reason his wedding to Chalisa away, he admired their moxie and the very romance of their endeavour.

"Anand, Krishna and Chalisa won't last," Auntie Kay said flatly. She got up, too, and folded her arms over her wild printed dress.

"Eh!" Anand pointed directly in her face. "You is not an expert in relationships."

Auntie Kay flinched, a subtle flutter of her black lashes. "Bas was a mistake." She brushed Anand's hand away and stood bravely before him.

"And who you think paying for that mistake, Kaywattie?" Anand turned his finger on himself, jabbing his chest again and again. "Me! I paying for it. Every damn day that pass, I paying for it!"

Krishna sensed his father had waited a long time to utter those words.

Maya tried to take Anand's arm, but he twisted from her hold with a growl.

Auntie Kay's eyes flashed. "Yes, Anand, I know your precious reputation damage because of my divorce." Her voice trembled. "I know I am a blight on the family name."

"An expensive blight!"

Krishna stepped around Anand and squeezed his way between the two. Dutchie threw Krishna a warning look, a look that urged him to intervene. Did Dutchie know what he did? Had he known it all along?

"An expensive blight?" The fire in Auntie Kay ebbed to a mere glow. She tipped her head to the side and searched Anand's face.

Maya averted her gaze and strummed her fingers against her mouth as if to keep the truth locked in.

"Oh, Kaywattie, you real naïve, girl," Anand said. He trailed his fingers over his mala. "Don't you know I have been sending money to Bas for years now, trying to buy back that kiss-me-ass piece of land you living on in Tobago?"

Auntie Kay opened her mouth and closed it again. Her hands found her belly, where her belt was tied in a looping bow. She swayed on her feet. Krishna imagined her thoughts: had she lived a lie these past years; was the independence she had so delighted in non-existent?

Anand, blinded by his own vexation and the burden of his sister's debt, seemed not to notice Auntie Kay's effervescence fading into something frighteningly tragic. He blustered on. "But when Krishna marry Chalisa—"

Krishna laid a firm grip on his father's shoulder. "Pa, there is no need for all of this. Auntie Kay only come here today because she want to see me happy."

Auntie Kay leaned into Dutchie. "When Krishna marry Chalisa . . .?" she prompted Anand.

Anand shook Krishna off like a fly. "I go finally have enough money to pay off Bas the Ass and retire."

Dutchie draped a protective arm around Auntie Kay and for the first time Krishna saw a single line of worry etch itself across his shining forehead.

Auntie Kay stared at her slippers. The veranda fell quiet and the gaiety below swelled around them like some cruel joke. "Allyuh open a next bottle of Puncheon!" Roop G. Kapil hollered from behind the ixora bush. "We pundit marrieding he son today!"

A cheer rose.

Auntie Kay met Krishna's eyes, took his large hands in her small ones. "Did you know?"

Krishna lowered his gaze. "Yes."

The Wedding Barat

The loudspeakers hummed and crackled to life. Mohammed Rafi's voice blared over Kiskadee Trace and a cheer flew up from the procession of cars winding bumper to bumper from the Govinds' home to Mahadeo's shop. People honked their horns, broke into song at random, knocked back their first drink of the day. Sangita Gopalsingh shimmied into the road and gave the district a dance they would remember for years. The sun glittered off rooftops and car tops, and rings and bangles on hands that draped out of windows to strum car doors. The air was so thick with merrymaking Vimla could barely breathe.

"That woman really have no shame," Chandani muttered, fixing the hem of her skirt over her ankles. "And what the hell she have that shitting periwinkle pin up all over she head for? She feel this is Carnival?"

Vimla saw Faizal Mohammed lean out of his window and drink Sangita in with insatiable thirst. Vimla knew that look well—she had seen it on Krishna's face just hours ago; only then it had been muted in pre-dawn shadows and nerves.

She had left him at the gates without looking back. A stolen glance over her shoulder could have shattered Vimla's resolve and hurled her back into limbo where other people—bigger, more influential people—manipulated her destiny. But Vimla wouldn't throw away her last shot at freedom for a glimpse of Krishna's tumble of black curls. Not this time. So she fixed her eyes forward, marched past Chandani and Om on the veranda stairs and lowered herself into a chair.

Chandani and Om stared at Vimla in what Vimla imagined was awe.

"We wasn't going to same way," Vimla said, gazing at the sky, where the stars were receding like memories. "Let we go to the wedding."

"We ain't—"

"Ma, nobody know about Anand and the deed except we and the Shankars. According to the district Chalisa and Krishna was marrieding all along. How it go look if you ain't go? You go have to live nice with Pundit Anand after the wedding. You might as well start by seeing he son marry."

Vimla knew she'd been right. No matter how Anand and Maya had shamed her family, they could not avoid Krishna's wedding. In attending they would show they supported Krishna's union to Chalisa Shankar; that there were no hard feelings about Vimla being passed up; that Vimla and Krishna's tryst had been innocent puppy love—something to laugh at and forget about. All lies, of course, but essential to Chandani's and

Om's peace of mind and restoring Vimla's own reputation.

Chandani had watched the way Vimla's eyes drifted from one star to the next like she was charting her course around the world. "And tell me, Vimla, why you want to see Krishna marry that girl?" she'd asked.

"I always wanted to be at Krishna's wedding," Vimla had said, wryly. "Is the last thing for me to do before I go."

Chandani looked at Om. He reached out and patted her back—awkward thumps that rattled her small frame. They both knew that Vimla would find her way to Canada with or without their permission. They knew now how she hitched her heart on perilous dreams and held on until the end.

Chandani snorted. "Miss Lady, you think your father does fly plane for BWI?" She nudged Om in the gut. "How we daughter come out so wayward?"

This is how Chandani gave Vimla her blessings.

"Watch Puncheon," Om said, looking in his rear-view mirror.

Chandani and Vimla twisted around as Puncheon on his bike weaved in front of the car behind them. The car screeched. The driver cursed.

Puncheon held up a hand. "You brakes working nice, Boss!" he said, bicycling on until he reached Om's car. "Hello. Hi!" He slapped the hood.

Chandani leaned forward so she could see Puncheon around Om. "Is like you looking for someone to bounce you down."

Puncheon dismounted and transferred the two Guinness Extra Stouts from his basket into his pockets with a grin. "You have place?" He abandoned the bike at the side of the road, opened the car door and climbed in next to Vimla before Chandani could object. The heady mixture of Vaseline, sweat and beer wafted through the car.

"People charging five dollars a man for a ride to the wedding," Chandani said. But she didn't reach back to accept the payment—she didn't even turn to look at Puncheon getting himself comfortable in the back. She was merely making a point, communicating the rules.

Puncheon whispered to Vimla behind his hand. "Going to see your lovah-boy get married?" He showed his yellowing teeth in a grin and opened a beer.

Vimla turned her face to the road as if Puncheon didn't exist, as if his boozy breath hadn't assaulted her cheek. If she stretched her neck far enough and squinted just so, she could make out the car with the pulsating loudspeakers secured to the roof, leading the procession to the bride's home. The tassa group followed close behind them. They stuffed themselves into one car with their drums wedged beneath their armpits and up against their bellies, tapping the rhythm from the loudspeaker on their knees. And in the third car, the one festooned with garlands of red and white dahlias, plastic pompoms, and streamers, the one floating like a white phantasm before Vimla's eyes, sat Krishna and his family. She imagined him sunk against the back seat, the embroidery on his *jamajura* digging into his flesh, his lovely curls flattened under a jewelled turban. How many times would he knock it askew in an attempt to rake his fingers through his hair, she wondered with a small smile.

"Excuse me!" a voice shrilled, interrupting her thoughts. "Good morning! Excuse me!" Gloria Ramnath zigzagged through the cars, her bottom swishing. "Allyuh see Dr. Mohan?" She pushed herself through Om's open window so that her fleshy bosom hung perilously close to his face. Chandani recoiled, although she was far enough away not to come in contact with the perspiration rolling into the abyss of Gloria's cleavage. "Fatty-Om, Dr. Mohan say he have place for me in he car, but I can't find he." She shoved her hand down the front of her dress and withdrew a handkerchief that already looked moist. Six rings glittered on four fingers.

Om shrugged. "I ain't see Dr. Mohan, but he must be here somewhere. It have plenty car behind me."

Gloria heaved a sigh and looked pleadingly at Om instead of the trail of cars.

Vimla thought of riding two hours in a car, jammed between Puncheon and Gloria Ramnath. She could almost feel their sticky skin pasted to hers, the sickening sensation of peeling free when they arrived in St. Joseph.

"You see that Austin Cambridge?" Chandani pointed to the Gopalsinghs' car ahead of them. "Them have plenty place. You could sit in the back with Minty."

Gloria squinted against the flashing metal. "Oh gosh. With Sangita? I go have to watch she wave and skin she teeth at everyone from here to St. Joseph and back!"

Chandani blinked stoically at her. She would not be dragged into gossip about her neighbour, however much she agreed.

Gloria peered into the back seat. "Go around, nuh?" she said to Vimla. "I could ride in the back with you and Puncheon. He could fold up small and sit in the middle. He hand and foot like bamboo stalk, anyway." She laughed. Her bosom bounced toward Om's eye.

Puncheon cuffed the back of Om's seat. "Tell she walk, nuh? Maybe she go loss some weight and get small like me."

Gloria scowled.

A cacophony of staccato car horns worked its way from the head of the convoy down the line. Om shifted into drive. "The barat leaving. You going with we or them?" he asked Gloria.

Puncheon flung his legs and arms out to show there was no room. Vimla glowered at her to show she had not forgotten Gloria's nastiness in the market.

"Humph!" Gloria huffed, and bustled away. She scrambled into the back seat of Rajesh's car just as it rolled forward.

They arrived in St. Joseph in great fanfare: music blaring, cars honking, people cheering and almost everyone—apart from the Govinds and Narines—blissfully tipsy. The people of Chance district poured out of their cars a block away from the Shankars' estate and fell in behind the tassa players and Pundit Anand and Maya on the road. *Patang!* The first strike against the drum resounded through the air. A charged lull ensued. Vimla saw a few people nudge each other and exchange knowing smiles. Someone whistled. The woman in front of Vimla bent her knees, thrust her bottom out, hiked up her skirt and waited. And then it happened: an explosion of rhythm rolled off the drums and the pound of heavy bass fell in sync with their hearts. The barat broke into a joyous frenzy of swivelling hips and swept Vimla forward down the road.

In the distance Chalisa's tassa group answered back. They came over the incline in the road with red tassels dangling from their drums, and behind them, a barat that shimmered in their movements. All the young women could have been brides, all the young men grooms. Vimla gasped. What must Chalisa look like? She pictured her tucked away in the big house, swathed in raw silk and diamonds, listening to her wedding celebrations with a sense of impending doom. Vimla pushed her guilt away and leaned into Chandani, who poked her arm and said, "Them people could really show off." She walked stiffly, her mouth pulled into a disapproving frown as the people from Chance district revelled around her. "You see how they trying to make style on we? All that glitters isn't gold, Vimla."

And yet everything that glittered was indeed gold. Drum tassels, sari borders, jewels, even the dainty bindis suspended between the women's eyebrows. Gold. Everything was gold and everything glittered. Vimla caught a glimpse of Pundit Anand's face as he turned his head. He didn't look slighted at all; in fact, he positively glowed.

The tassa groups met in the middle and engaged in a rhythm clash that excited the wedding guests to no end. This is when the most eccentric or obscene dancers pushed their way into the centre and exhibited their talents. Puncheon stuck his tongue out to the side, clasped his hands behind his head and thrust his pelvis back and forth as if he had a motor in his pants. The people went crazy for this, whistling and cheering him on. A young man from the bride's side challenged Puncheon's display. He pulled up his pant legs, spread his legs wide and squatted low to the ground. When the tassa switched tempo, he gyrated his waist in a circle an inch at a time the way a second hand goes round a clock. Both sides were joyfully scandalized.

The crowd churned and carried Minty, Sangita and Rajesh

ahead. Vimla followed Sangita's bright-blue sari in the sea. The gossamer material revealed the dizzying spiral of her waist, which Rajesh admired as he orbited around her. A few feet away Faizal Mohammed stood in a yellow checked shirt with the collar turned up, and gazed, bewildered, after the couple. And Minty lingered just behind Faizal Mohammed; her glossy ponytail swung from side to side as she scoured the crowd for Vimla.

"Ma!" Vimla yelled in Chandani's ear. "I going by Minty. I go meet you in the tent." She slipped away before Chandani could object.

As she wriggled through the crowd, Vimla snatched at conversations partly drowned out by the tassa:

"Whey! Watch how coconut man's head shining like crystal ball in this heat!"

"Wait, nuh, man. Let the pundit and them settle up by the mandap and we go knock a few drinks by the car."

"I glad we pundit find a nice girl for he son to marry."

"Nice? You ain't hear about *Mastana Bahar!*"

"Allyuh see Sangita sari? She couldn't put on a dress like the rest of we? She dress up like the bride self!"

"I think Bulldog have sugar. I fine he looking old and dry up these days. Watch, nuh?"

"Haul your ass! You think this road pave for you alone to dance?"

"I hear the Shankars does fan fly with money. Pundit Anand must be get rich now."

"Allyuh see Kay? I hear she married a creole captain."

Vimla passed Headmaster Roop G. Kapil. He held his head high, pinching the lapels of his jacket between two fingers as he danced off-beat. His salt-and-pepper bangs flapped over his left lens in his merriment. Headmaster looked confident, pleased with himself even. Much different, Vimla thought, from the sputtering fool Chandani had reduced him to at the school weeks ago. He caught Vimla's eye and smiled. She looked away, embarrassed by the freeness of his movements.

A man careered through the crowd, barrelling into Vimla on his way to the front for a dance. "Sorry, darling!" he yelled. Vimla pitched sideways and saw the asphalt rising to meet her, when a wiry arm caught her around the waist and steadied her on her feet. She glanced up. Faizal Mohammed shook his head and folded his arms.

"How you going?" he asked.

Vimla straightened her dress and mumbled a thank you. "You have my money?" she asked.

The top two buttons of his shirt were undone; his fat chain gleamed. "I find you real boldface."

Vimla shrugged. "And you not?"

"What you going over for?" His eyes were bright with curiosity.

"To study."

"And you plan to come back?"

"Yes."

"That is a shame." He stroked his long neck, scratched just at his bulging Adam's apple. "And wouldn't your mother wonder where you get money for passage to Canada?"

"I done tell she is scholarship money."

Faizal raised his eyebrows. "Eh, gyul, you does ever tired lie?"

"You does?" She twisted through the labyrinth of people away from him.

————

Minty and Vimla stood still with their shoulders touching and the crowd swirling around them. Something had shifted between them since they'd last spoken; Vimla sensed it in the prolonged moments they allowed tassa to fill the place of conversation, in the way they leaned into each other but each avoided the other's eyes. It was Vimla's fault, of course, flying away and leaving Minty behind after all she had done for Vimla, after all she would yet do to send her off. The more Vimla thought of Minty's inevitable hurt, the sharper her guilt gouged the pit of her stomach. She considered saying thank you, but then realized how insufficient, how flimsy, it would sound in the cacophony of Krishna's wedding.

Vimla finally said, "He come for me last night, you know."

"I know. I hear the car pull up by your gates."

Vimla laughed despite herself. "You come just like Faizal Mohammed, studying people's business all hours of the night."

Minty looked sheepish.

The tassa groups drew to the side of the road and allowed Nanny, Anand and Maya to embrace and exchange malas of jasmines and marigolds. When Nanny went, with Pundit Panday and her closest companions, to fetch Krishna from the confines of his air-conditioned car, Vimla's stomach somersaulted. Minty's fingers closed around hers and squeezed.

Dream Girl

Sunday September 1, 1974

....

ST. JOSEPH, TRINIDAD

Chalisa was spent from a night of crying and now she stood like a mannequin in the middle of her parents' bedroom while Delores fussed around her with an assortment of safety pins and hairpins clamped between her lips. Avinash lay on his belly on the bed, knocking his ankles together, his chin tucked in his palm.

"She pleats crooked, Delores," Nanny said, whisking into the room. She brought with her the scent of incense, perspiration and the faintest hint of rum.

Delores froze, pins protruding from her mouth like teeth. She had just finished dressing Chalisa and it had taken her well over an hour. She watched, horrified, as Nanny unpinned the phaloo from Chalisa's shoulder and yanked the pleats from the front of Chalisa's petticoat. Chalisa should have felt sorry for Delores as she spat the pins into her palm and sank onto the bed next to Avinash, but her heart was too full with pity for herself.

Two weeks ago Chalisa could not have imagined her decision to audition for *Mastana Bahar* would inevitably yoke her to an aspiring pundit. Now she understood that Nanny's pride was as brittle as her bones, that her own flirtatious performance had erased some smugness from Nanny's face. But Nanny's reprisal was excessive. Just as Chalisa stretched a toe in the vast realm of stardom, Nanny yanked her away. What Nanny didn't see was that Chalisa needed to sing and dance; it was the one thing that dispelled her loneliness and made her feel that her mother was nearer somehow.

Nanny crouched; her knees cracked. She wove the crimson silk between her gnarled fingers until a dozen perfect pleats swept from Chalisa's navel to the tips of her toes. "Like that, Delores," she said, her face contorting in discomfort as she straightened. She took a step back to admire her work. "Make sure my pleats look so before you light the funeral pyre. If my pleats look twist-up for Bhagwan, I go come back and haunt allyuh."

Delores was frightened already. She nodded and studied the folds and drapes of Chalisa's sari as if she were stamping the image in her mind.

"How you feeling, Chalisa?" Nanny asked. Her smile seemed distant, like she was seeing someone else.

Yesterday Chalisa had pleaded with Nanny to undo this scheme. Her cries had echoed through the house and spilled into the yard, until Nanny ordered Delores to shut the windows up and draw the curtains. The house grew hot and more oppressive than ever. It was only when Chalisa's tears had run dry and her throat had gone hoarse that Delores threw open the windows again. In the morning Chalisa woke with eyes so swollen she looked like she'd been devoured by mosquitoes. And here was Nanny, after Chalisa had held a cold compress to her eyelids for two hours, asking her how she was. The very sight of Nanny made Chalisa sick. She turned her face away and said nothing.

Nanny huffed; rum vapours wafted into the air. "Is some good licks you want, Chalisa!" she said. "Don't think I wouldn't beat you one last time before you get married." She shook her finger in Chalisa's face.

Chalisa rolled her tawny eyes boldly. Nanny hadn't laid a hand on her since her parents had died—not even after her sultry performance on *Mastana Bahar.*

"Bring the jewellery, Avinash," Nanny said.

Delores guided Chalisa to the vanity. Her blouse dug into her ribs when she moved.

Avinash brought the velvet cases one by one. He lined them up on the vanity in a neat row and stood like a soldier by Nanny's side waiting for his next duty. Delores and Nanny unlatched the cases and opened the lids as if they'd done this together once before.

"Switch on the lights, Avinash."

The jewels sparkled. Chalisa couldn't help herself; she fingered a necklace, lingering on the emerald paisleys skirting a ruby the size of Avinash's fist. Chalisa noticed Nanny's lips twitch and she dropped her hands back into her lap.

Without a word, Nanny and Delores fell into a dance, circling Chalisa with pieces of jewellery in their hands. Nanny lifted her right hand and Delores her left, simultaneously sliding identical sets of gold and opal bangles over her wrists. Nanny disappeared behind her and Chalisa saw a bejewelled choker hover at her eye level before it closed around her slender neck. This was followed by two longer necklaces that draped across the red silk of her sari like ropes. Delores clipped a flower nose ring with a delicate diamond in the centre to Chalisa's nose and hooked the fil-igree chain attached to one of Chalisa's enormous earrings. The nose ring pinched her nostril and the earrings stretched her earlobes.

"Lift your foot," Delores instructed. She crouched and placed Chalisa's heels in her lap so that she could fasten the *payals* around her ankles. When Chalisa lowered her feet back to the ground the gold anklets tinkled a joyful sound that seemed out of place.

Avinash's mouth made an O. "Pretty," he breathed.

The last thing they did was pin the phaloo over Chalisa's intricately twisted hair, cutting into her peripheral vision. She wondered then if Indian brides were so tightly wrapped and heavily ornamented to prevent them from running—and seeing.

"Nice," Delores said.

Nanny folded her arms and nodded. Chalisa thought she glimpsed melancholy in her cataract eyes, but it dissolved before she could be sure.

Delores pulled Chalisa to her feet and motioned for her to look in the full-length mirror leaning against the wall. Chalisa refused. She let the weight of her bridal trappings pull her back into the chair, clinking in a dozen places. She didn't need a mirror to see what was plainly written on Nanny's and

Delores's faces: Chalisa looked precisely like the film star she'd always dreamed of becoming.

Her heart felt black.

When they came for her, Chalisa was sitting alone, a picture of her parents lying idly in her lap.

Delores kissed the picture and set it on the vanity. "Ready?" she asked.

Panic exploded behind Chalisa's thick lashes. She gripped the sides of the chair and wondered if the women would drag her to the mandap. She clenched her jaw and resolved to stay until she was certain Vimla would not save her.

Avinash placed his hand over Chalisa's. Her breath quickened at the scratch of paper against her skin. His eyes were the roundest she'd ever seen them, frightened and excited at once. She extracted the paper from his fingers. Delores busied herself with sliding yet more pins into Chalisa's hair. Chalisa thought she heard her whisper, "Do fast before Nanny come." But the thudding in her ears made it impossible to know for sure.

Chalisa's hands trembled. She unfolded the scrap, tearing the edge in her haste.

Chalisa,
Do what you must. I am leaving Trinidad.
Vimla

Chalisa released the breath she was holding and for a moment felt nothing. She watched her fingers curl around the scrap, her knuckles turn white.

Somewhere tassa was rolling and growing louder. A woman cursed the heat. A baby cooed. A child exclaimed, "I see the bride, Mammy! Why she face vexy-vexy so?"

Chalisa fixed her gaze on her fist. "Avinash. Did Gavin reach?"

Avinash drew his solemn face close to Chalisa's and murmured, "He say you still his Dream Girl."

Nanny appeared in the doorway. Additional Xs around her mouth marked her impatience. "What going on here? The people waiting!"

Chalisa squared her shoulders, inhaled deeply and prepared for the greatest performance of her life. "Let we go."

A Bacchanal Wedding

Sunday September 1, 1974

....

ST. JOSEPH, TRINIDAD

K rishna looked like the god his father had named him for, sitting beneath the wedding mandap, a pergola, in fabrics finer than anything Sangita had ever worn. His ornamented turban, jammed tightly over the tips of his ears, flashed in the guttering diya light. As he waited with his forearms just resting on his thighs, Krishna's gaze skipped from face to face like a pebble over water until it fell on Vimla and drowned in her unblinking, bottomless eyes.

While Pundit Panday twiddled his thumbs in his lap and beamed at the wedding guests seated in rows beneath the adjoining white tent, Pundit Anand admired the grand columns, where sprays of hibiscus, coxcombs and fragrant jasmines wilted in the heat and fire smoke. He wiggled his toes in the swaths of Indian textile cascading to the mandap floor in pools all around him. He caressed a gold braid tied round a drape of orange organza and his eyes twinkled.

"Watch how we pundit making a ass out of he self," Chandani muttered to Vimla. Chandani had insisted they sit in the very first row, where the Govinds could see them and be reminded of their vacillating loyalty, of their base greed. Chandani pressed her spine into the back of the chair and knotted her fingers into a brown labyrinth.

Behind them Faizal Mohammed whistled. "Whey, sir! Watch style!" he exclaimed.

A collective gasp swept over the guests as Chalisa stepped from her home with Nanny, Delores and Avinash crowding about her like security. Nanny wound her veiny arm around Chalisa's waist and Delores gripped her hand. It looked to Vimla like they were preventing Chalisa from running.

"Let we stand for the bride," Pundit Panday said into the microphone. It crackled back at him.

The tassa group came around the house then, drumming and clashing their cymbals, eyes glassier and smiles broader than when they'd first arrived, and everyone knew Nanny's best rum was rushing through their blood.

Avinash waited for the sea of people to rise, then he thrust his chest out and led the way to the mandap, marching and blowing wisps of hair from his face. He reminded Vimla of the roosters at home, but she was too wrought with nerves to smile. Avinash nodded at Krishna as he clambered up the three steps to the mandap and plunked himself down even before the bride. The familiarity of the look that passed between Krishna and Avinash somehow widened the gulf separating her from Krishna.

Chalisa flounced after Avinash and Vimla noticed Nanny's grip tighten around her waist."Oh gosh! Look how Chalisa running down she *dulha!*" someone laughed.

"You ain't see how the boy good-looking? I don't blame she."

Chalisa glided by Vimla, the silk of her sari just brushing Vimla's toes. Vimla couldn't imagine why she was hastening to her fate this way. She wondered if Chalisa had received her note and knew that Vimla was leaving Trinidad. She crossed her feet at her ankles and tucked them beneath her chair.

Chandani followed Chalisa's movements and sucked her teeth. "No behaviour."

Chalisa made her way past Pundit Panday and Pundit Anand, but instead of sinking onto the peerha next to Krishna and hiding her eyes behind her lashes as all brides do, Chalisa Shankar disentangled herself from Nanny and Delores, stared directly at the crowd and flashed a smile so brazen even Sangita Gopalsingh dropped her fan into her lap with a gasp.

Krishna stared, bewildered.

The crowd murmured.

Nanny gripped Chalisa's elbow and tried to push her down. Delores inched away like she would slip between the cascading textiles and vanish altogether. But Chalisa payed them no attention. Instead she lifted her arms in the air, sending her bangles clinking at her elbows, and twirled to show off her exquisite sari. Her payals tinked with each step. She was radiant and nefarious at once.

"Watch, nuh. She feel this *Mastana Bahar!*" Vimla recognized Gloria Ramnath's voice.

Pundit Anand's grey eyebrows gathered on his crinkled forehead like storm clouds. He threw Maya a troubled look;

his jowls quivered. Maya pressed her fingers into her lips and shook her head in response.

Chalisa came full circle and winked an eye at the crowd, but Vimla suspected it was meant expressly for her. She found herself nodding back, silently urging Chalisa to do what she must—however outrageous—to see her through this day. It was the least she could do.

"I never see more." Chandani pursed her lips, although Vimla sensed her mother was enjoying some secret thrill at the audacity of Chalisa's actions.

Finally Chalisa sank to her peerha and Nanny made grand ceremony of straightening her phaloo, fanning her pleats and adjusting her jewellery. It was as if she would distract the crowd from Chalisa's sass by emphasizing the richness of her attire. But Chalisa worked against her: she watched the guests watching her and let her red lips curl into a slow, flippant smile.

Pundit Panday closed his eyes against Chalisa's pageantry and gushed forth a warble of Sanskrit. Suddenly the ceremony was underway again. Pundit Anand glowered across the bedee at Pundit Panday, raising his voice a decibel higher and jabbing the air as he rolled his tongue over the tricky bits. But Pundit Panday was oblivious to the showmanship.

Krishna did as he was told. Vimla felt her chest constrict and her palms grow clammy as he placed flowers here and circled incense there like a beautiful marionette in a theatre. For a moment Vimla's resolve faltered. She tore her gaze from Krishna and reminded herself that it was her choice to watch him wed Chalisa. She could have stayed home. She could have fled with him to Tobago and struck this moment from history altogether. Chandani reached over and stilled her bobbing knee with a firm hand. The strength in that touch made Vimla's vision of springing onto the mandap and intercepting the spurious union waver then fade away. She had chosen her path. It was up to Krishna to choose his. But even as she thought this, her heart leaped up against her ribcage and shattered.

Pundit Panday called for the dowry. Nanny bustled forward.

"On behalf of my late son," she said, handing a woven basket lined with red cloth to Pundit Anand. The ragged corner of the deed peeked over the edge of the basket. Nanny stole a glance at Chandani, whose face was pinched in a black scowl, and Vimla felt yesterday's shame boil hot in her veins all over again.

Pundit Panday chanted a mantra as he dipped the tip of a mango leaf into a lotah of water and flicked droplets onto the deed to bless it, and Vimla thought that no amount of prayer could undo the evil of this exchange.

Chalisa wet her lips and held Vimla's gaze. The gold flecks in her eyes glowed luminous against the outline of black kajal. Vimla leaned into Minty. "Watch how she looking so pleased with she self, Mints."

"I see she look like that before. That is how we end up at Maracas Bay," Minty said.

Pundit Anand drew the basket to his heart and bowed his head in a show of humility.

Chandani rustled at Vimla's side, unclasped her fingers, fixed her skirt, folded her arms. "God go punish he," she said.

Suddenly a young man carrying a picture frame sprang nimbly onto the mandap. Even before she saw his face, Vimla knew who it was. She thought, not for the first time, there was something gallant about him.

Avinash hopped up. "Gavin!" he exclaimed. He flung his

arms around Gavin's waist, and Nanny face became a shrivelled prune of disapproval.

"Who is this now? Chandani wondered aloud.

Faizal brought his head in close to Vimla and Minty. "That
witch there," he said, nodding to Chalisa, a smirk on his lips,
"have more tricks than two allyuh put together."

Pundit Panday froze with his mango leaf arced in the air.
"Yes, son?" he said to Gavin.

"Excuse me, Baba." Gavin knelt beside Pundit Panday so
that his words fell into the microphone and carried to the
back of the sprawling tent. "Sorry I late, Nanny," he said.
"Here is the deed for the Shankar estate on Orange Field
Road. I frame it and thing like you ask." He bowed, showing
off the big poof of his hair.

Chalisa's smile was as red and sweet as sorrel.

The colour from Nanny's face drained away; her skin
appeared more translucent than ever. She grabbed the frame
from Gavin's hands and pressed it against her small body. A
bark of a laugh escaped her. "Never mind he, Baba." She gestured for Pundit Panday to carry on. "The deed done bless. It
there in the basket!"

Chandani sat forward in her chair. Her small eyes darted
from Gavin to Nanny to Pundit Anand and back. "Lawd
Father!" she breathed. "What it is really going on here?"

Pundit Anand frowned. "Wait, nuh! Ain't the deed for the
estate on Orange Field Road in the basket?" He beckoned to
Maya, who lifted her sari pleats and climbed the stairs to the
mandap. Her silver fly-aways curled in the heat. Anand plucked
the paper from the basket and brought it close to his face.
"This deed for a orchard in Quinam!" He passed it to Maya

for her scrutiny. "Ain't you tell we you was giving we the big-gest orchard allyuh have? It have more orange in Headmaster's tree than all of Quinam orchard!"

Headmaster, seated across the aisle, pushed his glasses up on his nose and nodded at the compliment.

The crowd's murmuring rose to outright chatter.

"That Chance pundit real greedy, boy."

"But Nanny real fooling he. The man right to ask for he correct dowry."

"I want to know how that young man get that next deed."

"What happen? You blind? You ain't see how Chalisa skin-ning she teeth all over the place? Is she self who give that boy the deed."

"What the ass is this?" Someone sucked their teeth. "Big man and woman shitting up the children wedding for greediness!"

Nanny hunched and placed her wrinkled hand over her heart. "Baba," she said to Pundit Anand, "you expect a old and elder lady like me to keep track of every piece of land, orange and deed I own? It must be slip my mind." She held her head with her arthritic fingers.

Pundit Anand darkened. "I find thing slipping your mind steady these days. You also forget to tell we Chalisa was per-forming on *Mastana Bahar*." He whipped the deed from Maya's fingers, dropped it back into the basket like a piece of debris and wiped his hands on his dhoti.

Maya nodded. Her fly-aways framed her face like smoke.

The people gasped.

Chandani sprang to her feet. "It good for you, Anand! Allyuh is like family already—crooked same way!" She pointed at him and he recoiled.

Startled, Krishna attempted to drag his hand through his hair and knocked his turban off his head and into his lap.

The vein at Pundit Anand's temple leaped beneath his skin and fell into a steady throb. Maya placed her hand on her husband's shoulder as he spoke. "Chandani, sit down. This matter does not concern you."

Vimla felt embarrassment prickle under her skin but she made no attempt to stop her mother.

In his excitement, Faizal Mohammed leaned forward and draped his arms over the chairs in front of him. The fingers of his left hand grazed Vimla's shoulder, the fingers of his right, Minty's.

"Does not concern me?" Chandani stomped her foot in the grass. "Mr. Pundit Man, it look like thing slipping *your* mind and all!" She stalked to the mandap and wrestled Pundit Panday's microphone from its stand. "Let me tell all allyuh how this matter concerns me, too. My daughter there"—Chandani pointed to Vimla, who sank low in her chair—"supposed to marry Krishna today."

The crowd exclaimed.

Amusement softened Krishna's stoic stare. Vimla's heart turned over in her chest. There was no place safe to rest her gaze.

"Pundit self invite my family to he house just yesterday to ask we for Vimla to marry Krishna because he, and the rest of allyuh, see Chalisa wine she waist on *Mastana Bahar* like she playing Carnival." Chandani swept her arm in Chalisa's direction, and as if on cue, Chalisa rotated her slender hips as best she could sitting on the peerha in her lavish sari. The crowd tittered. Nanny blanched. Whistles flew up from the back of the tent.

Chandani thundered on. "But then, Miss Nanny come to Pundit Anand's house same day, and wave up she orange estate deed under he nose. Allyuh done know how Pundit greedy already." Chandani paused for the rumbling of agreement that followed. "Well, he get stupid when he see that deed and now for now he fling my daughter away and tell Nanny he go marry Krishna to she granddaughter, Chalisa, just to get he hands on that orange estate money. And then allyuh know what he do?"

"What he do, Chand?" Pudding shouted from somewhere in the back.

"He leave we standing by he gap like three stupidies. He didn't even watch we self!"

The crowd hurled a volley of insults and questions at the mandap.

"Pundit Anand get so take up by the money he ain't even check to see what it is he really getting, and now, after he shit we up, look Nanny shitting he up same way. Pundit Anand does steady be preaching about *karma* and *dharma* and thing. Well, watch karma take he in he ass now!"

Out of the corner of her eye, Vimla saw Om, Rajesh and Puncheon powering up the centre aisle. Om attempted to peel Chandani's fingers from the microphone, firm yet gentle, but she had come too far and she would not be stopped now.

"One more thing!" Chandani declared.

Om shrugged an apology as Chandani pulled the microphone to her face again. "My daughter ain't no duncy-head girl," she said. "In case allyuh ain't hear, Vimla Narine going over to study!" She nearly hopped she was so excited.

Sangita's mouth fell open. Puncheon hooted. He threw

himself into the air and landed in a pile in the grass. Rajesh pulled him to his feet and pushed him into a chair.

The tent erupted in applause.

Chandani glared at Pundit Anand and Maya. "I done with all allyuh! Bhagwan go fix you to suit. Allyuh real sorry, yes. And I sorry for allyuh." Chandani dropped the microphone and allowed Om to take her hand and lead her back to her seat. She sat with her chin held so high she was nearly the full height of an average woman.

Vimla stole a glance at Krishna. Last night, she had not mentioned her plan to leave Trinidad.

For a moment he blinked at her, once, twice, three times, but then his face crumpled and he did the unthinkable: he tucked his bejewelled turban under his arm and strode across the mandap, down the stairs and along the centre aisle. Pundit Anand called his name, but this only quickened Krishna's steps.

A SHIVER TRAVELLED up her spine and Vimla woke with a start. Tiberius was pawing at her door. The house smelled of buttery pancakes and greasy sausages.

She rubbed her feet together, trying to create heat, but the icy feeling was in her chest this time. She took a breath, exhaled slowly and threw off the patchwork quilt. The window was covered in condensation. Vimla leaned her head against the cool windowpane, her smile wistful. She remembered how she had stared at Krishna's tumble of black curls as he walked away. She had known where he was headed.

Now she wiped a circle clean and stared out at the maple trees glowing auburn and gold under the Canadian sun. A leaf drifted lazily to the ground, twirling then coasting on its belly until it fell into the growing mound below. She touched her lips to send Krishna a kiss, and found that she was smiling.

ACKNOWLEDGEMENTS

My heartfelt thanks to:

The University of Toronto School of Continuing Studies Creative Writing program, from which the early pages of this story first emerged.

My agent, Martha Magor Webb, who fell instantly in love with this book.

The kind folks at Doubleday Canada; and especially my editor Lynn Henry, who said yes to this book before it had an ending, and who, in her kind, gentle way, has guided me through the publishing process.

My teachers: Elaine Anderson, who saw the makings of a writer in a twelve-year-old girl; Lawrence Hill, who read my first short story and liked it; Rabindranath Maharaj, for seeing potential early on; Kathryn Kuitenbrouwer, mentor, believer, spirit bolsterer.

Shasta Townsend and the lovely yoginis at Balanced Life Yoga for helping me find stillness, peace and courage.

My friends at Woburn Jr. P.S. for helping me balance my passions of writing and teaching in equal measures.

Sharon Overend for commiserating, encouraging and drinking tea with me.

Nithya Addageethala, who has been reading alongside me for a lifetime.

Shane Ramnanan for his encouragement and for giving Chandani just the right words in the end.

Neil Kowlessar, my husband and best friend, for his support, his belief in this dream, and for the endless snacks.

Molly Ramnanan, sweetest, most loving mom in the whole world.

Ram Ramnanan, best dad, best storyteller, best hugger, best everything.

My families in Trinidad, for welcoming me into their homes over the years.

Trinidad, for being delicious and magical and infinitely beautiful.

Chance Kowlessar, for arriving in all his perfection.